ELEORA

a fantasy novel

MELISSA KEASTER

Printed in the United States of America

First Printing, 2017

ISBN 978-0-9988493-0-0

Phoenix 61 Publications
Farmerville, Louisiana

www.phoenix61publications.com

To the Declans in my life—

To Superman, who has loved me, served me,
and laid down his life for me in countless ways.

And to Jesus, who deigns to love this harlot's heart.

You've both won me a million times over.

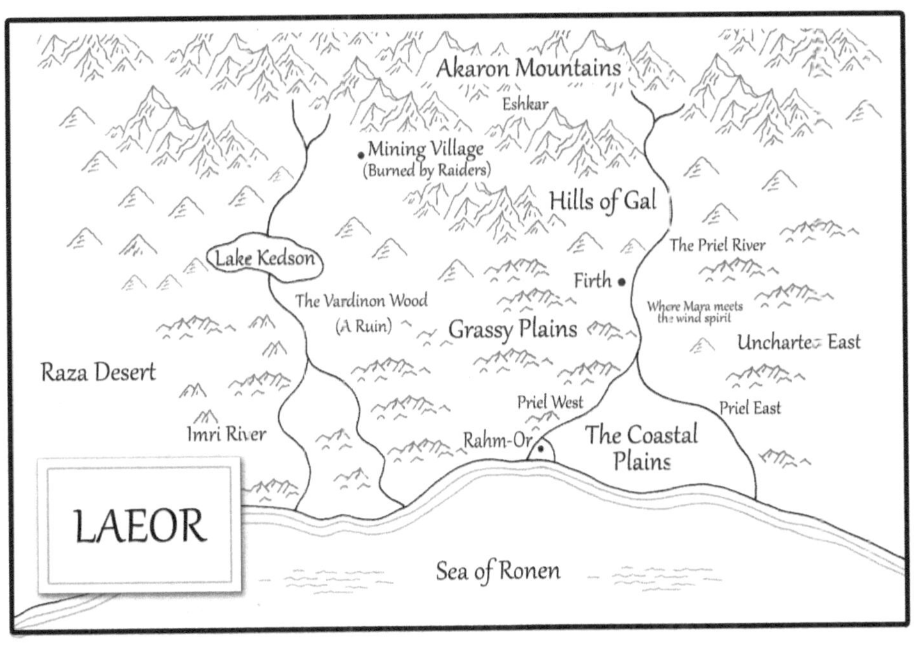
Akaron Mountains
Eshkar
Mining Village
(Burned by Raiders)
Hills of Gal
The Priel River
Lake Kedson
Firth
The Vardinon Wood
(A Ruin)
Where Mara meets
the wind spirit
Grassy Plains
Unchartes East
Raza Desert
Priel West
Priel East
Imri River
Rahm-Or
The Coastal
Plains
LAEOR
Sea of Ronen

PROLOGUE

Zev knelt at the edge of the lonely river bank, dipped his fingers into the water, and waited. Rivka liked to make him wait. He wouldn't tolerate her nonsense if he had a choice, but for good or for ill, he must comply with her whims and idiosyncrasies. For now.

Cool moisture wisped against his skin, and Zev beheld the form of a woman who could beguile even the least appreciative of men. Her mouth parted and curled into an inviting smile, revealing the pointed tips of her teeth. Zev counted them to clear his head. He hadn't yet become immune to her charms.

"Where's the child?" Rivka asked.

Zev looked toward the rising sun and shrugged. "Tending to animals, I'd wager."

"She should be here. What I have to say affects you both," she said.

Like a cat, Rivka liked to play with her prey. Terrorizing Mara was a favorite pastime of hers.

"Leave Mara to me," Zev said. "I'll pass along your message."

Rivka's eyes turned shrewd. "Your fondness for the child will be your undoing."

"I only fulfill my oath," he said.

"You can't protect her from me."

Zev grinned sardonically.

Rivka continued. "You leave for Rahm-Or in a fortnight. One of my spies has informed me that the stone has been sighted in the city. It's time to act. The child will remain here until she comes of age."

Zev fought to hide his surprise. Leaving Mara had never been part of the plan—his plan, anyway. He'd worked too hard for the fragile thread of trust between them to abandon her now. The plan would never work if she didn't trust him.

"You need distance," Rivka said. "And if you are still set on revenge against your father, there is work to be done."

"Nothing has changed," Zev said, aware his words weren't strictly true. Five winters had passed since the night he and Mara had sworn themselves to Rivka, Mara a newly made orphan of nine winters with a sister to care for and he a desperate rebel of fifteen. Everything had changed—except his demand to see his father pay in blood for the blood he'd shed.

Rivka studied him as though she knew his entire mind. If she did, he and Mara were both doomed. The sooner they were free of her, the better.

"What do you want me to do?" he asked.

"Build a trap fit for a king. It will take time, but all the best traps are laid with patience and sprung at opportunity." Rivka wouldn't say more until she was ready.

"What do you want me to tell Mara?"

Rivka's green eyes burned into his. "Tell her if she forgets her oath at the time to fulfill it, I will bring it to mind." She stepped back into the water. "Beyond that, I don't care what you tell her. I'll give you further instructions when you reach the city. Farewell, Akaronian."

With a provocative simper, she was gone, and Zev was left alone to decide how to tell Mara he was leaving. Only recently had that awful haunted look begun to fade from her eyes. He dreaded its return. Her pain reminded him too much of his own.

CHAPTER 1

Mara stepped outdoors with a shiver and cursed herself for having allowed Selene to venture into the uncommon dampness. It threatened Selene's frail constitution, but she wouldn't be persuaded to miss the annual harvest festivities no matter how Mara raged. Mara begrudged a smirk of pride, remembering the set of Selene's jaw as she'd declared herself too old to be ordered around by her sister. If Mara had taught her nothing else, Selene had learned her own mind. But every victory came at a cost, and Mara worried the price would be Selene's health.

When she'd freed the chickens from the coop and tended to the livestock, Mara opened the hog-pen gate and whistled. The hogs followed her out along the familiar trail away from the farm, grunting and squealing.

The mist grew thicker near the river, obscuring the bank on the opposite side. A familiar feeling settled in Mara's belly. Someone watched her through the haze. It could be anyone this morning. The woods, usually serene, were full of people shouting, blasting horns, and crashing through thickets in search of autumn foliage—a prelude to the harvest festivities scheduled to begin at noon the next day. Any one of them might pause to spy on Mara, who was a common topic of small-town gossip.

Mara and Selene's parents had both been half-Razan, a rare people whose brown skin contrasted with the paler skin of the people of the hills. One uncle was the town drunk. The other managed a questionable business, which Zev had established before he'd left so abruptly six winters ago. Though Selene was well received by all who encountered her, Mara didn't mingle much with the townsfolk, and so they liked to fabricate motivations to explain her behavior. Some thought her a witch, but Mara didn't mind. They were right to fear her.

Regardless of who the eyes belonged to, Mara stayed clear of the river, as she always did. She scratched the prickles at her neck, catching the chain of the lodestone necklace with her fingernail. She leaned against the mossy trunk of an oak, her fingers fretting the stone, and whispered a wish that the wearer of the necklace's counterpart would stay safe and well as she frolicked among the noisy revelers.

If they navigated the forest paths without getting lost, it would be a harvest miracle, never mind finding items for decoration. The weather wasn't right, and the vegetation knew it. Leaves drooped from tree branches, waiting for dry heat and crisp breezes to free them. The grass wouldn't dry, and fruit rotted on the vine before it ripened.

But the hogs weren't troubled by the gloom. The odd weather produced a bounty of mushrooms and truffles, and they didn't need sight to spot their prizes, only their precocious snouts. Mara closed her eyes, focusing on the sound of rooting and contented grunts. The scent of dank earth soothed like a lullaby.

A twig snapped. A hog startled and froze. Mara whipped out her dagger, squinting in the direction of the sound. "Who's there?"

"Sorry to frighten you," a man's voice said. A hulking figure stepped out of the mist, and Mara made out Loed's small head and bulging eyes.

"What are you doing here?" she asked.

Loed, her uncle and leader of the Ring's outpost in Firth, rarely sought her out himself. He usually sent messages by one of his goons.

"Urgent message came this morning, and my boys are out celebrating," he said.

Sheathing her dagger, Mara stepped through a huddle of hogs and snatched the letter from his massive hand. Her nostrils filled with the stink of musk. "Were you watching me just now?"

"Wanted to be sure you were alone. I see you remember Zev's lessons. Believed you might actually gut me." A noise that began as a laugh ended with a phlegmy cough. Loed spat to the side and wiped his mouth.

Mara didn't want to talk about Zev but wouldn't encourage Loed by saying so.

She frowned at the letter. The seal was broken. She unfolded the paper and read the familiar scrawl.

> Mara,
>
> Our friend grows impatient. We are two years beyond our agreement. She's given you until next harvest to fulfill your oath. I fear there will be consequences if you delay much longer. I urge you to depart for the city immediately.
>
> Zev

Underneath Zev's name, two circles linked together to form the insignia of the Ring. Mara handed the letter back to Loed. "Tell him I'll come at springtide."

Loed grunted, reminding Mara of a hog. Only she liked hogs far better. "Sounds to me like you need to leave tomorrow," he said.

"I can't. It's harvest, and I'm the only one fit to manage the farm."

"I'm no farmer, but I don't see how you can mow or reap in this mist."

"It has to lift sometime. Besides, you know I can't leave Selene till after winter. Not with Ramzi," she said. Ramzi wasn't fit to care for himself, let alone anyone else.

"I'll make arrangements for her," Loed said.

"I don't particularly approve of how you manage your affairs."

Color rose into his fat cheeks. "Don't know what all Zev means here, but doesn't sound like you manage your affairs all that well either. Let me help."

"No, thank you," she said.

"Stubborn wench," he said. "Seems like you'd go for Zev's sake anyway, after all he's done for you."

"Please leave."

With a roll of his toadish eyes, he said, "Let me know when you see reason." He left, kicking a hog as he went. The sow squealed in offense.

Mara called after him. "Easy on my hogs, if you please."

He answered with a mock salute and faded out of sight.

Her thoughts a flurry, Mara wandered farther down the path, searching for a pocket of clarity in the roiling gray. She had one year to fulfill her oath. A time limit was something new to consider. This day had hunted her for more than half her life and had sniffed her out at the worst time. If she left Selene and Ramzi in their season of need, she'd be guilty of the very thing for which she so resented Zev.

The woods had grown quiet except for the wren calling from a nearby tree. The townsfolk must have abandoned their quest. Mara straightened. Again, she felt someone's gaze. Not far from the river's edge, the mist converged and smoldered a sickly green. She scoured her eyes. When she looked again, the apparition was gone. Her focus didn't shift from the spot until a hog brushed her skirts, startling breath back into her lungs. Trembling, she reached down and patted its head. "Time to round up the others. We need to get out of these woods."

The next day, the town green teemed with activity. The men huddled around the roasting pits, laughing and drinking ale, while the women sliced bread and set out roasted vegetables and an array of meat and fruit pies upon the tables set up for the feast. The children shrieked in delight as they played some sort of running game with a small, round squash. A brother and sister played a lively jig on their fiddles—a signal the parade would begin soon.

Mara searched for Selene from Old Man Fuller's fence, which crowned the slope above the green, well away from the commotion. Nearly as dark as Mara and thinner than her blossoming friends, Selene was easy to spot. Her nimbus of almost-black curls matched Mara's tresses, contrasting with the fawns and blonds around her. The gold, orange, and russet scarves Selene waved animated the sound of her laughter, which rose from the valley.

Mara frowned. Selene shouldn't overexert herself in the damp air.

"No smile on this festive day?" Ben's long, lean frame ambled up the hill toward her.

Mara humphed at his lopsided grin. "The hay won't make and the world will rot if this mist doesn't lift. Strangest harvest weather I've seen. Smiles don't seem appropriate."

Ben chuckled and leaned against the fence at her side. Selene stopped midtwirl and waved the scarves at them in happy greeting, her dark curls bouncing like springs.

"Excepting smiles for Selene," Ben said as they waved back.

Mara turned to him, her face frozen in a satirical grin. He snorted.

A sheep's horn bellowed, announcing the arrival of the harvest king and queen. The pair waved from a horse drawn cart, bedecked in corn husks, wheat stalks, and a few late summer flowers. Ben and Mara exchanged a wry look. If the honored guests were outfitted in corn husks and grain, yesterday's expedition into the woods had been fruitless indeed. The fiddlers danced before the cart as it went along the perimeter of the green. Townsfolk showered the couple with seed and dried leaves, shouting well-wishes and other nonsense.

Mara recognized the two chosen for the ceremony. She sold a hog every year to the girl's family, and the boy was an apprentice in the smithy Mara favored. Beyond business transactions, she knew little of them or anyone else her age, save Ben. And even her friendship with him had begun as a business relationship.

Ben was the grandson of Hedya, the town healer. Four winters ago when Aunt Phi and Selene had fallen ill, Hedya had left Ben to manage the night watches. Together, he and Mara had sweated over the patients, applying poultices and distributing medicines. In the end, Phi had died, and Selene never fully recovered. But the trauma of it all had delivered Ben from shyness and Mara from her spiny shell long enough to form a bond.

Ben picked a sprig of sweet weed. "I nominated you queen," he said and stuck the stem between his teeth. His cheeks flushed from stooping.

Mara barked a laugh. "Felt sorry for the only girl in town without a vote, did you? What a queen I would make—dirt under my fingernails and smelling of swine."

"Just means you deserve it," Ben said with a shrug. "It is a harvest festival, after all. You're the only woman I know who runs her own farm."

But it wasn't her farm. It belonged to Ramzi, her uncle. Not long after she and Selene had arrived in Firth, he'd frowned at the two of them and said, "If my wife insists upon taking in her dead sister's whelps, they'll earn their keep."

He'd taught Mara to care for livestock, slaughter hogs, plow, sow, and harvest when she was still a child. Had he not, things may not have turned out so well for her and Selene. The winter Phi died, Ramzi had all but died along with her. Now he squandered his days drinking and complaining. Occasionally, he staggered into the fields just long enough to annoy the hands with drunken rants.

The only business matter in which he took real interest was payment. Though he did no work, he took it all and spent it on fire whiskey and nighttime diversions. The customers knew it and sometimes gave Mara a few coins in secret, which she collected in a box buried in the woods.

In spite of his gruffness and slovenly ways, Mara appreciated Ramzi. Sometimes she imagined he cared for her.

Mara cocked her head at Ben. "What do you think it means to deserve something?"

He grimaced. "Mara, I—"

"Forget it," Mara said with a wave of her hand. Not that she would. Every day she wondered what it meant that so many she'd cared for were dead. That Selene was sick. That Zev had deserted them. That her first home had been destroyed by marauding filth.

As she'd learned to account for hail, drought, and untimely freezes, she'd learned to expect an evil shadow, ever ready to frustrate her plans. For Mara, a seed sown was a crop failed, and the only way to change her fate was to do the thing she couldn't. Selene was too frail to abandon. And though she didn't care as much, so was Ramzi.

Mara wanted Ben's smile to return. "Thanks for the vote, but I would look ridiculous in corn husks."

Eyes crinkling at the corners, he took her hand and ran his thumb over her callouses. "Do you ever wish you didn't have to work so hard?"

"I don't give it much thought," she said. "The farm has to be worked, or we starve. As it's the only thing I'm good at, I hope Ramzi will leave it to me."

"So no, then." He snickered. "All right. What if you marry?" His light tone didn't match his twitchy movements.

Mara peeled her eyes from Selene to look at him. His cheeks were pink, and he wouldn't return her gaze. She retrieved her hand. "I won't marry. Not until Selene does, anyway. And maybe not then."

Below, the parade came to an end. The harvest royalty climbed out of the cart and made their way to seats of honor at the tables centered on the green. The feast had begun.

"Better get down there. I only sold four hogs for the roast," she said.

Ben stayed where he was. "Selene wants you to be happy, you know. She loves you as much as you love her."

Selene sat at a table crowded with young people. She whispered to her friends, giggling at their responses. Selene made Mara happy. "Tell her to wrap one of those scarves over her head, will you? I want to know how much she eats, and be sure she rests between dances."

Ben rolled his eyes. "Surely you aren't heading to the fields. All the hands are here."

"Exactly," she said. "All this work to do, and the entire town is at a party."

"You're insufferable."

"And yet you suffer me." Mara grinned.

"Go on then, you old hardnose. See you tomorrow? Mist or shine?"

"Sunrise. Don't be late, or I'll dock your pay. And be sure to wear thick gloves to protect those soft lady hands." Mara ran away chortling.

A wad of dung sailed past her head.

Mara spent the afternoon in the fields but left the sickle in the barn. She strolled between the barley rows, enjoying the tickle of the grain's feathery heads on her outstretched palms, pondering Zev's message.

Selene returned home at dusk, her face pale and eyes bright. After administering a clove of honeyed garlic and a steaming mug of lungwort tea, Mara tucked Selene into bed with a warm water bottle and extra blankets.

Too worried to sleep, Mara kidnapped a rooster from the coop. Working by memory more than by sight, she killed, plucked, and dressed it in the yard by the dim glow of a lamp. Clouds obscured the moon.

Ramzi rose when he smelled broth. The sour stench of sweat and alcohol exuded from the bed. Mara fought a gag. He tugged the ring in his ear, peering down at Selene. Mara and Selene had commissioned the goldsmith to turn Phi's wedding band into something he could wear at all times. It wasn't hard for Mara to guess the color of his thoughts. She missed Phi too.

"Sick again?" The words slurred.

She nodded. "Hungry? The broth isn't ready, but there's pottage."

Ramzi found the bowl on the hearth. "Fever?"

"Some," she said. "Not enough to postpone reaping. I'll make a soup before

I leave in the morning. She needs rest." Mara didn't want Ramzi ordering Selene around, as he was prone to do.

"I'll keep an eye on her," he said.

A sincere offer, but given the choice, Ramzi would rather drown than bleed. He wouldn't surface from the whiskey bottle until Selene was well. Not that Mara blamed him. The sounds and smells of the sickroom sharpened painful memories. She'd join him if Selene wasn't depending on her.

Soon after the cough began to rattle Selene's chest, Ramzi left.

Only a few hands arrived at the appointed time the following morning. Ben wasn't among them. When she asked after the others, they answered with yawns and complacent shrugs. Those who'd come fumbled sickles and were slow at bundling the grain. The midmorning yield was pitiful.

Mara tossed a bundle of grain into the cart, which should've been almost full, and turned to the men. "Did you all stay out drinking after the party?"

Some blushed. Several faces shone pale in the gray light. Dark circles shadowed several eyes.

Mara scowled at the sky. She needed to be with Selene, but the men would get very little done if she left them. Disgusted by the situation, she dismissed them when they finished the row and ordered them to return the following morning only if they were fit to work. When she returned to the house, she regretted having left at all.

Selene tossed. Damp ringlets framed her flushed face. She sucked the stone of her necklace. She hadn't left the bed, not even for a drink. Ramzi snored in the corner, oblivious. The sound made Mara's scalp prickle with fury.

Mara offered Selene a cup of water, urging her to drink. Selene sipped, but not enough. Broth, tea, and honeyed cloves failed to entice. After cooling Selene's skin with a damp cloth, Mara collapsed into bed beside her and fell into a fitful sleep.

Mara woke with a start. The sun had set, but Ramzi still slept. By her side, Selene labored to breathe. Faint crackles accompanied the rise and fall of her chest.

The dangers of Firth after dark didn't dissuade Mara from a ride into town. The King help the man who crossed her tonight. Whispering a soft apology to the mule, she mounted, not bothering with a saddle. The night air felt heavier—damper—than it had that morning. Very little moonlight shone through the thick cloud cover. Mara sank into speculation and found herself outside Hedya's home without recollection of the ride.

Ben answered the door wild haired and glassy eyed, with his undershirt half-tucked into his breeches. His shoulders sagged at the sight of her. "Selene?"

Distracted, Mara brushed by him and stepped inside. Hedya's orderly home was littered with open bags, herb pouches, and glass vials. "What's happened?"

Ben's eyes hollowed. "Gram and I are trying to figure that out. Over half the town is sick. It may've been bad food at the festival, but the symptoms aren't consistent with poisoning. Some are far worse than others. I'd say it's the weather, but healthy people aren't usually affected by climate changes."

"That explains where my hands were today," she said.

Ben's eyes flew wide. "I'm so sorry. The knocking started before dawn."

"It's fine," Mara said. "But I need you to come with me. Selene sounds—" She couldn't finish.

A curt nod. "Let me pack a bag."

Ben turned grim as he assessed Selene. He administered medicines and poultices, avoiding Mara's stare. Selene rested easier when he finished, but her breaths sounded the same.

Mara grabbed Ben's head and made him face her. "Well?"

He closed his eyes. "It isn't good."

Mara felt her backbone dissolve. "What can I do?"

"Not give up," Ben said. "I need to talk to Gram. But for now, do what you're doing. I'll leave a couple of tinctures that will ease her discomfort. Steal a little of Ramzi's whiskey if you think she needs it."

In essence, keep her comfortable. The last time he'd given those instructions,

Mara had buried Phi in a deep hole they'd dug together.

Ben helped her into a chair and left. When the sound of his horse faded down the road, Mara lit a lamp and raced out of the house toward the river. The clouds concealed the moon, and darkness hung thick among the trees. Mara lost the path, but followed the smell of silt, catching on briars and tripping over rocks along the way.

When her boots sank into the soft earth along the bank, she plunged a hand into the water. She waited, out of breath with fear as much as exertion. Nothing happened. "Rivka?" she whispered.

Mist, cool and wet, swirled at Mara's ankles and traveled upward until it engulfed her body and quenched her lamp. Caught in Rivka's magic, Mara couldn't see or move from where she stood and was reminded of the ill-fated night she and Rivka had met. The sound of her own breaths echoed off unseen walls. The nighttime music of the forest muted, and Mara wondered if Rivka had transported her to an unknown world of black silence. Fear quaked her heavy limbs.

"So you haven't forgotten me."

The voice was everywhere, reverberating inside Mara's mind, vibrating her skin. It rushed like waves and ebbed far away, undulating in hues of pitch and putrid green, which Mara sensed more than saw. Mara was glad to be blind. "I'm sorry," she said, her words hurrying together. "I—I should've come sooner. I should've gone like you said. But Selene's been sick, and now she's dying."

"At whose fault, do you suppose?"

"Mine," Mara said and felt sick.

A tendril of mist coiled around Mara, sliding against her skin. "And after winters of neglect, you come to me for help. How touching."

"Please," Mara said.

Rivka answered nothing.

"I'll do anything. I'll leave tomorrow." Mara had never begged in her life before now, but she couldn't lose Selene, not to death. While the idea of leaving Selene was unconscionable, the prospect of Selene leaving her was worse. Selene was all Mara had, and without her, Mara wasn't sure life was worth living.

A sigh hissed in Mara's ear. "The time for fruitless promises has passed. You were supposed to leave when you came of age, but for two years you've delayed. I no longer trust your word."

Mara's stomach dropped. Selene would die, and it would be her fault.

"There is a way you can save her yourself," Rivka said slowly.

Mara was sure she'd misheard. "How?"

"A flower with magical healing properties still grows in the ruins of the Vardinon Wood. Someone mad enough to venture there learned how to harvest it and turn it into an elixir. It's rare, as you may guess, but Loed will find it for you. For a price."

"I don't have the money," Mara said, sinking again.

"You're a resourceful girl. I'm certain you can make some sort of arrangement," Rivka said.

The mist constricted, wringing the air from Mara's chest. A touch, cold and cruel, caressed her cheek.

"I expect you to depart for the city within the week. Don't fail me again. I won't be so forgiving next time."

An easterly wind gusted across the water, dispersing the heavy vapor. Fresh air filled Mara's lungs and cleared her head. The woods came alive again with the noise of insects and nocturnal rodents. The palest light glowed inside the clouds above. Rivka was gone.

Mara tested her legs. Able to move them again, she stumbled up the river bank and through the woods to the place her box of savings was hidden. She needed every coin she could find, and even then it wouldn't be enough.

CHAPTER 2

Mara stared at the wooden sign, which featured two linked circles painted in black. An eerie silence, interrupted by an occasional cock crow, settled over the town. No one stirred in the early morning light except the smithy's dog and a few feral cats. It was her first visit to the outpost. Zev hadn't allowed her to go there, and she hadn't wanted to since he'd gone.

She blinked as she stepped into a large hall. Lush carpets. Polished wood. Bronze fixtures. A shocking contrast to the crude town, the finery of the outpost heightened the surreality of what she was about to do. She spotted a passage to the corridor.

Meg, Loed's wife, bustled through it and stopped short. "Mara?"

Mara brushed the smaller woman aside and followed voices to a closed door. Meg almost ran to keep pace. "Let me tell Loed you're here."

Mara opened the door. Two stunned faces snapped up, one a belonging to a stranger. The air, thick with sweat and musk, unsettled her stomach. Loed sat behind a cherrywood desk. Dressed in a fine tunic trimmed with gold thread, he had the look of a distinguished businessman, very unlike the sloppy thug she'd encountered in the woods two days ago.

"I need to talk to you," Mara said to Loed and glanced at the strange man. "Privately."

Loed's eyes bounced between Mara and the man. "I'll be with you in a moment," he told her.

"It's urgent."

He looked at her hard and sighed. Loed asked the man to wait in the corridor while he spoke with his niece. "What's this about?" he asked as the door closed.

Mara explained Selene's condition and described the medicine she needed. "Do you know it?"

Loed folded his hands, resting his elbows upon the desk. "I do." His expression was uncharacteristically sagacious, as if he'd already worked out her problem and anticipated what she would ask.

She focused on a crack in the wall behind him. "I was told you could get it for me. Is that true?"

Loed relaxed back in his chair and fought a grin. "Probably."

Her fist banged the desk. "I don't have time for games, Loed. Will you help me or not?"

"I'm a businessman, Mara, and your uncle. Of course I'll help," he said.

"How soon? Selene won't make it if you don't hurry." She hated the desperation in her voice, but it couldn't be helped.

"I'm not worried about getting the medicine in time," he said. "I'm concerned about the price."

Mara reached for her purse and poured its contents onto the desk. His eyes flicked from the coins back to her. "It's not enough."

Mara shoved the coins toward him. "Count it. I'll pay the rest after harvest."

"You don't understand."

"Then explain," she said through gritted teeth.

"It's a matter of supply and demand, sweetheart, which should be a familiar concept, having worked a farm all these years."

"Name your price," she said. "And don't call me 'sweetheart.'"

He considered her a moment. "It'll cost everything you're worth."

She stared at him, uncomprehending.

"I can't get the medicine for less than thirty silvers," he said.

The price of a slave.

"Don't look so shocked. People sell themselves for much less. One man staked his freedom on a card game." Rummaging through a stack of papers on the desk, he continued, "As a slave, you'll have rights to food and shelter. And don't worry—you won't have to stay with me." His mouth curled in a wry grin. "I'll escort you to Rahm-Or and sell you to Zev. You need to go anyway, and there's no better placement for a woman your age. It's your best chance to earn your way out."

A paper slid across the desk. Mara could only stare at it. When she managed to speak, her voice was distant and airy, nothing like her own. "Suppose I do it, and it doesn't work."

"The price of the medicine is the price of the medicine."

She nodded. Her head felt oddly light. "I need time to make arrangements."

"We'll leave at dawn after tomorrow."

Two days. If Selene lived through this, she'd never forgive Mara. But Mara could live with Selene's hatred better than she could her death.

"Have you ever slept with a man?" Loed asked.

Her attention snapped back to him. "Why do you need to know that?"

"Answer the question," he said.

Heat rose from her neck into her face. "I'm not pregnant."

"That's not what I asked."

Mara shielded her face with the papers, pretending to read. "No."

"What about that healer boy who follows you like a pet sheep?"

The paper flew down with a loud rattle. "What? No! He's my friend, nothing more. I'm not pregnant—I can't be—and I've never been with a man. Hills!"

Loed turned, busying himself. His shoulders shook. Mara ignored him and read the document in earnest. It contained no stipulations for release. When her face cooled, misery settled like a brick in her stomach. A dangerous ache tugged behind her eyes. She blinked hard. "I can't leave her like this."

"You won't," he said. "I'll have the medicine in hand by nightfall. She'll be out of bed tomorrow."

It took Mara a moment to comprehend what he'd said. "The medicine works that fast?"

He offered a ready quill. "Like a miracle, so they say."

Mara drew her mark, and Loed collected the coins scattered across the desk.

～～～

When Mara stepped into the corridor, the man Loed had dismissed from his office appraised her with obsidian eyes. His brown skin was almost as dark as her own. She was wondering about his heritage when she noticed the way he looked at her.

Mara was accustomed to second glances, even curious stares. She was tall with dark skin and a powerful build. No woman in town looked anything like her. Strong cheekbones, a full mouth, and large dark-brown eyes—inherited from her Aunt Phi—might've been beautiful, except they were set upon her father's wide, angled face.

"Odd-looking child," she'd overheard one woman comment several winters ago.

"Striking, I'd say," had said another.

But this man didn't look at her face. His eyes lingered at her neck, chest, and waist. "How much for her?"

Loed stepped between them. "More than you can afford." Guiding Mara away from the man, he said, "I'll deliver the medicine to the farm this evening."

Mara peered around Loed's wide girth at the other man, who continued to stare. Her insides squirmed at the glint in his eye. "I don't want you at the farm." She wasn't ready for the questions his presence would raise. "I'll be back to get it."

Loed nodded, his mouth grim. "Be here before sundown. I want you home by nightfall. Take no risks. Understand?"

A retort rose like fire in her throat. Then she remembered—he owned her now.

Selene struggled to breathe throughout the day. Ben came by once to see about her, but said little and avoided eye contact. Twice, Mara feared she might lose Selene before the medicine came, but whether by fate or magic, Selene pulled through.

Mara returned to the outpost midafternoon, musing over Loed's admonishment about her safety. In her case, risk mattered little. Nothing would happen. Only once—not long after she'd come to Firth—had someone been foolish enough to threaten her.

An associate of Zev had caught sight of her in town and had decided someone might pay a fine price for a Razan child on the underground market. People still whispered about what had happened to the man. His body had been found a small distance downstream—not with knife wounds as anyone who knew Zev might expect, but with his eyes burned out and his mouth hanging open in horror. After the incident, Zev had taught her to defend herself, but no one had dared to touch her since. The greatest danger to Mara had always been the loss of those she loved.

As promised, the medicine was waiting when Mara reached the outpost. She inspected the bottle. The liquid was crimson, reminding her of stories she'd heard about Eleora, the magical stone of legend. Unstopping the bottle, she inhaled. A vision of a citrus grove, warm and fragrant, formed in her mind.

"Day after tomorrow at dawn. Careful until then," Loed reminded her.

She nodded and hurried home.

Ben was waiting when Mara crossed the threshold. Selene looked pale and weary of life but was awake. She managed a weak smile in greeting.

Mara pulled the bottle from her bosom and held it to the light streaming through the window. A bright-red globe shone on the opposite wall. "I've brought medicine," she announced. "Supposedly, it works miracles, so I thought we'd give it a try."

Ben snatched the bottle from her hand and sputtered. "Is this? Gram told me it existed, but how did you—"

His relieved laugh cut him off.

"Magic." Mara winked and handed him the bottle.

Ben studied her as he took it.

"Prepare a dose for our patient, healer. I'm going to see about the men and feed the animals." Mara ducked out of the house, relieved to escape the weight of Ben's frown.

She joined the men in the fields, working alongside them until dusk. At day's end, they hadn't harvested as much as she would have liked, but not many had come.

"Half the town is taken ill," one said.

Another gazed in the direction of the river. "My wife swears it's the work of spirits. I almost believe her."

Mara didn't reply but thanked the men for their work. When they had gone, she drove the loaded cart back to the barn.

Ben waited at the hog pen when she returned to the farmyard. Her stomach curled in fear. She put away the mule and rushed out to meet him. "Selene?" she asked, out of breath.

He nodded toward the house. "Selene's fine. Already better."

Relief broke over Mara. But when she reached to embrace Ben, he made no motion to receive her. The set of his shoulders wasn't as easy as usual. "What's wrong?" she asked.

"What have you done?" he asked. The question came no louder than a whisper but fell with the weight of a gavel.

She didn't like his condescending look. "I found medicine to help Selene."

"Don't play coy with me. Where did you get it?"

"Does it matter?" She crossed her arms.

He stepped close, inspecting her face in the dim moonlight. His jaw flexed. There was no hiding from him.

"I went to Loed for help," she said.

"And?"

"And he said he could get what she needed. He did."

Small puffs of steam blew from Ben's nose, one after the other.

"I didn't have enough money, so I sold myself," she said.

A sharp intake of air drew her eyes to his face. He looked as if he'd been horse-kicked. Unable to bear it, she threw her arms around him. "I'm sorry, but I had to."

He stopped breathing. Every muscle in his body went taut. He pushed her off, a dazed look in his eyes. "I need to see about my other patients."

"Ben—"

He disappeared into the shadows.

Mara sat by the fire, watching the steady, soundless rise and fall of Selene's chest. The fever was gone. Color had returned to her face. That morning, Selene had been on her deathbed. Now she was a portrait of serenity.

Ramzi rose from bed; ate a bowl of stew, which Ben had made earlier in the day; and left, his jug of fire whiskey in tow.

The door squeaked open, and cool air rushed into the room. Ben appeared, a hard look in his eyes. A confusing tangle of relief and anxiety filled Mara's belly. Ben had always been a refuge for her. Now he was an impregnable fortress she couldn't breach. She didn't know what to say to him, so she said nothing.

The fire cracked. A log broke and settled in the ashes.

"I left my bag," he said.

Mara picked up the bag at her feet. When he didn't come for it, she stood with a grunt and carried it to him. He set it on the dirt floor and stepped closer. Picking a barley stalk out of her braid, he said, "How long did he give you?"

His proximity made her nervous. A joke would ease the tension, but she couldn't think of one with him standing so close. "At dawn after tomorrow."

Heaviness filled her chest. Despite the losses Mara had suffered in Firth, she liked her life there. She enjoyed her work and the challenge of it. Strained limbs and a sweaty brow were a particular satisfaction. The farm was her home and purpose. Ramzi, Selene, and Ben were family. In a few short hours, she would lose it all.

"Which brings us to this—I need you to ask Hedya to take Selene."

Ben stared through her.

"She can't stay here alone. It isn't safe. I'll send money when I can, but you know Selene. She's no trouble and so helpful. She'll earn her—"

His lips cut her off. She stiffened and almost resisted but stopped herself. She wouldn't hurt him again. Not today.

He pulled away, his breath racing. "Let me talk to Loed. I want to marry you. I'll offer him free services. I'll do whatever he asks."

Marry her? Mara shook her head to keep him from kissing her again. "It won't work. I'm as good as sold to Zev."

Ben's jaw clenched. His hard look returned.

"Zev and I were friends once," she said. "Maybe he'll free me after I've worked for him awhile."

Ben stepped back, pulling a stalk of sweet weed from his pocket. "You don't know what you'll become, do you?"

Mara frowned.

Ben chewed, watching her. "They'll make you a prostitute. Every night, strange men will come into your bed expecting things from you, and it will be your job to please them."

"Zev wouldn't—"

"He will."

Selene stirred and sighed, drawing their attention. Mara picked up the bag at Ben's feet and extended it toward him. "You need to leave."

"You don't plan to tell her," he said, disbelief plain on his face.

"I will. But in my own way, in my own time." She pushed the bag into his chest. "Please leave."

"I'll speak to Loed in the morning." Taking the bag, he left.

"Mara?" Selene's eyes fluttered open at the sound of the door.

Mara knelt beside the bed and brushed a ringlet away from Selene's face. "Shh. Go back to sleep. I'm sorry we woke you."

Selene stretched and looked around the room. "No, I feel good. And hungry. Is that stew I smell?"

Her eyes were bright but no longer glassy. She struggled to sit up. Mara propped her upon the pillows and brought a bowl, warm to the touch.

When Mara tried to feed her, Selene shook her head, reaching. "Let me do it." Under Mara's astonished supervision, she ate every bite and asked for more.

"Let's give it a while," Mara said, still unsure about Selene's recovery.

"It's good. Ben made it, didn't he?" Selene's cheeks dimpled.

Mara pretended offense. "No remarks against my cooking."

"If that's what you call it," Selene said and climbed out of bed.

Mara watched her wash and change without assistance. "Thirsty?" she asked when Selene returned.

"For milk. I'm tired of water."

"All right, then." Mara danced to the cupboard, accompanied by Selene's laughter.

It was worth it. All of it. Even though Mara was a slave. Even if she became a prostitute. Even if Ben never forgave her. To see Selene eat, drink, and jest when she should be dead would sustain Mara in the days ahead.

CHAPTER 3

Mara and Selene lay side by side on fresh, lavender-scented sheets. Selene amused herself with the matching necklaces, playing with the stones as Mara had when she was a girl. Her father had brought them from the mines before Selene was born. He'd given Mara stones of far greater value, but these were her favorites because he'd sat her on his lap and explained them. It was the most affectionate moment he had ever given her. The worthless stones had been the only items in her pocket the night their village had burned.

Selene held the stone of her necklace a finger's breadth from Mara's and smiled when they came together. Mara toyed with Selene's curls. "I leave for Rahm-Cr at daybreak after tomorrow," Mara said. "Zev needs my help with something."

The only sound was the clack of the stones coming together after being torn apart. "At harvest?"

"It's urgent. And—"

"We owe him." Selene sighed.

Mara shook her head. "I owe him."

Selene inspected the stones in the candlelight, her shoulders tense. "How long will you be gone?"

Mara breathed in the sweet, hay-like fragrance of Selene's skin, putting it to memory. "I don't know. But I'll be back as soon as I can."

Selene pulled the stones apart. "Will you read me a story about the King?"

The abrupt change of subject startled Mara. "Why? You know them all by heart." She goosed Selene's ribs, hoping to see her dimples again, but Selene twisted out of reach.

The stones snapped together. "If you laugh at me, I'll never forgive you," Selene said.

Mara placed a hand over her heart in mock-solemn pledge.

Selene's eyes turned distant and dreamy. "While I was asleep, I saw him—the King. He wore the Eleora stone. Did you know it's the same color as the medicine Ben gave me?"

Mara masked her cynicism with a smile. She never spoke of the King or his stone unless Selene asked her to.

"Anyway," Selene continued, "he smiled at me and told me I was safe and would feel better soon. I know it sounds crazy, but I felt his magic working in my body, healing me. I feel more alive than I have my whole life."

Mara could think of nothing helpful to say. It wasn't that she disbelieved Selene. Rather, she knew how easy it was to believe something she wanted to be true. "And what does your King look like, pray tell? All of Laeor wants to know, since no one's seen him in more than a hundred winters. Are we looking for a ghost or a corpse in a crown?"

Selene punched her shoulder. "You swore."

"I'm bad at promises."

"The medicine came from him. I know it."

Mara strove for gentleness. "The medicine came from a flower. The King's gone. That's why we have councils now."

Selene scowled. "Magical beings can't die."

"I love your confidence. But they're only stories to keep children from fearing the night." The stories had stopped working for Mara when their home village had burned to the ground. No living king worth his crown would allow raiders to pillage his kingdom and slaughter his people without acting.

"Aunt Phi believed the stories," Selene said. "They gave her hope."

"Fairy tales are a shaky thing to build your hope upon," Mara answered, thinking of Aunt Phi lying in a hole in the ground.

Mara expected anger and received joy. "Fairy tales are everything, and all the happy endings are true. I wish you could feel what I feel. See what I saw," Selene said, her countenance radiant.

Mara kissed Selene's dimples. "Today I believe in happy endings."

Selene fixed serious eyes on Mara's. "Good. Take that with you to Rahm-Or."

A lump formed in Mara's throat. The sun would rise in a blink. One day gone. She wouldn't tell Selene she'd sold herself. Not now, maybe not at all. Selene needn't fret.

The girls woke, hands clasped and necklaces intertwined, when Ramzi stumbled into bed. Selene readied for the fields, laughing at Mara's disapproval, and said, "I imagine I feel better than you at the moment, and like it or not, I plan to spend your last day in Firth with you."

Mara consented and tried to ignore the growing weight in her chest.

Selene entertained the hands with folk songs as she bundled grain. Wonder shone in their smiles. Winters had passed since Selene was well enough to work outside. Now she shamed them all.

For the first time in many days, the mist lifted with the mounting sun. By midmorning, Mara could see the whole farm from the rise above the fields. Ben joined them near noon wearing defeat like a heavy cloak. He worked a little, but mostly he cast forlorn glances at Mara and gawked at Selene.

Selene paused between songs, turning to him. "How are your other patients?"

"Not as well as you, but better," he said.

"You and Mara should fetch more of that medicine," she said.

Mara and Ben exchanged a side glance. His expression unreadable, he left. If Selene had noticed his odd behavior, she didn't say anything.

Selene excused herself after lunch, promising to return before dark. She didn't say where she was going, and Mara was too preoccupied to press. It was time to talk to the men.

The man she appointed steward had worked the farm as long as Mara. He was discerning enough to handle Ramzi and manage the hands. Curious, the men asked questions until they wearied of her vague answers. One offered to do whatever he could to help her stay—as long as it didn't require money. Others promised to watch over Selene. A hot, invisible hand gripped her throat as the last man wished her well and faded into the dusk. Winters would likely pass before she saw them again.

The house was dark when Mara returned from the fields. She stoked the embers in the hearth, added wood, and gasped. Selene glared from the shadows, her tearstained face a snarl of heartbreak and fury. She wheezed something Mara couldn't understand.

Alarmed, Mara ran to her side. "What's happened? Are you all right?"

Selene shook her head and wheezed again. Mara checked for injuries and fever. Finding neither, she brought a glass of water and rubbed Selene's back, making soothing sounds. Still Selene couldn't talk.

Mara put a pot on to boil. Eggs dropped into the water with six plops and a hiss. She sliced vegetables and placed them in a pan to roast, the process slowed by anxious glances in Selene's direction.

Selene cleared her throat. "I went to see Hedya today. To ask about the medicine."

Gone was the docile girl Mara had raised. In her stead was a young woman both familiar and foreign. Selene's eyes glowed with the fire that so often burned within herself. Maybe the fire had always been there, and years of illness had contained it.

"Hedya said the medicine you gave me is rare, and the only person in town who could afford it was Loed." Selene choked on his name.

Mara set down the knife and steadied herself against the table. She'd lied before and had even been caught, but never over something like this. Never when the blade would cut so deep.

"I found Ben so I wouldn't have to go to Loed alone, but Ben already knew."

Mara stooped and pulled a flask from the underside of the table. The whiskey burned its way down her gullet and spread to her limbs.

"He said you sold yourself," Selene said.

A bellow from the corner of the room. "What?"

Their heads jerked in Ramzi's direction.

Mara tossed back another swallow and returned the flask to its hideaway. "Nothing, Uncle. Dinner isn't ready. Sleep awhile longer."

He stood on clumsy legs, grumbling. "What's this about?"

Mara groaned, knowing he had to be told. She'd be gone in the morning, and Selene with her. "Selene needed a particular medicine to live. I did what was necessary to get it."

Ramzi brought the jug of fire whiskey to his lips and gulped. "Why didn't you ask me for help?"

Mara didn't answer.

"Ben says you'll become a prostitute," Selene said.

"Well, he didn't hold anything back, did he?" Swearing, Mara took the jug from Ramzi, who stared slackjawed at his hands as if he'd forgotten what they looked like empty.

Selene shot up from the chair. "Stop drinking, and say something for yourself. Why did you do it? My life isn't worth your soul."

Staring hard at Selene, Mara took another swig of whiskey. Ramzi snatched back the jug and clutched it against his chest. In silence, Mara removed the pot of boiled eggs from the fire and stirred the vegetables in the pan.

Ramzi toyed with his earring. "Who'll run my farm?"

"I've appointed a trustworthy hand to manage. It'll be in good hands until I return," Mara said.

The jug sloshed behind her. A gulp. "If you leave with Loed, you won't come back. I won't have a whore sully my house. Selene'll have to run it."

His words stung, but Mara wouldn't let him see how much. "Selene leaves when I leave. You'll run the farm, or the hands I've chosen will."

Ramzi's fist crashed onto the table. "I took you whelps in, fed you, clothed you. And what did I get for it? A dead wife."

Selene winced.

His face purpled. "How dare you abandon me in my old age? You owe me. Loed can't have you unless Selene stays."

Mara didn't care that he was drunk. No one threatened Selene. "We owe you nothing. You'd have lost the farm—starved on your bare bottom—if not for us. And please warn me if you decide to confront Loed. It's something I'd like to watch."

With a loud thud, two of Loed's thugs burst through the door. Mara stared at them in confusion. Before she could stop him, Ramzi crossed the room toward them, bellowing obscenities with his jug raised. One of Loed's men drew a dagger.

"Uncle!" Selene cried.

Ramzi didn't stop. "Get out of my house!"

Mara leaped. If Ramzi hadn't been drunk, she couldn't have saved him. Just before he ran into the man's blade, she caught his free arm and yanked with all her might. Grunting, he tried to fling her off. When Mara didn't let go, his raised fist swung down, and the cherished whiskey jug slammed against the side of her head.

Tiny bursts of light preceded an explosion of pain. A loud ringing accompanied her fall to the floor. Selene screamed, and heavy feet stomped away. Anxious voices. Someone yelled. Mara tasted metal, warm and liquid. As though one of the lodestones had melted in her mouth. The sharp smell of alcohol overpowered her senses. When a dark abyss rose up to swallow her whole, she gave herself to it gladly.

A familiar touch, light as goose down, beckoned her. Ben's face blurred and rippled. "You're not allowed to be hurt. I'm not finished being angry with you yet," he said.

A spoon pressed to her lips. Sweet liquid poured down her throat, mingling with blood. Her stomach rejected the offering.

"Okay, okay. We'll try another way." Ben placed a lozenge under tongue. "Let it dissolve there."

A small hand, smelling like hay, held on to hers. Warm drops splashed against her wrist. Mara squeezed, hoping to reassure Selene, but she lost her grip.

Ben said, "It's only the herbs. Is the water warm?"

Selene moved away and returned. Water squeezed from a cloth into the basin. "Mara, I need to clean the wound."

She wished Ben would stop talking to her that—like she was dying.

The warm water lifted the stickiness from her skin. Pain purred beside her like a placated wildcat, lurking but not attacking. She was almost asleep when the door swung open. A draft needled her damp head.

Loed's voice was harried. "Any sign of the damned uncle?"

No one answered him. Mara was too tired to laugh at the fine irony he'd served.

"She's awfully still," Loed said.

Whatever Ben muttered in response sounded more like an invitation for Loed to drown in the Priel than reassurance.

Coins jangled nearby. "I'll be outside," Loed said. "When you're finished, I'll help you load her."

Ben's hands disappeared. "You must be joking."

"Don't joke about business, boy. Meg'll need some of those herbs to keep her easy on the drive."

"She stays until she heals," Ben said. Mara had never heard him speak so assertively.

"Listen," Loed said. "There's nothing you can do; I've already told you. We leave for the city today."

"What good is she to you if she dies on the road?"

"Please, Uncle Loed," Selene said. A decent man wouldn't have been able to refuse her.

"There, now. Zev expects her. In a few days, she'll have access to the best healers in Laeor. Sorry, Selene, but she'll be better off there." To his credit, he did sound truly sorry.

After Loed went out, Ben and Selene kept quiet. A gentle tugging on her cheek lulled Mara to sleep. She woke when she rose from the floor. For a disorienting moment, she thought her spirit had taken flight to the Otherworld.

She forced her eyes open. Clusters of colored lights floated on a midnight sea. Mara thought she might join them until they disappeared behind a canvas roof. The scent of hay was all around.

"Selene?" Her voice sounded feeble even to herself.

"I'm here." Selene embraced her hand.

Soft curls tickled her arm. Ben and Meg spoke in hushed tones at her feet.

Selene's mouth brushed her ear. "If you can hear me, listen. I'm going to save you. I'm going to save you like you saved me. I don't know how, but I'll figure it out. We'll be together again. So don't die, okay? Promise."

Mara squeezed Selene's hand.

"I love you." Selene kissed her and moved away.

Another hand, larger than Selene's, cupped her cheek. Moist lips touched hers. "Be as strong as I know you are, and survive this. I'll take care of Selene." Ben slipped a second lozenge under her tongue and was gone.

Reins snapped. The wagon lurched and rolled forward, bumping over every hole and rut in the road. Mara's teeth clattered in her skull, but the expected pain didn't come. She hoped the gratitude she felt would find its way to Ben.

Hands braced her head, holding it still. The second lozenge took effect. As Mara faded into sleep, comprehension blazed through her mind.

Stars. The floating lights were stars.

The mist had vanished.

CHAPTER 4

The journey was agony. Outside Firth, the late summer weather was as it should be. The temperature rose faster than the morning sun, leaving Mara's skin damp and mouth dry. Meg put a wet cloth to her lips, which offered some relief, but the scent of cool water from the well at home haunted her dreams.

Meg was not as careful as Ben. At first, she administered too few lozenges. The pain crouched a long while and then pounced all at once, impossible to control. Mara thrashed and moaned until Meg overdosed her. When she regained consciousness, it was night again, and the wagon was still. The smell of sweat and urine overwhelmed. She retched.

"She's awake!"

Loed carried her into a home where Meg and a strange woman pulled off her damp clothing. Too weak to care, she surrendered to the enemy, who sponged and dressed her in fresh clothing. They tucked her into bed and offered broth but took it away before she had her fill. Another lozenge was placed under her tongue, and she was left alone. She woke in the moving wagon the next morning.

Such became the rhythm of the next few days. Meg made fewer mistakes, but Mara worsened. Pressure mounted in her head, pounding behind her eyes. At times she forgot where she was and why she was there. Fever took hold, spreading pain from her head to the rest of her body. Dreams were indistinguishable from reality.

Had it not been for nightly stops, Mara might have let herself die despite her promise to Selene. Regardless, she doubted she'd reach Rahm-Or alive. Pain gnawed relentlessly. Since overdosing her, Meg had been too conservative with the lozenges. The gift of oblivion wouldn't come. The only thing left was to writhe.

The road changed. Uneven jolting transposed into measured staccato. They'd reached Rahm-Or, Meg told her, but Mara couldn't muster relief. The bustle and smells of the city nagged. Every clip of the horses' hooves was a blow to her head.

The wagon stopped. The air sat on her chest like a tub of steaming bathwater. A fly buzzed close to her head. It lit, tickling her wound. An attempt to swat it told her she'd lost command of her limbs.

"Why didn't you come by boat?" a man said.

Loed answered. "Girl's got eyes. She wasn't out the whole time."

"How is she?"

Mara's memories stirred at the voice, at the force of his questions, which demanded immediate answers.

"One foot in the Otherworld. She ought not be moved till the healer comes," Meg said.

Something shattered. "You were supposed to be watching her."

Loed sounded defensive. "Old sot surprised us. All he does is drink, sleep, and gripe. Never raised a fist at either of 'em."

The man's voice dropped. "I'll kill him."

The wagon shook as someone climbed inside. Each step was an earthquake. The visitor leaned over, pouring off hot emotion. Desperate to match a face to the voice, Mara willed her eyelids to lift.

Sharp blue eyes. A powerful jaw. Jet-black hair. Thick, arched brows drew together.

"Zev?"

The brows relaxed. "You know me. That's a good sign. I was beginning to wonder if Loed brought me the right girl. You don't look much like yourself." A smirk.

Horses approached. "Healer's here!"

"You'll feel better soon, Mara," Zev said, leaning back. "I sent for the best healer in the city."

Mutters. Footsteps. The wagon rattled again as someone new came aboard. This one moved gently and smelled like soil and summer rain. His touch was light like Ben's. "Is this her only injury?"

Something about him recalled the times she'd pressed her cheek to sun-warmed earth, finding it ready for seed. She used to rest like that, smiling in the dirt before reporting to Ramzi.

Mara didn't hear an answer. There was movement, a clink of glass bottles. The odor of alcohol stung Mara's nose.

"This won't be pleasant, but if you keep it down, you'll sleep," the healer said.

Fingers pressed her nostrils. When she no longer smelled the tincture, she was able to swallow. It burned like fire whiskey, but the moment it hit her stomach, the pain crawled out of the wagon and into the street.

The healer's tone sharpened. "I need a cot, a clean table, boiling water . . ."

Before Mara gave way to sleep from which she might not return, she needed a look at this healer who reminded her of home. Her eyes fluttered opened and shut. In the instant they were open, they locked on his. Those brown eyes made her feel safe, something she wasn't sure she'd ever felt before.

The homey scent of an applewood fire nudged Mara awake. The pressure in her skull had receded, and the aches and chills were gone. A down mattress shifted beneath her as she sat up. Lifting her hand, she watched the mattress slowly rise like dough. Never had she slept on anything so luxurious. The large room was dim and devoid of windows. Monstrous heads of mountain beasts protruded from the wall, made ghoulish by the flickering light. A candle rested on the table, revealing another cot next to hers. The steady rise and fall of the blanket told her it was occupied. Too warm, Mara kicked off the quilts and looked around for a pitcher of water.

From the neighboring cot rose a petite figure Mara almost mistook for a kindly sprite. Creases gathered at the corners of the small woman's eyes, which were large and soft like those of a fawn. White hair cascaded down her back in a straight stream. She drew near, smiling. The dimple in her cheek endeared her to Mara at once.

"Hello, Mara. I'm Kali, your nurse. Will you have water or tea?"

Mara unstuck her tongue from the roof of her mouth. "Water."

Not only did Kali have the eyes of a deer, but she moved like one, with unhurried poise and silent feet. Kali returned with a full mug and watched Mara empty it. "Broth?"

At Mara's nod, Kali went to the door. Outside was a lighted corridor, walls planked with varnished wood and finished with glowing sconces. Muted laughter and music drifted from somewhere. Kali spoke to someone Mara couldn't see and returned. "How do you feel?"

"Confused, but better," Mara said.

"Please tell me your name and the name of the town you came from, and I'll be happy to answer your questions," Kali said.

"Mara. Firth. Where am I?"

"The King's city, Rahm-Or, at the headquarters of the Ring," Kali answered.

"So I'm not dead."

Kali's dimple made a shadow in her face. "Not today. Declan is an able healer."

Declan—the man who'd given her medicine and reminded her of home.

A maid delivered a steaming bowl of broth. Lamb and herbs. Mara's mouth watered. Kali leaned in to feed her. "I can do it," Mara said.

"I'll let you try tomorrow," Kali said.

Mara sipped. "Do you work for Zev or . . . Declan?"

Kali squinted, pursing her lips. "I'm an ambassador, so you could say I work for the King, though I don't serve on the Council. I sometimes work with Declan. I met Zev for the first time yesterday."

Mara raised a brow and winced when the movement tugged her wound. "You know the King?" She wanted to know whether Kali was a deceiver or simply deceived.

"Yes." The word was said with care.

"You've seen him?"

Kali smiled. "Would you like more broth?"

"No, thank you." Mara would've pressed the question, but the door swung open. Zev strode into the room. A maid followed, casting curious glances over her shoulder as she lit the sconces. Zev stood over Mara, arms folded. "I heard you were awake. How are you?"

In the time since he'd left Firth, Zev had grown. He was taller, broader. Light glinted off gold rings that decorated his large hands. His arms looked strong enough to toss grain sacks like straw dolls. Black clothing offset his light eyes and pale skin. He was the kind of beautiful that hurt to look at.

"Mara?" He waited for her answer, and she was staring.

Heat flushed her cheeks. "Better. Much better. Thank you."

"Good. Because you look dreadful."

It took a moment for her to realize he teased her. He seemed to want her to tease back, but she wasn't sure she wanted to give him the pleasure. She smoothed the wrinkles from her bedclothes. "Is Loed still here?"

Zev adjusted his rings, watching her. "He's here for a few days. Would you like to see him?"

"Hills, no," she said flatly. "I only want to send a message to Selene."

"I'll send parchment and ink," he said with a snicker. "You're as tart as I remember. That should serve you well." He whispered something to the maid, who scurried out. "In any case, I'm glad you feel better. Help yourself to the library and the kitchen. Don't hesitate to ask for anything you need or desire."

His manners had improved, which made him foreign to Mara. "Thank you," she said, not wanting to seem uncouth.

With a nod, Zev excused himself. Mara tried to ignore the strange queasiness she felt watching him go. Self-conscious, Mara returned to Kali with her previous question. "The King. Have you seen him?"

Kali's face, which had grown thoughtful, softened into a motherly grin. "Declan will be pleased. You are alert, observant, and responsive. And now, I imagine you're tired."

She spread the quilt over Mara once more and dimmed the lamps Zev had ordered lit only a moment ago. Then, climbing into her own cot, she said, "The King walks among us, Mara. Only most of us fail to recognize him. Sleep well."

Mara's mind erupted with questions as Kali closed her eyes. She hadn't yet decided whether or not Kali was trustworthy. Nevertheless, Mara pondered what Kali had said until she fell asleep to what sounded like a party at the end of the hall.

∽ ∽ ∽

Declan came by the next morning as Mara finished her breakfast of broth and dry toast. Mara noted his worn, simple clothing and wondered why the best healer in the city dressed like a pauper. He was neither large nor very tall. His wiry frame tapered from broad shoulders, which sagged as if they carried too much weight. Had it not been for such a young-looking face and dark beard, Mara would've guessed him to be twice her age, but he was probably only a little older than Zev.

After greeting them warmly, he listened to Kali's report and checked Mara's injuries, flashing bright smiles at her with abandon. They came like springtide gusts through the hills back home—predictable yet unexpected: one when Kali told him how alert Mara had been, another upon hearing how well she was eating and drinking, another at the offer of porridge. And one for no reason at all. Mara had never seen anyone smile like him, not even Selene.

Dark circles framed wise, kind eyes that at times laughed and at others drew her in with secrets she wanted to know. Apart from the eyes and grin, he wasn't handsome, and now that she saw him clearly, he didn't remind her of Ben or anyone. He was other, entirely unique. The heavy-laden man with the luminous countenance was a breathing paradox.

Satisfied with his observations, he sat. "Your wounds are healing, but I'm afraid you'll be left with a scar."

"A scar?"

"On your cheek where you were cut."

Touching her cheek, Mara shrugged. "I don't mind scars much."

"I doubt very much Zev will take the news so well. Which brings me to some unpleasant business," he said.

Kali placed a bowl of porridge in his lap. Steam danced above it with a lithe grace. Mara focused on the movement as Declan took a bite and then looked up at him, wary. He stared back like she was a riddle to solve. "When a slave—new or veteran—requires the attention of a healer, the Council asks questions. Abuse isn't tolerated. First, I must know who injured you."

Odd that he hadn't been told. Or maybe he had and wanted to hear the story from her directly. The answer was simple, but Mara hadn't untangled the events in her own mind and wasn't prepared to verbalize them to a stranger. A patient frown formed as he waited. He wouldn't leave until she answered.

"My uncle," she said. "Not the one who brought me here. It was an accident."

His frown deepened. "Why are you here? Were you forced?"

Yes. No. She didn't know. It was an impossible question. "I sold myself."

"May I ask why?"

"To save my sister," she said.

His dark expression compelled Mara to elaborate. "She was sick—dying—and needed a particular medicine. I didn't have enough money, so I went to my uncle who works for the Ring."

"How much did he charge you?"

"All I'm worth," she said. Loed's words.

He cocked his head at her, his mouth a grim line. "I doubt that."

A headache formed behind Mara's eyes. Massaging her forehead, she said, "Thirty silvers is the price of a slave."

"But not necessarily the value of one." Declan took another bite. "Did you consider going to the King's consulate for help?"

"What could they have done? As long as I've lived in Firth, the consulate has been little more than a nice building doing nice things for nice people who don't need it. And I'm not a nice person."

Mara stole a glance at Kali, who sat by the door dabbing her eyes with a handkerchief. Annoyed by pity and pain, Mara added, "It doesn't matter. I would've ended up here anyway."

The fire snapped and flickered. Chagrined by her outburst, Mara ducked her head. Declan didn't question her further, though she felt he wanted to. His business complete, he told her she was doing well and asked Kali to help her stand several times a day. Looking Mara in the eye, he gave her the gift of one more smile.

The hall Mara slept in had no windows, but by long habit, she woke each day at dawn. Every morning, her first objective was to stand. Dizziness and poor coordination made walking more difficult than she'd anticipated, but she pressed on, determined to regain independence. When she discovered the door beside the fireplace accessed the garden, she coaxed Kali into walks outside.

The garden was poorly tended, but Mara found comfort in the smell of green things and salty breezes. The Ring kept a pair of milking goats and a few chickens. Kali laughed aloud when Mara stroked and cooed at them like young children. Among the plants and animals, she felt almost happy. On these early morning excursions, Mara would sometimes peer into the open door of the kitchen. Gathered around a large table, four women ate breakfast and drank tea. Satin bathrobes draped their elegant postures. Each was striking in her own way. One in particular drew her gaze. Tall and willowy, the woman was as pale as Mara was brown, with snow-white hair and a young, beautiful face. More than once, Mara caught her staring back and was left with an impression of the woman's dislike. The others didn't seem to notice her at all.

Declan performed checks every morning. Part of the time was spent in conversation, which made Mara uneasy. She lived in fear he would unearth the comment she'd made about the inevitability of her fate. He hadn't forgotten. He had the look of someone waiting for an opportune moment to broach a sensitive topic. While she enjoyed his company, she breathed easier when he was gone.

Rest and nourishment were the staples of Mara's care. Maids served food several times a day in growing portions. Kali insisted upon three rests per day and an early bedtime. At home, Mara would have resisted such treatment, but in a foreign city and without purpose, compliance became reflex.

Mara liked Kali. She was unobtrusive and observant. Mara wanted for nothing. Little by little, she told Kali about Selene, Ben, and the farm she missed. In turn, Kali spoke of her time in the King's cavalry many winters ago and of how she'd met her husband, now deceased, during her service. He'd been a healer in the army. She'd taught him to handle a sword, and he'd taught her to care for the wounded and sick.

"Of the two of us," Kali said with a nostalgic grin, "he was the more successful teacher."

It was difficult for Mara to imagine Kali holding a sword in her tiny hand. Her nurturing temperament led Mara to ask whether she had children. She'd given birth to two. The first had been stillborn. The other had died as a young child, but she claimed four living children. She and her husband had adopted a girl some years ago. She was near Mara's age now. Kali's dimple shone when she mentioned her sons. Declan and a pair of brothers who served with him on the Council frequented her table and saw after her.

The Council piqued Mara's interest. At her request, Kali explained the Council of Ambassadors, which the King had appointed before his disappearance. It consisted of thirteen members who governed the city and sought the good of the kingdom, though many provinces valued autonomy above guidance and protection.

"Is that why the provinces go undefended from Akaronian raids?" Mara asked. "Because they won't accept the King's ideals?"

Kali smiled, unperturbed. "The reasons are varied and complicated, but many of the provinces and even portions of the city reject us, which may be why the King left. We maintain the consulates in hope they'll one day receive our help."

"I thought you said the King walks among us. How is that possible if he no longer lives in our world?"

"Surely you don't impose the limits of your imagination upon a magician powerful enough to build worlds and move between them," Kali said.

The conversation wasn't leading anywhere Mara wanted to go, so she asked what she really wanted to know. "Is it true the Council keeps watch over the King's magical stone?"

"Something like that," Kali said, "but I prefer to think Eleora keeps watch over them. At least until the King returns and sets things right again."

Mara tried not to roll her eyes. The King was likely dead, and yet seemingly intelligent people expected him to one day return with everyone who'd joined him in the Otherworld. Supposedly, he would unite the races, subdue enemy spirits, and heal the land. But dead people didn't live again. While she believed there once had been a just king who wore a legendary gemstone, she doubted the sensational nature of the stories. Every problem she'd faced, she'd solved herself, and if more people were honest, they'd say the same. The sooner they gave up hope of being rescued by mythological beings and accepted they were alone in the universe, the better off they'd be.

"How does it work?" Mara asked. "Do they keep it in a vault in the palace?"

Kali looked up from her knitting, her features aglow with an ethereal radiance. "Eleora is neither hidden nor flaunted but leaves traces of its magic wherever and upon whom it goes. Only the wearer knows where it is, but anyone with eyes to see can discern where it has been."

Mara asked nothing more. To do so might make Kali suspicious. For the time being, it was enough to know Eleora had a wearer.

As strength and balance returned, Mara lengthened her walks. Each day, she roamed farther down the corridor, edging closer to the mysterious door at the end, behind which frivolities ensued after dark. She fell asleep to the noise every night. Whatever took place on the other side, Kali didn't approve. Whenever the noise swelled, she pursed her lips and closed her eyes in what Mara assumed to be prayer. Mara had forgotten that people did that—pray to the King like he was some kind of god. Her mother had before she'd died, as had Phi.

Zev, another source of curiosity, frequented her room. He asked after her and made light conversation but never broached the subjects of her oath or slavery or how he'd left her behind in Firth. His visits left her restless. Her stomach bucked in his presence and dropped at his departure. Kali sensed her discomfiture. Unable to order him away, Kali shot him disapproving glances for the duration of his stay and tried to distract Mara with a treat of warm milk or a strategy game afterward.

One day, Zev announced he would escort Mara on her morning walk. Consternation was drawn plain on Kali's face, but she uttered nothing more than a warning not to let Mara overtire.

Straightaway, Zev led her down the corridor, through the mysterious door, and into a hall four times the size of the one she slept in. Massive wrought-iron chandeliers hung from high-pitched ceilings, casting a glow upon lacquered pine walls. Large gilded mirrors spaced evenly apart doubled the effect of the black-and-white carpet. The room was very fine but thoroughly masculine and devoid of real color.

Mara caught her reflection in one of the mirrors. The face wasn't the one she was accustomed to seeing in the silver plate back home. Purple, green, and black splotches about her eyes gave her the visage of a coon. Her eyes moved to Zev, who met her gaze. Next to him, she looked like a filthy swineherd on the arm of royalty.

If Zev guessed her thoughts, he didn't comment. "This is the grand hall. When you're well, you'll entertain here every night."

"Entertain." The word pulled her out of a daze.

"Men," he clarified. "You'll facilitate conversation, seduce them, and lead them upstairs to your chamber."

Mara blinked. Ben had told her she'd be a prostitute, but she hadn't considered what that meant until now. The image of her seducing men was ludicrous.

"Some stay until dawn, but most will leave earlier. You'll listen to everything they say and report to me. That's all you have to do."

That's all. Mara's stomach clenched. "Zev, I can't do this."

He smirked as if he'd expected that answer. "Of course you can. It'll be easy after running a farm."

Before she could tell him it wouldn't be anything like running a farm he scooped her into his arms and climbed the stairs. Mara stood eye to eye with most men and could lift heavy sacks of grain with all but the strongest. To be carried like a child was an odd sensation. She rested her head against his shoulder, inhaling frankincense. Something alive woke in her belly, overpowering her resentment toward him.

At the top of the stairs, there was a small corridor lined with several closed doors on either side. Zev opened the first door on the left, which revealed a lavish bedchamber. A large bed outfitted in red satin angled out of the corner by the window. A black velvet settee stood against one wall, an ornate vanity on the other. Beside the vanity was a large armoire. A tapestry and lace doilies provided decoration. Spices scented the air.

"This is your room." He placed her upon the settee.

She looked around, avoiding his eyes.

"What do you think?"

She stared at his rings. One featured a stone, gray and watery, like the Priel on a cloudy day. "I think there's a man in my bedchamber."

"You'll adapt," he said. "The job's easy. Our patrons think they come for pleasure, but they really come for companionship. Make them feel important. Listen to them. Ask them what they like and remember. You'll get everything you need."

Her face felt hot. "Surely there's another way to do what needs to be done."

"There are many ways to collect information. I employ them all. And this, by far, is the most effective. Rich men are well connected. They know everything of consequence that happens in the city, but they share very little unless they feel at ease."

"And they'll feel at ease with me." The words rang false in her ears.

"Naturally. You're a woman." His grin turned wicked. "Men chronically underestimate the fairer sex."

Mara's knowledge of how the sexes related didn't extend far beyond the mechanics of pregnancy and childbearing. She had no idea how to weaponize her sexuality. "Zev, I—"

"You're going to tell me in some awkward way you've never been with a man. Loed told me. Lack of experience won't hurt you. Patrons pay extra for it."

The bed in the corner drew her gaze. The thought of sharing it with strange men night after night sent a shudder down her spine. It hadn't met its end when Zev carried her back downstairs.

He showed her the kitchen, the garden she'd visited many times before, and his office, where she'd give her morning reports. He indicated his bedchamber when they passed and told her to look for him there if she had urgent information and couldn't find him.

By the end of the tour, Mara was eager for her cot but had questions she couldn't ask with Kali in the room. "I assume the plan hasn't changed."

Zev pulled her into his office and shut the door. "Not at all."

She eyed the neat desk, the large window, and the library on the far wall. The space smelled like him, an observation that made her insides lurch. "Who knows of it?" she asked.

"You, me, and Rivka, of course. Don't speak of it to anyone."

"Loed seems to know something."

"Loed knows only what he needs to know."

"And the women? How do they decide what to tell you?"

"They tell me everything. As will you. I decide what information is useful."

Her mouth fell open. "You don't trust your own people."

"I don't trust anyone," Zev said.

Mara understood distrust but couldn't conceive a way for Zev to execute the plan alone. Not that it was her business. At least, she hoped it wasn't. "So, I find the stone, and I get to go home, correct?"

"Close," he said. "I need you to bring the stone to me. After that, you can run home to the pigs if you wish. Once you've earned back your freedom. Or you can stay with me and see the raiders answer for their crimes."

"I don't think the stone will be easy to steal," Mara said. "Kali said it's worn by a Council member."

"Already spying, are we?" Zev seemed amused.

"No," Mara said. Kali was her friend. "But if what she said is true, I don't see how I can help you find it here, doing this. And if I were to miraculously succeed, I don't see how I can take it from one of them." Zev had trained her to defend herself in emergencies, not to take on a sword-wielding warrior.

Zev placed a hand on her shoulder and made her face him. "One step at a time, Mara. First, we'll find out who has it. Then, we'll make a plan to steal it. Trust me."

Mara couldn't decide whether to wrench away from his grasp or to take comfort in his touch. As angry as she was, Zev was the only person in Rahm-Or she knew well enough to be angry with. More importantly, he was her only way to save Selene.

Selene, who would despise her if she ever discovered what Mara planned to do.

Mara gave him a tight smile. "I don't trust anyone," she said, echoing his own words, and realized it was true.

CHAPTER 5

The weight of a millstone hung from Mara's neck as she returned to her cot. She tossed through the morning, nipped by chills. When she refused her midday meal, Kali sent for Declan. On the edge of sleep, Mara heard her say, "She came back to me like this after an hour with Zev. I warned him not to tire her."

"Why don't you go home for the night? I'll stay," Declan said.

Sometime later, a cup pressed to her mouth. "Drink this."

Thirsty, Mara gulped down cool willow-bark tea. Declan rubbed a lavender-mint salve into her feet, watching her. His smile wasn't as carefree as usual. "Better?"

She nodded. "Thank you."

Stretching backward, he yawned and mussed his hair. "You don't seem to have an infection. You overextended yourself today, but I can't find the cause of your ailment. Why don't you tell me what troubles you?"

As Mara opened her mouth, Declan pressed a finger to his lips. He turned to the maid who reclined on a couch near the door. "Thalia, would you please fetch two bowls of whatever the cook prepared for dinner?" When she was gone, he leaned forward. "Now."

How much did Declan know about the Ring? He at least seemed to understand conversations weren't private, and he knew what she would become. There was no need to pretend. "Zev showed me the building today, told me what's expected of me. I have no idea how I'll manage."

Declan shrugged. "You don't have to."

She answered with an incredulous frown.

"All you need to do is write a letter requesting redemption. I'll scribe it if you can't write."

"I don't understand," she said.

His smile was patient. "Redemption is a provision of the King. You apply by letter to the Council, which will purchase you from Zev. You'll live in King's Quarter for a few seasons as a kind of rehabilitation. Learn a trade, save some money, and decide what to do from there."

She sputtered. "How? I mean—do people know about this? And if they do, why are there slaves in Rahm-Or?"

"That's what I'd like to know. I suppose the Ring and masters like them don't discuss it, but you'd be surprised how many slaves know about redemption."

Thalia returned with two bowls of stew. Declan thanked her and said, "I'm sorry to trouble you again, but will you bring a warm glass of milk for my patient?"

With a huff, Thalia flounced out the door.

"How many errands will you invent for that poor girl?" Mara asked.

Declan pretended offense. "She's been bored all afternoon, I'll have you know. Besides, we're hungry, and you need the milk. But to answer your question, she'll be busy until we're through here."

Mara snickered at his wink.

"There now," he said. "That's the first real smile I've seen from you. It's nice."

Mara slung surreptitious glances at Declan as they ate. He was hungry, tired, sad, apparently poor, and the happiest person she'd ever met. She was relieved he wore no chain around his neck—not that the Council was likely to entrust their youngest and least experienced member with their prized gem. But she liked him and wouldn't want to betray him.

His eyes flickered when he caught her watching. "So?"

She stirred her bowl. "I can't. I owe more than a slave's debt."

His tone was gentle. "Whatever you owe, the Council will pay."

"It's not money that I owe."

Without meaning to, she told him of the night the Akaronians had attacked and burned the mining village that was her childhood home. How her father had plucked her and Selene out of bed when the drums first echoed off the hills. After hiding them in the brush by the stream, he'd left them to fetch his gems and tools. His back fading into a cloud of smoke was the last she ever saw of him. For Mara, the King of her mother's stories had burned to ash with everything else that night. Declan listened, his mouth forming a grim line.

"You must pretend I never told you this, but Zev was among the raiders. Selene and I should've been his First Blood. It's the rite of passage that would've made him one of them. But he defected and saved us."

"For a price," Declan said.

"Yes, well. Zev's always had an eye for profit."

After a thoughtful silence, he fixed Mara with a shrewd gaze. "There's something you're not telling me. Something you're more ashamed of than selling yourself. What is it? Maybe I can help."

She'd make a terrible spy if she didn't learn to conceal her thoughts. She shut her eyes. "I accepted help long ago and have regretted it every day since. No one can help me now but me. I have no choice but to fulfill my oath."

Her teeth clamped her tongue. Wary, she studied the man who made her secrets spill like water from a spring.

With a wistful smile, he said, "I suppose we have our answer. I imagine there are as many slaves in Rahm-Or as there are reasons to be enslaved." He didn't say it unkindly, but the words sliced to the bone.

Thalia returned with the milk. It wasn't as warm as Mara wished it to be, but she didn't dare send her out again. For Thalia's sake and her own.

Kali returned the following morning. Mara suspected Declan had stayed not because she required his expertise but because Kali needed reprieve and he'd wanted to discuss redemption. Mara was grateful to him but glad at Kali's return. Kali didn't ask provoking questions.

Loed came for the letter Mara hadn't written, so she dictated a short message—*Alive, as promised*—and hoped Selene would forgive the brevity.

That afternoon, Zev entered the hall with the largest man Mara had ever seen. He introduced Boz, his friend and bodyguard. "You'll see a lot of each other," Zev said. "Boz patrols the gaming hall every night. No man harasses his girls. Right, Boz?"

Boz answered with a slight smile and placed a box on the table next to Mara's cot.

Mara tried not to gawk. She couldn't imagine anyone fool enough to cross such a daunting figure. At full height, the top of her head reached only to his chest, which was as broad and solid as a boulder. Muscle rippled beneath ebony skin. An angular face made him appear chiseled from stone.

From the box, Boz retrieved a bronze instrument as intimidating as his physique. Several needles, flat and wide, were attached. Mara paled.

"Today, you'll get your first marks. Don't worry. Boz is very good," Zev said and disappeared before she could object.

Kali asked whether Mara wanted her to stay. Mara grimaced. "No. I might squeal, and I don't want more witnesses than necessary."

Kali patted Mara's hand. "I'll be back by dinner."

Mara tugged her lodestone necklace as Boz mixed the ink, wishing she was as brave as Selene. Boz offered her a flask. Mara accepted it with a grateful nod and drank.

"Tell me about your necklace, Miss Mara," Boz said.

"It's lodestone, one of a pair. My sister back home has the other." Her words jittered and scurried out.

Boz filled the needles. "It's nice you have something to remember her by. Tell me about your home."

His speech was an unhurried melody that rattled her chest with its depth. She wanted to hear more. And thoughts of home were painful. "Would you tell me about yours instead?"

He raised his brow. "Only one other has ever asked."

He took her nearest arm and pushed up her sleeve. A needle pricked the underside of her forearm a handbreadth above her wrist. Mara looked away, pulling a sharp breath through her teeth.

"I was born on a small island south of the Sea of Ronen, where there are no seasons and the water is always warm. Balmy winds toss the hair of the palm trees day and night and carry scents of coconut and spice to every home."

Mara lost herself in the cadence of his speech until she tasted his mother's coconut prawn curry and rubbed grit between her toes. "Why did you leave? I wouldn't."

His brow creased.

"Forget I asked."

Boz finished one arm and moved to the other. "A tradesman took me away when my father died. I was payment for his debts. Later, he sold me to the Ring."

"You're a slave?"

"I was and would be still if not for a black-haired boy from the outpost at Firth."

Mara forgot the needles. "Zev freed you?"

"Not exactly," Boz said. "When he first arrived, the leader assigned him menial tasks, such as slaves do. We met this way and became friends. But a man like Zev will always rise. He tried to carry me along, but in the Ring, a slave will not go far. He found out about King's Redemption and applied for me. I could not read or write, you see. After four seasons in King's Quarter, I returned here to help my friend."

"So the slave becomes a master." The words sounded harsher than she meant them to.

If he was offended, he hid it. "I see myself as a protector."

Boz finished and applied a salve that soothed her angry skin. As he cleaned and put away his instruments, Mara inspected her arms. The insignia of the Ring was drawn black on each one. Frowning, she reached for Boz. "May I?"

He extended his forearms. His marks weren't black. They shone pale against dark skin. "They don't fade," she said.

"I don't mind," he said. "They remind me of what I was saved from."

A reminder of hope for him. For her, a seal of fate. "Thank you, Boz."

"For what? Not the marks." Ivory teeth shone from smiling lips.

"Your home. I saw it, and it's lovely."

"It's yours. To visit when the moment isn't kind."

Declan paid his final visit the day Mara moved to her bedroom upstairs. She expected the good-bye to be uncomfortable, but Declan showed no offense that she'd scorned his offer of help. Zev interrupted to discuss the matter of payment.

Declan held up a hand. "No charge." When Zev pressed, he said, "Well, I may spend an evening with the lady."

Surprise looked out of place on Zev's face, as if the muscles weren't accustomed to sitting that way. "Of course. But not for a time, you understand. A virgin is worth—"

Mara's face burned at the word "virgin." Declan cut him off. "Understood. I'll book sometime next season." With a solemn nod to Mara, he left.

Mara tried to picture him in her bed and couldn't. He hadn't seemed the type to seek the company of a prostitute, and the idea of taking a friend into her chamber sickened her, no matter what she could learn about Eleora's location. Maybe by next season, Zev would have dismissed her as a lost cause and chucked her out on the street.

Kali helped Mara move upstairs and spoke a tremulous farewell. Mara kissed Kali's cheek and cocked her head. "Are your eyes blue or gray, Kali?"

Kali smiled, wiping away her tears. "They can't decide, but today, I imagine they're gray."

A rap on the door startled Mara awake. Zev leaned against the doorframe. Laughter and the tinkling of glass rose from the stairwell. "Come on. It's time you see what we do."

For a terrible moment, she thought he meant to throw her into the fray, but he led her down the back stair, through the kitchen, and into a small room furnished with two stools and a small table. Walking in, she looked through a darkened glass into the activity of the great hall. She pressed a finger against the pane. "Is this one of the mirrors?"

Zev nodded. "Magic glass. We can see them, but they can't see us."

"Where does it come from?" she asked in wonder, inspecting the edges.

"The desert people make them."

She whirled. "That's impossible. The fire spirits killed them all."

"Why would you assume that?" he asked. "Now, sit and watch."

With a flat look, she obeyed, knowing he wouldn't answer the questions he'd created. "How many of these do you have in this place?"

He smirked. "The women will come down any moment. Notice the way they enter the room. Observe how the men respond."

A moment later, a woman burst from the staircase with the energy of a flying star, full, green skirts billowing in her wake. Raven hair enhanced a bold silver streak that fell like a waterfall over one shoulder. Every man in the room grew in height. One claimed her hand and whispered something, which she answered with a dazzling smile that didn't reach her almond eyes.

The next woman descended like a queen, peering down a regal nose. She wore a close-fitting gown the sunset shade of lavender trimmed in black lace. As her subjects bowed, the corners of her fine mouth turned up in a puckered smirk. Men from one table beckoned, but she passed them to sit at another next to an older man who reeked of coin. Mara smelled his silvers through the glass.

Behind the queen bounced a petite blonde in an off-the-shoulder cobalt gown. A smattering of freckles decorated her small nose, which wrinkled when she smiled. She was the plainest woman in the room, but the way men responded to her reminded Mara of lodestones. Her presence drew them in with an irresistible force. Four escorts attached to her the instant her feet touched the carpet. She greeted each, causing them to beam in delight, and spellbound the lot with a giggle.

The white woman was last to emerge. A plum-colored gown offset her milky skin and waved and flowed along her graceful frame like willow branches caught in a breeze. The haphazard pinning of her hair had a bewitching effect. Mara suspected the style required more effort than it belied. If the green-gowned woman was a star, the white woman was a bolt of skyfire, jolting everyone in the room. She selected the arm of a handsome man, younger than most, and whispered something in his ear. Hot color crept above his collar as he chortled.

Mara now understood the hall's lack of decoration. The women were the centerpieces. Neutral tones framed the brilliance of their gowns. Mirrors echoed their exquisite features. Each moved through the room with ease and finesse, belonging in a way Mara suspected she never would.

Night after night, she observed them as she waited for her bruises to fade. She practiced their movements and gestures in her vanity mirror, a suspicious object now that she knew about the magic glass in the grand hall. Her efforts usually dissolved into morose laughter and self-loathing.

A crisp breeze nipped her face the morning Zev met her in the garden and declared her fit to work. Autumn had come in earnest. "You'll need all the time she gave you," he said. Mara could no longer delay the inevitable.

All day, she quivered and paced, neglecting meals. Sleep was impossible.

A knock surprised her midafternoon. Mara opened her door to the woman she'd dubbed "the Queen." She wore only her underthings.

"You must be Mara. I'm Cadha." She offered a languid hand. When Mara didn't take it, Cadha strolled in, perched on the settee, and inspected Mara's face. "You need wine."

Cadha pulled a cord Mara hadn't noticed before. A moment later, an unusual-looking girl of no more than eight winters appeared at the door. Dark-blue eyes shone from brown skin, a different shade from Mara's. "Two glasses of wine, darling," Cadha said.

The girl scampered off. Cadha smiled after her. "My daughter, Nuri."

Horror froze Mara's jangling nerves. "Is she . . . ?"

"A slave? No. Zev took us in when she was an infant. He helps me see to her education and dotes on her as well as any uncle."

An inner pang took Mara by surprise. Zev had once seen after her and Selene, but she couldn't imagine him doting on anyone.

When Nuri returned with the wine, Mara gulped hers down without ceremony. Cadha arched a brow. "Be sure to take small sips this evening. Men don't pay well for slovenly company."

Grimacing, Mara set down her empty glass.

"Come now, speak," Cadha said. "Is your shyness the reason you haven't joined us for meals?"

Mara appreciated frankness. She hadn't expected to find it in someone like Cadha. "Partly. And our schedules have been different till now."

"Levanna's convinced you're snobbish, but you don't appear to be. You're pale as a cucumber. You should eat."

Nuri delivered sandwiches. Mara forced small bites under Cadha's supervision. "That's how you should take your wine," she said. "Now, how shall we arrange your hair?"

Without Cadha, Mara would've been lost. She'd always worn her hair in a braid. Cadha showed her how to pin it up. "Have you ever used makeup?"

"The idea of tricking men into thinking I'm beautiful makes me ill." Too late, Mara realized she might've offended her new friend.

Cadha tittered. "The makeup isn't for them. It's for us. It helps us become what we need to be. We're actors, Mara, and the hall is our stage. You'll find the work easier if you play a character. Makeup helps."

Cadha traced the edges of Mara's eyes with kohl and rubbed rouge into her cheeks. "I can't hide your scar. You need to invent a story for it."

"A story?"

"Yes, and another to explain how you came here. The patrons prefer fancy to truth, so make it good."

Mara cursed Zev for not warning her and scrambled for ideas as she applied rose oil to her wrists and neck. Cadha helped her into a gold gown she pulled from the armoire. The color was lovely against Mara's skin, but the plunging neckline made her feel naked. When she peered at her reflection, she didn't know herself.

Cadha inspected her work, her expression victorious. "You look the part. The act is up to you. Now, listen closely. This is your first night, so no one expects anything of you. There's no need to volunteer conversation, but be attentive. There's much to be learned in the little things. And laugh at any attempt at a joke. Even if it's not funny. Even if you don't understand it."

Mara blinked. If she didn't understand a joke, how could she laugh?

"These men aren't like the ones who attend the lower-class brothels. They treat us well, so we treat them well. Tonight, you'll go to the highest bidder. Pray it isn't Jed, but if it is, bear it bravely, and know he's the worst of his kind. You're the newest, so you'll walk downstairs last. Be sure not to let Levanna trip you once you're on the floor." With that, she left.

Cadha had intended comfort, but Mara felt every mite as terrified as before and anxious to avoid this Jed character, whoever he was.

Mara sat at the mirror, working herself up to go downstairs, when Zev entered the room carrying a bundle of red roses. She stood to meet him, and his eyes scanned the length of her body. "You're stunning," he said. "Even with that scar. It makes you more exotic somehow." His fingers brushed the white line across her brown cheekbone, sending a pulse down her spine.

"Back home, 'exotic' is another word for 'strange.'"

"You aren't in Firth anymore." He set down the flowers and took hold of her arms. "You'll be fine. You may even enjoy yourself."

Her face flushed. How could he sympathize with Boz and Nuri and be so cavalier with her, whom he'd known since she was a child? Tonight, she would give something away she'd never get back, and to a stranger no less.

He chuckled. "You're a vision when you're angry." His lips brushed her cheek, and she was left alone.

The white woman, the one Mara assumed was Levanna, walked by her open door. Uncanny eyes raked over Mara's person, and with a sneer, she passed out of sight. Mara stepped into the hall, wondering how she'd made the girl her enemy. But she couldn't think of that now. It was time to fulfill her oath. Taking a deep breath, Mara pictured Selene. Everything she would do tonight was for her.

Mara's head spun as she descended the stairs. All her thoughts were consumed with staying upright. Only when both feet rested on the floor did she remember to breathe. She coughed, choking on cigar smoke. Unfamiliar faces gathered before her. Overwhelmed, she fought the urge to bolt and tried to ignore the itch at the middle of her back.

A pair of men guided her to a table where a short man with white hair and a trim beard shuffled an expensive set of lacquered cards. He studied her with an unsettling mix of desire and disdain. "You gentlemen remind me of my cat, Mr. Gray," he said. "Every time you leave my side, you return with a mouse."

As the laughter died, Mara realized she should've joined them. Hills—she hadn't smiled since she'd entered the room.

"We thought you'd like to meet the new girl, Jed. Name's Mara. Where you from, honey?"

Mara's stomach dropped at the short man's name. The one person she'd been warned against was the first she'd gone to. Her mind swore at her.

Five faces stared, waiting. Jed sneered. "What's the matter with you, girl? Are you mute?"

His biting tone snapped Mara to attention. "No, sir. I suppose Mr. Gray here caught hold of my tongue." She squeezed the arm that had led her into the trap and was tempted to sink her nails into the man's flesh.

To her surprise, the men guffawed. Success didn't ease her dread, but it helped her talk. "I grew up in Firth. Up north along the Priel."

"Firth, huh?" Mr. Gray asked. "Got family there?"

"A sister." The conversation, the room, the gown—none of it felt real. She reminded herself to breathe.

"A sister," one of the men said. Mara didn't like the way he smiled. "You have the look of a desert woman. Rare, these days. Were either of your parents Razan?"

Mara didn't smile back. She wouldn't mention Selene again. "My parents were both half-Razan."

Leaning back, he nudged Jed in the ribs with his elbow. "Half-Razan. She may be even more exotic than Lev, Jed."

Jed sniffed, staring at his cards. Mara felt sick. She was up for auction, and Jed's friends were trying to make a sale.

"How'd you get that scar?" another asked.

Fighting a scowl, she fumbled for an answer to the question. It had come before she was ready, so she said the first thing that came to mind. "Thorn bush. Last summer. Something spooked me in the woods."

The man leaned in. "What was it?"

Cadha had said to make it good. Mara dropped her voice to a dramatic whisper. "A spirit."

It was the right thing to say. The men looked up grinning and shuddered in delight. She released a breath she hadn't realized she'd been holding.

"Your ships sail by Firth, don't they, Jed? Your crews ever see spirits?"

"Aye. And harpies, sirens, and man-eating fish. A sailor tells a fine tale, but never trust him for the truth. Nor a woman." Jed skewered Mara with a sharp eye as he spoke.

A shooter of whiskey was placed before her like an offering of goodwill. She swallowed it down and clunked the glass upon the table. The whiskey was mild, almost sweet, compared to Ramzi's, and she was sorry there wasn't more.

The men gaped at her. She'd done something shocking, but couldn't think what. She relaxed against the back of her chair. "Perhaps tales are a pretty way to tell the truths we can't face."

Mr. Gray said, "Well, gentlemen, here's a thing—a virgin poet who takes her whiskey like a man. I'm in love."

Laughter erupted. They all drank to her, except for Jed, who took his shot some time later, eyeing her like one of the colossal predator fish he didn't believe in.

CHAPTER 6

Mara had never enjoyed fortune's kiss. Cadha's warning proved as good as prediction—Jed secured Mara for the night. After several rounds of card play, he stood, the top of his head reaching her neckline. "Let's go, Little Mouse."

Some of the men heckled and congratulated Jed as he took hold of Mara's arm. Others seemed sad to see her go. The world took on a nightmarish quality, filling her with an instinct to flee, but there was nowhere to go. Boz caught her terrified gaze as she passed him on her way to the stairs and quickly turned away.

Aunt Phi had explained physical intimacy at Mara's first show of blood. Mara had recoiled from the image, but reality proved worse than expectation. When they reached her chamber, Jed closed the door, took a seat upon the settee, and ordered her to undress. Sipping upon a glass of wine, he analyzed her as she would new livestock. "You're built for labor."

Panic emptied her mind of retorts, which was just as well. If she'd been able to speak, she would've said something insufferable and gotten into trouble with Zev.

Jed made her stand there until she shivered. "Not so talkative now, are we? That's good."

He swilled the last of his wine and told her to lie down on the bed. Humiliation capsized her. What followed wouldn't have been survivable if not for Boz's island. She made it her home until it was over.

In spite of the tremendous bid that granted him rights until morning, Jed dressed when he finished and walked out the door. Alone, Mara inspected the welts his belt had left upon her skin, vowing to never again strike an animal.

Her wounds throbbed beneath her robe on her way to Zev's office several hours later. Fatigue clouded her mind, her body ached, and soon she would have to endure it all again. Mara shut the office door behind her and sat in an empty seat with a soft hiss of pain.

A document on Zev's desk held his attention. "Well?"

The tone and manner of his greeting doused her in white-hot fury. "It was worse than I'd imagined, and he said nothing useful."

"You must've done something wrong," he said, looking up.

"I did nothing."

"And doing nothing would be wrong. Your job is to convince the patrons that you want them as much as they want you. No wonder he left so early."

Mara looked at the door, longing to run away. As a child, she'd idolized Zev as a sister might an older brother. Despite everything, his disapproval hurt worse than the welts.

"Really, Mara, you can do better. Jed is our wealthiest, most well-connected patron. We could learn a lot from him if you would only try."

Mara didn't tell him about Jed's belt. Apparently, its value made its crimes forgivable.

The four women fell silent as Mara took her seat at the table. A china cup of greenish-black tea steamed next to her plate. Mara sniffed it and cringed.

"Be sure to drink it all," Cadha said. "The world can't sustain another Jed, even in miniature."

The blonde slid a bowl to Mara with a smile. "Sugar helps. I'm Elise, by the way."

Cadha peeked at Mara over her teacup. "How was your first night?"

"It went as well as you predicted," Mara said.

Elise wrinkled her freckled nose. "Jed is horrible."

Mara gagged as she swallowed the tea. "Hills. This is worse than Ramzi's fire whiskey."

"Well, it's over, and you survived," Cadha said.

Levanna rolled her strange eyes, which appeared to be violet. "We all have to endure Jed from time to time. Get used to it."

The woman with the streaked hair smirked. "At least he has his own whorehouse to keep him occupied some of the time. Poor girls." She turned to Mara, extending her hand. "Joss. That's Levanna." She pointed. "She doesn't like you, but don't take it personally. She doesn't like anyone."

Levanna glowered at Joss, but something in her expression made Mara suspect she didn't entirely disapprove of what Joss had said.

"What's your story?" Elise asked. "Did your family sell you?"

"My sister was sick. I sold myself to buy her medicine." Mara shrugged, feigning indifference to avoid further questions.

"Well, don't expect pity," Levanna said. "We all have woeful pasts. Except Joss here, whose only woe is that she doesn't really enjoy men."

Joss stiffened.

Smirking, Levanna took a bite of toast. Mara stared, mesmerized by the way Levanna chewed. Somehow, she made even the vulgar task of eating sensual. Joss watched too, her face turning scarlet.

Cadha seized the conversation. "I was the daughter of wealthy landowners from the Coastal Plains. When my parents discovered my pregnancy, I was disinherited and thrown out. Nuri's father was their slave, you see. Elise was sold by her mother to pay for her sons' apprenticeships. And Levanna—"

Levanna's beautiful face distorted. "I'll tell my story if I want her to know it."

"Don't be such a witch," Joss said.

Mara turned to Joss. "What about you?"

"I'm not a slave," Joss said, scowling at Levanna. "I volunteered to earn. Zev takes a percentage and saves the rest in an account. In a couple of winters, I'll have enough to buy my own land and build a winery."

"But you don't care for men?" Mara didn't mean to pry, only to understand.

Her scathing gaze pinned Mara to the chair. "Do you?"

Mara still tasted the bitterness of the tea. "Not really."

"All right then."

Levanna watched everyone like they were pieces in a strategy game she was winning.

Haunted by the night, Mara couldn't sleep on the bed. But when she tried the settee, it smelled like Jed, so she made a pallet on the floor. Stiff muscles and stinging flesh greeted her when she woke. Staying awake through the night and sleeping through the day made her ill, but there was no time to lament. She must prepare for another night of work.

Downstairs, Mara avoided Jed and his men, but it did no good. Jed purchased her again. She didn't understand. He'd left her bed unhappy. She couldn't guess why he wanted her a second time. The night passed like the first, but worse. Jed seemed to enjoy hurting and humiliating her. He whipped harder, tempting her to yank the belt from his hands and return the treatment, and this time stayed until morning. The following night, when Boz told her Jed had asked for her again, Mara approached Cadha, who was surrounded by admirers. Mara explained the problem in hushed tones, pretending light conversation.

"He wants to break you," Cadha whispered out of the side of her mouth. "Flatter. Seduce him. You're an actor, remember? Show him a good time, and he'll leave you alone."

Mara followed Cadha's advice. Jed's belt stayed on the floor, but afterward, he said, "You're stiff as a corpse, whore."

Zev embittered the small victory. When she had nothing to report after three nights, he accused her of not being serious about fulfilling her oath. "What will happen to Selene if you fail?"

Mara heard the threat. Determined not to be thwarted by Jed, she altered the character she played to one that suited. She left her hair down and applied minimal makeup. Kohl and rouge didn't help her as it did Cadha, but the way her hair fell down her back made her feel more feminine than the fancy gowns. She approached Jed the moment she entered the room, passing several suitors on the way. Curling over his chair, she wrapped an arm around his chest and brushed her lips against his ear. "You haven't tired of me, have you?"

Jed grinned at his associates. "See, boys? Women are like dogs. Once you break them, they love you forever."

She swallowed her disgust and forced a smile.

That night, Mara became a shadow of herself. Keeping the pieces men responded to, like her wit and candor, she tucked away the rest in a box that she buried in the darkest corner of her heart. When self-loathing burned hot against her, she doused it with whiskey. When her bed was unbearable, she escaped to Boz's home. Sometimes, to assuage her guilt, she pretended Selene was dead. Selene would loathe what she did every night. Mara couldn't bear the thought.

Cadha was wrong about Jed. He didn't leave Mara alone. He became a regular patron. Gasping, he'd chuckle and say, "I love how you hate me," and she'd reach for the flask under her pillow.

On occasion, he revealed information, which pleased Zev, but nothing about the Council or its members. Jed didn't like her to ask questions. Mostly, his comments targeted Zev, which helped her understand why Zev never came near his women in sight of patrons. He wanted Jed to believe he saw them as Jed saw them—like chattel. Jed's low regard for Mara made him complacent. He spoke freely, hiding neither his dislike for Zev nor his plans to gain control of the Ring.

One night, he told her, "When you belong to me, Little Mouse, I'll take you as my mistress."

She smiled, knowing if that day ever came, he'd wish it hadn't.

After Jed, the job was easy, as Zev had promised. The power Mara held over the men astonished her. Most who borrowed her skin were eager to share their secrets. They were lonely, trapped in unhappy marriages, and in need of what she gave—pleasure, certainly, but also an interested ear.

Spy work wasn't so different from watching Selene's face for early signs of illness or anticipating how weather changes would affect the crops. It was all attention to detail, observation of patterns, and asking the correct question at the appropriate moment. She disclosed all kinds of confidences to Zev, some of which he found amusing. His laughter and compliments gratified, but still, she was disappointed by how little she learned about the Council and Eleora. Zev, however, no longer seemed worried.

❧ ❧ ❧

Winter's icy breath had carried away the last of autumn's splendor the night Mara spotted a new face in the crowd. He stood near the door tugging his coat, eyes darting about the room. He was out of uniform, but Mara noted his military posture, having seen a number of kingsmen while visiting shops with Cadha and Boz. Curious to discover what business a kingsman had with the Ring, Mara weaved through the crowd, greeting patrons as she went, until no one stood between her and the stranger. Careful not to look at him, she brushed his arm as she passed.

"Pardon me." She flustered.

He marveled at her face. "Seas, you look like her."

Mara waited for an explanation.

The man's throat bobbed. "How do I? I mean—how can I be alone with you?" He turned three shades of crimson, an apology in his eyes. This man was not her usual fare. He saw a woman, not a prostitute, and seemed embarrassed not by his artlessness but his coarseness.

Her amusement checked her. How worldly she'd become during her short time with the Ring. She felt sorry too. The last man who'd seen a person when he'd looked at her was Declan. She pointed to Boz, who stood in the opposite corner of the room. "Find me when you're done."

Mara pretended interest in a high-stakes card game while she waited, but she kept watch from the corner of her eye. Boz clearly disdained the man, flaring his nostrils in disgust, which was odd. The man wasn't well dressed or acquainted with Zev's establishment, but she didn't see how ineptitude mattered if his money was good—unless he was a spy, in which case he was a poor one, and she would find him out.

His business complete, the man loitered near the bar, staring to draw Mara's attention. After he downed two shooters, she glanced over her shoulder and smiled as if she'd just noticed him. Her arm lassoed his. "Shall we?"

Blushing again, he set down his glass and accompanied her upstairs.

Mara motioned to the settee and poured a glass of wine. "What's your name, stranger?" The people of Firth had asked her this question many times. She'd hated it. It had emphasized her lack of belonging and ignorance of their ways. But the stranger must perceive her as the expert and consent to be led by her whims.

"Griggs," he said, clearing his throat. "Captain Griggs."

Mara placed the glass in his trembling hand. "A sea man?"

"Yes, ma'am." Half the glass vanished with a single gulp.

Griggs reminded Mara of herself before Jed had corrupted her. She sat beside him. "Are you in trade?"

"You might say that." He inhaled the last of the wine.

"More?"

"Please."

She poured, smiling. "How's business?"

"Dismal." He stared into his glass, swirling the contents.

She patted his thigh and let her hand rest there. "Tell me about it."

After another gulp, he said, "It's this damnable mist."

Mara dropped her glass. Wine soaked into the wood floor.

"Let me help with that." The captain reached for a towel and began dabbing up the mess. "You're fortunate. I don't think your gown caught a drop."

The sight of him kneeling jarred her. She snatched the towel. "Sit, Captain, and tell me about this mist."

"It formed overnight at the end of summer, just off the coast," he said, relaxing as the wine took effect. "A small cloud on the sea, nothing suspect. But it never moved, and it grew. The navy launched a few vessels to take a closer look, but they never returned. Ships due at port haven't arrived, including the runners we sent out to warn surrounding territories. It's a mess. The Council has ordered the navy to stand down and prepare to defend the harbor, but we don't know what we're fighting."

When the captain looked at her, she could only blink. At length, she selected one question from the swarm in her head. "Am I to understand, Captain, that you are not in trade at all but a member of the King's Navy?"

He colored violently. "I didn't lie to you. I'm a naval captain. But I also oversee trade vessels and inspect their cargo."

With his responsibilities came a wealth of information, but he wouldn't content himself to talk all night. She must choose what to ask. "Why did the Council order the navy to stand down?"

"The Council, I think, understands the nature of the mist and doesn't want to lose any more ships. Or men."

"And what is the nature of the mist?" she asked.

He looked as if he expected her to disbelieve him. "Preternatural. I believe we're dealing with spirits. And the Council's right. We aren't equipped to deal with them."

"Surely someone is," she said. "What about that magical stone?"

The corner of Griggs's mouth twitched. "You tease. I understand. Lots of people think the stories are a hoax."

"But you believe them. Have you seen it for yourself? The stone, I mean."

"I haven't, but I know it exists. As I know the King exists."

The floor was as clean as she could make it, and she'd lost Griggs's attention. She sat down next to him so their legs touched. "And you would live and die for a hopeless cause and a king you haven't seen?"

His eyes traveled far away. "Yes."

Caressing his face, she kissed him. When he tensed, she spoke into his neck, smelling wine on her own breath. "Why are you here?"

Griggs blanched and drew back as if she'd burned him. The response surprised her. She'd intended to seduce him and resume conversation later when he was more relaxed, but she'd lost him. His feet twitched and angled for the door. He'd misunderstood.

"I haven't ambushed you, Captain. I meant the question honestly," she said.

He picked her hand off his leg and held it in his, which was as rough as hers had been when she'd come to Rahm-Or. "To answer you honestly—I don't know. I'm lonely and rather frightened, but that's no excuse. The Ring opposes everything I stand for, everything I do. I should free you, not use you. I'd be discharged if the Council knew I was here."

"They won't know." Her free hand circled his chest.

He seized it, kissed it, and stood. "I'll know."

She reached for his arm, desperate to keep him in the room. "Captain, you never said who I looked like."

A nostalgic smile softened his features. "My wife. She was lovely. Part Razan, like you. Enjoy your rest tonight." Gently, he freed himself and fled.

Mara stared after him. He'd wanted her, paid for her, but he'd run. Because staying would've been wrong.

Maybe the King was more than a story after all.

～ ～ ～

Zev looked out his office window, toying with his rings, as Mara reported the conversation. He was disappointed she hadn't found out more but praised her nonetheless. "I watched you from the glass last night. You're the reason he didn't leave right away. You were clever. Subtle. More so than the others would've been, and they never saw him. You've been at this one season, and already you're my best girl."

Mara's cheeks warmed. She almost forgot her questions. "What is Rivka up to? Is she here because of me?"

"Why do you think it's her?"

"It's her."

Zev moved from the window and perched on the edge of the desk. "Rivka's always had her own plans. She doesn't share them with me. The mist probably doesn't have anything to do with you. You're where you're supposed to be." He handed her a sealed envelope. "This came for you."

He'd dismissed her, but at the sight of Selene's fluid script, Mara threw her arms around him. The scent of frankincense and the firmness of his chest sped her pulse. Embarrassed by her childlike behavior, she breathed thanks and sped to the garden to read the letter. Puffing steam into the icy air, she unfolded the sweet-smelling parchment.

Mara,

Thank you for the message. I'm well. I decided not to trouble Hedya and Ben. A few weeks ago, I swore myself to the King and joined the consulate. I like the work, but I find my fellow kingsmen dispassionate—all but an older couple who once lived in the city. The others don't listen to them or to me, but they do listen to the Council in Rahm-Or. We recently received an interesting letter warning us of an upcoming investigation. The Council demands to know why a young woman from our town did not consider the consulate as a source of help when she needed medicine for her dying sister and felt she had to sell herself to the Ring to obtain it. I look forward to the results of the investigation. It's something I want to know as well. No one has seen Ramzi. Loed confiscated the farm. Claims he's holding it for you. Ben's still angry but says he'll forgive you if you run away this instant and return home. Don't do it. I've heard the things that happen to runaway slaves. My plan to free you is cleverer than his.

Selene

Mara reread the letter several times. She worried for Ramzi. News of Ben made her chest ache. The idea of the farm in Loed's fat, grabby hands infuriated her. But three golden threads weaved through the tangle of her thoughts.

Declan hadn't forgotten her. He was behind the investigation of the consulate, and he'd done it for her.

Angry though she was, Selene was well and seemed content. She had friends and a purpose.

And the mist had followed Mara to Rahm-Or.

CHAPTER 7

The snows came, and Declan still hadn't claimed his evening. Mara had been looking for him since receiving Selene's letter. While part of her worried he'd changed his mind, she was also relieved. Declan was a friend, and friends shouldn't do to one another what she did to the men who came to her bed.

On the night of Winter Solstice, Jed threw a party. While Rahm-Or suffered recession due to the trouble at sea, his business flourished. He was never without money or friends to help him spend it, despite his repugnant personality. This night, he'd brought them all.

Mara squeezed beside Joss at the bar and downed two shots to prepare for the evening ahead. "I don't envy you tonight," Joss said out of the side of her mouth.

Mara didn't know what she meant until she found Jed, his face blotchy and eyes swimming their sockets. She'd never seen him so drunk. The alcohol made him surly. "Just the woman I wanted."

He clenched her arm in his fist and lugged her across the room to a raucous crowd huddled around a table. Of the men seated, one stood out. He was young, not much older than Mara, with baby skin and rosy cheeks, and was quickly losing the battle against bourbon.

"Wendol." Everyone looked at Jed, the young man with trepidation. "Meet Mara, your promotion gift." Jed flung her toward the table.

Loud cheers erupted all around. Wendol's pink cheeks turned redder. Sweat beaded his brow. "Thank you, sir, but that isn't necessary." Like everyone else, Wendol was afraid of Jed.

"It is necessary. You'll leave with her after this round, so you'll have time to tell us about it before we're too drunk to remember." Jed chased the ultimatum with another man's whiskey.

Wendol stood at the end of the round accompanied by huzzahs. His hands shook at his sides.

Jed wanted a spectacle. Mara squeezed Wendol's arm. "He's adorable, Jed. A shame you won't let me keep him."

The men guffawed, Jed with them. "Be gentle, Little Mouse. He's green."

Which was a suggestion to do the opposite. Wendol looked ready to faint, so Mara ended the game and led him upstairs. When they were alone in her room, he turned to her with a beseeching expression.

"I'll pay whatever sum you name if you promise not to repeat a word of what I'm about to say," he said, his eyes wide in desperation.

"Go on," Mara said.

"I need you to lie for me."

She slinked past him, skirts swishing, and poured herself a glass of wine. "Explain."

Wendol gulped and fidgeted. "Jed says he's throwing this party to honor my promotion, but my promotion has nothing to do with it. It happened weeks ago. But last week, he found out about my engagement to my sweetheart. He said some crass things. I tried to ignore them, but somehow he guessed . . ."

"Guessed what?" Mara knew perfectly well what but was entertained by the tomato red of Wendol's face.

He took out a handkerchief and dabbed his brow. "That we've never . . . well, you know. Anyway, this look came into his eye, and the next day he organized this party. He means to force me to give you what should be hers."

She sat hard on the settee, staggered by the sentiment. Excepting Ben, the men she knew didn't speak this way. "So why did you come?"

Wendol's baby face turned shrewd. "You sleep with the man. Tell me, have you been able to refuse him anything? What he means when he calls this a 'promotion party' is that if I don't bed you, I'll lose my job, and then I can't marry Ana. So you see the mess I'm in. Will you help me?"

Mara pitied this man who was too good to betray his lady and too weak to stand up for himself. "Fooling Jed will be the most fun I've had since I came here. But first, the price for my silence."

For a price. The words echoed in her thoughts, startling her. Rivka had said them. Zev lived them. Was she becoming like them—addicted to power? She closed her eyes, pressing down the uncomfortable feeling in her chest. "Three secrets. Things Jed would hate for me to know. You may choose, but make them good."

Wendol dabbed his face again. "Why?"

"Leverage. Surely you understand."

"If he finds out who told you . . ."

"He'll never know."

Taking a deep breath, he sucked in his lower lip. "Not one of Jed's ships has been lost to the mist at sea."

Mara sighed. "Obviously. Tell me why. Fast ships?"

"No. I think Jed knows what's in that mist."

That the mist could be hiding something hadn't occurred to Mara. "Why do you think that?"

"He sends black runner ships right into it at night. They leave port loaded and come back empty. My friend works the night watch at the docks. Jed's men bribe him and the other guards to keep quiet."

Mara's charade was most difficult when she stumbled upon good information. She squashed her excitement, pretending detached interest. "That's two. Surprise me with number three."

"He recently hired two ruffians to be his bodyguards. They have the look of hardened criminals. I wouldn't be surprised if they were."

After the first two secrets, the third disappointed her. "Did they come with him tonight?"

"They come with him every night, but your guard makes them stay outside."

"What do they look like?" she asked.

"Tall, broad, pale. Arms thick as logs and covered in colored marks."

Mara stared through him, through the wall, and into the past. The stench of charred flesh filled her memory. Screams echoed in her mind. Large, decorated arms wielded swords and maces, swinging and cutting through flesh and bone.

"Hello?" Wendol said. "Sorry, I forgot your name."

Wendol came into focus, and Mara rose from the settee. "Take off your clothes."

"What?"

Wendol's indignation irritated Mara. She didn't want him any more than he wanted her. "Relax," she said. "If you want this to work, we must crumple your clothes."

Scarlet faced and clumsy, he undressed. She gathered the clothes into a ball and pressed them against her chest, soaking them in her scent. When he was clothed again, she tousled his hair with her hands, which increased his agitation. Finally, she grabbed his face and kissed his mouth, face, and neck, leaving traces of lip stain on his skin. He froze. The last kiss he returned—and leaned in for more when it was over. His breath shook when she pulled away to inspect her work. "Those guilty eyes will fool him if nothing else does."

He checked himself in the mirror. "I almost believe it myself," he said, amazed.

"When Jed asks for your story, act embarrassed, and pretend you can't speak."

Wendol thanked her and left before the heat faded from his cheeks. The smile dropped from Mara's face.

All her life, she'd been consumed with Selene's well-being, but now that Selene was safe, a deep void opened its jowls inside her, hungry for what Wendol felt for Ana. Love. The desperate kind that made a man do foolish things. Of all the men who shared her bed, not one of them cared for her. Ben once had, but she'd return to him a ruin, and all the mortar in the world couldn't remake her. Mara was lost to an emptiness to which there was no answer. No man deigned to love a harlot.

Zev laughed as Mara shared the previous night's antics. Until she told him what she'd learned, at which point he sobered and rifled through the documents littering his desk.

When she was quiet, he said, "You did well, Mara, but this isn't what we need. Jed's trade secrets won't bring us closer to Eleora."

Clouds drifted over the sun outside, turning the room gray.

"I see. Sorry to disappoint." Her words clipped short.

Before she rose from her seat, Zev seized her wrist and turned it over in his hand. His thumb swept across the delicate skin, and her mind emptied. "I'm not disappointed, but Rivka grows restless without new information. I worry for you and Selene. Spirits aren't forgiving."

The warning overshadowed the effect of his touch and left her cold.

The morning worsened. Levanna's face soured when Mara sat down to breakfast. "What did you do to that little virgin last night? He wouldn't say a word when he came down. He's getting married soon. I hope you didn't traumatize him."

Cadha and Elise cast uneasy glances at Levanna and each other.

"Ignore her," Joss said with a yawn. "She's irritable because Jed took her in your place."

"At least I would've known what to do with a virgin. Jed requires no skill. You just lie there until it's over," Levanna said.

Mara detected a tremor in Levanna's stone-hard tone. And later, when Levanna walked out of the room, her hips jerked more than swayed. Jed had hurt her. And he'd probably been unkind, but Levanna was too proud to complain.

Hatred boiled beneath Mara's skin. Levanna was an enemy. Nothing would change that. She lived for Mara's discomfort, playing subversive games Mara didn't understand and usually lost. But some enemies were so despicable they turned lesser enemies into allies. Jed had caused Mara to empathize with someone who hated her, and he would pay.

Mara seethed at Jed's side, downing one shooter after another. Every noise, every movement grated. Crass jokes about her time with Wendol rang in her ears. It was good he didn't suspect they'd made a fool of him, though part of her wanted him to know.

She'd learned long ago whiskey was fine served over ice but should never be poured over fire. Cold emotions like sorrow, guilt, and loneliness melted in the amber liquid. Apply it to rage, however, and the house burned to the ground. But tonight, she didn't care.

"Little Mouse?" Jed slapped the table. "Did you hear me? I leave for Firth tomorrow."

Scowling, she gulped another shooter.

"Seas, you can drink," a man Mara didn't recognize said.

Ignoring him, she turned to Jed. "And?"

Her tone drew his sharp gaze. "And I thought about calling on your sister. I'm afraid I'll miss you and need a substitute."

"I don't have a sister," Mara said calmly.

Jed pushed two gold coins to the center of the table. "I distinctly remember you mentioning a sister the night we met. I've asked around. Her name is Selene, correct?"

Mara swore under her breath. Levanna was the only one who would've told him.

Stifling the urge to lunge for his throat, she lazed back against the chair and suspended a hand in midair. "Oh, my sister has far too much taste to enjoy the company of a teeny"—two fingers measured half a handbreadth—"tiny"—the fingers drew close together—"man like you."

Silence. If terror hadn't riveted the men to their cushioned chairs, they would've scattered. Murder blazed in Jed's eyes. Mara expected his fist, but he stayed where he was, glaring at her with perfect control. He'd try to kill her in her room, without witnesses.

Alarmed by the prolonged stillness, she stumbled out of her seat and across the room to Boz. "I've angered Jed. He means to kill me." She wouldn't let him, of course, but she doubted things would go well for her if she killed him—even in self-defense.

Boz frowned, trying to understand, and looked over her shoulder. Jed approached. With a step of impossible grace for a man his size, Boz positioned himself between her and Jed.

"Time to go upstairs, Little Mouse," Jed said. His tone froze her blood.

Boz whispered to her over his shoulder. "Find Zev. But stay out of the wolf's den."

Confused, she gaped at him like a netted fish. She was too drunk for riddles and proverbs.

Something happened Mara couldn't see. Boz urged her again. "Go!"

Taking the back way through the kitchen, she ran down the corridor straight to Zev's office. She knocked, but there was no answer. The door creaked open to a dark, empty room. Pulling her hair, she struggled to think where he might be and remembered to check his bedchamber.

By the time she reached his door, heavy footsteps pounded down the way. She pummeled the door with both fists. "Zev! Zev! It's Mara!"

The door swung open. Zev, half-awake and bare chested, snapped to attention when he saw her face. "What's wrong?"

Without thinking, she ducked under Zev's arm into his room and hid herself behind him.

"Send her out, Zev." Jed pointed at Mara, his face purpling.

Zev slammed the door in Jed's face and scowled down at her. "What's going on?"

She fought to control her breath. "He threatened Selene."

His brows snapped together. "Details."

Mara explained, mentioning Jed's belt and Levanna's limp before confessing the thing she'd said.

Zev was livid. "He beat you? And you didn't tell me?"

"I thought it was part of it." The room spun. She tilted and reached for Zev's arm, which caught her.

"You're drunk. Sit." He guided her to a bench at the foot of his bed. Kneeling in front of her, he looked into her eyes. "I don't let men hurt my girls."

"If you make me go with him—tonight or any night—he'll kill me. Or try, and I'll have to kill him. You didn't see the way he looked at me."

Jed bellowed at the door. "Zev! Send her out here!"

His face a stone, Zev donned a shirt. "Don't leave this room for any reason." The door opened, and she glimpsed Jed and his guards before it closed again. The guards were Akaronian, as she'd suspected.

"My office. Now. Boz, guard the door."

Jed's railings faded down the corridor and muted after a loud slam.

Mara looked around the dim chamber. The furnishings were more luxurious than those in her room, but all the colors were dark, reminding her of a cave. Her head pounded. Helping herself to a glass of water, she lay down on the bed. The scent of frankincense enveloped her, causing her to shudder with a feeling she couldn't name. Her consciousness drifted through a sea of red, black, and fiery blue until she heard the creak of the door.

Zev extended a steaming mug of tea. "Drink this. The tender said you drained half the bar tonight. From now on, he'll cut you off at six. Whiskey makes you stupid."

She sat up and took the mug. "Where's Jed?"

"Gone. He won't be back. And he won't dare go near Selene."

"Thank you," she said and sipped the tea, which was sweet and buttery on her tongue.

"It was a good excuse to do something I've wanted to do for a long time." He rubbed his eyes.

Mundane though it was, the gesture took her captive. Since she was a little girl, Zev had awed Mara. He seemed more spirit than man. Not only was he beautiful. The world wasn't the mystery to him that it was to her. He always knew what he was doing and why and what would happen next, while day-to-day living perplexed Mara. She never knew what to expect. In a way, life with the Ring was comfortable because it was predictable. No one's well-being depended on the outcome of her decisions. A hail storm wouldn't threaten her livelihood. So though she was a slave, she felt a kind of freedom. She only had to follow orders and leave the consequences to Zev, who understood the world and tamed it to his liking. But Zev was tired tonight, and his fatigue made him real to her. Human. Unlike a spirit, a human was attainable.

She placed a hand on his arm. He studied it before meeting her gaze. Slowly, as if weighing every reaction, he lifted her wrist to his lips. They caressed their way down her arm, lingering on the ink that marked her as his. A flare of heat, distinct from anger, surged from her arm down her body.

The tea disappeared from her hand. He tugged at her waist, pulling her toward him. His lips traveled up her neck, and her skin burst into flame. A gasp hitched in her throat when their eyes met. Boz's warning became clear. A shudder trilled down her spine. Ignoring the alarm in the back of her mind, she pressed her mouth to his. The closer he came, the more of him she wanted.

Narrow slivers of morning light nudged Mara awake. Memories of the night broke through the muddle of her mind, and she remembered where she was. Her hand wandered to the space beside her. The bed was empty and cold. A mug of cooled tea and a note decorated the bedside table. Her head pounded as she sat up, almost sending her back down onto the pillow.

> Drink up, and get to breakfast. Answer questions at your own peril. We'll talk later.
>
> -Z

The tea cleared her head but didn't dissolve the familiar, cold weight that settled in her chest. Disappointment was a familiar companion, but she couldn't pin down what it was she'd hoped for. She was Zev's property, after all. When the pain in her head dulled to a bearable ache, she dressed and joined the breakfast table.

"So, what happened?" Elise asked.

"Yes, please tell us all about your evening," Levanna said, cocking her head.

Mara sipped her morning cup of bitter tea, ignoring her.

Joss peered at her through narrow eyes. "How much did you drink last night?"

"I heard you outdrank every man at your table and insulted Jed's size," Elise said.

"She didn't mean his height, Elise," Levanna said.

"Oh my." Elise covered her mouth.

Cadha didn't share the others' amusement. "We saw Jed fetch those nasty-looking guards of his and go after you. I worried."

Mara sank against the chair and sighed. "Yes, I insulted Jed. I think he meant to kill me for it, but Zev sent him away. He won't be back. You're welcome."

Levanna's eyes flashed as Mara swilled her tea with a grimace. "Why are you drinking the tea? You hate it." When Mara didn't answer, Levanna slammed her own cup onto the table, clattering dishes and flatware. "You slept with him, didn't you?"

"Ah, no. He left," Mara said, confused.

"Not Jed, whore. Zev."

Answer questions at your own peril. Mara bit her bottom lip. "Honestly, I don't remember where I slept. I was very drunk."

"You're a terrible liar," Joss said. "And now Levanna has a real reason to hate you. Congratulations, Lev." Joss raised her teacup and swallowed the contents with a smile.

"Who cares where Mara slept?" Elise said.

Levanna turned her violet glare onto Elise. "You're an idiot. It's no wonder your mother sluffed you."

"Hey!" Joss leaned across the table toward Levanna. "Elise is your friend."

With a sneer for them all, Levanna stormed out of the kitchen, leaving behind a wake of sullen expressions. Before Joss left the table, she said to Mara, "You'll need to be careful. Levanna is every bit as dangerous as Jed in her own way. She doesn't know yet what a favor you've done her."

"I don't understand," Mara said when Joss was gone.

Tears dripped off Elise's nose and splattered onto the table. Cadha sighed, patting Elise's pale hand. "Before you arrived, Levanna frequented Zev's bed. He hasn't summoned her since you came. She's suspected all along you were the reason. Now she knows."

Mara strode into Zev's office and slammed the door behind her. "I won't be summoned."

Two pairs of blue eyes looked up into hers. Zev and Nuri sat side by side, nestled on the bench near the window. Each held a straw doll, their grins fading at the intrusion. Mara gawked at Nuri, coloring in dismay.

Zev smoothed the straw of the doll he held and tightened the twine around its neck. Handing over the doll, he tapped Nuri's nose. "There now. I think Nella will survive, but show her to your mother to be sure."

Nuri scampered out, inspecting Mara with wide eyes as she passed.

"I'm certain I didn't summon you," Zev said when the door shut.

His smirk might've riled her if not for the tenderness he'd shown the child. Images of the long journey from the mining village to Firth came to mind—the way he'd sat up with her after nightmares and carried Selene on his back when she was tired.

"I know about you and Levanna." It wasn't what she meant to say.

"When I advised you to avoid questions, I was looking out for you, not trying to hide anything."

"So, you have a little fun with your whores, and when you tire of them, you move on to someone new?" she said.

He stood, wearing a mock scowl. "First of all, you're spies, not whores. 'Whore' is a favorite term with Levanna, to use against women she dislikes. Are you surprised I tired of her?"

Before Mara could answer, he swaggered forward, pressing her back against the door. His hand swept her hair away from her neck. "Second, you aren't new. You came into my life long before Levanna—before any of the women I know—and you'll be in my life a long while yet. We make sense, Mara. You can't deny it."

He leaned close, his breath warm on her skin, and slid the bolt into the lock. "And as for fun, we could have a little more."

He leered at her like she was something to eat. Heart flying, she found the lock and slid it open. "I only came to say—"

His thumb dragged across her lips. "Shhh," he said. "Let's put that mouth to better use."

She forgot the point she'd meant to make. She forgot why she was angry. She forgot everything but his mouth and his hands and the desperate way they made her ache. A hand lifted from the small of her back. With a clack of metal, the door locked again.

Zev was like whiskey, but better. Drunk on him, she thought of nothing else. Everything disappeared—the endless men, Jed, Levanna, Rivka, even Selene—and without the discipline of a headache. Happy moments lit the drear of life.

One morning, Mara bounced into the kitchen to find Cadha alone. Concern pinched the corners of Cadha's eyes. "Lovers are nice, but never forget you're his slave."

Cadha's unwillingness to be happy for her irked Mara. She watched Cadha sip from a china teacup, draped in a silk bathrobe. Nuri skipped into the room dressed for school in clothes finer than anything Mara had worn before coming to Rahm-Or. She thought of her father running into flame and fray for a handful of shiny rocks.

Mara poured a splash of whiskey into her morning tea. "We're all slaves to something."

"I only meant you should mind your heart," Cadha said. "Things rarely work out for the slave who sleeps with the owner." Her eyes saddened.

Mara gulped down the tea and carried the rest of her breakfast upstairs.

CHAPTER 8

The last snow of winter melted under a heavy rain that lasted for days. The storm kept the men at home, which gave Mara more time with Zev and a greater appreciation for inclement weather. Late one afternoon, the clouds parted, and Boz knocked on her door. He asked her to accompany him to Zev's office, which was curious. She'd been with Zev until late that morning. The men would arrive before long, and she needed to get ready. Nevertheless, she threw her robe over her underclothes and followed Boz, who kept silent.

Since the night she'd fled from Jed, Boz had distanced himself. Mara surmised that he disapproved of her trysts with Zev, though she couldn't discern a reason. It hurt that none of her friends shared her joy.

Mara heard a familiar voice when she rounded the corner near Zev's office and burned with mortification when she saw it belonged to Declan. Behind him stood two armed kingsmen with matching auburn hair and similar faces, both several winters older than Mara. The younger one, near Zev's age, was broad shouldered and stocky, only reaching his brother's chest in height. His bashful glances contrasted with the older one's avoidance.

Gathering her robe close around her, Mara shot Boz a silent accusation. "I'm sorry. I should've dressed."

Declan smiled. "Actually, I brought something for you to wear, so it's just as well." To Zev, he said, "Are we agreed? The guards are capable, and she isn't likely to be recognized."

Zev turned to her, scowling in annoyance. "Declan asks to take you to dinner in King's Quarter. As payment."

When Mara recovered from the surprise, she cast Zev a calculated glance. "That's nice. I haven't seen King's Quarter."

"It's not a good night."

"The weather is perfect."

He clenched his jaw. "I don't usually let men ride off with my girls."

Mara didn't know what to make of him. Did he not see the opportunity? "Declan is an ambassador. He won't steal me."

Zev appraised her with a suspicious glare. Declan fought a smile. She'd made a joke everyone understood but her.

"If Jed's men spot you . . ."

Mara's eyes flicked to Declan and the guards. "If I'm dressed like them, no one will even look at me."

"I'm offended," Declan said, his eyes crinkling at the corners.

"I'll be fine," Mara said. "The risk isn't unreasonable, and I can carry a dagger if you like." The younger brother's mouth twitched at the word "dagger."

Zev gave a curt nod, and Mara left to change into the gown Declan had brought. It was plain, closer to what Mara was accustomed to wearing in Firth. The white fabric covered skin her current gowns exposed. Unused to the fit, she tugged and adjusted until she itched. She twisted in front of the mirror, feeling alien in the King's color.

To enforce the disguise, she braided her hair. Jed hadn't seen it styled that way. As she worked, she considered the problem of Jed, who'd vanished from her thoughts the night Zev had thrown him out. She could bet all she was worth he hadn't forgotten her. If Mara survived Rivka, Jed waited on the other side, and he might not be as kind.

The Council had acted on her behalf before. Maybe it would help again.

She crossed the hall to Cadha's room and borrowed parchment from Nuri. Cadha cast her an odd look when she made the request but didn't comment. Rushing back to her room, Mara tore the parchment in half and scribed hasty notes, one to the Council and another to Captain Griggs, who would be in the best position to apprehend Jed's runner ships sailing to and from the mist. Zev wouldn't like her sharing the information, but he needn't know. Captain Griggs could plausibly stumble upon a ship making an illegal run.

Mara rolled up the papers and stuffed them into her bodice. Spinning on her heel, she found Levanna looming in her doorway, her eyes narrowed. "Why are you wearing that?"

"The healer who cared for me is taking me to King's Quarter tonight. I'm late," Mara said, hoping she didn't appear as startled as she felt.

Levanna stepped out of her way. "You look ridiculous. Like a peasant."

Rolling her eyes, Mara bid Levanna good night and raced down the stairs. If Levanna had seen the notes, there was no way for her to guess what they said or who they were for. Mara tried to relax.

Declan stood to receive her, wearing his springtide smile. "White is your color."

Zev handed Mara a dagger in its sheath. "I prefer her in red."

A carriage waited for them on the street. Mara questioned Declan with a look.

"A gift from the Council," he said, opening the door.

Two horses awaited the guards behind the carriage, and the driver was armed. Declan also carried a dagger at his waist.

"Do you know how to use that?" She nodded to the blade, her mouth fighting a smile.

"You mock my clothes and now question my skills?"

Mara grinned as he helped her into the carriage. "Speaking of the Council, my sister wrote. It seems there will be an investigation of the consulate in Firth."

Declan slid in across from her, his face serious. "Yes."

The carriage pulled forward, bumping over cobblestones. "I'd like to thank the Council for taking an interest in Firth."

"Why don't you write and tell them so?" he suggested. "Now, I know you didn't get to see the city on your way in, so let's open the windows."

They passed a familiar commercial street, and the carriage turned south toward the sea. The smell of brine wafted in. Mara breathed deeply. Declan pointed to the palace as they passed. White stone turrets towered above the city like giant watch guards, contrasting with an azure sky. The sea cliffs, Declan explained, served as the wall's foundation. All the palace stones were hewn from the rock. From the sea, the cliffs and wall appeared as one solid piece. Where one ended, the other began. The ornate gates awed Mara. Through them, she glimpsed lush gardens, greener than she expected so early in springtide.

King's Quarter charmed Mara. Quaint homes, uniform in size with orderly gardens, lined the clean-swept streets.

Mara turned from the window to Declan. "The gardens are too small for many vegetables. What are they for?"

"Beauty," he said. "Soon, they'll be full of color and fragrance. I love to walk these streets in early summer."

The carriage stopped. The door opened, revealing Kali's dimple and soft eyes, shining blue. Laughing Mara's name, Kali wrapped her in skinny arms. "I'm so pleased to see you."

Seasons had passed since Mara had been embraced this way. She squeezed the small woman, swallowing the tightness in her throat.

A girl near Mara's age stood on the stoop. She wasn't unattractive, but the rigidity of her mouth gave her an austere look. Mara noted the lift of her ears and wondered if her braid might be too tight. Kali introduced her as her daughter, Sabra. Mara smiled at the girl, who nodded but didn't smile back. Sabra opened the door for everyone, releasing a wholesome fragrance of herbed meat and roasted vegetables into the street.

The guards followed Declan inside. They were brothers, Kenrik and Gavan, raised in the northern Hills of Gal. She didn't ask, but like Mara, they probably knew what it was to be attacked by Akaronian raiders in the night. They also served on the Council.

Mara saw no evidence of a gemstone necklace hanging around either of their necks. She turned to Kali. "So they're your other sons. This is your family."

Kali winked in reply.

Declan explained he'd asked them to come along as chaperones and protection, if need should arise. Mara suppressed a smirk at the word "chaperones" but sobered when she realized he'd probably asked for his own sake. Ambassadors weren't likely allowed to keep company with prostitutes.

The bond between Declan and the brothers was unmistakable. They told entertaining tales and said terrible things to one another at which everyone laughed and no one became offended.

"You obviously know each other well," Mara said during a brief lag between jokes.

"Astute." Declan grinned, receiving a bowl of potatoes from Sabra.

"How did you meet?"

Declan looked to his friends. Kenrik attended his plate, content to let his brother answer. "King's service. Declan's saved our lives a few times over the years," Gavan said with a dramatic sniff.

"A few?" Declan raised his brow.

Gavan shrugged. "Lost count, really. Don't see why it matters."

"Get into much trouble as a kingsman?" Mara asked.

"Nah." Gavan gave an exaggerated shake of his head.

"Please tell me trouble is specific to you," Mara said. "My sister is a kingsman in Firth."

Gavan's expression lit. "Is that so? Well, I wouldn't worry. Girls are much too clever to get into scrapes."

The irony struck Mara like skyfire. "When you're ready to shatter your delusions about women, ask for my story."

She met Declan's gaze and found his smile warm and eyes sad.

The meal and company were the most pleasant Mara had enjoyed in a long while, but as the sun set, she began to feel unwell and anxious.

Kali took hold of her trembling hand as she placed a nut cake on her plate and leaned toward her ear. "Are you all right, dear?"

"I will be. Thank you for the meal. I've never had better," Mara said.

As soon as dessert was eaten, Declan announced it was time to leave. "Here," he said when they were seated in the carriage again. He extended a flask.

She looked at it and turned to gaze out the window, resting her aching head against the door.

His voice was gentle. "Don't be ashamed. If I had your life, I'd drink too."

It was whiskey, but barely. Her eyes watered as she swallowed. Coughing, she pounded her chest with her fist. "Hills, that's bad. I hope you don't drink that."

He chuckled and admitted he only used it for patients.

"Do them a favor, and buy a proper bottle." She took another swig and stared at the rising moon. The white cobbled streets glowed in its light. Closing her eyes, she let the spring air cool her face.

When she'd drunk enough to relax, Declan cleared his throat. "Speaking of your life, the Council received a letter requesting your redemption."

She blinked at him.

"It's done, Mara. Your freedom is paid for."

"What does that mean, exactly?" she asked.

"It means you're free to leave the Ring. We can return to the Quarter right now, and you'd never have to go back. Zev knows."

When she recovered from the shock, she huffed a laugh. "So you were trying to steal me. That explains Zev's pleasant mood."

"Know that when you leave, you must make your home in the Quarter for a time. Rehabilitation is an important part of the King's policy," Declan said.

Mara sat back in her seat, overwhelmed. "Do I have to leave?"

"No." He leaned forward, his brown eyes penetrating hers to uncomfortable depths. "I know the decision comes down to your oath. So I'll ask you this—is there any way to fulfill it outside of the Ring?"

Mara worried her lip. "I'm not sure. Zev says no."

"Leaving is your decision. If you believe there's another way, there is. I'll help you if you let me."

"I'll think about it."

His smile slipped. She'd disappointed him again. "Send word to Kali the moment you decide to leave," he said. "She'll come and collect you. She volunteered to take you in."

They had nearly arrived at headquarters when Mara remembered the papers. She pulled them from her bodice. "I almost forgot. I need you to deliver these papers for me as soon as possible. Zev would ham me if he knew about this, so please be careful. This one is for Captain Griggs of the navy."

Frowning, he took the extended papers. Uncharacteristic gruffness roughed his voice. "How do you know Captain Griggs?"

"Never mind that. He's a good man and in a position to do something important. For me and the city. This one"—she pointed to the other—"is for the Council. It contains the same information along with an appeal for the arrest of Jed of Sardor."

"Why are you risking the wrath of the most powerful men in the city?" he asked.

When Mara woke that morning, she'd expected the day to be like all the others since she'd come to the Ring, but Declan had interrupted, presenting her with choices she hadn't anticipated: Act against Jed or hide behind Zev's limited protection. Accept redemption or remain a slave. Tell a lie or risk Declan's opinion with the truth.

"I'd like to tell you it's for the crown, but my motives are entirely selfish," she said. "I've already earned Jed's wrath. If I left with you tonight, it wouldn't do me any good. Jed would find me, and I'd be dead. My information against him comes from a reliable source. If you get this to the captain, he might be able to save me."

He took both papers in hand, his expression serious. "You honor me with your honesty. I'll do what I can. But remember, you can leave at any time. We'll protect you from Jed."

She smiled, touching his hand. "Thank you, Declan. For everything." For the evening, his help, the offer. For not once treating her like a whore.

The Ring's door guard let her inside. She turned to watch the door close on the carriage. Heaviness washed over her when it clicked shut. A sense of missed opportunity gnawed at her belly, urging her to chase after them. But no. She needed time to think.

Noise drifted from the hall down the darkened corridor. No one was in sight. She rounded the corner that would take her through the kitchen when a figure emerged from the shadows. Preoccupation and lack of practice slowed her reaction. Air shot from her lungs in a painful gasp as her back slammed into the wall. She unsheathed the dagger, but the assailant grabbed her wrist. Swiveling, she jabbed at his ribcage with her free elbow, but he was ready. With a quick step back, he seized her free arm and pinned her between his body and the wall. The cold blade pressed against one cheek; the other stuck to the lacquer on the pine. She struggled, preparing a scream. Whiskey-laden breath blew fast and heavy on her neck. A familiar chuckle sounded in her ear.

"Zev? What in hell are you doing?"

"I wanted to see if you can still handle yourself. I'm disappointed."

The dagger disappeared. He released her, and she slugged his arm. Laughing, he herded her against the wall. "You're exquisite when you're angry."

"I could've gutted you," she said through clenched teeth.

Cupping her chin, he tugged her mouth open. His whiskey-sweet kiss made her clay in his hands. "How was your evening? Learn anything interesting?" he asked.

His lips explored her jawline, which made it difficult to think. Or breathe. "Nothing more interesting than my redemption."

He tilted his head, his features sinking into a dark frown. "What did you decide?"

"I don't know yet, but it's an appealing offer. No more sleepless nights or bad jokes. No Levanna."

"No me." He caught her lower lip between his teeth.

She wrapped a hand around his neck. "So convince me to stay."

With a wicked grin, he attacked. Mara shoved him back. "That's not what I mean."

Frustration flashed through his eyes, compelling an explanation she wasn't ready to give. She entwined her fingers with his, fearing how he'd respond to the hope she'd never intended to express. "Forget the mission, Rivka, all of it. Pretend it's you and me. I'm not asking for a declaration, only a reason to stay."

Mara tilted his face to hers. "Look at me. See me."

A moment passed. He released a heavy breath. "We can't forget Rivka, whether you stay or go."

"All I need is a reason."

Mara thought he would walk away, but he stayed, analyzing. Weighing. His blue eyes flickered. With a slight retraction of his grip, his fingers transformed from claws into cradles. His lips gentled. Taking his hand, she led him to his chamber, where he conjured a fiction so convincing she might've believed him had she not known better.

Mara admired the effect of her brown hand against Zev's pale shoulder, avoiding his eyes. It hurt to look into them. Zev carried ice in his soul, cold and sharp, and his best efforts at love couldn't melt it.

She tucked a lock of black hair behind his ear. "Why did you save us all those years ago?" She felt his gaze bore into her. "I took my oath for Selene. What was your reason?"

With an exasperated sigh, Zev rolled out of her arms onto his back. "I've trained you too well. Relax. You're with me, not a patron."

"I ask as your friend, not a spy."

He was quiet so long Mara gave up hope for an answer. Drifting into an unhappy sleep, she startled at his voice. "My people are barbaric, especially to women. Some men marry. Few treat their wives well. Mostly they see them as animals to be bred. To stock their armies and take over. Sons are more desirable than daughters. Captured women are expendable. My mother was captured by my father, who was a man of . . . influence. He added her to his harem and liked her so well he chose her to produce an heir. Mothering a son should've protected her.

"She cared for me five winters. During the first blizzard of the sixth, my father threw her out into the storm, told her to leave, and locked the door. No explanation. I listened to her cries until the wind drowned them out. I found her frozen to the door the next morning."

Mara swallowed the pity lodged in her throat. Zev wouldn't like it.

"I would've done anything to avenge her, even kill you and Selene." His fingers traced an apology and other pretty lies along her spine. "I planned to complete the Rite, rise through the ranks, and destroy my father over time, but Rivka convinced me my way wouldn't work and showed me one that would."

"Rivka never showed me anything," Mara said. "She just kissed me and made me swear."

"You were a child. You didn't need to know anything. You only needed the magic to do your part. That's what she gave you that night, not a kiss." He demonstrated the difference.

When he pulled away, she asked, "What will you do? Kill them all?"

"My father and anyone who stands in my way."

His detached tone chilled her blood. Then she remembered she hated the Akaronians and didn't care what became of them. "Will you be their king?"

"Something like that." He lifted her chin and searched her eyes. "Did I convince you?"

She almost asked how Eleora fit into his plans but stopped herself. No more talk about Rivka tonight. They were supposed to forget her, and she wanted to enjoy the first genuine moment they'd shared. With a smile, she nestled against him and closed her eyes. "For now."

The next morning, Zev invited her to stay in bed as long as she liked, but when he left, she rose and searched for her white gown, which she found in a heap on the floor. A large wine stain covered the front of the bodice. Odd, she didn't remember drinking. The loss saddened her, but part of her felt relieved. All evening she'd felt wrong in it. An imposter. And the sharp contrast of white against her skin ached her eyes.

CHAPTER 9

The balance of power shifted, but not enough to benefit Mara. Zev ranged from gruff to wary, which hurt until she understood—she knew his secrets, and it unsettled him. She spent all her warmth on him only to be met with chill. Under the influence of his touch, hope came easy, but his passions lied. The moment she caught her breath, he was gone. Cold. Asleep. In his absence, agitation and despair had their way, fretting even her dreams. Loneliness burrowed inside, eating away what little contentment she'd managed in her new life, reminding her of the hard days after he'd left her behind in Firth. Better circumstances and fresh information waiting in King's Quarter tempted her to leave, but Zev had offered her a glimpse of his real self. She wanted to see what would come of it.

Another series of storms rolled off the sea when the air warmed, and business slowed. Boz knocked on her door one evening with an urgent summons from Zev. Flushing, Mara followed him to the office. When she stepped inside, Zev stood with his back to her, staring out the window at the torrent. "I thought I told you I won't be summoned," she teased, wrapping her arms around his waist.

He whirled, throwing her off. "What have you done?"

"What?" She drew back, stung.

"I trusted you."

A hard slap stunned her. Tears sprang to her eyes. She placed a hand over her throbbing cheek, gaping at him.

"Jed just left. Thinks I betrayed him. He lost a runner ship to the King's Navy last night. A Captain Griggs intercepted it on its way back to port. Explain to me how a man only you know discovered a secret only you were told."

Mara swallowed. "It's the captain's job to apprehend illegal vessels."

He stepped toward her. "Levanna told me you took papers with you the other night. I defended you. Told her notes were a common way to express gratitude. Why did you do it?"

His eyes skewered hers. Lies would get her nowhere. "To sink Jed. That's all. I don't understand why you're so angry."

"What you learn here belongs to me and no one else," he said, shaking her.

"I only wanted to protect myself." She whimpered at his grip on her arms, and he released her. As she rubbed where his hands had been, a troubling question came to mind. "Why does Jed think it's your fault? How could he know you knew about the ships?" Her mouth fell open at the set of his jaw. "You're in business with him. You knew about the mist, the ships, all of it. Why would you work with that imbecile?"

Saliva sprayed into her face. "Who I do business with isn't your concern."

"Right. What do I know? I'm only the sex."

Zev hit her again. His ring caught the corner of her mouth, flooding it with the sharp taste of metal. Glaring, she spat red into her palm and held it up for him to see. "You aren't so different from your father, you know. Or Jed, for that matter. You deserve each other."

She reeled and fell over his desk. He'd hit her again. Picking herself up, she swung a fist at his jaw, which he caught midair and forced down. The opposite hand grazed him at a poor angle. His face twisting into a snarl, he grabbed her throat and pushed her onto the desk. She tossed and scratched, desperate for air, but he was too strong for her. When she met his gaze to plead for her life, he looked through her with eyes that had fled somewhere cold and far away. She shoved a lamp and a stack of papers off the desk, hoping to reclaim his attention. To no avail.

Patches of darkness spotted Mara's vision. Her lungs burned for air. As she became too weak to struggle, a door opened.

"Zev? Zev, no!" Boz barreled into Zev, knocking him away.

Air rushed in, searing Mara's throat. She tried to get up but fell back coughing. When Boz picked her off the desk, Mara glimpsed Zev staring wide-eyed at his hands. Boz carried her to the hall that had been her first room at the Ring and placed her on the couch.

"I'll be back for you in a moment," he said and left.

In the dark room, clarity flooded her mind like a light. It was time to leave, run away, from Zev and from this awful place. Her reason to stay in hell had burned her. Trust was broken, all hope gone. Except that she had somewhere to go.

Unsteady on her feet, she slipped out of the room and down the corridor. With a deep breath that riddled her chest, she thrust open the street door and dashed into the rain. The guard called out behind her, but she ran on, every breath knifing her throat as she slogged through the streets, heavy skirts weighing her down.

Mara rounded a corner and stopped short. A woman fleeing in the rain in a conspicuous gown was sure to draw unwanted attention, and a man like Jed was never far away. She needed to rid herself of the gown and hide her hair. Turning up a residential alley, Mara searched for laundry forgotten on the lines. A large pair of men's trousers and an undershirt was all she found. Not caring who peeped from darkened windows, she stripped in the street and pulled the clothes over her chemise. She hung the gown back on the line, hoping the man's wife could turn it into a fancy set of curtains.

The sky faded from gray to black, and Mara lost all sense of where she was. Cold ravaged her body with tremors. Her wounds, more diverse than she'd realized, throbbed. The clothes clung sour to her skin, tickling her nose. She sneezed and staggered at the pain but forgot all discomfort when she heard her name bellowed over the noise of the storm. Zev's men were close.

Mara hid behind a pile of empty bins. Boz and another guard came into view. They split and searched either side of the street. Boz paused when he neared the bins, and Mara was certain she'd been found. She held her breath. To her surprise, he passed.

"All clear. Zev's right. She probably headed south for the Quarter. They'll have found her two streets back. Let's get out of the rain."

She waited until she felt sure the search had been given up, headed two streets back, and continued south. All night she walked. Her joints froze. Her slippers ruined in the rain. She staggered and fell and almost couldn't continue, but she did. It was still dark when Mara reached Kali's stoop. She beat the door until she collapsed. A gasp followed a long creak, and warm light spilled onto her face.

❧ ❧ ❧

When Mara tried to speak, the words came out in incomprehensible wheezes. Kali changed her into dry clothing and then went out into the rain to fetch Declan. Mara dozed on the couch until they returned.

Cool hands touched her throat. She focused on Declan's mouth, which was grimmer than she'd ever seen it. "Her airway seems to be intact, but we'll have to watch her. Mara, can you look into my eyes?"

She tried, but everything—including her eyes—felt too heavy to move. Poultices were applied to her face and neck. The offered sleeping tonic wasn't needed. Time distorted, measured only by bowls of broth. Figures moved around the room. Voices buzzed, but she understood nothing until Zev's broke through. He called her name.

Pain ambushed when she stirred, causing her to moan.

"It's all right, dear," she heard Kali say. "The guards will get rid of him. As they have the last two days."

"How long have I been here?" Mara's voice was a thin rasp.

"Three days."

Zev called her name again.

Pursing her lips, Kali glanced at the door. "He's persistent. I'll give him that."

"Help me." Mara reached up.

Indecision creased Kali's brow.

"There's something I need to say to him," Mara said.

Kali's lips stretched into a thin line, but she pulled Mara to her feet and led her out the door. The auburn-haired brothers Mara had met before stood shoulder to shoulder, blocking Zev's passage and her view of him. She touched Gavan's arm.

"We'll take care of him. Go back inside," Gavan said.

"Let me see her," Zev said.

She nodded to Gavan, who stepped to the side but otherwise held his position. Kenrik looked as if he smelled rot and remained where he was.

A sharp intake of breath. "I don't know—I wasn't myself," Zev said.

There was nothing to say, so she waited. Zev approached, and Gavan closed the opening between them.

Zev cast an annoyed eye at the guards and looked past them. "Forgive me,

Mara. Come home. It won't happen again, I swear."

Part of her wanted to throw herself into his arms, another to rip him to shreds. "This is my home now. I accept my redemption."

"She knows you left," he said.

Dirty of him to use Rivka against her. "I'll send word if I have something for you. Good-bye, Zev."

Fatigue rushed over her as she turned from him. How had it come to this? Kali took her arm and helped her to the door.

"Wait."

Mara paused but refused to look at him. He was too beautiful to turn from twice.

Zev's voice softened. "The charges against Jed didn't hold. No one could prove the boat was his. And he knows you're gone. It's not the kind of thing I can hide for long. I won't tell him where you are, but his men are looking. Be careful."

Her knees buckled the moment the door shut behind her, and a lifetime's worth of convulsing sobs ripped from her chest. Mara couldn't remember her last cry—even when she'd thought she'd lose Selene, she hadn't cried—and this one threatened to unravel her. Kneeling, Kali wrapped her arms around Mara's waist and held her as she wept.

Exhausted and sore, Mara pulled herself up from the cool floor. Nothing moved in the dusky light of the house. Kali was gone, but voices murmured on the stoop. Assured she was alone, Mara made her way to the kitchen, lit only by a candle and the fire.

Candle in hand, she searched shelves and cabinets until she found what she was looking for. Dusty and covered in cobwebs, a dark bottle hid behind a stack of pots. More than four days had passed since her last drink, and she was thirsty for oblivion, no matter how pungent the taste. The wine burned as badly as Ramzi's fire whiskey but lacked the pleasant warming effect.

Little remained when Sabra stumbled upon her reclined against the wall by the fire. She snatched the bottle from Mara's mouth, her stretched-tight face agape. "What do you think you're doing? Do you know what this is?" She shook the bottle in Mara's face.

"Terrible wine?"

A gust of air huffed out of Sabra's mouth, and she stalked out of the kitchen calling Kali's name. The front door slammed. Mara located a flask buried in a basket of medicine. Its contents were also terrible, but at least it was whiskey. Her head jerked up when she heard a light step. Sighing, Declan sat beside her and extricated the flask from her fingers.

"What happened to 'If I had your life, I'd drink too'?"

He was neither harsh nor patronizing. "You're too ill to risk poisoning."

"What does it matter? I'm dead anyway," she said. "Jed's looking for me, and he will find me. I should leave. You're all in danger as long as I stay."

She made to stand, but Declan took her hand and eased her back down.

"You can't leave. Redemption requires you to stay in the Quarter for a minimum of a season. And you aren't upset about Jed."

She glared at him, hating his scrutiny. "So the Council offers freedom, but it's really slavery of another kind? How generous."

He said nothing.

She mocked him with a smile. "Why are you here, Declan? If you wish to bed a whore, all you need is money. Or am I expected to pay for your services, after all?"

He shut his eyes, and his shoulders sagged. "You're trying to bait me. It won't work."

"You think those all-seeing eyes tell you so much, but you barely know me. So I ask again—why are you here?"

He turned the flask in his hand. "You're sick, and I'm a healer."

The fire whispered secrets into the silence. After a time, Declan stood. "Your next few days will be difficult. Kali will clear out all the alcohol tonight, which means you have to find another crutch until you can walk on your own again. I'll be back tomorrow. In the meantime, consider apologizing to Kali. That bottle of wine is the last thing she and her husband made together. She'll never let on, but the loss is a blow."

Mara watched him go. Why did everything she survived lead to something worse?

The tremors started before noon. When Kali slipped outside to deliver lunch to Gavan and Kenrik, Mara searched every possible hideaway for bottles Kali might've missed. Nothing, not even a tincture, was found. Food was unpalatable. Strong drink was the only thing Mara craved. She smelled it, tasted it, felt its heat. She'd become Ramzi. Ramzi, whose weakness she'd scorned.

That afternoon, Mara paced in agitation. Time in Kali's back garden eased her some. An evening storm blew in, tearing at her hair and gown and the invisible creatures crawling over her skin. She stood in the downpour, clawing her arms, ears, and neck, until it waned into a drizzle. Turning, she found Declan watching her from the doorway.

She glowered at him. Her misery was his fault.

Ignoring her expression, he said pleasantly, "Fancy a walk in the rain? The streets are quiet, and we're both already soaked."

She brushed past his offered arm and waited by the front door. He followed. As he opened it for her, the corner of his mouth gave the slightest twitch. Gavan offered her a canvas covering for the walk, which earned him an incredulous brow. Closing her eyes, she let the sky cover her in light, cool kisses and listened to four pairs of boots splash along the puddled sidewalk.

Declan's voice was soft. "Look there. The first buds of spring."

A cherry tree, days from blooming, decorated a street corner. Tight-lipped buds littered the ground beneath. She stooped to retrieve a fallen clove and cracked it in her trembling hand. A slip of pink peeked through a crack in its armor. Had it clung to the tree, it would've made a lovely flower.

When they returned indoors, Kali offered them all dry clothes warmed by the fire and hot cups of tea. It was the first nourishment to please Mara since she'd arrived in the Quarter. A meal followed, but she couldn't manage more than a few bites. Afterward, they moved to the cozy sitting room. Declan chose a book from Kali's shelf, took the empty seat beside Mara on the sofa, and read aloud to everyone. The book was a collection of stories about the King, the same ones her mother and Phi had told her when she was a little girl, only with more detail.

The comfort of familiar stories didn't ease the task of sitting still. Once, Mara almost dashed out the door. She didn't notice the violence with which she was shaking until a hand took hold of hers, steadying her. Declan massaged her fingers and palm as if it was an everyday gesture. Glancing from his hand to his face, which remained attuned to the book, she considered pulling away. But she relaxed and found his touch was what she needed.

Several monotonous days dragged by, and the tremors subsided enough for Mara to contribute to the household. Too ashamed to mention the wine, she seized the opportunity to apologize to Kali through action. She swept, scrubbed floors, washed dishes, laundered linens. Work eased her agitation and gave her a place.

One afternoon, the sun shone warm on her shoulders through the kitchen window as she scrubbed vegetables. Sabra chopped beside her in a pleasant rhythm. The scent of rain-soaked soil wafted in. Declan had come early.

Arching a brow, she glanced over her shoulder at him. "Unless you carry whiskey in that bucket, go away."

The way Sabra's face stretched made Mara want to touch it to discover whether it was really made of skin.

"Don't talk to him like that." If Sabra wasn't so polite, she might've spit. "He's been nothing but kind to you. Too kind, if you want the truth."

A droll smile curved Declan's mouth. "It's fine, Sabra. If she won't be pleasant, I won't share my ice cream."

Mara faced him, wiping her hands on her apron. She hadn't had ice cream since Phi was alive. "Ice cream? Isn't that a winter treat?"

Declan shrugged. "Not when you have access to the palace kitchens. Would you like to vent your frustrations on the crank once you've properly flayed the potatoes?" With a mischievous grin, he set the bucket on the table. "I'll be outside with Kali. Join us when you're done."

Shooting sharp looks at Mara out the corner of her eye, Sabra chopped feverishly. "You should be more respectful."

She was probably right. Sabra was good at being right. "He knows I'm not really angry with him," Mara said.

"That isn't the point. Didn't your mother teach you manners?" Sabra asked.

"My mother died during my fifth winter." After an uncomfortable pause, Mara sighed. "Do you know what it's like to be a prostitute?"

"I should think not," Sabra said, tossing vegetables into a pan.

"It's a life of lies. We pretend all the time. Back home, I was free to be what I was and say what I felt, but I learned if I was going to survive the Ring, I couldn't be Mara of Firth. So, I dressed her up in satin and lace until she disappeared." Mara fussed over a scrubbed-naked potato. "I'm bone-tired of pretending."

Sabra sniffed. "You shouldn't have to pretend with Declan. He's better to you than you deserve."

The words stung, but Sabra was right even if she saw the thing upside down. Mara didn't pretend with Declan because he didn't want her to. She knew the difference between polite conversation and true interest. Declan wanted to know how she was, and she told him—without the trouble of finding words to describe the indescribable. But these were things she doubted Sabra could understand.

When the potatoes were all scrubbed, she grabbed the bucket and escaped the frigid kitchen. Gavan and Kali greeted her with warm smiles as she plopped down beside Declan. Kenrik ignored her, as usual.

Declan's eyes lit with humor as he watched Mara toil at the crank. "I hope you don't mind, but I did the easy work on the carriage ride here."

Mara humphed.

"I've spoken with Kali," he continued. "We think you're ready for a project of some sort. Something of your own. What did you like to do back home?"

"Farm work mostly—plowing, planting, reaping, all of it. I miss my hogs. And taking care of Selene," Mara said, struggling to churn and talk at the same time.

Gavan's jaw dropped. "You can plow?"

"You can't?" Mara teased.

With a hand over his heart, Gavan declared in mock-solemnity, "If you can cook, I'll marry you this instant. I'll buy some land and let you work it. You can even darn my socks."

Mara heaved a dramatic sigh. "That's quite the offer, but alas—even my generous sister complains of my cooking."

"So no cooking," Declan said with a wry look for Gavan.

"My garden hasn't grown vegetables since Dak died," Kali said. "Is there time to get seed in the ground?"

Eager to do Kali a kindness, Mara nodded. "I think so."

"And maybe you can join Sabra and me at the shelter some mornings," Kali said.

"The shelter?"

"A temporary home for refugees and ex-slaves," Declan said. "There's plenty to do. You'll find a niche."

The ice cream was ready before dinner, but Declan insisted they eat it right away. Mara accepted the full bowl he offered her. When the spoon scraped the ceramic at the bottom, she glanced down in surprise. It was the first bowl of anything she'd finished since she'd come to the Quarter. Without looking at her, Declan exchanged her empty bowl for his full one. His eyes crinkled when she took a hesitant bite.

Something inside of her rallied as she ate. When the last bite disappeared, the world was greener, life less impossible. Sabra's stew had flavor. Mara thought of Selene and let herself miss her again.

After dinner, Declan peered into her third empty bowl of the evening. "Never underestimate the medicinal properties of ice cream."

Mara rolled her eyes but failed to suppress a grin.

CHAPTER 10

Selene,

I'm free, redeemed by the King's Council, and now reside in King's Quarter. Not certain how it happened. My healer, who serves on the Council, tells me they received a letter but won't say who wrote it. You'd like this healer. He took away my whiskey. Ask Ben if all healers are irksome. I'd ask you both to come, as I can't leave for a season or two, but I'm too busy for nonsense. I've planted a vegetable garden for Kali, the woman who took me in, and I help at one of the shelters where the homeless stay until they're able to manage for themselves. No one asks me to cook, of course, but I clean, play with children, and teach anyone interested how to grow food. Don't gloat. I'm not a kingsman yet. Write soon. Tell me how you are and how things go in Firth. Any sign of Ramzi? I plan to set eyes on you and <u>our</u> farm by harvest.

Mara

Terror that Selene would visit the city with the mist still in the harbor and Jed's men prowling about outweighed Mara's desire to see her. She'd have to wait. To distract herself, she questioned shelter residents about the Council and the ambassadors, determined to capitalize on her time in the Quarter. As a whole, the residents didn't know much. Most were like Mara—there because they needed assistance, not because they felt any loyalty toward the King. Mara asked Kali if these were turned away once the required season passed.

"The King built this city for the grateful and the thankless alike," Kali said. "Some of them come around and are helped. A few become loyal kingsmen. But many stay exactly as they are, taking advantage to their disadvantage. It's sad to watch."

"I don't know why the Council doesn't chuck them out. Set limits and be done," Sabra said.

Sabra didn't mind helping those she considered to be truly needy. She was excellent with orphans, widows, and the sick and dying but brisk with recovering drunkards and hearty folk who'd lived at the shelter many winters. Favoring the practical work of feeding and nursing, Sabra had little patience when Mara animated over ball games and growing seeds, so Mara learned to keep her joys private until Kali or Declan asked to hear them.

Bright-green shoots sprouted from the soil of Kali's garden, promising good things to come. Declan stopped by most afternoons to watch Mara fuss over them. Smiling at the tallest shoot, he said, "Growth is miraculous—invisible at first and then happening all at once."

Mara squinted up at him. "Farming is the closest to magic I'll ever come." Digging up a bean sprout, she held it up. Her fingertip caressed the hairy roots spilling out of the broken seed. "To grow, the seed has to die. Monster that I am, I throw it into a shallow grave, where it's torn apart. But only then can life happen. The death of this one bean yields scores more. If the little fellow could speak, I imagine he'd say it's a worthy sacrifice."

Declan cleared his throat. "I've long thought farmers were the keepers of deep wisdom."

Her shoulders tensed at the tenderness in his voice. She replanted the bean. "Don't mock me, healer. I'll throw dirt."

His chuckle was different from Zev's. Warm. Happy. Safe. "Kenrik tells me you're curious about the Council. That you've asked questions of everyone except those who can answer them. Why is that?"

So her little interviews hadn't gone unnoticed. She scratched her nose. "It's . . . well . . . you seem so secretive about it."

"Ask me anything."

"All right," she said, hesitant and a little suspicious. "How often do you meet?"

"Two mornings per week. It seems someone should've been able to answer that one."

She ignored his teasing smile. "But what about Gavan and Kenrik? Aren't they on the Council? They've been with me every morning."

"Yes, well, we take leave when necessary," he said. "For example, I send a note when I must attend to patients. But we aren't frivolous with absences. We all take the work seriously."

"And guarding a prostitute every moment of every day is necessary?"

He squatted and looked into her eyes. "You're a special case. You've managed to anger the two most powerful and dangerous men in the city. One has threatened to kill you. The other has tried. We can't imprison them, so the Council voted to protect its investment, even at the expense of Gavan and Kenrik. And you aren't a prostitute anymore."

She worked in silence, feeling a gentle pressure in his words. He'd encouraged her to charge Zev with assault, but she wouldn't. There was no reason to revisit the disagreement. "What do you do in these meetings?" she asked.

"Why don't you join us one morning and find out?"

The invitation took her aback. "I'm allowed?"

"Whenever you like," he said. "All scheduled meetings are open to the public."

She chewed her lip, contemplating. "Maybe I will."

But of course she would. She had to.

The Council sent a carriage on the appointed morning. Mara, Kali, Gavan, and Kenrik piled inside. Warm sunshine and a cool ocean breeze made Mara wish to be in the driver's seat rather than cupboarded away with Gavan's incessant jokes and Kenrik's ongoing aloofness. Kali buffered the effect of the brothers, but not enough to make Mara easy. Much depended on what she learned today, and she longed for a few moments of preparatory solitude.

The palace gates opened to a large, decorative garden. A verdant lawn featured a variety of flowering trees and shrubs she'd never seen. Domestic blooms filled beds of dirt lined by white stone, dazzling to the eye. Their ambrosial fragrance filled the carriage. The concept of a piece of land dedicated to admiration bewildered Mara, but she found the effect pleasing nonetheless.

The carriage stopped at the entrance. Gavan leaned toward Mara from the opposite seat and said in a grave voice, "Now, Mara, there's going to be a huge crowd of very important people who will all be watching your every move, so be sure to maintain your usual level of charm."

Mara gulped, and Kali patted her leg. "He's teasing, dear."

Gavan helped Mara out of the carriage with a wink. Kenrik stepped out last, trapping Mara in a hard gaze. Unsettled, she followed Kali up the palace steps, which were of the same white stone as the palace walls. Polished oaken doors, more than double her height, led to a spacious foyer with marble floors and cedar-paneled walls, which gave off a sweet, woody scent. Vivid tapestries depicting tales of the King added color and character to the space. A glass dome filtered sunlight high overhead, and briny air swept through open doors that led to a balcony overlooking the sea.

Her companions were called aside, and Mara found herself alone. Giddy with the small freedom, she passed the tapestries and answered the draw of the sea. The wind rushed at her, loosening tendrils from her braid and exciting her lungs. She leaned over the balcony edge. The sheer drop made her lose her breath. Deep-blue waves crashed onto the rocky shore below, churning and frothing as they returned home.

To the west, she spotted the cloud of mist, as large as an island not far off the coast. What was it hiding? Her stomach roiled with the tide. For a wild moment, Mara wondered what Rivka would do if she threw herself off the parapet to the water and rocks below. Save her? Let her drown? Could Rivka's plan unfold without her help?

The plan. Today, she would memorize the names and faces of each ambassador on the Council and note which ones were most likely to have Eleora. How she was to investigate them, she had no idea, though she could guess Zev's suggestion. And then what? Betray the people who had freed her? A long dive seemed preferable.

A voice startled her. "Beautiful, isn't it?"

A man with silver-flecked hair and beard stood beside her. His regal posture gave the impression of military training. He was handsome and trim—for a man old enough to be her father. A commanding tone and refined intonation bespoke wealth and power. Memories of her time with the Ring shocked through her. He was the kind of man who had frequented her bed, except that his skin, turned golden by the sun, creased at the corners of his eyes and mouth instead of on his brow, and he seemed cheerful without reeking of alcohol.

"Beautiful, wild, dangerous, free." Everything she'd like to be.

"A poet," he said warmly. "You've either water or fire in your soul. Maybe a little of both."

She straightened. Maybe he wasn't so different from her old patrons after all.

"I'm Lazar of Rahm-Or, and I mean no harm." He smiled, extending a hand.

Pressing down distrust, she shook it. "Mara. Of Firth." Nervous fingers toyed with the lodestone hanging around her neck. Where was Kali?

Lazar's eyes flicked to the marks on her forearms and brightened. He bowed. "Honored to meet you, Mara of Firth." He didn't mock. She sensed respect, the kind people usually had to earn.

A bell sounded. "Ah. Time to begin," he said.

Not knowing what else to do, she took his proffered arm. He led her to a meeting hall. At its center stood a handsome table of dark, polished wood. Mara spotted the back of Declan's head in one of the straight-backed chairs surrounding it. Kali sat in the gallery along the western wall. Lazar escorted Mara to the empty seat beside her and took his place at the table.

Kali leaned over. "I see you've made a friend of dear Lazar."

Declan smiled from across the room. Mara answered with a wave and whispered back. "He made a friend of me. Though I'm not sure what to make of him."

"Lazar is one of the good ones. They all are."

When Gavan and Kenrik took their seats, Mara counted eight men and five women. She'd met a third of the Council already and would have to meet the others soon. If they were, as Kali said, all good people, could she betray them to Zev? To Rivka?

She could. For Selene, she could do anything.

The gallery filled, and more seats were brought in. Lazar called the meeting to order. He appeared to be the most affluent member of the Council, and she counted at least two gold chains at his neck, which required closer inspection.

What followed fascinated her, even when the topics lacked interest. She'd learned the particulars of male hierarchy at the Ring but couldn't discern a trace of it in the room. No one dominated. If anything, each seemed subservient to the rest. Age, rank, and gender carried no weight.

They discussed gutter repairs, street sweeping, and plans for new shelters to accommodate the influx of refugees and then opened the floor to attendees. A tradesman asked if the Council had information about the mist and sea travel, but there was nothing new to report. Neighbors in the Quarter disputed responsibility for wall repairs. To Mara's disappointment, no redemption letters were read. Throughout, she was struck by how attentively the ambassadors listened, how respectfully they argued, and how fairly they governed.

When it was over, Lazar approached. "Well, what did you think, my dear?"

Caught off guard, Mara frowned. "It wasn't what I expected."

"A diplomatic answer if I ever heard one. It's too bad you came on a slow day. I fear I won't see you again," he said.

Declan appeared at Lazar's shoulder. "Prediction is no good with Mara. She'll always surprise you. How are you, Laz?"

People milled and chatted, the atmosphere warm and easy. Back home, she'd never attended council meetings. Had they been like this?

Declan spoke low in her ear. "Every time I looked at you, cogs were spinning between your ears. What were you thinking?"

His earthy scent mingled with the brine in the air. She smiled. "That maybe the world's not as hopeless as I thought."

So close, she noticed how warm and deep his eyes were. He squeezed her elbow. "I'll see you tonight," he said.

Her foolish mouth settled back into place as she watched him go. Looking around the room, nearly empty now, she cursed herself. She'd forgotten why she'd come.

CHAPTER 11

Lost in routine and rigor, Mara often forgot her investigation of the Council. It was nice to have a sense of purpose without losing her dignity. Once a week, Kali, Sabra, and Mara stayed late at the shelter to clean, which granted Mara a rare hour of complete solitude.

On the next cleaning day, Mara headed upstairs, as usual, while Gavan and Kenrik kept an eye on the street door. Hearing voices in the corridor beyond the foyer, Mara clattered her broom and bucket to alert the speakers to her presence. A door clicked shut. A frightened cry followed.

Mara dropped the bucket and rounded the corner, broom in hand. No one stood in the corridor, and all the doors were closed. Not wanting to barge in on a resident, Mara pressed an ear to each door. At the third, she heard a low, grating laugh followed by a whimper. She threw it open, and two men turned from the woman they pinned to the bed.

Outrage set Mara in motion. The broomstick smacked against the side of one man's head, splintering. As he howled, his friend lunged for what was left of the stick. Mara struck his jaw. The jagged wood tore his face.

Mara ran to the woman and struggled to pull her up, but she curled into a trembling ball on the bed. The second man snatched what was left of Mara's weapon and tossed it across the room. His mouth twisted in a feral grin. Blood dripped from his jaw. "Lookee here. One for each of us."

When he closed in, a well-aimed knee doubled him over. His partner, recovered from the blow to his head, was untrained and easy to deal with. Mara dodged his swing and thrust her palm against the underside of his nose. "Gavan!"

The bleeding man slammed into her, taking her down. Through a storm of fists, elbows, and knees, she kept him from pinning her and had him subdued by the time Gavan and Kenrik arrived. Breathless and slack jawed, they glanced between the woman still frozen on the bed and Mara gasping next to the groaning men. After they hauled the men away, Kali checked Mara and the woman for injuries and made a pot of chamomile tea. Sabra continued cleaning because, as she said, someone had to do it.

The woman's name was Carina. She'd been a prostitute servicing one of the Ring's less-reputable brothels. Hearing of redemption, she learned how to secure her own. Her attackers had watched her since she'd arrived, which was no surprise. With fiery-red hair, Carina was as eye catching as any of the women Mara had worked with.

Kali alerted the kingsmen on duty to the problem and partnered Carina with Wenny, an older woman who would watch out for her. Wenny's wild salt-and-pepper hair and over-bright eyes made Mara question her ability to keep Carina safe, but when she expressed her concern to Kali, Kali assured her Carina was in capable hands.

On the walk home, Gavan leaned over to Mara. "The amount of blood coming out of that guy's nose was impressive. And the other one still can't talk. It's a shame you didn't leave us anything to do. I enjoy hitting jerks."

Mara gave a halfhearted smile. "I don't regret my bruises. What they were doing was—"

"You should've called for help first thing," Sabra said. The admonition cracked like a whip.

"There wasn't time. You didn't see—"

"As a prostitute, she's had worse. She chose worse. You should've taken the time. You're lucky you weren't hurt."

Mara halted, causing Kali to bump into her, and scowled down at Sabra. "You think she deserved to be treated that way? Because she was a prostitute?"

Sabra's mouth set. "That's not my point, but it isn't a surprise. There are consequences to the choices we make."

Mara stalked by, grazing Sabra's shoulder, and lengthened her stride. Gavan jogged to catch up but left Mara to her stormy thoughts.

That evening, Declan discovered her, shovel in hand, hacking and tearing at the ground along the back wall of Kali's garden. "I hear you did a good thing today. Though Gavan complains you could've called for help a bit sooner."

Mara plunged the shovel into the ground, hauled up a clod of dirt, and tossed it over her shoulder. "Sabra thinks the girl deserved it. Because she chose to become a prostitute. But Sabra doesn't know her story. Maybe"—the shovel bit into the soil—"her mother sold her. Maybe she embarrassed her parents, and they threw her out. Or maybe she's cursed. But I'd bet Ramzi's farm she didn't do it because it seemed like so much fun." A clump of dirt landed near Declan's feet. "She left. Of her own volition, she left the life. Wrote her own letter and everything."

Carina was the braver woman.

Mara leaned against the shovel, catching her breath. "What does it mean to deserve something, anyway? Who decides?" She dropped the shovel and grabbed the hoe. "And what about spirits and invisible kings and magic stones? What part do they play?"

Mara hacked away at the clods. "The world doesn't care about our silly, made-up rules. It moves on. From one season to the next, no matter how many good people die. The world doesn't care that someone like Jed is the richest man in Rahm-Or or that a ship-eating cloud terrorizes your merchants. It wouldn't care if Carina had been raped. And as Sabra so eloquently points out, she's had worse."

She threw down the hoe, gasping. "Does anyone deserve anything? Maybe there's no such thing. Maybe we're all beggars in need of a way out. A choice. Seems to me, until there's a choice, we do the best we can on the way to hell."

She straightened, meeting Declan's intent gaze. "But someone has to care for there to be a choice. Someone like you. You gave me my first real choice. Before you, I did what I had to do."

"The King gave you the choice," Declan said.

"Have it your way. All I know is when I was given a choice, I chose wrong. Does that mean I deserve what Zev did to me? Or should I think of it as a favor because it brought me around?" She clutched the cramp in her side. "And did you and Kali deserve me? I've been a nightmare." She paused, wiping tears with the back of her wrists. "But you did choose me, and that's important."

Attentive soil-brown eyes encouraged her to go on.

"So I've been thinking—let's give them a choice. The prostitutes, I mean. Think the Council might redeem them all? Without letters? Is it rich enough?"

Declan's mouth quirked, but he said nothing.

"It's a fair question. Look at what you all wear. Anyway, they need somewhere to go. I know that's why you brought me here that night—to show me I had a place to go. The shelters won't do, obviously. They need a place of their own where they won't be harassed or condemned for their 'choice.'" She slung him a disgusted look. "A building the city isn't using. I could fix it up and invite them all to live there. What do you think?" Wary, she searched his eyes.

"I love it," he said with a grin.

"Really? Do you think the Council will help?"

"Really," he said. "Why don't you ask at the next meeting?"

He chuckled at her expression. "You fought two men by yourself today in defense of one woman. Surely you aren't afraid to propose your idea to a group of friends on behalf of every prostitute in the city."

Mara felt sick at the thought.

"Why don't you write a letter? You can read it." He glanced around. "But first, maybe put Kali's garden back in order."

Mara appraised the chaos. "Right. What do you think? A few citrus trees?"

His eyes smiling into hers, he stepped toward her and wiped grit from her cheek. "Why don't you give Kali a choice?"

With a mischievous grin, she wiped both hands down his face. "A little dirt never hurt anyone, healer."

Declan rubbed at the grime, his mouth droll. With a short laugh, Mara wiped her hands on her skirt and brushed away what remained. Before she finished, he said, "Don't think for a moment what Zev did to you was a favor. Wrong is always wrong. But I'm not sorry it led you here."

Inexplicable terror sped Mara's pulse. Her limbs tensed to flee.

Until he wriggled his eyebrows. "Even if you are a nightmare."

⌁ ⌁ ⌁

Lazar attached himself to Mara's side the moment she entered the palace doors. Leading her from one tapestry to another, he explained each one, detailing the artist, the date it was completed, the materials used, and the particulars of each depiction. He watched her as she lingered at one that featured the King subduing a water woman and a dragon belching flame. "You don't believe the stories, do you?"

"I don't know what I believe," she said, gazing at the water woman. "Terrible things have happened. Things that shouldn't exist in a world of heroes and magic. No one was there to save me." No one could save her now.

Trouble clouded Lazar's expression. "How do you cope without something to set your hope on?"

"The truth?" she asked.

"That would be refreshing."

"I keep my mind on what comes next. And if that isn't enough, I drown myself in work and whiskey. Or I did until a certain healer banned my habit."

Lazar followed the direction of her gaze. Declan greeted him and turned to Mara. "Nervous?"

"If I lose my breakfast in front of you all, will it hurt my chances?"

Declan patted her shoulder. "That depends on your aim."

"What are we discussing?" Lazar asked.

"My proposal." Mara waved the letter she'd written.

"Which is?"

"You'll see. If I don't faint before I get it all out."

Mara clung to the parchment like a lifeline and attempted a deep breath, which was rejected by a dry throat and ornery lungs. She met thirteen stares: Lazar's kind and interested, Gavan's mocking, Declan's encouraging. The words tripped off her tongue too fast. "Dear Ambassadors of the Council: As some of you know, I'm Mara of Firth. You voted in favor of my redemption last season even though I hadn't written a letter of my own. Without your generosity, I would still be trapped in a life I despise.

"What you may not realize is that your preemptive action was vital to my acceptance. With my freedom ensured and a home waiting for me, I was able to escape when I needed to. A choice made all the difference."

Mara shared Carina's story. "No one wants to leave a bad situation to find herself in a worse one.

"So I propose you redeem all prostitutes in the city, without letters, and request a building to shelter them. If my proposal is accepted, I'd like to lead the project. After renovations, I'll visit the brothels and announce freedom to the women. A program including basic education, apprenticeships, and life-skills instruction would be offered to each woman until she becomes self-sufficient. The women will maintain the facility themselves. Responsibility has proven important to me.

"In addition to the price of redemption, I need funds for renovations, furnishings, staff, clothing, food, and probably a lot more I haven't thought of. It seems an impossible request to me. I don't have the slightest idea of what it will cost, but I ask you to consider the benefits.

"You can help women reclaim their dignity and grant them resources that will benefit the city in time. You won't win them all, but if you're patient, some will come around."

Mara looked up from the letter and saw Declan. Inspired by an unexpected surge of boldness, she said, "When my sister found out I'd sold myself to buy her medicine, she told me her life wasn't worth my soul. I don't know about that, and you wouldn't either if you knew Selene, but you seem the kind of people who value souls more than money. Thank you for valuing mine. I can't pay you back, but I'll help if you decide to do more."

At first, Mara couldn't tell whether the stillness was a sign for good or ill. A woman shared her handkerchief with the man beside her. Emotion of some kind seeped into Kenrik's perpetually bored expression, and Declan beamed pride. A lady ambassador assured Mara they would discuss her idea at the next meeting and vote whether or not she should present it to the full council to which Kali belonged.

Mara sat hard in the seat next to Kali and let out a long breath. The prospect of having to say it all again made her queasy, but when the meeting was over, each ambassador came to meet her and told her how delighted they were with her idea. Even Gavan and Kenrik complimented her. Mara studied each face, wondering which she'd have to betray. They all seemed so kind. Fortunately, Eleora wasn't in sight, though some wore tunics loose enough to conceal the stone.

Lazar was last in line. "My darling Mara, I'm inclined to disbelieve your disbelief. You belong too well to the world of heroes and magic, and one cannot embody ideals she does not at least partially accept."

Mara wasn't sure how to respond.

"Will you lunch with me after the vote next week? I'd like to discuss the particulars of your plan and know you a little better," Lazar said.

"What if it doesn't pass?"

"It will," he said blithely and patted her shoulder in parting.

Deep, even breaths and an occasional groan punctuated the stillness of the dark house. Sleep eluded Mara, as it had since the whiskey went away. She spent most nights lying awake, aching for Zev until she was rescued by the dawn. But tonight, her mind flurried with plans. She rose from bed, careful not to wake Sabra, and crept into the kitchen. Silver moonlight poured from the window, lighting the room better than a candle.

While Mara waited for a pan of milk to warm, she hunched over, filling a slip of parchment with her ideas. When she was done, she marveled. With words, she'd made something from nothing. Like magic.

A shuffle behind her made her turn. Kenrik walked around the table and took a seat across from her. "Can't sleep?"

Before the meeting today, he hadn't once spoken to her. Now, twice in one day. Maybe he was warming. "What's sleep?" she asked. "Want some milk?"

The pan bubbled over the fire. Kenrik nodded. She served two mugs and sat back down. Her insides squirmed when she saw him reading the parchment.

"A few rough ideas," she said.

"They're good. Develop them, and bring them to the next meeting." He sipped the milk and winced. "Tell me, do you burn everything you set over a fire?"

Mara grimaced. "I'm talented in the kitchen."

"I see." He set the mug down and studied its contents. Unspoken words burdened the air. As much as Mara wanted to escape whatever it was he'd come to say, she stayed.

"I don't agree with Sabra," he said. "Prostitutes are people with complex histories, like the rest of us, and more vulnerable than the fortunate can imagine.

I'm glad the King instituted redemption before he left Laeor. I'm glad you have a second chance."

He paused. Mara thanked him because she felt he expected it of her and she was afraid of him and she didn't know what else to do with the pregnant silence.

"But I know what you are. I know what Zev trains his women to do. I hear every question you ask. I see every movement of your eyes."

Mara shivered, despite the warmth of the fire.

All emotion drained from his face. "Steward well your second chance, Mara. Because if you betray the King or the Council, if you bring harm to any of my friends, I'll kill you."

He left, and she released a forgotten breath. She didn't know how Kenrik knew Zev's secrets, but he'd watched her with far greater attention than he pretended and had waited for an opportune moment to tell her. His dispassionate threat scared her worse than Zev's temper.

Three knives poised at her throat. Rivka would kill her if she failed to find Eleora by harvest. Kenrik would kill her if she succeeded. And she couldn't forget Jed, who searched the city, thirsty for her blood, and would kill her when he found her, no matter what she did. She stared at the wall long into the night, her plans forgotten, and tried to make peace with the likelihood she'd never see Selene again.

CHAPTER 12

As Lazar had predicted, the Council voted to bring Mara's proposal before the full council, which included lesser ambassadors like Kali. They would meet the following week. The day after the vote, a servant from Lazar's household delivered an invitation for Mara to lunch with him the next day. She fingered the linen paper and crimson seal, frowning at the servant's fine clothes as he mounted his thoroughbred horse.

Gavan swiped the paper from her hands the moment the servant rode off. "Yes." He grinned.

"What are you so happy about?" she asked.

He pointed to the words "and your guards."

"So?"

"So Lazar's chef is amazing. Maybe you should take lessons while you're there." He laughed when she punched his arm but sobered at her frown. "What's wrong?"

Everyone she met wanted something from her. She hadn't yet ascertained what Lazar wanted—or Declan for that matter. Not knowing made her uneasy. But it wasn't something she could explain to Gavan. "He doesn't seem very concerned for his reputation."

His cheeks pink, Gavan rubbed the back of his neck. "Lazar's a careful man. He asked you to lunch, not dinner—in the light of day, when his entire staff will be working. And he invited us." He nodded to Kenrik, who leaned against the house, snoozing. "But I imagine it's all for you. To protect your reputation and help you feel comfortable."

Her reputation? There was nothing left to protect. But if Gavan was right, it was a thoughtful gesture.

Surrounded by lush pasture, Lazar's home perched on a rise above the Priel in view of the sea. Stables and a corral dotted the landscape to the south. Mara tried not to gawk when a servant helped her out of the carriage. The mansion was larger and finer than it had appeared from the road. Gavan nudged her forward.

Lazar strode out of the entry with warm greetings and extended an arm to Mara. The inside of the house was more impressive than the facade. Her eyes widened until they ached. Her feet refused to keep pace.

Lazar paused as she peeked into a library larger than Kali's entire house. "Would you like a tour now, or do you prefer to dine first?" he asked.

Catching Gavan's pointed gaze, she said, "Lunch first, but the tour starts here."

Gavan winked, and Lazar led her on. "Excellent. Do you read, my dear?"

"I do. Or I did before I took over my uncle's farm." She didn't mention Zev, who had taught her to read, or the pain that accompanied the memory.

A slight frown creased his brow. "What do you mean when you say 'took over'?"

"I managed and worked it."

Lazar blinked at her.

"She can plow," Gavan said, as if such a thing was as impressive as Lazar's library.

"And sow and reap and thresh and manage hands and livestock. I hated figures but loved raising hogs. Though I never cared to slaughter them," she said.

Lazar guided them to an outdoor patio overlooking the mouth of the Priel. The sea sparkled in the distance. Gulls called overhead. Under the partial shade of a vine-wrapped pergola, a cloth-covered table was set with ocean-blue china and crystal goblets rimmed in gold. Pulling out a chair for Mara, Lazar asked, "Did your uncle die?"

"My aunt did. After that, he slept all day and drank all night."

Lazar took the seat across from Mara, his face stern.

Her lips pressed together. "I'm sorry. My history isn't fit for polite conversation."

His answering smile didn't quite reach his eyes. "I invited you here to know you better, not for polite conversation. But I'll change the subject. Tell me more about this plan of yours. I want to know exactly what you need."

Four servants, all dressed in fine linen, walked outside and, in one synchronized motion, served each guest a bowl of crab chowder—warm, creamy, and perfectly seasoned. They left and returned with three gold platters, which offered four varieties of cheese, an array of meats, sweet and savory jams, green and black olives, roasted peppers, sun-dried tomatoes, and warm bread. A short while later, a glazed lamb shank with spring vegetables and cream sauce was brought out. The lamb featured a flavorful crust with tender meat that juiced in Mara's mouth.

Over the finest meal she'd ever eaten, she told Lazar her ideas for a health clinic, basic education, sewing classes, and lessons in gardening, food preservation, and self-defense.

His brow rose. "Self-defense?"

Mara swallowed a bite of roasted asparagus. "Knowing you can defend yourself from someone who means you harm gives security and confidence, which most of these women either lost or never had. And they may need the skills. The girl at the shelter did."

"I'd like to think most will find a nice man to marry and will never have to worry about such things," Lazar said.

"Nice men don't want a prostitute for a wife. Not even the men who use them. My own uncle, who needs my help, won't have me back in his house."

Lazar's countenance descended into a frown. "What will you do when you return home?"

"I won't worry about that until I'm on my way." If Jed found her, she wouldn't worry about it at all. "Now I have a question for you."

"Go on," he said.

"Would it be bad manners to lick my plate? This sauce is amazing."

The men chortled, including Kenrik, and Gavan seconded her assessment.

The meal complete, Gavan and Kenrik excused themselves to the stables, leaving Lazar and Mara to the tour. As agreed, Lazar showed her the library first. She felt his eyes on her as her fingers ran over the fine, gold-engraved bindings. When he told her to borrow whatever she liked, she checked the contents of a history of Laeorian peoples.

"Looking for anything in particular?" he asked, peering over her shoulder. Traces of cigar smoke and peppermint fragranced his clothing. There was comfort in the smell.

"I'm interested in the people of the Raza Desert."

"Curious about your heritage?" he asked.

Hearing both questions in the one, she smiled. "Yes. And to find out if they somehow survived the fire spirits. Zev once implied they did, but I'm not sure I believe him."

Lazar crossed to another shelf, pulled a volume, and placed it in her hand. She flipped through a beautiful copy of *Stories of the King*, complete with illustrations and commentary. An illustration of the spirit rebellion caught her eye. The King had created elemental spirits to serve him and the people of Laeor. A number of fire and water spirits had rebelled and tried to supplant him. Earth and wind spirits had remained faithful. Mara remembered her mother saying, "The wind carries secrets to and from the King, but water lies."

The next illustration depicted the battle between the fire and water spirits. Though they both opposed the King, they weren't friends, and their wars eventually destroyed the Vardinon Wood—once a flourishing, fruitful place that separated the grassy plains from the desert. Mara's mother had taken her to see the black scar of land when Mara was very young. The sight had left an impression. The charred remains of trees, once magnificent in beauty, had haunted her nightmares until worse things took their place. It had been a surprise to learn the ruin grew anything at all, let alone flowers with medicinal properties.

Spirits of the river that flowed through the ravaged wood kept the fire spirits bound in the desert. In a fit of temper nearly a century ago, the fire spirits had turned on the inhabitants of the land. A few desperate Razans had fled through the cursed wood, some consumed by water spirits along the way. Until Mara had learned of the magic glass, she'd believed her grandparents had been some of the last pure-blooded Razans.

Lazar's voice interjected her musings. "Do you remember what spirits eat?"

"Magic, the stories say."

"Yes. And rebel spirits are no longer fed by the King. So where do they get their food?"

"Human souls." The idea of being made of magic was too fantastic to embrace, but she knew for a fact spirits fed on souls, whatever the reason. "And sometimes they eat each other."

"Spirits are fiercely clever," he said. "They wouldn't consume their most valuable resource at once. Not when they can control them by offering them what they want."

"Such as?"

"Oh, the usual things. Health, wealth, power, revenge."

Beset by a sudden headache, Mara massaged her temples. "So why haven't we seen more Razans on this side of Vardinon? Are they trapped in the desert with the spirits?"

"I think not. I suspect they prefer to stay hidden for reasons still unknown. Somehow I doubt those reasons bode well for us. But help will come when it's needed."

Hands clasped behind his back, he walked over to a painting of the King. "Do you ever wonder what the stories mean when they say he'll bring the kingdom to life through death?"

"I'm not sure I believe in the King."

"But you believe in spirits?" His question was a clear challenge, but he didn't ask it unkindly.

"Spirits, I've seen," she said.

He whirled, his mouth open. "Have you?"

She approached the painting, deciding how much to say. "When I was a little girl. But I've never seen anything like the King." Before he could ask questions, she turned the conversation back to him. "Do you believe the part about the King returning from the Otherworld?"

"I must," he said, his voice low.

"I'm sorry," she said. "Who have you lost?"

"Wife and daughter. My daughter would have come of age this summer." He released a heavy sigh. "Sorrow, death, and evil are wrong. Things aren't the way they were meant to be. I know it in my bones. I'll see my wife and daughter again."

He cleared his throat. "Come now. Allow me to show you the rest of the house."

A perfect host, he led her from one breathtaking room to another, explaining its history and pieces of interest. He pointed out vaults where family heirlooms and fine jewels were kept. But she couldn't take it in. This man, of whom she was growing so fond, was likely the bearer of Eleora. Lazar was affluent, powerful, and experienced. His home boasted elaborate security. He seemed sure of the stories, as if he'd held proof of them in his hands. And now she had to tell Zev.

But not yet. Not before she found Eleora.

When Lazar kissed her hand in farewell, she couldn't bear to look for a telltale gold chain peeking from his tunic. If he indeed had Eleora, she didn't want to know. Not until she found a way to save him.

When Captain Griggs spotted Mara smiling at him from the gallery of the meeting hall, his face burned scarlet. Understanding, she averted her eyes, which found Declan. An uncharacteristic darkness clouded his face as his gaze flicked from Griggs back to her. She'd have to explain, clear Griggs's name.

Her nerves weren't quite the little tyrants they were at the previous meeting. More bodies somehow helped—a mystifying observation. The ambassadors peppered her with questions. Thanks to Lazar, she was prepared for them.

One posed a concern. "The idea is brilliant, and I believe the program is maintainable, but the initial cost will bankrupt us. Even if we manage to purchase every prostitute in the city, we can't afford to renovate, furnish, and supply a space large enough to house them."

A chair scraped against the stone floor. Lazar stood. "Which is why my associates and I have agreed to donate the required funds. We will also support maintenance costs, which should help the treasury recover from the initial blow."

A murmur swept through the crowd, and Mara's mouth broke into a wide grin. With an answering wink, Lazar proposed a vote on whether or not to proceed to figures and accounts. The results in favor were unanimous.

After the meeting, Mara pressed through the crowd, threw her arms around Lazar's neck, and kissed his sun-browned cheek. "Why didn't you tell me?"

Chuckling, he said, "I thought it would make a good surprise. I wasn't wrong. Now, you have duties to fulfill." He nudged her toward the waiting ambassadors.

A torrent of names, faces, and questions blurred together. Until Griggs reappeared. She extended her hand, expression demure, and pretended not to know him. He took it, leaning in. "I apologize for my behavior earlier. You surprised me."

"Don't fret, Captain. I understand."

"I think your idea is splendid," he said. "And I'm honored you asked for my help last season. Please, never hesitate to do so again." He squeezed her hand and was gone.

Feeling the pressure of a gaze, she looked up. Declan watched her with an unreadable expression. Tilting his chin toward the balcony, he invited her to follow. Away from the crowd, the fresh air and salty spray washed away her stupor, of which she hadn't been aware until it was gone. Propped upon his elbows, Declan leaned against the railing and studied her face. "Please tell me why I shouldn't bring Griggs before the Council and throttle him for good measure. I'm afraid I require an excellent reason. I'm very angry."

Mara kept her eyes on the sea. "It's not what you think. We didn't . . . nothing happened."

"Not good enough."

The mist, unchanged, drew her eye. Swallowing the bile of self-loathing, she gave an account of the night, careful to tell him Griggs might have left had she not stopped him. "And then I asked a question meant to seduce him. Instead, it woke him up. He told me he should free me, not use me, and he left. This may sound odd to you, but watching a man run from me out of moral obligation to the King almost made me believe—for a moment—that maybe he exists."

She risked a glance at him. He seemed unmoved. "Don't forget that he helped me," she said.

"And then he pretended not to know you."

"I startled him, that's all."

"When are you going to stop assuming responsibility for the wrongs committed against you?" he asked. "You have compassion for others. Have a little for yourself."

Mara wanted to tell him how responsible she was and that he should stop wasting his kindness on her.

"You aren't who you were when you met him," he said.

A wave slammed into the rocks below. The cliffs seemed indestructible, but the shoreline testified to the truth—the tireless waves would, in time, break them all. She glanced at Declan's profile. Was he the rock or the wave? Which was she?

His eyes met hers, and his anger faded. "If I may pry a bit more, what did you ask him? Do you remember?"

It was the question she asked every man in her life, whether or not she spoke it aloud. It was the question she'd asked Declan the night he'd taken away her whiskey. "Why are you here?"

His countenance transformed from stunned to sad to something she couldn't read. He faced the water and nudged her with his shoulder. "You are remarkable. Did you know?" There was no mockery in his tone. "Heartbreaking, but remarkable."

He didn't explain, and she didn't ask. They watched the waves roll in and crash against the rocks, a comfortable silence between them.

CHAPTER 13

The Council approved Mara's proposal and gave her an empty storehouse in the Quarter. With Lazar's help, renovations were soon underway. Every morning, under guard, Mara, Carina, and wild-haired Wenny worked with a group of women from the shelter, emptying the space, overseeing repairs, and cleaning. Council members sometimes joined them. They pieced together partitions, which formed bedrooms, a sitting room, a corridor, and a foyer. The kitchen, they decided, should be in the open corner near the window, door, and spigot. Mara threw herself into planning and work, sparing few thoughts for Jed, Rivka, or Kenrik's recent threat.

Any question she had concerning Kenrik's ability to fulfill his threat was answered on the walk home after a long day at the shelter. The hot sidewalk warmed her feet through the soles of her shoes. Sweat trickled between her aching shoulders. She scratched and stretched, listening to Gavan and Kenrik murmur behind her. Weary, hungry, and lost in a windstorm of thought, she didn't see the beggar on the street until she was nearly upon him.

A strong arm hooked her waist and swung her out of the way as the beggar rose, his sword clashing with Kenrik's. Gavan dealt with a figure that lunged from a shrubbery, keeping Mara close at his back. She didn't see the passerby approach from the street. Gavan whirled in time to save himself from receiving a blade to the back. The attackers didn't seem interested in Mara at the moment. Through the frenzy, she watched Kenrik spar and deliver a killing blow. She stood gaping at the four bodies on the ground when a fifth sprang for her. Gavan intercepted him and wrestled the blade from his hands.

Tucking Mara behind his back, Kenrik questioned the struggling assailant. "Who sent you?"

The man spat red onto the white sidewalk. "The bitch knows." He stretched out his neck to grin at her, white teeth dripping blood. "He misses you, sweetheart."

When he launched into a graphic description of what would happen to her when she was caught, Kenrik punched him in the mouth. He leaned toward the man, shaking out his hand. In a quiet, detached tone, he said, "Lucky for you, I feel merciful today. This is what will happen: My brother will let you go. If you make a move against me, my brother, or the lady, I will kill you. But if you leave, as you should, you will do so in peace. You will tell Jed his assassins are dead, and if he sends more, they'll be the same. And the kingsmen will pay him a visit, of course, because we can't have thugs attacking citizens in the street."

Gavan let go. Flapping his arms, the man spat again. "Never said it was Jed, did I? Don't know who it is. Could be anyone. Even ol' Zev." The man grinned at Mara again. She shuddered.

"Leave," Kenrik said. "Before I regret my decision to let you live."

With a mocking bow to Mara, the man said, "He'll see you soon enough."

When the man was out of sight, Kenrik looked Mara over for wounds. Her limbs jittered, and a headache hammered her skull, but she assured him she was fine.

"Get her home," Kenrik said to Gavan. "I'm going to see that our friend makes it out of the Quarter." He glanced around his feet. "And find someone to help with the mess."

Blowing out a heavy breath, Gavan watched him go. "I hate it when he talks like that. It's creepy." He glanced at her. "Are you all right?"

"I'll live," she said.

Gavan scratched the back of his neck, grinning. "Five assassins. Five! A respectable number, but I think we could've taken eight at least."

She didn't disagree. Her guards had proven their worth. But neither could she celebrate. Jed had found her and had sent five assassins to kidnap her and kill her friends. Five.

One humid morning at the shelter, not long after the incident on the street, a woman offered Mara a cup of water, which she accepted with gratitude. She was so thirsty that the strange taste didn't trouble her—until the room began to spin. The last thing Mara remembered was the woman's satisfied smirk.

In the darkness, she smelled earth and peppermint. Voices rumbled nearby. A hand stroked her hair.

"As far as we can tell, she accepted a drink from a female worker, who turned out to be a bounty hunter," Gavan said. "We found her male partner waiting in the side alley. Thank the King for Wenny and her frying pan."

Wild-haired Wenny? She'd saved her?

Lazar's voice sounded tight. "Will it be safe for her to continue the work?"

"No," Kenrik said. "She won't be safe anywhere now that he's found her."

"I could send her away. Hide her somewhere outside of the city." Lazar was so kind.

Declan sounded tired. "You can offer, but I doubt she'll accept. And the choice will be hers. We won't force her to do anything."

There was comfort in kindness and being understood, but she wouldn't eavesdrop a moment longer than she could help. With a giant effort, she pushed through the wall pinning her down.

"She's stirring." Kali's soft hand touched her face.

At the table that evening, Mara propped her head upon her hand, too drowsy to eat. "I think I'd like some training. With a blade."

Gavan smacked his fingers, grinning. "Sure, but start with Kali. I'll lose respect for you when I flatten you left handed with my eyes closed."

"And who taught you to blindly level an opponent with your weak hand?" Kali asked.

Gavan leaned over and planted a greasy kiss on Kali's cheek.

Cringing, Kali wiped the spot. "I'll be happy to give you lessons, Mara."

"Good. Because I have to go to the brothels soon, and I can't neglect Jed's," Mara said.

Five sets of eyes blinked at her. Kali frowned. "Surely someone can go for you."

Mara shook her head, which slipped out of her hand. She recovered with a jerk. "It has to be me."

Kali appealed to Declan, who'd been pensive all evening. Playing with a napkin, he looked up at Mara with troubled eyes. "Mara's right. But you'll take extra guards." It wasn't a suggestion.

"Extra guards?" Gavan scoffed but silenced at Declan's expression.

Mara noticed Sabra's uneaten meat pie. She'd been subdued since the day the assassins had attacked. "Is something wrong?" Mara asked. It wasn't worry for her.

Sabra glared at her. "You're going to get us all killed."

Mara tried to think of something comforting to say that wasn't a lie. Sabra wasn't the warmest of the lot, but she was rarely wrong.

"Nonsense," Gavan said. "I, for one, enjoy the excitement."

Standing, Declan set an envelope beside Mara's plate. "Sabra, will you join me outside? The weather is perfect, and the roses have begun to bloom."

The envelope was addressed to Mara in Selene's writing, but instead of a happy flutter, Mara's insides gave a sharp twist. Sabra disappeared around the corner on Declan's arm.

Excusing herself, Mara took the letter to the bedroom.

Mara,

I laughed, cried, and danced when I received your letter. In worrisome moments, I pull it out and read it again. You can't imagine how happy you've made me. Your healer and I will be great friends, I can tell. Ben says if you find him irksome, he's probably exactly who you need. I agree. We too are busy. Please don't fret, but the Akaronians have amassed in troubling numbers and now camp thirty leagues north of Firth. The Council sent reinforcements to help us fortify and protect the town. Their presence keeps our kingsmen in line. I'm training again and plan to humiliate you in our next match. Ramzi hasn't been found, which is hopeful. What danger are you in that you pretend not to want me? Answer honestly, or I'll come. See you soon—in King's white.

Selene

Thirsty for strong drink, Mara returned to an empty kitchen to check Declan's basket, which held neither tinctures nor bad whiskey. Growling in frustration, she stomped out to pace the garden. She wasn't sure of the precise reason for her angst. Her mind filtered Selene's news piece by piece. She didn't like the Akarnian army so near her hometown nor the idea that Selene was in enough danger to need training. Nor that Selene was becoming someone she didn't know. Maybe the words "your healer" bothered her. On her next turn, she collided with her healer.

"What's wrong?" he asked.

"You never pack whiskey anymore." She pushed off him.

"She told you about the raiders."

"How do you know everything? Did you read my letter?" she demanded.

He wouldn't be riled. "I'm on the Council."

"If you're so important, why are you here all the time? Surely, you have more urgent things to do than act as my personal healer, especially now that I'm well." She marched away, her anger purging the effects of the drug.

He waited for her to pass again. "I work where the King sends me. Right now, you are his particular concern."

Mara stopped. "Where the King sends you. What in hell does that mean?"

His gentleness equaled her ferocity. "Just because you can't see the King doesn't mean he can't be known."

The urge to roll her eyes was strong, but she refrained. For Declan's sake. "All right. I'll play. Why did he send you? What does he want from me?"

Declan shrugged. "Everything, I imagine."

She extended empty hands. "Look at me, Declan. I don't have anything."

"Nothing is all you need."

Weary of enigmatic responses, she scowled at the moon.

"The King isn't unreasonable," he said. "He won't ask what you can't give. He won't demand a thing from you until he's given you everything."

She searched the vast black sky. "How can a person who never shows his face give me anything? As far as I'm concerned, he's like my father. Absent."

"The King redeemed you. He gave you a home and a family."

"You gave me those things."

He inhaled, preparing to answer, and stopped himself. After a long pause, he asked, "What do you want? From life? From the King?"

Her eyes darted in every direction. Tugging at her hair, she sank into a heap in the grass. "I don't know. What about you? You say you're here because the King has an interest in me. What about your interests?" Her heart bucked as she realized what she'd asked. But no matter how she snatched at the words, they were spoken, dissolved into the ether.

Night settled around them. Insects chirped in the grass. A whippoorwill called from a willow behind the wall. Hidden in a damp corner of the garden, a frog belched an ode of unrequited love into the dark.

With a groan, Declan sat down beside her. "My interests and the King's interests are inseparable."

"You don't worry about what people say? You're friends with a whore. A whore, Declan, which isn't very dignified of an ambassador. My uncle told me I could never go home if I became a prostitute, but you come calling every day. I assure you, people are talking, and none of it's nice."

"I'm not going anywhere," he said.

"That's not what I asked."

"Isn't it?" The gust of his springtide smile followed the question.

"Even at the expense of your reputation?"

"If you think I care one mite about my reputation"—the word tripped over a short laugh—"you don't know me at all."

"Even if I get you killed?" she asked softly.

"What makes you think I'm easy to kill?"

His hand glowed in the moonlight upon the grass. Mara covered it with her own. His head jerked to her hand, then to her face, and drifted back to the sky.

"Tell me something of yourself," she said. "Where did you grow up?"

"I was born north of the Coastal Plains. My parents were grain farmers, like you. They weren't wealthy, but we had enough. They didn't think me suited for farm life, so after my twelfth winter, I was sent to Rahm-Or to begin my apprenticeship . . ."

As he talked, Declan turned over his hand and wove his fingers into hers.

Lessons with Kali proved almost as rigorous as plowing. Each morning, Mara repeated drill after drill until her limbs jellied and sweat poured. Gavan observed from his seat on the ground, taunting her between yawns. He was especially critical of her footwork. Exceeding her limit for his nonsense, she challenged him to duel—an unfortunate decision.

Grinning wickedly, he rubbed his hands together. "Stakes?"

"If I win, you shut it."

He rose to his feet, chuckling. "That's fair. If I win, you eat this slug." He held up the juicy fellow for her inspection.

After that, she ignored him the best she could.

Over a breakfast of squash-blossom soup, Mara announced, "This evening, I go to the Ring," hoping she sounded more determined than she felt. "I'd like Cadha's help with the shelter. I need her nurturing instincts, and the Ring is no place for Nuri to grow up. If I can't convince my friends to come, I won't convince anyone."

Kali wiped her pursed lips and set down her napkin. "Sometimes, friends are the most difficult to convince."

A carriage came after a lunch Mara couldn't eat. The brothers lumbered in and sat side by side across from her. Her hands trembled, rattling the redemption papers.

"We won't let him hurt you," Gavan said.

Kenrik narrowed his eyes. "That's not what troubles her." Disapproval dripped from every word. "It's seeing him again. Because you're still in love with him."

Mara didn't comment. "Zev should be busy. If we enter through the hall, I can bypass his office. You can't follow, of course. Only patrons are allowed upstairs."

An uncharacteristic scowl settled on Gavan's face. "I don't like the idea of you up there alone."

"I won't be alone. Besides, Zev rarely goes upstairs."

Nerves firing and heart pounding, she stepped out of the carriage and into the street. A guard whose name Mara couldn't remember nodded and held the door open. When she hesitated, Gavan clapped her on the back. "Think of it this way—it won't be as bad as eating a slug."

Mara stopped cold when she walked into the hall. A hundred memories attacked at once. Whiskey and cigar smoke fragranced the empty space. In her mind, she heard the clink of shooters, the rustle of satin, and the slap-tack of cards hitting the table. Jed's voice. Forced laughter. Her head spun.

"We need to leave before anyone sees the carriage and reports back to Jed," Gavan said, guiding her forward.

With leaden legs, Mara trudged up the stairs she'd walked down every night, putting herself on display. Cadha's mouth fell open when she saw Mara standing in her doorway. Nuri ran at Mara, throwing scrawny arms around her waist. Mara knelt, smiling into the girl's face.

Motherly eyes passed over Mara's figure. "You're thin."

"Am I? Maybe it's the dress." Mara gave Cadha a squeeze.

A delicate crease formed upon Cadha's brow. "Why are you here? Zev lets Jed come now. If he catches you—"

"I won't stay long. Can you gather the girls? Levanna too. I have a proposition for you all, one I hope you'll be excited about."

With a timid nod, Cadha left. Nuri's eyes brightened. "Want to see my new dolly? Zev bought her for me."

Mara fawned over the porcelain masterpiece, fingering its fine features with a heaviness in her chest. Why did Zev have to be so difficult to love and impossible to hate?

Several pairs of feet shuffled into the room. Elise greeted Mara with an embrace, followed by Joss. Levanna lingered in the corridor. "What's wrong with you?" Levanna said. "You look ghastly—like you haven't slept in weeks."

Mara smiled wryly. "Hello, Levanna. You're pleasant this evening, as always."

"What's this about?" Joss asked. "I hope you haven't risked that pretty head for a social call. Jed's favorite conversation is how he plans to kill you."

Levanna scoffed at the word "pretty."

"I came to tell you the Council has redeemed you. All of you." Mara held up the papers. "There's a safe place for you to live if you choose to accept."

Mara was reminded of the vacant expressions of sheep.

Blunt, but not unfriendly, Joss said, "This conversation isn't for me. It's lovely to see you, but I need to get ready. And you really should leave." She pecked Mara on the cheek and left.

Posing against the doorframe, Levanna inspected her pristine fingernails. "I'd rather entertain Jed every night than live in a shelter. And you should know Zev came to his senses. He'd almost forgotten what it is to be with a woman who knows what she's doing," she said and slinked away.

Mara pressed a hand beneath her stomach where the words hit hardest and turned to Cadha and Elise. "Well?"

Cadha watched Nuri with her doll. "What has the Council promised besides a place to live?"

Mara made herself focus. "Um, food, protection, community. Also trade training and apprenticeships, if desired. You can learn to sew, garden, even educate if you wish, and when you're ready, they'll help you move into your own home."

"What about Nuri?" Cadha asked. "I've experienced poverty. I won't allow her to suffer as I did."

"You'll have all you need. I promise. And I could use your help when the girls start coming."

"Girls?"

"The Council has redeemed all the prostitutes in the city," Mara said, attempting a smile.

After a startled pause, Cadha said, "I don't think so. We're comfortable here, and Zev sees that Nuri receives the best of everything."

"But . . . I don't understand."

"It's a good thing the Council has done, especially for less-fortunate girls. I'll keep it in mind for when Nuri's older. Thank you for being so brave to come and tell us." Cadha fixed her attention on styling her hair.

Bidding Cadha a listless farewell, Mara sagged out of the room. Steps sounded behind her. Mara turned to find Elise gazing past her with wary eyes. She whirled. Zev leaned against the wall next to the stairs, a shadow sprawled across his face. "What are you doing here?"

Mara's heart pounded in her ears. "I came to see my friends."

"Bold, considering Jed has every criminal in the city looking for you," he said.

"Right. I should go." She moved toward the stairs.

He blocked her passage. "You avoided me. Why?"

She recoiled from the hand at her waist. "I need to leave. If you care about me at all, you'll let me."

His fingers traced the scar along her cheekbone. She closed her eyes, scolding herself for indulging his touch.

"Say you forgive me," he said.

Her eyes flew open when a finger brushed her lips. She slapped his hand away.

"What's this?" He snatched the papers.

"Proof of redemption. The girls are free to go. Lucky for you, they want to stay." Her spirits bolstered as he scowled at the print.

The papers disappeared. "You came to steal my girls?"

"Of course not. The Council redeemed them. They're paid for." She took in the angry set of his jaw and glowered up at him. "What are you going to do? Hit me again?"

For a moment, she thought he might. Instead, his arms enclosed her, drawing her body into his. Then he was everywhere, surrounding her, filling her senses with frankincense and whiskey heat. Herding her to her old room.

"No," she gasped, pushing him away.

"We don't have to be long. Unless you want to be." The look in his eyes breached her resolve. She searched for an escape.

His mouth quirked in amusement. "Why do you say no to something you clearly want?"

"I need to go."

"Wait." He grabbed her arms. His thumbs traced her marks. "Rivka demands a report. Tell me you have something."

"How are you communicating with her?" Mara asked, wondering why the question hadn't occurred to her before.

A noise at the top of the stair drew their attention. Boz cleared his throat. Mara sighed in relief at the sight of him.

"One moment," Zev told him and turned back to Mara. "Your report."

"Only that Jed will probably kill me before she has the chance. Tonight, if you don't allow me to leave this instant."

"That won't do."

"It's all I have. Good-bye." Mara twisted out of his grasp. Pausing to embrace Boz, she rose onto her toes and whispered, "Thank you. You saved me." She kissed his smooth cheek and fled down the stairs.

Gavan intercepted her before her feet touched the carpet. "What took so long?"

"One guess," she said, drawing Kenrik's perceptive gaze. At his sneer, she smoothed her gown and angled her face away, aware of her smoldering cheeks.

They led her out of the hall in long, swift strides.

"Well?" Gavan asked when they were inside the carriage.

"They didn't want it." Mara stared out the window.

Kenrik pulled down the shades, blocking her view, and leaned back. "That's not surprising. It's quite a descent from the finery of Zev's headquarters to a shelter."

"I don't understand," Mara said. "Why should that matter?"

A faint smile warmed Kenrik's face. "I might find your disregard for luxury charming if you didn't love a man who's poison to you."

"Please stop saying I love him."

Her insides writhed. Part of her wished she'd let Zev take her to her old room, which only increased her self-loathing. Any pride she felt at having denied him fizzled at the rush of heat when she remembered the pressure of his hand, the taste of his kiss. At once, she regretted their good-bye, longed for another meeting, and never wanted to see him again.

Declan greeted them upon arrival at Kali's home. Guilt smothered her as he offered smiles and encouragement. Unable to take any more of his kindness, she excused herself to bed without dinner.

Later, when her tossing disturbed Sabra, Mara abandoned the bed for a patch of grass in the garden. Immersed in moonless night among the bugs and the dirt, she sank into the peace of sleep.

Mara woke to something prodding her ribs. Gavan towered over her, the morning sun at his back. She jolted upright when he kicked her again.

"Sorry to frighten you, but as you've frightened the entire house, it seems fair."

He squatted down beside her. "That wall won't protect you from Jed's thugs. Do you mind telling me why you chose to sleep out here without your guards?"

Groaning, Mara rubbed her eyes. "Catharsis?"

His tone snapped teeth. "The next time I catch you out here in the morning, you'll wake with a mouthful of slugs. How's that for catharsis?"

Gavan grumped at Mara until her heart grated raw. His criticisms during drills were sharper, more constant than usual. On the way to the shelter, she walked ahead so he wouldn't catch her swiping moisture from her eyes. What had happened to her? She'd rarely cried before coming to the Quarter.

In the foyer, he stopped her with a dramatic sigh. He lifted her, squeezing so tight the air woofed from her lungs. He returned her to her feet and rested his chin on her head, tilting it at an awkward angle. "I haven't had a sister in a long time. Mine died when she was small. Sickness of some sort. This morning, I thought I'd lost another. Sorry to be an ass, but please don't be an idiot."

"All right. As long as you release my head."

Laughing, he mussed her hair. As she smoothed down the mess, he said, "Don't tell Declan I made you cry. He'd ham me."

Her cheeks warmed. Before she could deny her tears, she heard her name and spun at the familiar voice. "Elise?"

A petite figure launched into her arms. "I decided to come soon after you left yesterday. Zev brought me here this morning. He says you owe him."

Mara turned to Gavan and rolled her eyes, but he was too enamored with Elise to notice.

"It's a good thing I decided to come," Elise said, looking around. "No one will want to live in this dreary place until we brighten it up." She took Mara's arm and led her through the shelter, describing her plans for each room.

Gavan followed, jotting notes and muttering approval.

Elise wasn't who Mara would have chosen to help run the shelter, but watching how others responded to her, Mara realized how well suited she was for the work. Her warmth won over the cool ones Mara couldn't reach. Everyone fed off her bubbly energy. Elise was likelier to begin a new project than complete an old one, but she always solicited plenty of help to execute her vision and encouraged everyone as they went along.

The shelter wasn't ready for residents, so Elise shared Mara and Sabra's room. Mara worried Sabra would be rude to Elise, but she took to her better than she had to Mara. Not even Kenrik was immune to Elise's charms. The frigid atmosphere in the home thawed. Declan continued his evening visits, often joined by Lazar, who always brought something made by his chef to share with everyone along with a small jar of cream sauce for Mara. As she looked into each smiling face gathered around Kali's table, she realized Declan was right—she'd been given a family. For the first time in memory, she was content.

Spring was at its end. Everyone gathered on Kali's stoop to enjoy Sabra's berry pie as the sun set. Lazar seemed as comfortable sitting on hard stone as in a fine chair. He laughed boisterously at Elise, who entertained everyone by animating her attempts to catch the rats that infested the shelter.

"Mara was no help at all. When she saw it, she shrieked like a child, which sent the boys running with their swords. Kenrik was even worse. He rolled his eyes and walked away, but Gavan did try to save us. He bounced around, jabbing at it, but he never went close enough to do anything."

Gavan groaned. "They aren't rats. They're the stuff of nightmares."

"A couple of cats will take care of the problem and shame us all," Mara said.

A boy approached from the street. He was no more than ten winters and dressed in King's white. He held a small package in his hand. "I'm looking for Mara of Firth," he said, his eyes darting between Mara, Sabra, and Elise.

Mara set down her plate, smiling to put the boy at ease. "I'm Mara."

Eyeing the men, he carried the package to her and dashed out of sight.

Sabra gathered empty plates. "That was strange."

Declan swiped the package out of Mara's grasp. He sniffed, tasted, and shook it before handing it back with a shrug. Shooting him a teasing glance, Mara lifted the lid and brushed away the straw. Her fingers touched something cold and hard, something fleshy. She pulled it out and dropped it, blanching.

A large human ear lay on the sidewalk below. Through it, Aunt Phi's wedding band glinted rose and gold in the setting sun.

CHAPTER 14

Elise screamed. Gavan chased after the boy. The ear was tucked back into the box and taken away. Someone repeated Mara's name. Was it Lazar? Declan turned her face toward him, peering into her eyes. He asked a question she couldn't hear for the rush in her ears. Her attached ears.

The world shook with the violence of an earthquake until Declan wrapped his arms around her. When sounds and words made sense again, she was inside, lying on Kali's sofa. Declan rubbed oil into her feet. Bergamot and rose perfumed the air. She stirred at the sound of the door. Declan flicked concerned eyes to hers before looking up in question.

Gavan's voice. "The boy's gone. We can't find him anywhere."

"Do you think you can drink some tea?" Declan helped her up before she responded and placed a steaming mug in her hand.

No one said a word as she sipped. Her heart twisted at the new lines etched in Lazar's brow. She was teaching his face to frown. Questions hovered, unasked, weighing the air. With a sigh, she turned to Declan. "Someone's killed Ramzi. Zev will know who."

⌇ ⌇ ⌇

Gavan answered the knock at the door. Boz walked in after Zev, his bald head brushing the ceiling. He nodded to Mara with empathetic eyes.

Gavan glared at Zev. "Did you do this?"

Zev answered with a derisive scowl and sat next to Mara. "Let me see it."

Mara turned her head away as he inspected the box and its contents.

"Can we talk alone?" he asked.

At Mara's nod, everyone shuffled out the front door. Draping an arm over her shoulders, Zev asked, "Are you all right?"

She answered with a glare.

"He's not dead," he said. "But I wouldn't be sorry if he was, if you want the truth."

"Why? Because he hurt me? That's interesting."

Zev withdrew his arm. "I didn't come here to fight with you."

"Fine, but let me ask you a question. Don't answer. Think about it. You believe your father deserves to die because he killed your mother, and you suggest Ramzi's death would be fair. But what do you deserve? You made me your slave, sent me to bed with sick and dangerous men, nearly killed me—so who are you to decide what a person deserves? I suggest a little caution before doling out judgments. One day, your own words may try you."

His eyes fastened to the wall as she talked. "Are you finished?"

"Yes."

"Good. This"—he held up the box, shaking it—"is a message. To us both."

"From?"

"Guess."

"Rivka." Mara spoke the name like a curse.

"Yes. Cutting off appendages—that's Akaronian work. They do it to captives of value for ransom money. Some captives return to their kin alive. Others, piece by piece. It's barbaric but effective. To me, this says the raiders have pledged themselves to her, which is part of the plan. Now, she waits on me. And as you know, I wait on you. To you, she says the raiders have your uncle, and you'll continue to receive similar packages until you find the stone. Your time is limited. I suggest you forget your little project and new suitors and get back to spying."

"That's it?"

He rubbed his hand down her thigh. "Unless you want to show me your room.

But I think your time would be better spent showing it to someone who can answer your questions. Like those guards of yours. Or Lazar."

Laughing at her revulsion, he continued. "Rivka's kiss"—his thumb traced a circle on her brow—"draws men of power to you. One of them has Eleora."

"What?"

He touched her quivering lip, a cruel glint in his eye. "You must realize it's true. Jed. Your friends on the Council. Me. Do you think we stay because of your charm? Good night, Mara."

She flinched at the slam of the door. Lazar and Declan reappeared, and her heart wrenched. Declan's expression turned stormy. "What did he say to you?"

His anger and Lazar's distress blurred behind a sheen of tears. It wasn't real. None of it was real. "He says Ramzi is alive, but I should expect more packages."

"Why? Who's done this?" Lazar demanded.

"Akaronians, probably."

Declan studied her like he didn't know whether or not to believe her. He shouldn't believe. He should run.

"What quarrel could Akaronians possibly have with you?" Lazar asked.

A knot formed below her stomach. "I . . . could you please tell Gavan I'll be in the garden and that I'd like to be alone as long as possible?" She raced out of the house.

Hiding herself in a grassy corner that couldn't be viewed from the door or any window, she drew her knees to her chest and buried her face in her skirts. It was bad enough to be in Rivka's debt, but to entrap others was an unforgivable crime. Not one was her friend by choice. They'd all been compelled by dark magic.

Sometime later, she heard the door. She startled at the sight of Kenrik. Arms full, he eased down beside her and draped a blanket over her skirts. "From Elise. She threatens her miniature wrath if you catch cold and can't work tomorrow." He placed a hot mug in her hands. "From Kali. Chamomile, lavender, and mint. My personal favorite after unpleasant events." A handkerchief. "From Declan." Another slice of pie. "From Sabra." An arm hooked her shoulders and squeezed. "From Lazar and Gavan."

She wiped her face with the soft handkerchief and gave him a wry smile. "And what do you have for me?"

"Besides protection from my brother's well-intended jokes, taunts, and questions? An observation and advice. Zev seeks control over you. He'll help you, hurt you, love you, frighten you, lie to you, anything to keep you enslaved. I don't know what he said to you tonight, but don't be too quick to believe him, especially if doing so would serve his agenda in any way."

Mara sipped her tea, considering. "He isn't all bad, you know."

"Few people are."

"Jed is."

"I may agree with you there. Should Gavan and I bring out blankets of our own?"

"I'll come inside soon."

Kenrik nodded, closed his eyes, and rested his head against the house. When it became clear he had no intention of leaving, she went to work on her pie and tea, casting him wary glances between bites and sips. Was he there because of Rivka's magic or because he wanted to be? Had even Kenrik, who would kill her as soon as protect her, succumbed to her spell?

Another choice lay before her. Would she allow Ramzi to die a slow and horrible death at the hands of enemies, or would she betray a friend? She could go to Zev with her suspicions about Lazar, but suspicions wouldn't be enough for Rivka. Mara needed the stone.

Mara escaped her anxieties in the gardens—Kali's and the one she tended at the shelter. There, she cloistered the fear haunting every thought and fantasized about the relief of death. To run away from the mess she'd created and leave it to others would be a coward's act, but an unutterable weariness dragged her toward the ground, and she had a mind to let it have her. Buried in the soil, she could rest. Sleep. Her body would break apart and feed the earth—and finally do the world some good instead of drawing everyone and everything into the curse of her existence. Her spirit would be free, and no one could hurt her ever again.

But there was the shelter to prepare and the prostitutes who still awaited freedom.

No matter how she nettled him, Declan wouldn't stay away. If anything, he came more often, working alongside her until dinner. But if what Zev had said was true, he couldn't help himself. So she used the time to learn what she could, almost hoping he would become wise to her scheme.

"Have you ever seen the King's stone?" She ripped a handful of weeds from the soil.

"Eleora." A jealous correction more than a clarification. "Yes."

The answer shocked through her. But maybe all ambassadors saw it at least once during their ministry. "I've heard of it all my life. What's so special about it? They say it has healing powers. What else?"

"One of its names is the Spirit of the King," he said. "Any good the King would do, it does. Which is why it heals."

What could Zev and Rivka want with such a thing? "Let's say the King wanted to bring justice to a group of evil people. Could the stone help him do it?"

He gave her a quizzical smile. "I suppose."

"Does it give special powers to anyone who wears it?"

"Yes and no."

"Can you explain?"

"Well, not everyone can wear it," he said. "It's a magical—I hesitate to call it an object. It's an entity of its own. A personality. As I said, the Spirit of the King, which is like saying magic itself. It chooses where it goes and who wears it."

Mara scowled. "You're teasing me again."

"I'm not."

"It's a necklace. What kind of necklace makes choices?"

"It's not really a necklace. But to finish answering your previous question, it does empower the person who wears it to do extraordinary things. Now"—he stood, brushing his hands—"what shall we do with this lovely sack of manure you requested?"

With a snort, she emptied the heavy bundle and handed him a rake. "Spread it."

That evening, Mara wrote Zev a note, which she planned to send by Kali the next morning:

> Obtaining Eleora will be difficult without the cooperation of
> its keeper. More later.
> —M

∿ ∿ ∿

At Mara's request, Declan set up a healing room at the shelter where he could perform routine checks and treat the women as needed. This way, the women wouldn't be forced to use the crowded healing rooms at the shelters, and they could build trust with one or two caregivers. Declan had always made Mara feel safe. She hoped the women would sense that same safety.

As she and Declan stocked the room with herbs, tinctures, and cheap alcohol, he asked, "Will you be all right if I leave these here?"

"I think so," she said. "I'm happy when I'm here. Something about this work makes me come alive. Makes me feel my life is worth something."

Declan set a vial on the shelf, his mouth serious and eyes gentle. "I love that serving the King's people makes you happy. It's a happiness we share. But I want you to understand something. Your worth has nothing to do with your work. Your work is only what you do. Your value lies in who you are, in the magic of your soul. And someone needs to tell you—it far exceeds your father's gem collection."

He returned to the task, and Mara mulled over his words. Who was she, really, but a girl who'd given her magic away?

Lazar supplied Mara with three cats. The rat population dwindled, and the cats grew sleek and fat. Mara rubbed their bellies, lauding them the cleverest felines she knew.

When the shelter was safe for residents and all the furnishings were in place, Elise, Carina, and Wenny, who Carina refused to part with, moved in. With Mara, they set up the sewing room, secured master tradeswomen able and willing to accept apprentices, and watched over the growing garden. Only a few projects remained before the shelter was ready for more residents.

Wenny, whispering to herself, counted flatware while Mara inventoried dishes and pots. "How does the King fare, lass?" Wenny asked.

"I wouldn't know," Mara said with a startled laugh.

Annoyance flashed in Wenny's bright eyes. "Why wouldn't you? He's with you all the time."

"I'm confused," Mara said.

"Confused? The magic of his Spirit surrounds you. Are you so daft you don't notice?"

Staring at the strange woman, Mara recalled what Kali had said about Eleora some time ago. Its magic left traces. "Wenny, are you talking about the King's stone?"

Flatware clattered onto the floor. "Stone? The Spirit of the King is no mere stone, girl. If you insist on being difficult, I'll find someone else to work with." Wenny stalked out of the room, wild hair bouncing.

Kenrik passed by the door and glanced from Wenny's retreating figure to Mara. "Is everything all right?"

With an absent nod, Mara stooped to retrieve the scattered flatware and puzzled over what Wenny had said.

Zev,

A crazy old woman at the shelter seems to think one of my guards has the stone. I doubt her sanity. Kali doesn't seem to. Please advise.

—M

Search your guards. I trust you remember how to get a man out of his clothes.

—Z

Mara shredded the note, wadded it, and threw it into the kitchen fire. Plopping into a chair, she chewed a fingernail and watched the flames. Gavan didn't have it. She would've noticed by now if a clunky gem hung around his neck. They sparred daily, and he was rather demonstrative with his affection.

Kenrik was another case.

That evening, she studied him over her dinner plate. "Tomorrow, I'd like to spar with Kenrik."

Gavan burst into laughter. "Please, oh please, let me watch. What do you think, Kali? Disarmed in two breaths if he uses a dagger to her sword, blindfolded with his strong hand tied behind his back?"

"If that." Kali's dimples appeared.

"What am I missing?" Mara asked.

Kenrik pretended not to hear the conversation.

Gavan swiped the toast from Mara's plate and bit into it. "Kenrik may be the most accomplished swordsman to have served in the King's army. Ever. At my finest, I can't last more than a few minutes. If I best him, he let me."

"And why shouldn't I learn from the best?"

The expression that passed into Kenrik's eyes before he smiled unnerved her. "It's been too long since I've given a lesson."

Kenrik proved to be an excellent teacher. He offered different perspectives from those of Gavan and Kali, and he made Gavan be quiet. After several sets of drills, he let her attempt a complicated sequence and praised her when she did well.

Gavan gave a loud yawn. "I'm bored. Enough with drills. Mince her already. Mara, prepare to grovel. It's the only way I'll take you back."

"Let's see what you can do," Kenrik said, placing his sword in the opposite hand. "We'll start slow. Practice your drills and sequence. Concentrate on your footwork."

Kenrik allowed Mara to complete the offensive sequence before forcing her into defensive work. She did well until she fell backward over a shrub.

"Watch your footing." Kenrik offered his hand with a slight smile.

During the next match, Kenrik's motions sped, and Mara struggled to keep up. A padded blade swiped her abdomen.

Gavan folded his arms. "For real this time."

Before Mara felt it slip from her grasp, her own sword was pressed against her throat. Kenrik's eyes bore into hers. Gavan chortled. At her tense smile, Kenrik lowered the blade. Patting him on the shoulder, she thanked him for the lesson and slid her hand down across his chest. No stone.

CHAPTER 15

"You need me," Elise said.

Mara scowled. "Absolutely not. I won't put you in danger."

Elise stretched to full height, pressing her tiny fists into her waist. Mara focused on the freckles smattered across her nose. Indignation looked adorable on Elise.

"Elise is right," Gavan said. "You're as winsome as a nettle bush, and we can protect you both. There'll be so many guards; we'll be in each other's way."

Gavan tended to agree with Elise whatever the case.

Mara understood the plea in Elise's eyes. She longed to be useful, to be good for something other than entertaining men. Mara conceded, earning an enthusiastic hug.

"Get some sleep. Tomorrow will be long," Mara said, hoping she'd made the right decision.

They planned to visit all the brothels in one day, beginning with Jed's three. Mara hoped to surprise him so he wouldn't have time to intimidate his slaves into refusing. They would finish with the four remaining brothels belonging to the Ring. Zev knew they were coming and had assured Mara of his full cooperation. She wondered what he had offered the women to convince them to stay.

Dawn broke gray and wet. Mara, Gavan, and Kenrik clambered inside the carriage, mumbling sleepy greetings to Elise and Lazar, who had also insisted upon coming.

"To a man like Jed, I'll be the most intimidating person in the room," Lazar had said, though Mara couldn't imagine Jed being intimidated by anyone.

Horse hooves clop-splashed before and behind the carriage, the rapid tempo no match for Mara's galloping pulse. Elise chattered trivialities without a breath while the rest sat in silence. The carriage skidded to a halt on the wet pavement.

Gavan glanced between Mara and Elise. "Mara, you're with Kenrik and Lazar. Don't leave their sides. Elise, you're with me. Mara." He snapped his fingers. "Do you hear me?"

She nodded, noticing for the first time Lazar's cane, which he didn't need, and the dagger at his belt. Mara suspected he knew how to use both, though she hoped he wouldn't have to.

Whatever Mara had imagined Jed's brothel to be, she wasn't prepared for what it was. The facilities were pristine, perhaps finer than those of the Ring, but the women were pale, and there was something deeply wrong in their eyes. They were empty, lightless—until Mara announced her name and errand, at which point they widened in panic. Murmurs rippled, and the group dissolved. Not one of them accepted redemption.

Devastated, Mara nearly missed the youthful face that passed her. Placing a hand on the girl's shoulder, Mara squinted into her eyes. The girl, aware of what Mara saw, squirmed out of reach, casting terrified looks over her shoulder. Mara couldn't prove it, but the girl was no older than Selene, which was below the legal age for prostitution. Back in the carriage, she shared her suspicions. Shaking his head, Lazar told her nothing could be done without proof or testimony but promised to mention the problem to the Council.

Their reception was no better at the next brothel. Mara never stated her name, which helped to keep order, but fear radiated from every face, some of which looked very young. When Mara asked questions, they scattered.

The street in front of Jed's third establishment boasted a fine black carriage. The nape of Mara's neck prickled at the broad-shouldered man in the driver's seat. A deep scar ran through the center of his milky right eye, which was less terrifying than the look in his left one. Extra men covered each entrance, their weapons visible, but she and her guards were admitted into the building. She asked one of the brothel guards to gather the women in the hall and was instead met by Jed and a group of henchmen.

Many winters had passed since Mara had seen up close any Akaronian besides

Zev, but they were unmistakable. Blue marks decorated brawny arms and necks. Cold, practiced eyes studied the room. Her head spun.

Jed leered over a glass of amber liquid. "Good morning, Little Mouse."

Mara took a slow breath, which shook as she let it go.

"Are you here to accept my offer? I'd still like you for a mistress, and I hear you're available."

His grating laugh worked like smelling salts. Mara passed the redemption papers to the guard who stood between her and Jed's men. "Not today. I've come for the women who'd like to be rid of you."

He relaxed in a chair and glanced over the papers. "My women are happy where they are."

"I doubt that." Her words cracked like a whip. Gavan groaned behind her. "By order of the Council, they will hear what I've come to say."

Jed stared unblinking into Mara's eyes. Then, glancing at Kenrik and Lazar, he gave a curt nod to the man at his right. The women gathered a moment later. One glance told her none of them would come, but that didn't keep her from trying.

Ignoring Jed, she gazed into each frightened face. "In the name of the King, the Council has purchased each of you. Your debts are paid in full. A home waits for you in King's Quarter supplied with everything you need, including protection." She flung a pointed look to Jed. "You're free to leave with us this moment if you wish."

No one moved. Jed swilled his whiskey. One of the women hacked a troubling cough.

Sneering, Jed stood. "What did I tell you, Little Mouse? My women are happy. You might be too if you let me take care of you." Turning to the women frozen in place, he said, "Run along, ladies. We're through here."

They dispersed. An evil grin settled on Mara. "Be sure to tell the Council I appreciate the contribution. The ambassadors are welcome at my establishment any time. I'll see you soon, Little Mouse."

Mara opened her mouth to retort, but Kenrik spoke into her ear. "Let's go. Now."

When the carriage door snapped shut, Lazar said, "Vile excuse for a man." The carriage lurched as if the driver was also impatient to leave Jed behind.

Gavan shuddered. "Why does he call you that?"

"Something that was said the night I met him. You don't want details," Mara said, the weight of defeat settling on her chest.

"What did you do to anger him?" Kenrik asked. "Declan never said."

Elise snickered, and Mara buried her face in her hands. "Jed threatened my sister. I was very drunk. I wanted to hurt him, so I humiliated him in front of his friends."

Kenrik leaned back in his seat. "Did you want him to kill you? Because in one meeting, I know he's the kind of animal you have to put down. Wounding a man like that is suicide."

"Whatever Mara said or did is inconsequential," Lazar said. "It's who she is. Jed seeks out strong women and destroys them. It's a game to him. I've suspected for years he murdered his own wife. Not to mention that nasty business with his sister. If only we could prove something and lock him away in a dungeon to rot."

Strong. Mara didn't feel strong. She felt tired and beaten and ready for the day to be over.

At the next stop, Zev opened the carriage door and reached for her hand, his thick brows drawn together. "What are you doing here?" she asked.

His eyes darted from one guard to another as he set her on the street. "Helping."

Mara followed his gaze. Several of his own men had come, Boz included.

Lazar and her guards begrudged his presence, unable to order him away from his own brothel. He followed Mara and the others inside but kept out of sight when Elise announced the women's redemption. A few accepted. Zev insisted his own men would escort them to the shelter later.

Mara hooked his arm on their way back outside. "What's wrong?"

"Someone plans to take you today and frame me."

"That's ridiculous. With all these guards?"

"You're a fool to trust everyone who wears white." He handed her back into the carriage and shut the door.

At the next stop, she demanded an explanation. A patronizing chuckle rattled his chest. "Mara, you wear white and spy against the Council. Why shouldn't others capture a nameless prostitute for a fine sum of gold?"

Mara tensed at the reminder.

His lips brushed her ear. "Why haven't you slept with your guards?"

Mara shoved him back, drawing Kenrik's eye. Lazar edged closer.

She kept her voice low. "They don't have it. The old woman is crazy."

"Have you tried Lazar?"

"No," she said too quickly.

"Why? He's smitten by you. It would be easy. You wouldn't even have to sleep with him."

Mara was relieved when Elise called her forward to answer questions about the shelter. Zev lost half his women at that location. When Mara returned to his side, he leaned against the wall with his arms crossed, scowling. "You're drawing more than I thought you would."

His eyes narrowed at her gloating smile. "Check Lazar."

The way he said it—the suspicion in his voice—doused her in cold. She avoided him until the day's work was complete.

Outside the last brothel, she faced him. "Are you aware that Jed has hired Akaronians?"

"Yes."

Mara glowered at his condescending tone. "How involved is he in Rivka's plans?"

"Less involved than he thinks."

The rain had stopped, and the puddled streets glowed in the afternoon sun. Mara breathed in the scent of rain-soaked soil and exhaled some of her tension. Glancing about for eavesdroppers, she spoke loud enough for Kenrik and Lazar to hear. "So if I told you he has underage girls working his brothels, what would you suggest?"

Zev jerked her hard to face him. Kenrik snarled in warning and removed Mara from Zev's hold.

"Are you certain?" Zev asked.

"Yes, but I don't have proof," Mara said.

Zev swore. "Then I suggest you alert the Council and that captain friend of yours—Greg or whatever his name is. Tell them to search every boat that comes downriver. And be sure to let them know if they don't arrest him soon, I'll kill him myself."

Zev turned to Kenrik. "Get her home. And never have her out with this many guards again unless you'd stake your life on every one."

"Did he hurt you?" Lazar asked, his eyes bright with fury.

Mara gave him what she hoped was a consoling smile. "I'm sturdier than I look."

"Help me understand," Gavan said. "Zev runs the largest prostitution ring in the kingdom, but he feels particular about the rules. He won't abide underage prostitutes and threatens to murder the man who uses them. And he has no qualms killing you with his bare hands, but flag the cavalry if anyone else looks at you cross-eyed."

Mara inspected the dirt under her nails. "Zev is complicated."

Lazar humphed.

"Complicated." Gavan shrugged. "Insane."

Elise's voice was small. "He was always nice to me."

"But he wasn't. He used you," Gavan said.

Mara patted Elise's hand. Zev probably did seem nice after living with a mother like Elise's.

The carriage door shut. Kenrik tapped the ceiling. "Zev follows a moral code of his own making, one I can't entirely disrespect. But Mara, neither can I understand why you tolerate him."

"Let's talk about something else," Mara said. "How many accepted, Elise?"

"Eleven!"

Mara's shoulders drooped. She'd hoped for twice that many.

"Smile, Mara," Gavan said. "That's eleven free women who were slaves when they woke this morning. Eleven women who don't have to sell their bodies tonight."

Though the perspective helped, Mara couldn't smile. The idea of a quiet meal at Kali's tempted Mara and Elise, but as hungry and exhausted as they were, they agreed they should be at the shelter when the women arrived.

The scent of stew greeted Mara on the street. Her stomach growled, and her feet led her to the kitchen. Wenny eagerly served Mara and the others, hovering as they ate her offering. Her anger at Mara seemed to have evaporated. The stew tasted every bit as good to Mara as the lamb shank Lazar's chef had made.

Between bites, Mara scribbled notes to both Captain Griggs and the Council and handed them to Lazar. "Can you get these where they need to go?"

Lazar scowled at Griggs's name, but he nodded. "Mara, will you oblige me by accepting another invitation to lunch? I'd like you to come in a couple of days when the women are settled."

"Of course," she said. "Thank you for coming today."

"The pleasure was mine, my dear. You are an extraordinary woman. It's always a thrill to see you in action." He kissed her cheek and left.

Mara busied herself, setting out linens and garments. When she next looked up, several women fidgeted in the entry. The evening scurried by. Mara and Elise greeted new residents, showed them to their rooms, and dispersed clothing. The women's wide-eyed aimlessness reminded Mara of her first days at Ramzi's farm, Zev's brothel, and Kali's home. Change was terrifying, even when it was good. And they weren't sure it was good yet—she could see it in their eyes as they looked about. It would be a miracle if she didn't lose them all back to Zev by the end of the week.

Mara longed to comfort them as Kali and Declan had comforted her. Unable to do much else, she offered steaming cups of chamomile tea and assured them that the fear would pass and a new sense of purpose would come.

Exhausted in every possible way, Mara drifted to sleep on the carriage ride home. The scent of damp soil beckoned her consciousness. Insects chirped and chattered, and a cool breeze caressed her face. Someone scooped her off the cushion and passed her out of the carriage into another set of arms. Too weary to open her eyes, she rested her cheek against a firm chest.

"How did it go?" Declan's voice was a soft rumble, vibrating her ear.

Gavan spoke low. "We had a few surprises this morning. Met Jed. What a snake. She was scared spitless, but said what she had to say. Even sassed him to his face."

"Our Mara? I don't believe you."

A snicker. "Eleven accepted. She's disappointed, but she doesn't understand how comfortable Zev makes it for them, even after living with him. But you should've seen her tonight. She was different. Happy. And weirdly good with them. They all came in scared as kittens. She gives them a cup of bad tea—I was dumb enough to taste it—and tells them they're brave and they'll be fine. And they were. Like magic."

Mara felt Declan's smile and a light pressure on top of her head. "That, I believe."

The opportunity to check for Eleora would never be better, but Mara couldn't stir herself. She didn't want to. She wanted to surrender. To the comfort of his smell, the safety of his arms, the warmth of his heart.

Declan set her on the bed with a quiet groan and draped the blanket over her shoulders. Light fingers rested on her temple as he whispered something indiscernible into the dark.

What she wanted in that moment scared her more than Jed did. More than Rivka even. More than the possibility that Declan could be hiding Eleora and she'd have to betray him. Because those futures were all possible. The one she wanted wasn't.

CHAPTER 16

After another delectable lunch, Lazar proposed a walk by the river. Gavan and Kenrik stood to join them, but when Lazar told them about a new stallion he'd acquired, they traipsed away like eager schoolchildren. He turned to Mara. "Shall we?"

There was a tightness in his tone and expression she didn't understand. She hugged his arm, hoping to ease whatever troubled him.

Brine and silt scented the breeze rushing at them from the water. Mara closed her eyes and enjoyed the flutter of her lashes and the summer heat on her cheeks. Whether or not she found Eleora, she wouldn't have many more days like this.

Lazar brought them to a halt. "If you could ask for anything and be certain of getting it, what would you want?"

Mara pondered, watching a bird soar away from shore. Not long ago, she had only wanted one thing—for Selene to enjoy a long, happy life. Now, she could scribe a list that would read like a fairy tale. "To be free. Truly free."

"You would ask for something only the King can give, wouldn't you?" he said.

She rested her head on his arm. "You already give me too much."

With a deep breath, he took her hands in his. "I'd like to give you more than cats and cream sauce, Mara." His mouth twitched once and then set with the rest of his face. "I'd like to give you my protection—take you away from the city, out of Jed's reach."

"Lazar, I—"

"Please allow me to finish."

She pressed her lips together and nodded.

"I have connections in the plains. They'll hide us until it's safe to return. You may send for your sister, if you like. And when it's safe, we can return here, and I will give you my home, estate, name, and utmost devotion until my dying breath, if you'll let me."

He knelt before her, his gaze locked with hers. A trembling hand reached into his pocket. Placing a simple gold band in the palm of her hand, he closed her fingers around it.

"I know I'm too old for you, and the idea of taking me as a husband is unlikely to have entered your mind. And truly, I never intended . . . I approached you as a friend and might have loved you as a daughter, but you've so completely stolen my heart it no longer belongs to me. If you would honor me by being my wife, I would seek your happiness and welfare above my own."

His countenance faltered as she sat on the ground, stunned. "See now, I've shocked you," he said. "Shall I take you back to the house?"

How had she let this happen? How had she missed the signs? Zev had warned her, but she'd dismissed him, because Lazar knew what she was and what she'd done, and he was a good man—good enough to care for a prostitute and too good to fall in love with one. One less than half his age. Not that his age was a problem. His forty-something winters had been kinder to him than twenty and one had been to her. But Lazar was the father she'd been denied. Until now, she hadn't realized how much hope she'd placed in him.

Sickness struck her stomach. Were his affections even his own? Or were they contrived by Rivka's kiss?

He pulled at the grass, waiting for her to say something. What came out of her mouth surprised her. "How could you leave? Your work, your home, the Council. It's all here."

Squinting over the water, he said, "I'd give it up. I'd leave my work and home in the hands of trusted stewards, and I'd resign my position on the Council. It would seem a negligible sacrifice, I assure you."

Did real men speak this way? Skies and sea, she almost agreed. "I don't understand. How could you leave the Council?"

"I'm not irreplaceable. None of us are."

"Untrue," she whispered.

A bouquet of daisies and violets appeared. "I expected immediate refusal." Taking the band, he placed the stems inside. "As long as you aren't on mission to rescue my feelings, I'd like you to take some time to consider."

She nodded, trying to smile.

He kissed her hand and wrapped her fingers around the bouquet. "And know this—regardless of whether you accept or refuse, you will always have my friendship. If you refuse, I may distance myself for a time out of necessity, but I intend to love you however you'll let me."

Distance himself. Leave. Accept or lose him.

On the ride home, she stared out the window, lulled into deep thought by Gavan's snores. She resolved not to tell anyone what Lazar had asked. Twisting the band around the flower stems, she imagined herself as Lazar's wife. It wasn't an impossible scenario, and there may be a kind of happiness to be had in it. And maybe she could save him, if he required saving. His readiness to leave the Council made her wonder.

Could the keeper of Eleora be so careless with his responsibility? Could he give up his life for love?

Her neck prickled. Kenrik frowned at her fingers. No, at the band. When her hand covered the gold, he looked into her eyes with an unreadable expression. Then, leaning back, he pretended to sleep. Pretended, because no sleeper took such shallow, rapid breaths.

There was little time to consider Lazar's proposal. Every morning after combat lessons, she tended Kali's garden, wolfed down a few bites of breakfast, and left for the shelter, often returning home after Sabra and Kali were asleep. Kali spoke her concerns about Mara's hours but allowed Mara to choose how to spend her time.

Kali and Sabra stopped by the shelter every day to help where there was need. Impressed by Mara's zeal, Sabra warmed and offered advice. But in place of disapproval, another kind of tension arose.

When Mara shared her observations with Gavan, he shrugged. "She envies you. But don't worry; she fights it."

"What in my life is the worth the energy of envy?" Mara asked.

Gavan grinned at her. "You're so lovably daft about some things."

"Well?"

Straightening, he cleared his throat and counted fingers. "Well, you have several friends, friends who really love you, which I find highly suspect." He squinted at her. "How have you duped us all into forgiving that spiny exterior?"

Mara blanched.

"Two extraordinarily handsome, charming, and fearsome guards. The ear of the Council. Seems to me, all you have to do is ask for something, and it's done."

Mara opened her mouth to argue. Gavan covered it with his hand. "Hush. I'm not done. Based on my observations, with the single, unfortunate exception of cooking, you can do anything you decide to—a quality even I envy. And I rarely envy anyone anything, being this handsome, charming, and fearsome. Also, I think Declan may be sweet on you. But that I definitely don't envy."

Mara blinked at him several times and then busied herself with the next task.

While the work fulfilled Mara in many ways, something deep inside her ached. A sense of loss gnawed at her as she pulled weeds, rushed through dinner, and tossed in her bed, but she couldn't discern what the lost thing was.

The encounter with Jed renewed her fervor in combat lessons. In the event of capture, she determined to deliver a well-placed blow or two before facing whatever torture Jed had in mind. Kali showed her how to use an opponent's superior strength against him. Gavan demonstrated how the body itself could be a weapon when handled well. Kenrik reminded her to remain vigilant of her surroundings and observant of her opponent. The smallest detail could alter the outcome of a battle.

Long days and sleepless nights wore on her. The rigor affected her friends as well, even indefatigable Gavan, whose gibes came slowly between yawns. Dark circles framed Kenrik's eyes. Mara's sword arm drooped. A resistance slowed her feet, as if she moved through water. She lost match after match.

Gavan stretched and leaned against the house with a groan. "Lazar's right. You should marry the first man who'll take you and forget this whole thing because you are hopeless."

Mara swung the padded sword at his head, catching his triumphant smirk as he whipped out his own blade. He parried the blow and the one that followed and pulled a wooden dagger from his belt. The tip rested underneath her chin. "Next lesson—take inventory of your opponent's weapons before rushing him in blind anger. Use them against him when you can."

"Your problem," Kenrik told her as she glowered into Gavan's face, "is that you let your emotions cloud your judgments."

"Is that necessarily a problem?" Declan asked, surprising them with an early-morning visit. He closed the back door and crossed his arms. "I don't like the idea of a detached Mara."

Kenrik's abashed face competed with the shade of his hair. "I only mean she shouldn't allow her emotions to consume her. You're too easily distracted by Gavan's taunts. You've heard them all by now. Ignore him. Be attentive. Make your environment work for you. Find your opponent's weakness, and exploit it."

"Like Gavan exploits my temper," she said.

The brothers rewarded her with a synchronous "Precisely." Gavan grinned.

Kenrik adjusted Mara's stance. "You had the advantage but made the mistake of warning him of your intention. Anger betrays. Had you controlled it, you might've surprised him and exploited his expectations of how you would respond. We'll try that another day. For now, complete the new sequence without allowing him to distract you."

Glee shining in his eyes, Gavan rubbed his hands together. Now distracted by Declan, whom she'd avoided since her last lunch with Lazar, Mara tuned out Gavan's heckling with ease. She lost hold of her sword a third time.

Declan asked to speak with her alone. The garden cleared. Mara wished to scatter with the rest.

"Where have you been?" The question was so soft, and yet it sliced to the quick of her heart.

"The shelter mostly. There's always a lot to do," she said with a shrug.

"Maybe you should delegate."

Gathering the practice weapons, Mara shook her head. "That's not necessary. I love the work."

Declan took the weapons from her arms and dumped them onto the ground, a challenge in his eyes. "As your healer, I can't help but notice you're exhausted. You've lost weight, and you don't seem as happy as you were. As your friend"—his smile was pained—"I miss you."

Mara's feet twitched in her shoes. "What do you want from me?"

Whatever response Declan had expected, the one he received wasn't it. His features fell.

Damn his pity. "Come on. Tell me. Am I your personal project to show everyone how skilled you are? If you can fix me, you can fix anyone, right? Or am I supposed to be beholden to you? What could you possibly expect from me, Declan? I don't have anything."

He drew his hand down his face, and his body sank. A part of her wanted to reach for him, another to strike him. He choked on her name and prepared to say more. The words had to be staunched. Because he would explain and say something wonderful, and he would win. Again.

"Except one thing," she said.

Too late, his eyes registered the wildness she felt. She lunged, grabbed his face, and accosted him with a kiss. He froze. Recalling what must be done, she dropped a hand to his chest—tugging, groping, searching. A laugh bubbled in her throat when she found nothing but fabric. Relief softened her mouth against his, and he began to return her kiss. Calmly, attempting to slow her. Indecisive hands rested at her waist, half pulling her to him, half holding her back.

Mara was aware of her own absurdity, but rather than resisting, she let it sweep her along. Her hands roamed down his chest to his waist, and as fast as skyfire, he restrained them in one of his. The other pushed her to arm's length.

Eyes blazing, he huffed through gritted teeth, and for the first time, he frightened her. "You aren't a prostitute anymore. You won't act like one with me."

To disguise her alarm, she lifted her jaw and sent him all the spite she could muster.

"I hate that look."

She struggled against his grip. "What look?"

He released her, and his awful grief returned. "The one begging me to hurt you."

He sat down hard upon the ground and buried his face in his hands. Guilt writhed under Mara's skin as she peered down at him. She would never win with this man. Every time she thought she'd seized power, he disarmed her.

So she grappled. "You want me. Tell me I'm wrong."

His weary eyes settled on the row of citrus trees they'd planted together. "You're not, but you see it wrong."

She'd forgotten his candor, and now, by her own fault, the conversation had careened off a cliff, and there was nothing for it but to fall. Their friendship would suffer an irretrievable change. She should leave. Run, for all she was worth.

She plopped down in front of him. "Help me see."

A stern brow measured her. "Yes, I want you. But only if you give yourself freely."

Her answering expression was met with an adamant shake of his head. "Not like that. What I want is you. All of you. I don't want your body if you won't give me your heart."

She should've run.

His anger dissolved. "Everything I want, I aim to give. More, if I can. The question is, will you have me? Because I can only give what you accept, and I won't take a thing from you I haven't returned."

"You do realize you propose marriage to a whore." She hadn't been so brutal with Lazar, but then Declan's sensibilities weren't as delicate.

His thumb sealed her lips. "Never use that word to describe yourself again." After a pause, he said, "Not today. You aren't ready for marriage. To give freely, you have to be free. And you aren't yet, are you?"

Declan understood her like no one else, unlike anyone had a right to. "Lazar asked me to marry him."

His shoulders stiffened. "Did he? Did you answer him?"

"I told him I'd think about it."

Reproach clouded his countenance. He threw a handful of grass. "I hope you aren't trifling with my friend. If Lazar proposed marriage to you, it wasn't done flippantly."

Mara stared at a speck on her skirt. "I love him. Not like he loves me, but enough to matter. He's given me so much. All I wanted was to give him something in return, and now I can."

After a long silence, Declan whispered her name.

She shook her head, and tears fell loose, splattering her white gown.

"Mara, look at me."

Her eyes lifted to his, lashes blinking away moisture.

"Lazar didn't help free you to see you sell yourself again. He wants you as his wife, not his slave."

"Then why give what I can't repay?" she asked.

"Love. He loves you. You can't earn what's already yours, and you shouldn't try." He gave her chin a gentle tug and leaned back, mussing his hair. "Well, I hadn't planned for any of this."

If he only knew how often he upended her plans.

"As much as I love Laz, I can't . . ." He frowned at her, working his jaw. "Here's what I propose: Consider choosing me because I love you, and there's no undoing it. And don't kiss me again unless you decide on me. And speak with Kali about all this. I know you aren't used to being nurtured by an older woman, but that's why she's here. And please agree to spend the day with me because I miss you, and I have big news to share, and you need my help today."

His words tumbled out like hers often did. A sly grin answered her arched brow. Yes, he mocked her, and she wouldn't reward him with a smile. Flopping back onto the grass, she growled in exasperation at the sky. "All right."

Amusement colored his tone. "You don't have to agree. I'll give you the choice."

"A choice between what? Conceding to another thorough defeat and digging in my hooves like the stubborn ass that I am?"

His laugh echoed off the garden wall. "Maybe one day you'll stop picking fights with me."

"Maybe I'll challenge you to a duel and be done with you instead."

Chuckling, he stood and pulled her to her feet. "What makes you think you'll fare better with a sword? Though, I must say, you took to your lesson this morning."

"What lesson?"

He plucked a blade of grass from her hair. "Exploiting your opponent's weaknesses."

"Ha! As if you have weaknesses."

A hand caressed her cheek. The warmth in his brown eyes caught her breath. Closing them, he took hold of her head and planted a reverent kiss at the center of her brow.

"Don't I?"

CHAPTER 17

Over breakfast, Declan told them of the warrant issued for Jed's arrest. Under cover of night, one of Jed's captains had anchored a cargo ship just past the river gates, where the crew lowered a boat and rowed several illegal slaves to shore. Tipped by Zev, Griggs had apprehended them there.

Word reached Jed before the kingsmen arrived. He eluded capture and disappeared with several of his men. All his assets were either absorbed by the crown or relinquished to the Ring per previous arrangements made between Zev and Jed himself. With limited resources and all outgoing vessels under careful watch, his arrest was imminent.

"So Zev benefitted from Jed's arrest," Mara said. But how had Zev managed to convince Jed to sign over his holdings? Jed hated him.

"Yes." Without further comment, Declan explained that the illegal slaves were either on their way home or newly arrived at the shelter, and nearly half of Jed's legal slaves had accepted redemption as opposed to working for Zev.

"We have to leave. Now." Mara said, standing.

Gavan cut wry eyes to her. "Maybe you should've told her after breakfast."

"We aren't leaving until your plate is empty," Declan said. "Besides, you'll have my help, remember?"

At the shelter, Mara assisted Declan with a clinic. Each woman from Jed's brothels required a thorough check. Many were wounded or sick. All were malnourished and traumatized. More than practical help, Declan needed Mara's female presence. As unthreatening as he was, Declan was a man, and these women had experienced worse things than Mara at the hands of Jed and men like him. They recognized Mara as the one who had come for them and responded to her.

Watching Declan work reminded Mara of her early days at the Ring, of how his kindness had held her up when she was sinking. She returned his frequent smiles in spite of herself. Her friendliness with him seemed to put the women more at ease.

At the end of the clinic, Mara's eyes glazed at the stack of orders she'd copied. Each woman had an individual prescription for nourishment, rest, exercise, teas, and tinctures, and Mara had no idea how to keep it all straight. Declan suggested she give the orders to Wenny.

"Are you sure?" Mara asked.

"Wenny is one of the sharpest people I know. She'll sort it out," he said without teasing.

That evening, near dinnertime, Declan caught Mara's arm as she bustled by him and told her it was time to leave. He was hungry. Elise, Carina, and Wenny could manage without her. The work would wait until morning. As the retort formed on her lips, mischief glinted in his eyes. "You agreed to spend the day with me, remember? I'm leaving. And Gavan threatens to toss you over his shoulder and carry you out if you give me trouble."

Down the corridor, Gavan waved, wearing an impish grin.

With a dramatic roll of her eyes, she smiled and took Declan's outstretched hand.

Kali tapped the wooden spoon against the pot of simmering vegetables and herbs and propped it against the lip. Mara's stomach growled. Judging from the smell, dinner was almost ready. Declan and the others sat outside on the stoop. Their voices drifted through the open windows with the breeze. Turning to the doorway where Mara stood, Kali startled and swore under her breath. Mara apologized with a grin. "Do you have a moment?"

"Always, for you." Kali invited Mara to help her make a salad with the lettuce, radishes, and tomatoes Mara had grown.

Over the chop of knives biting into wood, Mara told her what Lazar and Declan had offered. Kali's dimple pronounced itself. "I can hear them now," Kali said. "Lazar, eloquent. Declan, direct." She dipped a finger into a blend of oil and citrus, tasted, and wiped it on her apron. "It seems to me you have several good options before you."

Mara scowled at a perfect tomato. "But if I choose one, I lose the other."

"That's the nature of choice. Every yes brings with it an infinity of nos. But you don't have to choose either one. You can continue here as you are or return to your sister when the season changes. Those options are good as well."

Mara tried to imagine life without Declan and Lazar.

"However you choose to answer, don't tarry long. It isn't fair to them."

With a nod, Mara tossed the bleeding tomato over the lettuce and picked up a radish, which smelled of earth and spice.

"Slice it thin." Kali pilfered the thick slice Mara cut. When the crunching ceased, Kali said, "Be certain to answer the questions underneath the proposals. Lazar's estate could have no better mistress, but can you be his lover? Marriage is more than that, but it shouldn't be less. And can you give Declan your heart when you withhold it from the King he loves? Either man would make an excellent husband, but are you ready to be a wife?"

Mara and Kali turned at the scrape of a heel against stone. Sabra stood at the kitchen entry, pink cheeked, her eyes hot as brands. She grimaced as if she tasted something bitter. "I came to see if you needed my help. Looks like you have things well in hand." Her white skirt swung behind her, and she was gone.

The next morning during drills, over the clack of wood meeting wood, Mara asked Kenrik to order a carriage. His stance faltered when she told him she needed to speak with Lazar but not long enough for her to gain the advantage. He nodded and continued the lesson, saying nothing.

Lazar wasn't home when they arrived. A servant led them into the library, where Gavan blinked in boredom. Kenrik watched her pace and fidget. After refreshments, which she couldn't eat, she suggested the men go to the stables. Gavan narrowed his eyes and said, "I'm beginning to think 'go to the stables' is code for 'go away,'" but he followed Kenrik out the door.

Voices drifted down the corridor. Mara felt too anxious to read but thought she might enjoy a conversation with the servants. She followed their murmurs but stopped herself from turning into the foyer when she heard one of them say, "He and Declan will arrive any moment with the stone. Be sure to tell him Mara is in the library. He will want to stow it in the vault before he greets her."

Mara's heart dropped to her feet. Afraid to be caught lurking, she crept back to the library, rebuking her tears as she went. Lazar was the keeper of Eleora, as she and Zev had suspected.

Her mind raced. The stone would be within reach in a moment's time. Declan and Lazar weren't likely to hand it over, no matter how much they loved her, and even with Gavan and Kenrik distracted in the stables, she wasn't skilled enough to take it by force. What could she do?

Horses approached, scattering gravel in their wake. The shouts of their riders brought forth fresh tears. Mara battled for composure but hadn't quite won when the doorknob turned. Lazar spoke to someone in the corridor and walked inside, closing the door behind him.

With an assessing gaze and a smile that failed to disguise his disappointment, he said, "You've come to decline."

Taking a deep breath, Mara ordered her feet to approach him. His features blurred as she placed the gold band in his hand. "You, Lazar, are a miracle. You're a good man, something I didn't think existed last winter. I can't thank you enough for proving me wrong."

Lazar fumbled in his pockets, searching for a handkerchief. Finding none, he took her in his arms, stroked her hair, and told her she didn't have to say anything more.

Soothed by the scent of peppermint, she almost changed her mind. "I don't know much about love, but I do know I can't marry you because I'm afraid to lose you. And I can't marry you for what you can offer me. You deserve to be loved for yourself. And I do love you—more than you know—but not as a husband. I wish that weren't true." Kissing his hand, she whispered an apology and left him.

Gavan and Kenrik were still at the stables. To her horror, Declan stood with them. When he saw her face, he told his friends he'd see them later and walked toward the house. As he passed, a handkerchief pressed into her palm. Frowning,

Gavan opened his mouth but closed it again when Kenrik shook his head.

Nervous throat clearings and sniffles punctuated the monotonous rattle of the carriage. Gavan pouted like a child left out of a secret but said nothing. Kenrik napped—or pretended to. Grateful for the silence, Mara pushed aside her heartache to think. Now that she'd saved Lazar from an unsatisfactory marriage, she had to save him from Zev, who wouldn't hesitate to hurt Lazar to seize the stone.

She didn't have long. Summer was half-gone, and harvest would arrive in a blink. Mara saw only one viable course. She'd have to steal Eleora herself.

A lamp shone in Mara's eyes. She blinked into Kali's face, which was taut with concern. "Get dressed," Kali whispered.

Mara rose from bed and dressed in the dark, careful not to disturb Sabra. When she entered the dim living room, Gavan and Kenrik were dressed and waiting. "What's going on?" she asked.

Kenrik groaned, stretching his shoulders. "We aren't certain. All we know is an injured prisoner at the wall demands to speak with you. Only you. He claims it's urgent. He needs a surgery he may not survive, so Declan sent word."

It was a quiet drive to the city wall. Gavan and Kenrik dozed. Sleep wasn't possible for Mara. Her imagination sifted every dreadful possibility of who would want to see her and why.

The carriage parked next to the stables. The wall, taller than Mara had pictured, shone pale under a silver moon. The smells of hay and horse sweat tickled her nose, reminding her of Firth and of Selene. Mara breathed a prayer for her sister's safety, hoping the prisoner would have no connection with her.

White-clad guards blended with the stone wall. Mara didn't see most until they muttered in greeting. She startled at one, earning a gibe from Gavan. Not far from the stables, stone garrisons stood in shadow. Kenrik opened the door of the first and led her down a corridor to the hospital.

Declan met them outside the surgical chamber wearing an uncharacteristic frown. "We have a prisoner who claims to have a message for you. He won't name his source, and he won't speak to anyone else. The only thing we know about him is that he's an Akaronian from the camp north of Firth. You can talk to him or go home and return to bed. The choice is yours."

There was no real choice. "I'll see him."

"Would you prefer to speak with him alone?" Declan asked.

His inflection laid bare every suspicion. He knew her secrets lay with the Akaronian, but he wouldn't intrude unless she wanted him to. He was too good to her. Better to frighten him now and save him the heartache later. "No. You should be there. It's time for you to know the person you think you love."

Declan opened the door. A stout figure gasped for breath on a cot by the fire. Declan ordered the guards to wait outside and squeezed Mara's hand.

"How was he injured?" she asked.

"He arrived in this condition and won't say anything other than he must speak with you."

Slow, cautious steps brought her to the cot. Flames reflected off glassy eyes, which studied the scar on her cheek and the interlinked rings above her wrists. She followed the elaborate ink designs traveling down his arms. "I'm Mara of Firth. What is your message?"

Wheezing, the Akaronian reached inside his tunic. "First, a present." He ripped at the fabric and extracted a pocket. Mara remembered the box that had held Ramzi's ear.

Trembling fingers turned the pocket upside down. Something small and hard fell into her palm, and light glinted off a gold chain. The necklace fell to the floor as she lunged for the Akaronian's throat. "Where's my sister, you bastard? Where is she?"

Declan pulled her away, restraining her arms, and spoke into her ear. "The man can't breathe well as it is. You won't learn a thing from him if you kill him."

The raider chortled and choked. Declan held her until she relaxed against him. Retrieving the lodestone necklace from the floor, he placed it in her hand.

"Where's my sister?" she said again.

"Put my ring in the basin, wench." He twisted it off and held it out.

The gold band and gray stone looked familiar, though she couldn't place where she'd seen it before. Foreboding tightened her stomach as she dropped the ring into the blood-stained water of the basin. Nothing happened at first, but after a moment, the water swirled and bubbled. Mara stepped back as it transformed into vapor and took shape.

Rivka, tinged red with lurid green eyes, slinked over the lip of the bowl and stood before Mara, pulchritudinous even in this inferior form. Rivka cocked her head, mouth puckered. Leaning into Mara's neck, she inhaled slowly. Mara tensed. Rivka circled, hips undulating, pausing once to leer at Declan. Mara couldn't bring herself to face him. He'd know everything now.

Seductive alto tones sounded behind her. "Your time has nearly passed, child, and you've nothing to show for it."

"Where's my sister?" Mara didn't have patience for games tonight.

A cruel smirk curved her exquisite mouth. "Zev claims you're quite the woman—intelligent, observant, motivated. If I didn't know better, I'd say he's smitten. Perhaps you can explain something to which infatuation has blinded him."

Fear and fury warred inside Mara. Then she remembered the visage in front of her wasn't the real Rivka. This wisp of vapor couldn't bite. "My sister."

"I smell my magic on you. Your failure perplexes me. It may be that you've again forgotten what you promised. Or you believe I've forgotten what I promised."

"I won't answer a word until you tell me where Selene is."

"How gallant you are," Rivka said. "But you were always a fool for the brat. She's safe, for now. The Council and I have mutual acquaintances at the consulate. Tell me why I shouldn't order her killed tonight."

"You can't," Mara said.

"Have you located the stone?"

"No." Mara held her breath. Would Rivka hear the lie?

Mara forced herself to look at Declan then, but his gaze was trained on Rivka. A hand massaged his clenched jaw.

"Tsk, tsk, Mara. I save your wretched lives, and you fail in this one, simple task," Rivka said.

"Selene is innocent. Punish me. I'm the one who failed."

"I consider myself a reasonable spirit, not like those capricious fire spirits of the West. I'll give you ten days."

"I have until harvest," Mara said.

Rivka pretended not to hear. "Ten days to find the stone. Ten days until your sister meets your uncle's fate and I raze your precious farm to the ground."

"What have you done to Ramzi?" Mara said.

"My little gift of him didn't have the impact I'd hoped. And hacking away at a man piece by piece seems a tragic waste."

Rivka's figure dissolved. The blood-red mist reshaped into a moving portrait of a one-eared Ramzi kneeling by the edge of the Priel, Rivka looming above him. His face warped in fear and pain. When Mara reached out, her hand cut through the mist forming his head. She yanked it back, and the mist converged once more. Rivka seized him by the shoulders and opened her mouth, revealing the teeth Mara had glimpsed long ago. Like a leech, Rivka attached to Ramzi's brow. His screams for mercy died on the air. She released his body, which slapped against the wet silt like a dead fish. Empty sockets stared at Mara where his eyes had been.

"Ten days until I come for you," Rivka said, her voice fading into a whisper.

The mist returned to the basin. Choking sounds erupted from behind, waking Mara from her stupor. Declan went to the aid of the Akaronian. Quick, practiced hands reached for the necessary tools. A small knife drove into the raider's chest. A puff of air followed, and he breathed.

Declan took two lozenges from a tin and tucked them under the raider's tongue. Through the din of her thoughts, she heard him say, "This changes nothing between us, not for me. But we do need to talk. Would you like to stay while I work, or should I stop by Kali's when I'm through here?"

Mara stared at the subdued Akaronian, hating him. If released, he might return to Firth. He or someone like him would hurt Selene and burn her home and fields and barns. "I . . . I need fresh air." She made for the door.

"Send in Kenrik before you leave," he called after her.

She burst from the surgical chamber. "Let's go." She glanced at the guard on her right, but the guard wasn't Gavan or Kenrik. "Who are you?"

The guard bowed his head, fighting a smile. "Sorry, miss. A fire broke out in the stables. Your guards ran to save your carriage and the horses. My friend and I will stay with you until they're back."

Mara scowled at the guard on her left. Both were young, not much older than she. Their pleasant expressions melted her frown. An idea formed in her mind. "I need a horse."

"Of course, miss. This way."

The walk out of the garrison took longer than Mara thought it should. She needed to get away before Gavan or Kenrik saw her. Rivka had given her ten days. Ten days to steal into Lazar's mansion, take the stone, and get to Firth before anything happened to Selene. "Are you sure this is the way out?" she asked.

"Yes, miss. Here we are." He opened a door with a charming smile. Night air rushed into her face. Mara looked into the dark and made out a light-colored horse hitched to a cart. She turned, smiling, to thank the guard, but his smile had disappeared. He nodded to his friend, who stood behind her.

Alarm sang through Mara's senses too late. Powerful arms closed on her. She thrashed against the man's grip, clawing and kicking. It didn't give. The other guard yanked a small tin from his tunic. Mara screamed, and gloved fingers thrust several lozenges under her tongue. Before she could spit them out, the guard clamped his hand over her nose and mouth. The one who held her squeezed tighter. She struggled for air.

Mara set her mind not to swallow, but the lozenges dissolved on her tongue. Thought turned to liquid, and Rivka was forgotten. Resistance flowed out of her like blood from a wound. The lodestone necklace slipped from her fingers and clattered onto the floor.

CHAPTER 18

No headache born from her wild romance with whiskey competed with the one pounding her skull when she woke. A groan seared her raw throat. Blinking, Mara glanced around. Her bed was a bare plank floor. Sun slipped between boarded windows, providing not enough light and too much heat. With a heavy roll to the side, she crawled to the door. Locked. She meant to check the windows but collapsed, pulled under by a desperate need for sleep.

The door nudged her awake. A burly hand pulled her head off the floor and put a cup to her lips. "Drink."

Parched, she obeyed and almost uttered thanks before she realized she was in the arms of an Akaronian. Recoiling, she fell back onto the floor.

"Eat." A tray of food and a pitcher of water plopped onto a rickety board next to her. The door slammed shut. Metal scraped wood, and footsteps pounded away.

The water returned Mara to her senses. She understood who had her and what would soon transpire. Food repulsed her. Her only comfort was her own stench. Sour with sweat and dried urine, she hoped to repulse him.

The raider returned and yanked her to her feet. Too dizzy to resist, she followed him out of the room into a large space, which had been a grand hall at one time. Ornate wallpaper, fixtures, and covered furniture hinted former opulence, confirming her fears. Mara was thrust into a kitchen where a bath and female attendant waited. The woman, like the hall, had been beautiful once, but bitter lines furrowed her skin. She reached for the buttons at the back of Mara's gown.

When Mara dodged, the woman nodded toward the Akaronian. "If you refuse to cooperate with me, your friend there will take my place. Do you understand?"

Mara submitted. The woman dismissed the raider and helped Mara out of the gown. She washed Mara's hair and left her to soak. Mara distracted herself by contemplating Rivka's threat. Not that it mattered now. Her only hope was that Declan would save Selene.

The woman returned with a towel. When Mara was dry, the woman presented her with a thin gown of red silk, cut low with slender ruffles for sleeves.

"I'm not wearing that."

"Then you'll be naked."

Mara put on the gown.

The woman combed Mara's hair, running perfumed fingers through it when she was done. Rouge, kohl, and stain were pulled from a purse and set out on the dining table. Shivers ravaged Mara's body. She was being prettified for degradation and murder.

She grabbed the woman's hand. "Help me. Help me escape. This man will kill me."

Stooping, the woman smoothed rouge into Mara's cheeks. "I've been instructed to tell you there is no escape. There is only compliance and pain. Do what you're told, and you'll be spared pain. Don't misjudge me because I'm a woman. I'm as capable of inflicting pain as any man here."

As the woman packed away her tools, Mara caught sight of her forearms. Each featured a black mark, different from hers. "You're a slave."

The woman gave her a hard look. "I was, and I'll never forget it." She left Mara alone.

Hunching over the table, Mara cradled her head in her arms and thought hard. The window was too small to crawl through. Two men guarded the single exit. Even if she managed to escape them, there would be more, and she had no idea how to get out of the house. Her fingertips brushed something light, which rolled away across the tabletop. She caught it. The woman had left behind a thin application brush. A small gift from one woman to another. Mara snapped the brush in two and hid a piece in each clenched fist.

Her raider escort reappeared, accompanied by another. "Let's go."

She obeyed, if only to keep their hands off of her a moment longer. One led her out of the kitchen; the other followed. Her feet begged to run, but she watched for an opportune moment. Any attempt to escape now would be wasted.

Mara counted guards as she paraded barefoot and all but naked through the house. Probing eyes met hers, but no one approached. Hesitating at the staircase, she observed the raider who guarded the foot. Only one knife was visible. It slept sheathed at his waist.

The raider behind her pushed, touching the bare skin of her back. Shrinking from the contact, she trudged upward on quaking legs. Whenever she slowed, the raider prodded her on. His partner waited at the top. Yellow light spilled onto the floor at the end of the corridor. A giddy hum buzzed inside the chamber, sending a shudder down Mara's spine.

The guard behind leaned forward. "Run, and I'll hurt you."

Her eyes narrowed at the threat.

Lush red carpet swallowed her toes. The humming ceased. A massive bed stood at the center of the luxurious tomb. Dressed in a black silk robe, Jed greeted Mara with a hateful smile. "Good evening, Little Mouse. I told you I'd see you soon." He opened a bottle of wine and poured two glasses. "You seem anxious."

Mara accepted the offered glass, careful not to drop the broken brush handle. She sipped. Its sweetness made her retch. The hard smile fell from Jed's face. "Such refined drinking etiquette. The woman I patronized chugged wine like a horse."

Lethargy lapped the edges of her mind. She shut her eyes and fought for focus. "Tastes change."

"Mine don't."

The raider who had led her into the room opened a polished armoire and withdrew rope, a rod, and other alarming items. Jed leaned into her chest and inhaled, reminding Mara of Rivka. "So how will we do this?" he said. "Will you do as I ask, or will my men have to hold you down?"

Her mouth went dry. "Send them away. I won't give you trouble."

"They wouldn't appreciate that. I told them they could watch," he said.

Jed moved toward the bed. The raider nudged her from behind. Mara pivoted hard, sloshing the wine into his face, and jammed the broken brush pieces into his throat. The raider clutched his neck, sputtering. Mara gaped, aghast at what she'd done. Jed bellowed to the other raider. Grabbing the handle of the dying

Akaronian's knife, she yanked and ran. Footsteps pounded behind.

Flying down the stairs, Mara used her momentum to launch herself at the raider at the bottom. He saw her coming and braced to catch her. The knife sank into his shoulder. She elbowed his face and kept running.

A door with a lock flagged Mara's attention. She sprinted, begging it to be an exit. The door shut behind her, casting her into the pitch of night. She'd found the cellar. Her heart skittered to a halt. Out of options, she stumbled down the stairs, hoping to find an escape or a weapon with which to fight her way out.

At the bottom, she gagged. Foul odors mingled with the stale air. A sneeze followed a whimper. Someone was with her in the darkness. "Hello?"

The door opened above, and a shaft of light reflected off wide eyes an arm's length above the floor. Mara squinted, uncertain of what she was seeing. Boots thundered down the stairs, and Mara scurried into shadow.

"I know you're in here," a voice growled in a thick accent. "Come out and play—what does he call you—Little Mouse?"

Shaking from her core, Mara groped for a suitable weapon. Gasps and small cries masked her clumsy noise. Her fingers closed around something cold and heavy. Gripping it with both hands, she waited for the raider and tried to quiet the noise of her ragged breaths. When he was within reach, she swung it at his head, connected, and bolted up the stairs. The blow threw him off balance, but not to the floor. He pursued, snatching at her ankles. The raider she'd daggered at the foot of the stairs loomed in the doorway at the top. A stain spread over the right half of his tunic, and a stream of blood poured from his nose. The knife was gone. She ran at him, claws bared to sink into the wound. Blocking her blow with one hand, he caught her hair in the other and snarled into her face.

The other raider yelled something from below, but his injured comrade either didn't hear him or pretended not to. He flung her into the doorframe twice, smashing her head against the sturdy wood. Stunned, Mara fell backward into air and slammed into the raider below. They tumbled down the stairs in a tangled heap. She landed under him, and her head hit the floor with a snap.

Noise rushed like ocean waves, cresting in sobs and gasps. She surfaced for a moment, sighting a small, frightened face above her, before an irresistible tow pulled her under.

~~~~~~

A sharp odor wrenched away the peace of oblivion. A vial was capped and placed out of sight. Jed stood over her, rod in hand, his face red and dangerous. "There now. I forgot how feisty you are. You've killed one of my men and injured another. Ha!"

The rod smacked against her skin, sounding off the wall. The impact shifted her body, but she felt nothing. Jed frowned and hit her again, harder this time. She didn't flinch. "What's wrong with her?"

He hit her again and again, filling her ears with the destruction of her own flesh and bone. She tried to move, but her body refused to obey. Glaring, Jed removed his robe and climbed on top of her. She knew what he was doing, but apart from the involuntary seesaw of her head, she felt nothing. She couldn't spit or scratch, scream or kick; helpless tears pooled in her eyes. In the moment of her greatest need, death forsook her.

Jed swore, and the movement stopped. Heavy breathing screeched in her ears. The stench of him diseased her skin, her hair. Jed stood and sneered down. "What did you do to her?"   Voices growled at one another until Jed's rose. "She's no good to me like this. Bring me a girl. You can have her if you want her. But don't kill her, or we'll all be dead."

If there was a King, if he was good, he would let her die—and soon.

"Jed!" A banging noise. "Jed! I know you're in there." Two loud bangs. Wood splintered. A crash.

Zev stood in the doorway, violence raging in his eyes. They lit on her for the span of a breath. His voice dropped deathly quiet. "What happened?"

Jed sounded strange. Afraid. "I didn't do it. It was him. She wouldn't drink the—"

Jed's body dropped to the floor. He clawed his throat with panicked eyes. Blood gushed, darkening the red carpet. Zev turned to the raiders. Again, in the same tone of voice, he asked, "What happened?"

Voices rumbled. Another body fell to the floor, gurgling. Mara envied his swift death.

Zev bent over her, pulling down her gown. "I'm here, Mara. Talk to me."

But there weren't words for this, and when she tried to beg for his blade, her
~~~~~~

tongue wouldn't form the plea. Her eyes drooped.

"No. Stay with me. Help will be here soon."

Crashes sounded in the distance. Yelling. The clash of metal. Zev disappeared and shouted, "Declan!"

And then he was there—soil and rain and sun. His hands brushed her face, her head, her neck. Past him, Gavan supported himself on the doorframe, white faced and wild eyed. Kenrik dropped at her feet, panting.

"Is she?" Lazar's voice.

"She's alive, but Laz . . ." Declan's voice was wrong. Too thick.

Lazar stepped into the room and staggered. A hand covered his mouth. It was just as well, she wanted to say. Her death would bury his secret.

"How bad is it?" Zev sounded uncertain. Zev was never uncertain. No one sounded like themselves.

Declan leaned away. "Mara, blink twice if you can feel this. Zev, watch her for me."

"Nothing."

"What about this?" His voice was a pillow inviting her to sleep. With each question, fear faded.

As she slipped over the lip of a hungry ravine, she remembered she had something important to say before she could never speak again.

"Her neck is broken," Declan said.

Zev swore and paced away, tugging at his hair. In the doorway, Gavan slumped to the floor with a moan. Kenrik encouraged his brother to help downstairs, but Gavan didn't move. Lazar walked the room, avoiding corpses, mumbling to no one in particular.

Focusing what was left of her strength, Mara willed her lips to move. "Cellar."

Declan knelt, lowering his ear to her mouth. "I'm listening, love. Can you say it again?"

If it killed her, he would hear. "Children. Cellar."

Declan drew back, delivering sharp commands.

"Can you help her?" Zev asked.

"I'll do everything within my power."

Zev's icy eyes writhed, considering her, and then he left, punching the wall on his way out. Lazar frowned after him and resumed his low utterances. Kenrik touched her feet. It was strange to watch what she couldn't feel.

A frown gathered around Kenrik's eyes. "Are you absolutely certain?"

Mara puzzled at the question until Declan answered. "The most certain I've ever been. Will you guard the door?"

Declan knelt beside her. Unshed tears shimmered in his eyes. He drew a gleaming object out of his tunic. Gold and red glittered in the low light. "This isn't the way I wanted to tell you." He pulled Eleora from his neck and laid it on her chest. An offering.

"We have much to discuss when you're well. But for now, close those lovely eyes and rest." His lips touched her brow, releasing her into deep sleep.

CHAPTER 19

Two comforts anchored Mara when she woke—she was in her bed at Kali's, and Declan slept nearby. She listened to his exhalations a long while before opening her eyes. A morning slant of light fell through the window onto a vase filled with pink and yellow roses from Lazar's gardens. Scents of porridge and spice wafted into the room. Declan slept on a cot edged next to the bed. His hand relaxed over hers. Next to his pillow, Eleora sparkled in the sunlight.

Mara wiggled her toes and fingers and flexed the muscles in her legs. Rolling onto her side, she took Eleora in hand and shifted it in the light. Ruby beams burst onto the ceiling. The stone was exquisite, larger and purer than any she remembered from her father's collection. It felt warm in her hand. Alive. The gold chain glittered like a jewel. Her father would have salivated at such a treasure. For her, it held a wary attraction.

As she set it down, her eyes met Declan's inscrutable gaze. How had she so thoroughly entangled herself with this stranger? Familiar fingers caressed the side of her head. No, not a stranger, but not a friend. The prey to her snare. She was the enemy, and he'd rescued her.

With a groan, he pushed himself up. Gentle hands pressed her head, neck, shoulder, ribcage, hip, and knee. "Is anything tender?"

She shook her head.

His fingers tapped her palm, wrist, and elbow. "It's been three days."

Seven days left. "Why did you save me? You knew what I was."

He helped her sit. "I knew what you were before I invited you into my life. And I assure you—you were far beyond my ability to save. I don't know how you were alive when I arrived." A firm tap against her knee made her kick.

"You knew Rivka sent me to find you?" she asked.

His checks complete, he sat beside her. "I knew you were entrapped in a scheme beyond your power to escape. The only surprise was how much danger you're in."

"You mean how much danger you're in."

Unflappable as always, he smiled. At her, the enemy. "How did it happen?" he asked.

She focused on a dark spot on the wall and recounted the memory she'd wanted all her life to forget. "The night the Akaronians attacked, when it was over, Zev found us hiding in the brush by a stream. He would've killed us, but Rivka stopped him. She came out of the water and told him we could all help one another. Somehow she knew what we all wanted. Zev wanted revenge on his father. I had to keep Selene alive. Which I couldn't do. It was late autumn before my tenth winter. We were in the mountains with no shelter, no weapons, no food, and no one to take care of us.

"But it wasn't only that we were helpless. I was angry. Angry at the King for leaving me alone in the world. He was supposed to be good. Rivka offered Zev his revenge and me mine. Along with Selene's survival. All Zev had to do was swear fealty and keep us alive. I had to swear to help Zev find Eleora and let her kiss me.

"Her kiss was a violence. It had teeth. I still feel them sometimes." She rubbed her brow. "It wasn't so different from what Jed—"

She swallowed and took a ragged breath. "Zev says it wasn't a kiss. More like a spell or something. To draw the attention of people in power. To trap you. So you can't trust your feelings for me. They aren't real."

"May I hold you?" he asked.

Incredulous, her face jerked to his. What she saw made her want his arms around her, even if it was a lie. She leaned toward him. Gathering her into himself, he tucked her head beneath his chin and rocked her like the ten-wintered child she still was. "Listen to me. Evil seduces. It can't conjure love. I won't credit a rebel spirit with the King's magic, and neither should you. I love you. Kali, Lazar, Gavan, and Kenrik love you. That's the King's work. And while you may struggle to believe it, you are precious to him.

"Eleora drew me to you, not some evil spell. Of all the healers in the city, Zev asked for me. My responsibilities prevent me from accepting every case, but I had to come for you. I can't fully explain what I mean, but not coming would've been inconceivable. Eleora saved you that day and again two days ago. Some are saved once. The King saved you twice."

"He's a fool then," she said. "I'm allied with his worst enemy."

He nuzzled the top of her head. "The King possesses a marvelous knack for turning enemies into loyalists."

"You sound so sure."

"The King didn't only save you from death, Mara. He saved you for something," he said. "You need to speak with Zev as soon as possible. Gavan and Kenrik will take you when you're ready."

She lifted her head to meet his gaze. "I won't betray you."

Tenderness radiated from his eyes.

"She wants Eleora. Will you give it to her?"

"Of course not," he said. "But Rivka gave you ten days to find Eleora. Those were her words. You found it, and you're free to give Zev its location."

"She'll kill you to get it." Rivka hadn't said so, but it felt true.

"I will deal with Rivka," he said.

"I won't do it."

"You will."

Declan was the only person she knew who smirked without a trace of superiority. Tears flooded her eyes. "You think I'd hand you over after all you've done for me?" she asked.

He pulled a letter from a pocket and placed it in her hand. "I simply make a prediction based on what I know of you. Besides, you'll only say my name, and I give you permission to do that."

The letter was addressed to the Council in Selene's script. Mara slid out of his lap.

"I fell in love with you when I read that. I think we all did." He stood, stretching, and yawned. "Can I get you anything?"

Mara stared at the letter, sensing what it was. "A bath. I want the sandsoap."

The door opened and closed.

To the King's Council of Ambassadors:

I, Selene of Firth, your fellow kingsman, request the redemption of my sister, Mara of Firth, property of Zev of the Ring in Rahm-Or, Kingdom of Laeor.

I know it's customary for the slave to write her own letter or have it scribed, but I ask you to make an exception for my sister. After all, Mara is exceptional. Even if she hears of King's Redemption, she'll never write a letter—not because she enjoys slavery but because she won't consider herself a candidate. Her reasons are more complex and personal than I can explain in a public letter, but I'll do my best to present her case.

Mara sold herself to pay for the medicine that saved my life. Only after it was done did she learn she would become a prostitute, though part of me worries she may have done it anyway. Our mother died giving birth to me during her fifth winter, and our father was rarely home, so my care was left to her. She sacrificed her childhood for mine. Later, our father was killed in an Akaronian raid. That night, she shielded me from a raider's blade with her own body and swore a terrible thing to keep me alive.

She stayed the same throughout my childhood. When we were cold, she clothed me—and froze. When we were hungry, she fed me her rations—and starved. When I was sick, she nursed me. When Uncle yelled, she defended me. When things fell apart, she held them together. Until I was dying and she couldn't save me.

I was furious when I discovered what she'd done. It wasn't until she was gone that I realized—she's looked after me her entire life, but no one has looked after her. Everyone who should have taken care of her either died or abandoned her.

Knowing this, I can't feel angry anymore. Instead I feel loved, deeply sad, and hopeful that you'll look after my sister and offer her redemption. If she rejects it at first, be patient. She isn't used to receiving help. Please contact me at the consulate in Firth if you have further questions or require my assistance.

With gratitude, Selene

Mara crumpled the parchment in her fist. How much did Selene know? They'd never spoken of Rivka, but the letter caused Mara to wonder what exactly Selene had witnessed the night of the raid.

Selene made her out to be a victim, and maybe she was, but that made Mara no less a monster. She hurt everyone she knew. Phi and Ramzi had died from the curse she'd brought upon them, and all because life without Selene wasn't worth living. There had never been anyone she wouldn't sacrifice to keep Selene alive.

Agitation set her in motion. As she paced, whiffs of Jed's cologne brought to mind the terrible rock of her head, the noise of his breath, the inability to scream. She barreled out of the room. Eyes followed her until she passed into the kitchen, where she began tearing off her gown. She paused. Someone had exchanged the red silk for King's white.

"The water's not quite warm enough," Kali said.

A hysterical voice, nothing like her own, said, "I want him off me."

Kali helped her out of her clothes and into the tub. Mara didn't mind the cool water. She found it bracing. Grabbing the sandsoap, she attempted to scrub Jed from her life, one layer at a time, all the way back to the night she met him. Even in death, he held power over her, power she'd surrendered when she'd sold herself a slave. Worse than being taken against her will was having offered herself to that despot. Behind the memory was Rivka's kiss, how she'd consented to her cold, cruel touch. Mara squeezed her eyes shut to shield herself from an ugly truth.

She'd been whoring all her life.

Kali knelt beside the tub and pried the soap from her hand. Humming an old lullaby, she rubbed it over the places Mara couldn't reach and put it away. Tears gathered in Kali's watery eyes, cascading down her cheeks as she sang. Sabra tiptoed into the room. Without a word, she poured warm water over Mara's head and washed her hair.

Washed and scrubbed raw, Mara still didn't feel clean. She imprisoned the sobs thrashing her chest. She would not cry. She didn't deserve to.

Kneeling behind the tub, Kali wrapped Mara in her arms, planting kisses on her shoulders and neck, murmuring love into her skin. Finally, Mara's control succumbed to Kali's compassion, and Mara wept herself hollow.

Empty, Mara tried to eat. After a few tasteless bites of porridge and a cup of tea, she joined the men in the sitting room. "I'd like to go to the shelter," she said.

Kenrik frowned up from the sofa. Gavan wasn't in sight. Declan stood, reaching for her. "Are you sure?"

"Unless you have a bottle of whiskey."

Declan held out Selene's lodestone necklace. "I found this."

The way his voice hitched squeezed her heart. What had the last three days done to him? She turned, sweeping her damp hair over a shoulder.

He cleared his throat. "Do you understand what I meant about my prediction?"

"Yes. But I haven't decided what I'll do." She hoped Declan didn't hear the lie. Kenrik did. He scratched his beard, his gaze searching hers.

Declan's fingers fumbled at her neck. "Promise me that whatever you decide, you'll include us."

Mara nodded, relieved he couldn't see her face.

The necklace in place, he angled her to him. "And don't worry for Selene. We've sent trusted kingsmen to Firth. They'll keep her safe."

His eyes darted between her and the door. She counted the days. The Council would meet soon. He needed to go and wanted to stay. She embraced him, resting her cheek on his shoulder. "Thank you. Please thank Lazar for the roses."

"I will." He sighed the weight of the universe. It was the sound of desperation, desire to take the pain away and powerlessness to do so. Mara knew it well.

"Please forgive me, but I have to ask," he said. "You know Zev better than anyone, I imagine, and from what you said, he's in as much trouble as you. Do you think he can be saved?"

Declan was too good, and it would lead to his demise. She lifted her face to his. He must be made to understand. "Zev doesn't want to be saved. He doesn't even know he needs to be. If I tell him you have Eleora, you must count him your enemy."

With a nod, Declan swept his thumb across her cheek and left. Kenrik and Mara followed him out, stumbling upon Gavan, who lounged on the stoop. Mara nudged him with a foot. "Fancy a walk?"

A cumbersome silence fell. Gavan stared straight ahead as they went, misery hanging on him like a chain. Mara glanced at each brother. "It's not your fault," she said.

Their eyes flashed to her from either side.

"It's not. If it's anyone's fault, it's mine. I sold myself into prostitution. I angered Jed. I followed those guards out of the garrison." Irony lifted a corner of her mouth. "I let my emotions consume me. I forgot my environment."

"You're not funny," Gavan said.

"Maybe not, but I won't have you act like a scolded dog," she said.

Kenrik blocked her way, scowling down at her. Flinching, she prepared for the renewed threat. "What happened is not your fault," Kenrik said. He stepped out of her way and continued on. "We were too comfortable with the warrant for Jed's arrest. And something about it bothers me. It was well planned. Neat. Not at all like Jed's previous attempts to capture you."

She didn't want to think about Jed, but her curiosity prevailed. "How much time passed before you realized I was missing?"

"Long enough," Kenrik said. "We helped the driver with the carriage and corralled some of the horses. When we returned, we checked with Declan—the Akaronian was dead by then—and realized you were gone. A quick search turned up the necklace and the lozenges they used to drug you."

Mara stiffened.

"We don't have to talk about it anymore," Kenrik said.

She pretended not to hear him. "Have you caught the guards who took me?"

"No," he and Gavan said together.

"They were young," she said. "Close to my age. Blond hair, both of them. Handsome, with pleasant smiles. One my height, the other a little taller than me."

Gavan cursed under his breath. "We know them."

"Zev warned me some kingsmen were for sale," she said.

Kenrik's mouth turned down.

"How did you find me?"

"Declan asked Zev for help," Kenrik said, his disapproval apparent.

"Is Zev in trouble for killing Jed?" she asked.

Gavan shot her a quizzical look. "Zev didn't kill him. It was one of those Akaronians. He confessed."

"No, I saw him do it. He killed Jed and the one I stabbed," she said. "Or so I thought."

Gavan's brows shot up. "Dagger to the shoulder? Nice. Get anyone else?"

"I stabbed one in the throat with a broken makeup brush. I think I killed him."

Pride seeped into Gavan's face and lifted his chest.

Unwilling to ruin his improved mood, she chose not to tell him that fighting and running had almost been the end of her. "It's unusual for Akaronians to kill each other. They're very clannish. Why did he do it?"

Gavan and Kenrik exchanged a glance. Gavan said, "Jed killed the one you stabbed for hurting you, and his brother avenged him."

"That isn't what happened. Jed was killed first."

"You were really hurt," Gavan said. "I don't know how you were alive, much less conscious. You had a broken neck, a nasty head injury, and several broken bones besides. Is it possible you remember it wrong?"

"Absolutely," she said. "But it makes no sense for Jed to kill for me."

"It does," Kenrik said. "Think about the kind of man Jed was, what he wanted from you."

He had a point. Jed had wanted to be the one to hurt her. In his time, in his way. He wouldn't have done it so quickly. He would've leeched all her pride and self-possession until she begged for death and then made her wait longer still.

When they reached the shelter, Kenrik excused himself with a promise to return later. Gavan shrugged and opened the door, releasing the smell of home cooking into the street. Elise spotted Mara from the other end of the makeshift corridor. Mara didn't miss how Gavan's face lit when Elise launched into her arms. "Mara! We heard you were—"

Mara cut her off. "I'm fine. How can I help?"

Elise's eyes danced in thought. "There's really nothing to do. Wenny delegates tasks to everyone and chases us all with a spoon until they're done," she said with a giggle.

A brief inspection displayed neat rooms, women working happily, and a wholesome atmosphere. Mara's vision was realized. The shelter thrived even in her absence. She was unneeded and so soon.

Elise brightened. "Would you like to see the children?"

Mara stared, uncomprehending.

"The little ones you rescued? They're in the garden."

Eight little girls played under the watch of Carina and another woman. When Mara stepped outside, they froze like startled fawns. They were so young. Too young. The smallest approached. Like Mara, she was brown skinned with black hair. In those wide, dark-brown eyes, Mara glimpsed her own pain. Maybe Mara wasn't as rare as she thought. She knelt and smiled into the child's face. The girl reached toward her and caught the tears spilling from her eyes. Pulling the girl into her arms, Mara peeked behind her at the rest.

They gathered around her, pressing in, kissing and touching, until Mara toppled to the ground, laughing through her tears. They all lay down beside her, pointing out figures in the clouds. Mara took in their sweet scent, the earth beneath, the blue sky above.

Wildflowers and clover grew thick in the grass. Mara made crowns and necklaces for each one as her mother had done for her, and the girls agreed—blooms made better ornaments than jewels. One by one, Mara crowned them princesses, daughters of the King, beautiful and beloved. The little one asked why Mara hadn't made herself a crown and crafted one for her.

Before long, the girls itched and wiggled. Mara rose to play ball. She lost herself in their heady laughter and smiling faces. How did children so easily forget their pain and let the joy out? She sought their secret as she frolicked with them in the grass.

A picnic lunch was served. The women joined them in the sunshine. Mara peered into each face. Jaded eyes sparkled with a faint light. A season had not yet passed, and healing was taking place. The children, so full of life, were medicine to them all.

"You need to hire a tutor for the girls," Mara told Elise. "A mild-tempered man would be good. Ask Declan who he recommends."

"I will," Elise said.

"And the food-preservation classes. You should find someone to teach those as soon as possible. The tomatoes are nearly ready."

Elise's smile faltered. "Won't you teach them?"

"I don't think I'll have time," Mara said.

Gavan, who sat on the other side of Elise, cocked a brow at Mara until one of Elise's hearty giggles distracted him.

Mara let others pack up the picnic and enjoyed the children until late afternoon. Kenrik fetched her, his expression softer than she'd ever seen it. When the girls shied from him, she knelt, gathering them in her arms. "Girls, this is my friend

Kenrik. He's one of the men who rescued you. Kenrik is a good, kind man. He protects people like us. His brother, Gavan, is a good man too." Mara pointed to Gavan, who hovered in the doorway wiping red-rimmed eyes.

"It's time for their dinner," Kenrik said.

The little one reached for Mara. With a smile, Mara scooped her up and carried her to the door where Gavan leaned, sniffling. His swollen nose was as red as his hair. Mara pressed her cheek against the girl's. "Look at her, Gavan."

He obeyed, attempting a smile.

"When you see this precious face and think where she might be, doesn't it make you almost"—she choked—"glad it happened?"

Gavan burst into tears as the girl reached for him. Blubbering, he carried her down the corridor to the kitchen, with the others trailing behind.

Kenrik peered down at Mara. "Thank you for helping my brother. I wish we could help you."

"You help me by being good men," she said.

Kenrik offered his arm. "The guards who took you have disappeared. It may take some time, but we'll find them."

She let him lead her down the corridor. "I'm not worried about them," she said, her mind elsewhere.

Seizing the arm he supported, he stopped. "Don't do it, Mara. Don't make me your enemy." It was a plea, and in it, he laid his whole self bare.

Kenrik was an honorable man. Threats were as good as oaths to him. Nothing had changed except that she'd become his friend. He didn't want to end the life he'd fought to protect and wouldn't until she gave him reason. But the moment she betrayed Declan, her life was forfeit. Declan's permission counted for nothing.

Mara understood his loyalty and loved him for it. Declan was his Selene. "She'll kill my sister."

"We'll protect you both," Kenrik said.

"You'd try."

He winced. Ghosts from the past three days haunted his eyes.

Gavan approached, his eyes bouncing between them. "Everything all right?"

Kenrik's brow lifted as he strengthened his grip. But he wouldn't win this one.

With a sad smile, Mara patted Kenrik's shoulder. "Everything will be."

Mara waved good-bye to the children and wrapped an arm around Elise. "You are one of the sweetest, smartest women I know, and I couldn't have chosen a better partner to see this through." She kissed Elise's temple and leaned into her ear. "Encourage Gavan a little, will you? He's smitten."

"Really?" Elise mouthed, color rising to her freckled cheeks.

Mara winked and followed the brothers to the door.

In the encroaching dusk, Mara curled in on herself like lemon clover. The shelter was in good hands. Jed couldn't harm anyone anymore. She'd lived in the Quarter almost two seasons per the redemption agreement. Her time in Rahm-Or was done. All that was left was to fulfill her oath and save Selene.

She glanced at Kenrik, who brooded by her side.

Then the end would come.

CHAPTER 20

Soft snores pulsed the nighttime quiet. Mara peered at Sabra's still form. In sleep, her harsh lines relaxed into a lovely softness. Mara held her breath as she stood, willing the floorboards not to creak. A breeze drifted through the open window, stirring the bedside tablecloth that hid Mara's satchel. But first, she needed the stool.

Mara froze when the wooden legs scraped against the floor. Every sinew in Mara's body drew taut, but Sabra slept on. Relaxing, Mara carried the stool to the window. Hanging over the ledge, she eased it onto the grass and turned to retrieve the satchel.

Sabra perched on the edge of the bed with narrowed eyes. "What do you think you're doing?"

Mara clapped both hands over her chest and swore. "Leaving. Please don't make me bind and gag you."

A soft laugh blew through Sabra's nose. "Where are you going?"

There was no reason to lie. "To see Zev, and then on to Firth."

"Tell me why I shouldn't scream for Gavan and Kenrik this instant."

Mara reached for the satchel. "I don't belong here."

"That may have been true when you first came, but not now. You've earned your place."

It was a kind word, coming from Sabra. "My sister needs me."

"Fine. Leave in the morning," Sabra said.

"I can't. They won't let me go. Jed wasn't my only enemy. I'm still in trouble, and as long as I'm here, none of you are safe." A long pause made Mara uneasy.

Sabra stared at her hands. "Did anyone tell you Jed was my uncle?"

Mara could find nothing to say.

"He and my mother were the only children my grandparents had. As you can imagine, Jed wasn't a very good son. My mother received the larger inheritance when they died, so Jed poisoned her wine. But not enough to kill her at once. Little by little, he watched her waste. We all thought she was sick."

"That sounds like Jed," Mara said.

"I remember the way he watched me. So brazen, right in front of my mother. She was too frail to do anything about it. He touched me sometimes. I think he meant to kill me—or worse." She shuddered. "Declan was the healer who came. He found out what Jed was doing and rescued me. He brought me here and helped me disappear. It was too late for my mother."

"I'm sorry," Mara said. She and Sabra shared more in common than she could've imagined.

"It's over now, isn't it?" Sabra wiped her eyes. "I just knew you were going to lead him back to me. But you rid me of him. I suppose I owe you a boost over the wall."

Mara exhaled slow and heavy. "Thank you."

Outside, Mara memorized the garden. The square she and Declan had tilled and planted. The space she'd learned to handle a sword. The patch of ground where Gavan had kicked her awake. The nook where Kenrik had brought gifts and offered advice. The scene blurred. Mara blinked, squeezing away moisture. "They can't come after me. Not this time," she said.

Sabra nibbled her lip. "There's a stable around the corner. Borrow a horse. I'll fetch it for you later. In the morning, I'll tell them you want to be left alone and that you'll come out when you're ready, but I doubt I can give you more than a few hours. Declan can be pushy, especially concerning you."

"Tell them I threatened you or something. So they won't be angry."

"They'll know I'm lying," Sabra said. "Why do you think Declan brought you here and not to a shelter with a larger guard?"

Mara shrugged. "Fewer people for me to annoy and offend?"

"Ha! No. Kali's the most celebrated sword master alive. She trained most of the Council, including Kenrik, Gavan, and Declan. She also trained me. During sleeping hours, you're my charge. They all know I can best you."

"So what will you tell them?" Mara asked.

"The truth. I'll tell them you wanted to leave because you're a danger to us and I helped because Declan is too good to be within reach of a—" She paused. "Well, you know."

Mara hoped the darkness hid the effect of Sabra's words. Not that Sabra was wrong. Maybe she could help Declan see reason.

Sabra snapped her fingers and disappeared through the window. Before Mara could worry, Sabra returned with a hooded cloak in hand. "Wear this. You may be stopped if you're recognized."

The cloak was cut from dark velvet, soft and fine. Sabra tied it on and pulled the hood over Mara's head. "Be safe. I hope you survive whatever trouble you're in."

"Thank you," Mara said. "And thank Kali for me. Tell her I'm sorry for not saying good-bye and that I'll love her forever."

With a terse nod, Sabra made a stirrup of her hands and hoisted Mara up. The climb was precarious in the gown, but Mara managed without falling or ripping the fabric. She swung her legs to the other side and dropped. Whispering an apology Declan would never hear, she glided through the shadows to the stable around the corner.

The door guard at the Ring's headquarters gawked when she arrived. She wondered what he'd heard. Stepping aside, he held open the door. "Zev's in his office meeting with someone. Wait in the small hall. I'll tell him you're here."

"That won't be necessary," she said. "I'll wait in the corridor until he's finished."

To her surprise, he let her pass, staring as she went. Noise strayed from the large hall down the empty corridor. Cigar smoke spiced the air, and the clink of glass watered her mouth. She rounded the corner. A sliver of light splayed across the carpet outside the office. Voices murmured within. Mara crept to the edge of the doorway and peeked inside. Zev sat at his desk, out of her line of sight, and before him sat the dark-skinned man she'd met the day she'd sold herself to Lced.

He held a generous glass of whiskey.

The dark man belched. "The final shipment arrived last night. Ran it in myself. They're ready to move. Tired of drifting, they tell me."

"The only thing that can defeat us is impatience. A few more days, and I'll give orders. Tell them that," Zev said.

"Can't blame 'em for being nervous. That much magic fire could take out the whole fleet."

"Only if they're fools."

"I never hire fools," the man said with a tight-lipped smile and swilled down half his drink. "What are we waiting on exactly?"

"Something important. If nothing happens within a fortnight, I'll move to the next plan," Zev said.

"Don't trust me with specifics?"

"The ring of trust must stay as small as possible. You understand."

"All right, then." The man stood. "Got a girl for me?"

"If you're willing to part with your hard-earned gold."

He shook Zev's hand. Mara fled around the corner on her toes, her mind whirling. Dropping the hood of her cloak, she loosened her braid. The man plowed into her before she finished smoothing her hair and grunted an apology.

"Oh, good. I haven't missed you," she said, trying to remember how she used to smile. Her arm hooked his.

He gave her an odd look but consented to be led to the small hall. "I've seen you before," he said when she lit the lamps.

"Yes. I work for the Ring." Mara chewed her lip, her mind scrambling for a way to stall him. "Have you eaten?"

"Yes. But I wouldn't mind another drink." His voice deepened. "Or a woman to share it with."

A plan took shape. With trembling hands, she removed the key to the liquor cabinet from the hideaway behind the mantel and poured him a large glass. "I'm happy to offer you a drink, but I must speak with Zev about a woman."

He grasped her wrist when she offered the glass. "You'll do fine."

Mara knew enough of men not to struggle. If he used force, she'd learn nothing. Her mouth remembered how to simper. She leaned in. "Zev expects me, but I'll return. I promise."

He let her go, his eyes glinting over the top of his glass.

Covering her hair, Mara closed the door and stole to Zev's office. His head whipped in her direction the moment she stepped into the doorway, a terrible scowl on his face. She lowered the hood. His expression went slack. As soon as the door closed, arms wound around her. Tension seeped from his body.

"Tell me you have it with you," he said.

"I couldn't take it without their notice. I'm sorry."

"Never mind that. Who has it? Lazar or Declan?" he whispered into the soft skin below her ear.

Her heartbeat sped at the heat of his breath. Would she ever be free of this man? "Are you happy that I'm alive or that I have the information you need?"

"Both."

"I leave for Firth before dawn," she said. "I'd like you to take me."

Zev became more interested in her mouth than what it had to say. He'd never kissed her this way before—tenderly, without the heat of desire.

"I'll tell you which one has Eleora when I've seen Selene," she said, careful not to promise anything further.

He drew back, bristling. "Are you fool enough to think you can negotiate with Rivka?"

"Not at all. I'm negotiating with you."

His face turned dangerous. "What if I decide to kill them both and take the stone instead?"

Mara dismissed his response as an empty threat. If brute force could secure the stone, Rivka never would have needed her help. Mara began her prepared speech. "I need to see Selene alive and well before I give Rivka anything, and I need your protection. When Kenrik finds out I'm gone, he'll come after me. To kill me. You're the only one who might delay him long enough for me to save Selene."

"Why would your guard kill you?" he asked.

"Because he'll know I've betrayed the King and the Council."

He considered her a moment and chuckled low. "This isn't about him. You're trying to protect one of your new friends. You have to choose, Mara. Selene or them."

"Rivka killed Ramzi, threatened Selene, and shortened the time she allotted me. I don't trust her. She isn't above killing my friends along with Selene for the sport of it. Someone is going to survive this. I've accepted it won't be me."

The light leeched from his eyes. If he lost control tonight, Boz wouldn't be around to save her. She touched his face. "Come with me. I need you."

Mara held her breath. Scratching the back of his neck, he frowned at the water basin. "I need a few minutes to think. Wait somewhere out of sight. My chamber, if you like. Take a nap."

"Thank you."

"I haven't promised anything yet," he said.

She pecked his cheek and slipped under his arm and out the door.

The dark man looked up when she returned. "I was beginning to think you'd forgotten me."

"How could I?" She flashed him a coy smile. "Zev was telling me what a valued associate you are." She sat next to him on the settee, casting a longing glance at the bottle of whiskey. But she couldn't afford to drink tonight.

He grunted. "Fooled me. He doesn't tell me much."

"You know what he told me?" she said, placing a hand on his leg. "That you could tell me all about magic fire and how it works."

Setting down his glass, he pulled her against him. "Kiss me, and I'll show you."

She straddled his lap. "A secret for a kiss. The better the secret, the better the kiss."

The hunger in his eyes sank her. This one wouldn't be content with kissing alone, but she'd known that the moment she'd whisked him into the hall. She ran her fingers through his hair, assessing. He required a delicate tread, or it would be over too soon, and she wouldn't get what she needed. Closing her eyes, she told herself what she was about to do was for Declan.

Mara curled up on Zev's bed, relieved he hadn't arrived before her. It had taken all her concentration and skill to control the situation with the man in the hall. She'd managed, but what she'd learned and how she'd learned it sickened her. She'd committed a violence against herself. But there was no time to wallow.

A bowl of porridge clopped onto the bedside table. "Get up. Eat. We leave as soon as I'm packed and the horses are saddled."

She eyed the porridge. Whiskey would be preferable. She sat up, feigning a stretch. "You're taking me?"

"I'm taking you," he said, filling a satchel with clothing.

Her eyes narrowed. "Why?"

"What do you mean 'why'?"

"Don't insult me. Why did you change your mind?"

He slinked toward the bed, wearing a sly smile. "Be at ease. My intentions are entirely dishonorable."

Mara fended him off with the bowl. "Tell me."

He continued packing. "You can't walk into the Akaronian camp alone. You'd be raped and murdered before you ever made it to Rivka. And I hear your friend Kenrik's pretty good with a blade."

"You aren't telling me everything."

Zev threw a wad of black clothing at her. "Wear this. You're too conspicuous in white."

Chewing another bite, she untied the blue cloak. Zev leaned against a bedpost and watched her undress. "Between taking you and torturing you until you talk, taking you sounds more fun. Especially if you want to wager on how long you'll be able to resist me." His brow quirked at her scowl. "I'll be back for you when we're ready."

"We?"

The door clicked shut.

Mara was glad to shed the color she would betray, and Zev's clothes concealed her figure enough to cast doubt upon her gender from a distance, which might prove convenient. Digging through a drawer, she found a wrap to cover her hair and face. Her reflection resembled a young bandit.

Mara scanned Zev's desk. Spotting parchment and a quill, she scrawled a greeting to the Council with an unsteady hand. The quill was snatched away. She whirled and met Zev's penetrating gaze. "Not wise, Mara. Your little good-bye will cost us our lead. Write when you reach Firth."

He examined her costume. "As long as no one looks too closely, you'll pass for a boy. Still, they'll know who you left with when they check the logs at the gate."

As much as she hated it, Declan discovering she'd left with Zev was part of her plan. This betrayal, more personal than the one he'd encouraged, would wound him. He would know what it meant, and yet it must be done. Declan required every available reason not to follow her out of the city.

But he also required the information for which she'd betrayed herself, and now she had no way of getting it to him.

She picked up the blue cloak, lost in thought. Zev pulled it from her hands and laid it on the bed. "It might give you away," he said.

With a final glance at her white gown and cloak, she followed him to the stables.

Outside, Mara sensed the approach of dawn and forgot her sleepiness. Three men stirred in the stables. Boz surprised her. Who would stay behind to guard the women? Mara didn't know the other two. Curious eyes flicked to her as they mounted their horses but didn't light on her again. Boz's stare, however, scorched her flesh wherever it touched. Zev hadn't told them who she was, and in the dim of the stable, Boz didn't recognize her. She kept silent, testing the quality of her disguise.

Zev pointed to her horse, a lovely brown mare, which nickered when she approached. Patting the mare's nose, Mara tried to remember the last time she'd ridden. Too long. The next few days would be brutal.

Perched high upon the saddle, Mara pushed down the feeling of being small and feeble and clicked her tongue. Zev led the horses at a canter through the empty streets. The white city was lovely at night, particularly the bridge spanning the Priel, which shone like alabaster in the moonlight. A wave of loss rushed over her as she crossed. She'd yearned for Selene and the farm since the day she'd left Firth. But without permission, her heart had grown to include a new family and home, thus dooming itself never to be whole again.

Night faded as the small company approached the wall. Mara stiffened at the sight of the charred section of stable. But Jed was dead. Something worse was loose in the kingdom, something she'd empowered through seasons of amenability. Defiance came too late to do any real good, but she could give Declan the gift of time and preparation, if an opportunity presented.

The guards at the gate ordered the party to dismount and submit to a search of their belongings. Zev acquiesced, signaling the others to do the same. While he answered questions about their destination and purpose, Mara's eyes swept the grounds.

Guards stood at their posts, some alert, some yawning. All questionable.

After the other night, Mara didn't trust one of them. No one else was up and about except for a bored-looking stable boy, who tossed a stick for his golden-haired dog. Mara approached, whistling. The dog ran to her, wagging his tail, and nuzzled her outstretched palms.

Mara peered at the boy. "Is he yours?"

The boy gave her an odd look and a hesitant nod.

Mara cooed and babbled and laughed when the dog licked her between the eyes. "What a handsome fellow. But I prefer my suitors to be a little taller."

Scratching the dog's ears, Mara invited the boy to approach with a tilt of her chin. He ambled over on awkward, chicken-thin legs, his young face alight with interest.

She lowered her voice. "Would you like a job? It's important."

He squatted. "What do you have in mind?"

"I need you to deliver a message to someone. By mouth, if you're sharp enough."

"I can do it," the boy said.

Mara studied him. Pale fuzz lined his jaw. His eyes were clear and steady. "Aren't you going to ask about payment?"

His eyes widened, and Mara relaxed. She reached into her clothes and placed a silver coin in his hand. "Close your mouth, and stop looking at me like that. Smile and pretend I'm entertaining you with a tale."

His artless expression might have amused Mara in less dire circumstances, but she'd chosen well. Even if he gave her away, he was honest. "Go to King's Quarter. Find the home of Kali and Sabra, and ask to speak with Declan, the healer. Tell him I'm sorry, but I've gone to Firth with Zev. War is coming. Soon, the Akaronians will march on the city with a water spirit in command. The mist at sea hides a fleet of Razan mercenary ships. Zev commands them. I don't know their purpose, but they're armed with enough magic fire to destroy Rahm-Or. The fire burns everything, even water. It's the fire causing the mist off-shore. Only sand will put it out."

The boy drew back, horror in his eyes.

"Smile," Mara reminded him. "What time is your watch over?"

He grimaced. "Soon, miss."

She stared at him. Innocent eyes blinked back. Her voice must have given her away. Glancing over her shoulder, she met Zev's gaze. The guards were almost finished with the search.

"Rest for a while. Make your way to the Quarter sometime after noon. Don't repeat the message to anyone but Declan. Do you understand?"

The boy frowned. "Who should I say it's from?"

"He'll know."

"Why a healer, miss? Why not one of the senior guards? What will a healer know about war and magic fire?"

Clever boy. "Why don't you ask him?" she said.

After he repeated the message twice, she stood. Zev strode in their direction. She intercepted him before he came any closer to the boy. "I'm sorry. I couldn't resist such a beautiful dog."

"I'll buy you one before I leave Firth. Now, come on," he said.

On the walk back to the horses, Boz again trapped her in his uneasy gaze. With a brisk nod to him, she mounted and chased Zev through the gate. A league down the road, she glimpsed the shrinking wall behind her. Swallowing hard, she faced forward and lowered her head.

The eastern horizon stole her breath. The sun rose from slumber beyond the breadth of the Priel, its pink and golden tresses filling the sky. Mara longed to throw off the head wrap and feel it shine upon her face, but this close to the city, disguise was still important.

Declan, Gavan, and Kenrik would wake soon and in a few hours find her gone. Those hours would linger long for Sabra and the stable boy. By the end of the day, Kenrik would become foe. She didn't know about the rest. Maybe Gavan would help him track her down and end her. She cringed at the thought and focused on keeping pace.

CHAPTER 21

Zev rode the horses hard and traded them at an outpost of the Ring a few leagues down the road. Mara was sad to part with her mare but didn't begrudge her the rest. After a quick transfer of belongings from one horse to another, they were off again. Jarred by the ride, Mara gritted her teeth, wondering how long Zev intended to press them. When she felt like she would fall from the saddle, he stopped at another outpost.

He nodded toward the building. "There's a cot in the loft. Take a nap. The last thing we need is for you to fall off your horse and break your neck again. Of course, it wouldn't matter if you'd packed the gem."

Too weary to roll her eyes, Mara went inside, climbed into the loft, and was asleep before she settled.

Mara woke with a jolt. Boz loomed over her, scowling, the wrap in hand. "What are you doing here?" he asked.

Annoyed, she snatched the wrap. "Why do you care?"

"I care because I'm your friend." He seemed ready to say more, but Zev strode into the building, calling her name. When he spotted Boz in the loft, his face went slack.

"She's awake," Boz called down.

Zev folded his arms. "Couldn't get by you, could she?"

"I know my girls. Even when they try to fool me," he said, his countenance heavy.

Mara rewrapped her head, avoiding further eye contact, and tried to put him and all else out of mind. It wasn't hard—lost in the monotony of thundering hooves, jangling metal, and a constant flurry of dust—until nightfall, when Zev took mercy on her and stopped at an inn.

The doorframe of the inn featured a pair of interlinked rings, imperceptible to anyone not looking for them. Mara frowned. If the Ring owned inns, what else did they own and influence in the kingdom?

Mara opted to take her meal in her room instead of the noisy hall. She trudged upstairs, pulling the dusty wrap from her head. The mirror above the basin reflected grimy, lost-looking eyes. After washing, she sprawled upon the bed and waited for dinner to be delivered.

In the stillness, guilt twisted cruel tentacles around her heart. By now, Declan knew she was gone, that she'd lied and cut him out of her plans. Gavan and Kali were blaming themselves, and Kenrik would be plotting her death. She hoped no one had been too harsh with Sabra and the boy had delivered her message.

A kick pounded the door. She dragged out of bed. As tired as she was, she wouldn't sleep without food. A ravenous beast growled in her belly, louder than the rusty creak of the door. Zev stood before her, his hands occupied with two bowls of stew, a bottle of whiskey tucked under his arm.

Sighing, she stepped out of his way. He smirked at the sight of her. "You're out of shape. How will you cope with a plow?"

The bowls and bottle thunked onto the table. She ate without looking at him but felt every glance he fired over his bowl. When she emptied hers, he left and returned with another. "Why are you so thin? Hasn't Declan been feeding you?"

She daggered him with a glare.

He pulled two shooters from a pocket and filled each with whiskey. When she shook her head, he pushed one across the table, his mouth fixed in a wry curve. "Go on. You look like you could use a drink."

Mara stared at the amber liquid. A woody scent wafted to her nose. Her mouth watered. "You won't be able to wake me up," she said.

"I'll cut you off when you've had enough."

The battle was brief. She tossed it back, eyes closed, moaning at the sweet heat. Her insides relaxed.

"You act like you haven't had a drink since you left me."

"I haven't." She pushed the glass toward him.

He refilled it. "Maybe that's what's wrong with you." He drank his down. "Or maybe it's because you're in love. With Declan." His eyes narrowed when she drank at his name. "You're afraid I'll kill him when you tell me he has Eleora."

With a flat stare, she plopped her empty glass in front of him.

"Or is it Lazar you're worried about? Tell me, has he proposed yet?"

The muscles in her face reacted against her will.

At the scent of blood, Zev's grin turned devilish. "Well done. He's prosperous, respected, well connected. A little too righteous for my taste, but good looking for an old man, I suppose. Not to mention he holds the finest property in Rahm-Or."

Zev was being Zev, attempting to wheedle out information before she was ready to give it, aiming for her weaknesses, which he knew well. She needed to stop drinking. "I won't discuss this with you, and I won't confirm anything until we reach Firth."

He refilled their glasses. "How did he take it when you turned him down?"

She emptied her shooter. "I don't know."

Leaning back, he studied her. "I was right. You're in love with Declan." The bottle gurgled as he swigged. "No one has to tell me how he feels about you. I suspected way back when he delivered those damned redemption papers, but the last few days removed all doubt. Did you know he came to me for help?"

She tapped a finger on the table.

He handed her the bottle. "Take it easy," he said.

She wiped her mouth with her wrist. "Doesn't matter. I don't deserve him. Either of them."

A mocking smile. "So you'll settle for me."

"That's not why I asked you to take me. You're bad for me, and not only because you tried to kill me." She took another drink. "But I don't hate you. I've tried, and I can't. Not even a little."

Warmth flooded through her, loosening her tongue. "Sometimes, you're almost good. I've seen you with Nuri. I remember how you took care of Selene and me. You helped save those illegals. You do good things, Zev. It's your reasons that trip you."

He pried the bottle from her fingers. "You've had enough."

After another swig, he capped it. Mara's head swam as he lifted her from the chair. His hand reached for the end of her braid and untied her hair, combing it loose with his fingers. Her mind warned her to make him stop, but her body disagreed. An arm wrapped around her waist. Fingers sank into her hips. Her mind had better sense. She shook her head, dodging his kiss.

Undeterred, his lips brushed her jaw and traveled the length of her neck, hesitating only at her tears. If women ever cried when he touched them, it wasn't from sadness. Until now, Zev had never seen her cry at all. "Let me help you forget him," he said.

When she opened her mouth to order him out, his lips, damp and salty, pressed to hers. A hand reached under her shirt. His fingertips ran up and down her spine, circling at the small of her back.

What did it matter? She wasn't promised to anyone, and she'd ruined what she had with the man she loved. In truth, part of her had known it would come to this. When had she ever had the power to resist Zev? And now she was drunk and lonely, and even after a day of hard riding, he smelled good. The whiskey burrowed holes in her soul, which leaked pain like a roof in need of daub. Zev offered to patch her up. In this strange place, he was something she knew. What was more, they were the same—damned by the attentions of Rivka. They belonged together.

Her mouth answered his, giving into the oblivion she craved. But something was different. There had been a time when her skin had basked in the comfort of his. Tonight, he felt wrong pressed against her, and for the first time since their first night together, she yearned for someone else. Zev felt it—she could tell—as she felt how much he'd missed her. Some secrets couldn't be kept. Not between them. Not like this.

When it was over, he searched her eyes and rolled over with a frustrated sigh. Turning away, she covered her mouth, but the bed shook with every buck of her chest. Zev dressed without a word. The door screamed on its hinges, and she was left to cry herself to sleep.

A lamp came to life, barraging her reluctant eyelids. Bitter herbs mingled with the scent of porridge. A chair scraped across the room and settled next to the bed. Mara blinked awake. Every muscle in her body ached, but none more than her heart. Remorse, worse than anything she'd felt last night, ambushed as Zev's incisive gaze came into focus.

She sat up, massaging her head. He handed her the tea. She made herself meet his eyes. Her guilt wasn't his fault. "Afraid to father my children?"

"You aren't afraid to mother mine?"

Raising the mug in a mock toast, she sipped and grimaced. "Are you always so romantic with women you intoxicate and take to bed?"

Zev cleared his throat. "What happened last night won't happen again."

Her fingers drummed the warm ceramic as she waited for the tea to cool. Zev avoided her gaze, fidgeted. She relished his guilt a moment longer before releasing him from it. "Maybe I was using you. Did you think of that?"

"If you were, you were doing it wrong."

Mara chugged the lukewarm tea and retched. "What are we, you and me?"

"Friends, I think. I don't know. I don't have many." He rubbed his eyes. "Now, eat and dress. We need to leave."

Mara observed a pattern. For every outpost of the Ring, there was a consulate nearby. Which had come first? And how many traitors to the crown masqueraded in King's white?

The next thought came like a blow to her gut—hadn't she?

At one stop, Mara overheard two men discuss Akaronian supply lines over ale. Using the easterly branch of the Priel, supply vessels disguised as trade ships carried food and materials from the sea to the camp north of Firth.

"Think they'll use those shiny new weapons against us?"

"Not if we join 'em."

Mara scowled. How would simple villagers stand up to the threat of

Akaronians? Even if they weren't massacred, they'd be pillaged and forced to face winter without food. Many would turn traitor against a crown they hadn't seen rather than watch their children starve to death. Fealty would be easy to obtain given acceptable promises, assuming the raiders didn't simply kill everyone. The Akaronian numbers could swell before reaching the city.

While Zev tended to business, Mara scribbled notes to the Council and Captain Griggs and ran them to the consulate. The kingsman on duty accepted the notes with curious eyes.

"Can you send these where they need to go?" she asked.

His curt nod made her suspect they would be tossed in the fire the moment she returned to the street. As a postscript to the apology she planned to write Declan before her death, she'd recommend a thorough inquisition of all kingsmen, especially those stationed at consulates.

Zev grabbed her arm as she rounded the corner of the stable. "Where have you been?"

"Hills! You scared me," she said, catching her breath.

His face grew redder as she stalled.

"The consulate. I asked for word about Firth and Selene." As the lie slithered off her tongue, she wished it was true. Assurance, however small, would be welcome.

"Find out anything?" His anger cooled. His suspicion didn't.

At the shake of her head, he escorted her to her new horse.

Every few hours, she glanced over her shoulder. If Declan followed, her efforts to keep him safe would be wasted. As long as he remained inside the city wall, he could prepare for the impending attack. He could prevent Zev from returning.

At the next stop, Zev said, "They won't catch us."

"I hope they aren't following at all." Mara scanned the small fishing village, which had little more than a market, a consulate, and an outpost. Muttering a quick word to Zev, she set out for the consulate.

Inside, a middle-aged woman smiled in greeting. Mara pulled the wrap from her face to cool her head and build some trust. "Can you give me news of Firth? I have a sister there, and the rumors are worrisome."

"The Akaronian camp is only a league north of the town. Many have evacuated," the woman said with a sympathetic frown.

"What about consulate members?"

"According to policy, they won't evacuate until the town is empty or the King's troops arrive."

Mara latched onto the offered thread of hope. "Where are the troops now?"

"I'm sorry," the woman said. "I'm not privy to that information."

Mara decided to trust the woman and rewrote the notes she'd delivered to the previous consulate. "Is there a more direct way to send information to the Council than pass it from one consulate to another? I don't trust every kingsman I meet."

Amusement twinkled in the woman's eyes. "Nor do I trust every lady who walks through my door dressed like a bandit." She opened her hand to receive the notes.

Zev watched Mara walk out of the consulate toward him. "Bad news?"

"Probably nothing you don't know," she said.

Zev took the cloth from her hands and wound it around her head, kissing her mouth before he covered it. "She'll be fine."

"How can you be sure? Did Rivka ask your permission before she killed Ramzi?" she said.

His jaw clenched. "I wasn't consulted about Ramzi, but she won't hurt Selene. She knows we're coming and that you'll give us the location of the stone as long as Selene stays safe."

"How?"

"How what?" Zev stalked toward the stable, Mara at his heels.

"How does Rivka know we're coming?"

"I sent word."

The edge in his tone warned her off further questioning. "You'd better be right," she said.

Mara slipped dismounting her horse.

"Whoa." With a quick step, Zev caught her before she landed on her backside.

Dragging from the stable to the inn, she scowled at the others. They were all stiff, but no one else had difficulty walking. Zev told her he would have the innkeeper's wife draw a bath and sent her upstairs with a bowl of stew.

A rap sounded at the door as she finished eating. The bath was ready.

Gathering the fresh clothes Zev had given her, she stepped into the quiet corridor. A floorboard squeaked at her step, and a door opened to her right. An enormous black hand covered her mouth and pulled her into a room. The door slammed, and she was cornered against the wall.

"Boz! You scared the hell out of me."

He scowled down at her, arms akimbo. "You need to run away from here. Tonight. Wait until Zev is asleep. Steal a fresh horse, and ride it hard south. Do you understand?"

Mara cowered.

He took her shoulders. What was a gentle shake for him rattled her teeth. "You are riding into danger," he said.

Terror that he might kill her passed. She offered a tremulous smile. "Thank you for caring, but I've known about Rivka and the raiders all along. I'm going to save my sister."

Boz exhaled through flared nostrils like a riled bull. Angry men made her nervous, especially when their arms were thicker than her legs. Pacing in a circle, he rubbed his bald head and threw troubled glances in her direction. Mara melded to the wall as he advanced again. "If I have to drag you from your bed and tie you to the horse, you're going."

She stood blinking in the empty corridor before she realized he'd shoved her out the door. In a daze, she tromped down the stairs and into the kitchen. The innkeeper's wife hung a towel on a chair and told her the water had cooled enough. Half listening, Mara slipped into the delicious bath and tried to make sense of her encounter with Boz.

"I'd give a purse of gold to know what's spinning in that pretty head of yours."

Mara startled, splashing water onto the floor. She sent a spray at Zev as he chuckled. "Go away," she said.

"I will. But first, I wanted to offer you a massage." He held up a glass vial of oil. "I'll warm it for you."

"Not tonight." Her hands stirred the water. "What have you told Boz?"

A cold pause. "What did he say?"

"Nothing." She shook her head, unwilling to betray another friend. "He keeps frowning at me like he doesn't want me here. I thought he liked me."

Zev knelt behind the tub, kneading the muscles in her neck and shoulders.

"Boz loves his girls. If he frowns, it has nothing to do with you." His kissed her jaw. "My room is next to yours."

She'd thought she wanted to be alone, but when he left, a terrible emptiness gnawed her insides. A series of faces reeled through her mind. People she'd hurt. People who'd hurt her. The quiet suffocated. Gasping, she emerged from the bath and threw the towel over her dripping skin. A strong compulsion to outrun her ghosts almost sent her screaming naked into the dark. She ached for a sea breeze, the smell of earth, the calm of the night sky. To roll in the grass and feel her heart race. To act on the insanity besetting her. At the foot of the stairs, she chose insanity of a different kind.

She burst through the chamber door and kicked it shut. Zev blinked up from the table where he scribed a letter. A puddle formed at her feet. He lazed back in his chair, looking her over. A crescent formed above the corner of his mouth. "Yes?"

The towel dropped to the floor.

CHAPTER 22

In the predawn gloom, Mara discerned the angry set of Boz's face. He avoided her gaze. If he'd gone to snatch her from her bed as he'd threatened, he would've found it empty and known what it meant. From the look of him, he probably had, which was why she'd stayed with Zev. She couldn't turn back, no matter the danger. Not without Selene.

A ferry floated them across the river. Zev had opted for the rougher road, forfeiting speed. When Mara asked his reason, he told her it was safer and that they could afford the lost time. She would arrive in Firth before Rivka's deadline, and any pursuers would be slow to catch up. Zev told her to discard the head wrap. She wouldn't need it. The two men Mara didn't know seemed unsurprised by her feminine features, which made her wonder how long they'd known.

A giddy longing curled Mara's stomach as they neared her home country. One more night, Zev promised. They would reach Firth before noon the next day.

Zev stopped on the river bank at sunset.

"We're camping?" she asked him.

"Have I spoiled you?"

"I'll survive," she said flatly.

Zev pulled off his shirt and swaggered in her direction. "If you'll excuse me, I'd like a bath. Come with me if you like, or I'll find you when I'm done."

She'd lived on the Priel too long to risk bathing in it. "Don't get eaten."

His muttered innuendo earned him a dramatic eye roll.

Mara turned from the river and the final rays of light and located a mound to prop her back. Sometime later, she jerked awake, enveloped by night.

"Hungry?" Zev handed down a napkin filled with fish and biscuits and smoothed a blanket over the grass. "It took me a while to find you. Didn't help that you were sleeping like the dead. I worried."

She muttered an apology through the dry biscuit. A canteen plopped onto her lap. Folding his arms behind his head, he leaned against the mound beside her. "Does Declan know his friend threatened to murder you?"

"No," she said. The fish flaked in her mouth. Someone among them knew how to cook. "It's between Kenrik and me."

"It isn't. And Declan wouldn't like it."

"If it comes to it, he'll understand Kenrik's reasons and forgive him," she said.

Mara heard the scowl in his voice. "I wouldn't forgive anyone who killed you."

"Excepting Rivka."

He rolled onto his elbow. His eyes pierced hers. "Not even her."

"And yourself?"

He sighed, flattening his back. "I would've stopped."

Mara ate and kept her doubts to herself.

"You broke our trust. I was angry, but instinct would've won out. Twelve winters is a long time to protect someone. It becomes habit after a while."

Mara drained the canteen. "Maybe that's what we are. A habit."

His arm hooked her waist and swung her onto him. "You're not just the sex." The smirk was short lived. "You never were."

He believed what he said. Maybe she could believe with him if he'd ever wanted more than her body, but Declan had ruined her with his demand for her heart first and bed later.

Unexpected pity welled inside. Zev wasn't so different from her—unloved by his father, orphaned by his mother, enslaved by Rivka. Lonely. Terrified by real love. She forced the feeling down. It would grate him, and there would be war.

She raked her fingers through his hair. "Careful. You're dangerously close to telling me you love me."

His teeth gleamed silver in the moonlight. "Nonsense."

"Nonsense indeed."

Then his lips were on her throat. He began working off her clothes. She grabbed his face before she lost his attention. "If Kenrik kills me, you won't lay a finger on him. Understand?"

No longer in the mood to talk, he did his best to distract her.

"If you do, I'll become your personal poltergeist." Breathless, she didn't sound as firm as she meant to.

"I'll count on it," he said.

"I mean it, Zev. Let him be."

Laughing, he tossed her onto the blanket and leaned over her. "Shut up and kiss me."

At the sound of her name, Mara sat upright, tugging up the blanket to cover herself. Zev's arm fell loose beside her. Squinting into the dark, she half expected Boz to emerge from the shadows. But an attempt to steal her from Zev in the middle of the night would be foolhardy, and Boz was no fool. The grass swished. An insect chortled nearby. No one was there.

Turning into Zev, she settled again. He stirred as she arranged her hair behind her. In sleep, his perpetual scowl relaxed. He was only a man. A broken man who feasted on her soul and left her to starve.

Her lips brushed his. Kenrik was right—she loved him. Even though she shouldn't. Even while she loved Declan.

"Mara."

She froze, searching the dark.

The whisper came again. "Mara."

Trembling, she scanned the hills and valleys in every direction. A gust rushed from the east, washing over her nakedness, caressing her face, and then eddied back. Dust and debris spiraled up from the ground. A figure formed before her. It smiled and beckoned with an outstretched arm.

A wind spirit.

Her lips parted in awe. Rivka, she'd accepted. She'd known evil all her life. But this creature was something new. Other.

Mara leaned against the mound, considering. The spirit waited, its smile never faltering. Whatever it intended, it wasn't like Rivka. Rivka never smiled. Not without baring teeth.

The spirit tilted its head eastward and looked back, a question in its eyes. With a glance down at Zev, who slept through it all, Mara slipped out of his reach. Something cool and alive gripped her wrist, and she ran.

Laughing and gasping, the spirit led her faster and farther than should be possible. The airy melody delighted Mara until she laughed too. When she thought her heart would gallop from her chest, they stopped, and the spirit dissolved into the ether. Mara swiveled her head, looking for it. It was gone.

"What was that about?" she asked aloud. No answer came. No breeze either. Was she dreaming? With an absurd laugh, she threw out her arms and fell back onto the willowy grass. Air rushed from her lungs, but she didn't mind. There was a sweetness in the pain.

Overhead, the sky streamed black like a thick widow's veil, pinpricked by stars of various shades and sizes. They were tiny, not enough. Insignificant in all that darkness. Mara stretched until she hurt, and still she wasn't as vast as she knew herself to be. If she was the night sky, Zev was a single star, lost in an infinite void.

Another breeze swirled the grass, whispering. She rose to listen. Her mother's long-forgotten voice sounded in her head. *The wind carries secrets to and from the King . . .*

Mara searched the sky, disquieted. "All right. You brought me here. Now what?"

The universe poised to listen. And nothing happened.

"Are you there?" She shook her head. What would Zev think of her? What did she think of herself? "Kali once told me you left because the people didn't want you. For a long time, I didn't want you either. If I want you now, will you come?"

She sensed the farce in a naked woman lying in the grass talking to the wind. Declan with his scorn for dignity would approve. Thoughts of Declan made her throat swell hot.

"The truth is I need your help. Not that I deserve it. I've disbelieved you—hated you—and I'm going to betray your man to the enemy."

Tears filled her eyes. "I don't want to betray Declan, but I don't know how to save Selene if I don't. And protecting her is habit. It's what I am. I can't not do it. But if you're everything the stories say you are, you can protect Declan. You can help me save Selene. Hills—you can even save Zev."

A cricket chirped at the sinking moon.

"I dragged him out here, thinking I was free of him, but look at me." A wave of her hand indicated her bare skin, raised by dew and the cool of night. She groaned in self-disgust. "I know I've ruined whatever I had with Declan, but maybe you can help him forgive me. I don't want to be his enemy. Maybe I can make all this up to him somehow. If Kenrik gives me the chance. But then, you gave me a chance, and I chose wrong."

A pair of nightingales serenaded one another from a nearby coppice. Mara smiled to herself. The seasons had cycled since she'd last heard their song.

"Another chance is a lot for a traitorous whore to ask. Too much. But I never thought I'd see my home again, and here I am. Chances and choices seem to be what you do."

Wind breathed into her face, kissing her cheeks.

"As long as I'm asking for impossible favors, I'd really like to be free. Of Zev. Rivka. My own emptiness." She pressed a fist into the flesh below her stomach. "I think I'm more afraid of this damned hole than I am of Rivka."

A chill stole over her body. Mara wrapped her arms around herself, rubbing prickled skin with her palms. "Let's assume you're really here, and you hear me, and I'm not a crazy woman talking to herself. You should know—I can't offer you anything. I can't pay you back for saving my life or using your magic to help me. If I ever had anything, it's all used up.

"But Declan says you love me. That you saved me for something. Whatever that is, I'll do it. I don't know how, but I'll try. Because you're like Declan—you keep proving me wrong. Every time I begin to believe all the good's gone out of the world, you show me some."

The faces of her friends passed through her mind. A wistful smile shaped her mouth. "I suppose you can have what Declan asked for. He probably doesn't want it anymore, so it's yours if you do. What's left of it, anyway."

Another gust rustled the grass and swept up her hair, a prelude to the rising sun. Black faded to violet gray. The stars blinked to sleep as the sun burst over the horizon. Gold and crimson filled the sky, shimmering against the silhouette of the wind spirit. It smiled in front of her as if it had never left. Mara stood, reaching out to touch it.

"He loves you," the spirit said, its voice an airy soprano. "He won't leave you."

In spite of everything she'd seen and done, Mara decided to believe. "Help me believe."

The spirit stepped toward her and kissed her mouth. Mara gasped in surprise, breathing in the spirit's essence, tasting fruit, earth, and sunshine. The breath traveled beyond her lungs, filling and warming her insides like whiskey. Her empty places dissolved in the heat. Sweat formed on her skin, but she didn't turn cold, despite the cool morning. She exhaled, and the spirit retreated. The sun shone through it, healing Mara with its light. Mara felt alive. Whole.

With a parting smile that reminded her of Declan, the spirit blew away, disappearing with the night. Not ready to let it go, her hand closed over its arm, but it slipped through her fingers.

Zev called her name, but she couldn't turn from the beauty before her for the lesser behind. The swish of grass ceased as he entered her peripheral vision. He flung clothes at her, which she let fall to the ground. "We could've watched the sun rise from where we were," he said.

She marveled at the horizon, enjoying the breath of earth on bare skin. "It looks like Eleora."

"I wouldn't know." His voice was flat.

She smiled from within. "Isn't it amazing how fast it fills the sky? I'm already warm."

"Amazing. Let's go."

She dressed facing the sun and followed him back to camp, feeling unnaturally buoyant and chipper. "Red dawn. A storm's coming," she said.

He didn't respond. She skipped ahead and faced him, blocking his path. "When I fulfill my oath, Selene and I will return to the city. Come with us. Forget Rivka."

"To the city or to Declan?"

"Both, if he'll have me," she said.

Zev ground his teeth. "What about Kenrik?"

"Kenrik is a problem. One I'll risk."

"You're through with me then." His eyes iced over.

She rested a gentle hand on his shoulder. "I'm through with your bed, not with you. We need some time apart, but you're my friend. I love you." Her own words surprised her, but as they settled on the air, she couldn't regret them. They were true. His jaw flexed beneath her lips. "In case I forget to say it later, thank you for bringing me."

Turning, Mara noticed a dark cloud to the north. It couldn't be the storm this early in the day. Unsure of what she saw, she squinted and froze.

A column of smoke billowed above Firth.

CHAPTER 23

Mara sprinted to the horses; leaped atop Zev's, which was fastest; and snapped the reins. Zev swore after her, but she wouldn't slow. Not for him, not for anyone. She pressed the horse as hard as she could without causing harm, aware of the leagues ahead. Anxiety roiled her insides until it surged from her stomach. Slowing the horse, she coughed up bile and flicked the reins again.

As the sun rose, thirst gnawed her mouth and throat. She drank when she stopped for the horse and pressed on. The smoke burgeoned in the sky, too large to be confined to the farm. Assailed by the scent of ash, she was thrown twelve winters into the past. Skyfire thrummed under her skin. She couldn't lose Selene the way she'd lost her father.

Not far from the edge of town, the horse refused to go farther, at which point she sprang from the saddle and ran. A wave of heat plowed her over at the river bank. The air wisped thin. Towers of smoke and piles of smoldering ruins were all that remained of the town. A few stubborn citizens filled barrels and buckets near the docks, but little could be saved. Mara prayed the rest had given up and evacuated, Selene among them.

She kicked off her boots and dived. She'd never swum the width of the Priel, but today she would, no matter what lived beneath the surface. Halfway across, she heard her name followed by a string of curses. Zev had caught up.

Panting, she dragged out of the water and dashed to the consulate. Smoke blinded. Heat consumed her energy. Debris fell from flame-ravaged buildings, narrowly missing her head. The consulate was gone, except for a charred skeleton, which was too hot to approach.

"Selene!" Coughs racked her body. "Selene!"

No answer came. Her thoughts congealed. She couldn't decide whether the silence was blessed or cursed. Staggering down the ashy street, she called for Selene, Ben, and Hedya. No answer. She collapsed.

A damp cloth covered her face. Unyielding arms lifted her from the dirt and hauled her away. Who had her and where she was being taken mattered little. She'd come for Selene, and Selene was gone.

Boz waited in a rowboat by the water's edge. Zev dumped Mara inside, pushed off the silt, and leaped in. His sooty face set off livid eyes. "What in hell were you thinking? You could've died in there."

A drawn-out cough was all he received in answer. Boz paused rowing to pat her back, releasing black-tinged sputum from her lungs. Deep tones encouraged her. "There, there, Miss Mara. Now then. Deep breaths."

Coughs gave way to raspy sobs.

After his own coughing fit, Zev said, "It's good she wasn't there. It probably means she evacuated with the rest."

Suspicion cracked through her mind. She glared at Zev. "Did you know this would happen?" Without giving him time to answer, she lunged for his throat. "Did you know?"

Zev shackled her wrists in one hand and held in her place with the other. Looking her in the eye, he said, "I didn't know. But what makes you think I could've stopped it if I had?"

Her anger evaporated, and she sank against his chest, weeping.

From the safety of the opposite bank, Mara watched her town burn to rubble. Zev filled a canteen and made her empty it several times before he was satisfied. As promised by the red dawn, storm clouds approached from the west, carrying skyfire in their bellies. Zev urged Mara to leave. They needed shelter. The Akaronian camp wasn't far.

"I'm not going anywhere until I find Selene."

Zev growled in exasperation. "You've seen what Rivka's capable of. Why would you test her when she might have Selene?"

"Rivka lied," Mara said. "At first, I had until harvest. Then she gave me ten days—ten days—to deliver the information. It's only been seven. And if I had missed the deadline, she was only supposed to burn the farm. She burned the entire town. I will look for Selene, I will find her, and I will leave. Rivka won't get a thing from me."

"You're out of your mind if you think you can double-cross her," he said.

"Damn right I am."

She turned toward the boat, and Zev grabbed her arm. "I can't let you do something that will get you killed."

Mara scowled at his hand on her arm and remembered Declan's question. "Come with me."

"What?" He spat the word as if it tasted foul.

"Run away with me. Help me find Selene. We'll go back to the city and help the Council take them all down. She obviously needs Eleora. How much power can she have without it?"

"If you run, she'll come after you, and she won't stop until she kills you, Selene, and everyone you care about."

"Let her try." She snatched her arm away. "Are you coming?"

Zev peered over her head at the growing storm, grinding his teeth. "I'll come."

Stunned, she threw her arms around his neck. "See? Almost good."

Holding her, he tipped her face to his. "I'll help you find Selene. You'll tell me who has the stone. I'll tell Rivka, and you'll be free."

Her smile dropped. "Why would you help her? She lied to us both. That's what she does. This is what she does." She waved her arm at the ruins across the river.

Zev extended a flask. "You need to relax."

"You need to break free while you still can."

He uncapped the flask and thrust it into her hand. "I'm not going anywhere with you until you stop yelling every word you say."

Daggering him with a glare, she gulped and winced. Not so much at the burn as at the way it drew up her mouth. "What's wrong with your whiskey?"

Zev watched the storm, pretending not to hear. Mara sniffed the mouth of the flask. The oversweet odor matched the way it cloyed her tongue. A second taste gnawed at her memory. "Zev?"

She meant to say more but was struck by a sudden wave of listlessness. Her vision blurred, and when she blinked, it didn't clear. The flask thumped the ground. Gurgling, it emptied its contents onto the grass. The earth tilted. Zev caught her, easing her down.

"You're going to be very angry with me," he said. "But listen. Everything I've done, everything I'm doing now—it's all to keep you alive. You won't see it that way, but it's true."

His touch seared like a brand. She wanted out of his arms but had no strength to struggle. Foul and furious words zipped through her mind, jumbling into soup. Her eyelids drooped and closed.

"Boz," Zev called. "Help me get her onto the horse."

Before the drug pulled her under, she understood. Boz's warning, the extra men, Zev's relentless sexual advances. He'd wanted her in his bed where he could watch her. Control her. Steal information if he could. She'd intended to lure Zev out of the city and away from Declan, but the entire time she'd been on her way to the Akaronian camp as his prisoner.

CHAPTER 24

Consciousness returned in fragments. At first, Mara was only aware of water washing down her parched throat. Later, she noticed the cup when it pressed against her mouth. Rain pelted canvas. Boots slogged through mud. Someone brought stew, and she choked. A hand smacked her back, and she was left alone. She slept.

Arms lifted her and carried her out into the rain. The scent made her stomach twist in wistful knots. Drops splashed her cheeks until her eyelids fluttered.

"That's it," someone encouraged. "Come on. Wake up."

Her insides froze. The voice belonged to an enemy. "For a woman who could drown a cat in the whiskey she drinks in one night, you can't take a sleeping draught."

She was taken out of the rain and offered a rich broth. When she resisted, Zev's voice went wry. "You won't be able to fight me until your head clears. The broth will help."

She drank and fell asleep.

Apart from the iron in her limbs, Mara was herself the next time she woke. The rain had stopped, and night obscured her surroundings. She sat up with a groan, rustling a straw mattress. Boz's snores rumbled between her bed and the tent flap. Zev was gone.

Rage burned through her blood. Tripping over Boz, she fell through the flap into the mud. One of the men who'd traveled with her hauled her to her feet. Caustic eyes glared into hers. "Stay inside. If you come out again, I'll bind you. Understand?"

His grip and her poor balance almost ripped her arm from its socket. At her sharp intake of breath, Boz emerged from the tent with a growl. "Let her go, Arc. She won't go out again."

Arc obeyed, sneering. Boz guided her back to the mattress and placed a cooled mug of broth in her hands. Stone struck iron. With a spark, light glowed from a lamp. Boz sat in the only chair.

"Where is he?" she asked.

Boz rubbed his head. "Drink. Then we talk." His eyes swiveled to the tent flap. She nodded. Arc could hear everything and would report to Zev.

She displayed the empty mug. "Well?"

"He's asleep. He stayed with you last night and was in and out most of the day."

"I'm a prisoner, aren't I?"

Mara had never heard a heavier sigh. "Zev insists he be the one to explain."

"I'm sure he does." Wrapping her arms around Boz's neck, she whispered into his ear. "I'm sorry. I should've listened to you."

The grace in those large, dark eyes melted her. He gave her a gentle squeeze and a pointed look. "While you're here, do exactly as you're told."

But Mara wouldn't make any such promise.

Throughout the night, she sifted the days since she'd left Rahm-Or through her mind, collecting clues she should've recognized. There were plenty, but she'd been too self-absorbed to notice. Mara paused at the memory of the drugged whiskey, frowning at the canvas ceiling. A detail nipped the edge of her mind.

Flashes of her abduction at the wall merged with images of her time at Jed's rundown mansion. She tasted the lozenges under her tongue, the wine Jed had offered. The wine.

She wouldn't drink the—wine.

Her eyes flew open at the sound of Zev's voice. She sprang from the bed, every nerve rife with fury. "Let me explain," he said.

"Begin with why you had me abducted and given to Jed."

Zev blanched, betraying himself. She pounced, swinging, kicking, and scratching. They tumbled out of the tent into the mud. Zev blocked most of the blows but hesitated to fight back. Mara took advantage, clocking his jaw and kneeing his ribs before he pinned her down. Squirming beneath him, she cursed and spat in his face. In low tones, he told her to be quiet. But she wouldn't be quiet. Not if he wanted her to. He covered her mouth. She bit, loosed a hand, and slapped him hard across the face.

"Dammit, Mara," he said. "Now that you have the attention of every man in the camp, can we return to the tent?"

Chest heaving, Mara glanced up and around. A crowd stared down at her. Some grinned in amusement. Others leered, something sinister in their eyes. The moment she yielded, he yanked her from the mud and pushed her inside.

"Boz, see if you can disperse our audience," Zev said.

Boz left, casting Zev a dark look. Zev scowled down at her as she seethed up at him. "I did it to save you."

She slapped him again. He seized her wrists and bound them in a strip of cloth. Wrapping the excess around his fist, he reeled her to him. Mara thrashed against his touch. With a sigh, he tied her to the chair and squatted.

"I suppose binding me protects me too," she said and spat.

Closing his eyes, he wiped his face and fought for control. She took sadistic pleasure in watching the struggle.

"What do you think would happen if I let you run out of this tent into that crowd?" he said.

"How would it be different from what you let Jed do to me?"

His eyes flashed open. "It would be different."

At Zev's order, Arc brought another chair. Zev sat across from her and leaned forward. "I found out Jed had paid one of the guards at your shelter to take you. It happened before the warrant for his arrest. It was only a matter of time. Had the guard been successful, Jed would've killed you, probably before I could find you."

"My guards—"

"Your guards were incredibly easy to distract," he said.

A contradiction faltered on her lips.

"I also knew about Rivka's message." He pulled a gold ring from his finger.

Like the Akaronian's, it featured a gray stone. Zev hadn't worn it during the journey north. Had he, Mara would've recognized it and guessed Rivka had been the one to convince him to take her.

"Two powerful people thirsty for your blood, and I pitted them against one another. To save you," he said. "Jed accepted my help to get you. I gave him rules. He broke them and paid the price. Rivka demanded the location of Eleora, and you refused to do what needed doing. The only way to help you was to force the stone out of hiding. I knew either Declan or Lazar had it. Both would've done anything for you."

A cold realization settled inside her. "You sold me. You used me to get Jed's properties."

"I saved you."

Hot blood surged into her face and pricked her eyes as she yelled. "You subjected me to rape and torture—you risked my life—to help yourself, not to save me."

Zev paused and looked away. "You weren't supposed to remember what happened."

Standing, she swung the chair at him. But she was slow, and he was ready. He spun her around and fastened her ankles to the wooden legs.

"Eleora doesn't heal everyone," she said. "What if you'd been wrong? I'd be dead, and you'd be left with nothing." She almost wished he had been wrong. It would've served him well to foil his own plans.

"But I wasn't wrong. You're alive, and you'll stay that way if you do what I tell you."

"Go to hell."

"I'm sure I will," he said. "Now, listen. The immediate danger isn't Rivka. It's that horde of women-hating imbeciles outside. Don't even think of escape. Boz will fight to the death for you, but he can't take more than ten Akaronians at a time. Rivka has only so much . . . influence, so stay put. You'll be free tomorrow."

"What happens tomorrow?"

"Tomorrow, one of them—Declan or Lazar—will come for you, Eleora in hand."

"What?" she screeched.

Zev swore. "If you don't quiet down, I'll gag you. There's to be an exchange.

You for him."

"No deal," she said.

"It isn't your decision."

"I hate you."

"Two days ago, you loved me."

"If you hurt him, I'll kill you." She despised the crack in her voice.

"Should be interesting," he said, standing. "Ten silvers—we'll both be naked before you draw blood."

Weary and beaten, she asked the only question that still mattered. "Selene?"

He paused at the flap, his back to her. "Safe. And don't worry. I've hired someone to take care of Kenrik. When this is over, no one will say I didn't fulfill my oath to protect you. Not even you."

A sob tore from her throat before the flap closed behind him.

A fierce scowl furrowed Boz's face when he found her tied to the chair. He loosened the knots, catching her as she collapsed onto him. Ointment emerged from a knapsack, which Boz massaged into the raw skin of her wrists. No amount of coaxing could convince her to eat the gruel Arc delivered. She wanted sleep. Boz stood outside while she changed out of the mud-caked outfit into a fresh set of clothing.

She flopped onto the mattress as the fifth member of their traveling party entered the tent carrying a small washtub. Arc followed, a full bucket of water in each hand, which he poured into the tub. The other returned a few moments later with buckets of his own. After another appearance from each, the tub was full. Arc left. His partner lolled in a chair, trimming his fingernails with a knife.

Mara called to Boz. "Will you kindly explain to your friend that I prefer to bathe alone?"

Boz brushed aside the tent flap, glancing between the man and the tub. Mara didn't like the storm gathering in his expression. From behind him, Zev said, "Step aside."

"Zev." Boz said his name like a plea.

Zev stepped inside, looking grim. "Take a walk, Boz. You may not want to stay."

Mara sprang upright, her fingers clutching the edge of the mattress.

"Don't do this," Boz said.

Zev met Mara's gaze as he answered. "It's me or a specially trained Akaronian. Rivka's orders."

A chill washed from her scalp to her ankles.

Boz glanced at her, rubbing his head. "I'll guard the tent."

Zev nodded, his lightless eyes trained upon her. He took a gold bracelet from a pocket and shoved it onto her wrist. It shrank as Mara watched, until it was smaller than her hand. She tried to slide it off, but it clung to her skin. The bracelet featured a watery gray stone like the magic ring Zev wore. Her stomach lurched at the prospect of confronting Rivka.

Zev moved the empty chair in front of the tub and sat with a sigh. "I'll let you decide how you get clean today. Tell me what I need to know, and we leave. You can wash in peace, and you won't see me again until tomorrow."

"If I don't?" Mara asked.

"Donal here will help you. You won't like his standard for cleanliness," Zev said, his tone cold and detached.

"Rivka received these yesterday." Two slips of paper passed to Donal, who handed them to her. They were the notes she'd written to the Council and Griggs three—no, four—days ago, the ones she'd known wouldn't make it. But she hadn't considered having to answer for them.

"The first question is easy. Are these the only notes you sent with this information?"

Glaring, Mara thrust out her jaw.

Zev rubbed his eyes and nodded to Donal, who jerked her off the mattress, dragged her to the tub, and forced her head underwater until her lungs burned and her mind shrieked in terror. After what seemed like an eternity, she gulped air.

"Are these the only notes?" Zev asked again.

"Yes." She gasped and went under again.

Mara was certain she would drown before Donal pulled her up. Half-conscious, she slumped over the lip of the tub back into the water. A hand yanked her out. She sputtered like a dying fish on the ground.

"Tell me what I need to know, and it's over," Zev said.

Mara panted something foul and found herself underwater again.

Consciousness slipped before Donal gave her air. A fist pounded her back, and she vomited water.

"No," she said when she could speak.

"How many others?"

What did it matter? If the Council didn't have the information by now, they would never see it at all. "One."

Zev lapsed into a long silence, which she filled with gasps. "Next question. Tell me what you gave the stable boy at the wall."

Mara's eyes widened and found Zev. "Nothing."

Donal hauled her up by the collar.

"It's true! It's—" The water cut her off.

She came up and was face to face with Zev. His eyes bore into hers. "If you didn't give him anything, what did you tell him?"

She hacked, splattering his face. "That he had a beautiful dog."

He shook her. "I'm losing patience, Mara."

"Drown me then."

He flung her to Donal and snapped his fingers. A succession of lengthy dunks weakened her resolve, but she blacked out before she was given another opportunity to speak. Zev and Donal were waiting when she woke exhausted and cold.

Zev pointed to her wrist. "That bracelet allows you to survive repeated drownings. If you don't tell me what you told the boy, he'll receive the treatment you're enjoying now. Without a bracelet. I doubt he's as stubborn as you, but that may not be enough to save him."

Mara believed the threat. Groaning, she tried to push herself off the ground and slipped. She rested her head in the mud. "Have you hurt him?"

"Not yet. He was, however, detained after we left. Your message was never delivered."

Frustrated tears spilled down her cheeks as her fist pounded the damp ground. "Swear you won't."

"Must've been important, whatever it was," Zev said. "Your decision to involve him placed him in danger. The only thing I can promise is the boy won't be tortured if you answer the question."

"You have to do better than that."

Zev's eyes flicked to Donal. Mara cried out, clawing his wrist as he dragged her up again. Water replaced oxygen. As darkness pressed in, she saw Declan's face, eyes shining in assurance. Mara relaxed.

She was on the ground again, Donal beating her back. Mara emptied her lungs and lay lifeless in the growing puddle.

"Enough," Boz boomed. "Let her rest."

"I can't," Zev said. "If I don't get this soon, the Akaronian will come for her. There are no bracelets to protect her from the things he'll do."

"Magic fire," she said, praying she hadn't condemned the stable boy to death.

Silence. A sharp order. Boots splashed out of the tent. Zev scooped her up, supporting her lolling head. "What did you say?"

He would kill her now. There was a dark sort of comfort in the thought. "You heard me."

"How did you—"

"Your captain friend required a woman," she said. The words came slowly. "I know about the ships, the war. He gave me everything he knew."

Zev went rigid. A biting laugh gurgled in her throat and transposed into a fit of coughs. "I'm your best girl, remember?"

"Mara, you must never speak of this to anyone. No one can know, do you understand?"

She would promise him nothing. She was almost asleep when he said, "Last question. Who's coming for you?"

"No one." She hoped it was true.

Again, Mara was underwater, unable to move or breathe. Arms restrained her, her head seesawed, and teeth sank into her mind. Bolting upright, she gasped for air.

Scratchy woolen blankets wrapped her naked body, which ached all over. The lamp burned on the table next to a steaming mug of broth. Her clothes hung over one of the chairs, drying. Boz sat in the other, studying her with a troubled expression. She stiffened at the sight of the washtub and water-stained dirt.

"Does Zev have more questions?" she asked.

Holding up a hand, Boz leaned toward the flap and listened. A moment passed.

He brought the broth and pressed his mouth to her ear. "Drink and dress. I'm taking you away from here."

Without expounding, he left. Mara put on the damp clothing, which made her shiver, and sipped the broth until she was warm again. When Boz returned, he threw a cloak around her shoulders and covered her head with the hood. "It's a walk to the horses. Can you make it?"

Not that it mattered—they had no chance of success either way—but she nodded, willing to try anything to escape Zev, even risking a violent death at the hands of the Akaronians.

Nestled in the clouds, the moon offered enough light to discern the narrow walkways between tents. Mara latched onto Boz's arm, borrowing his strength, thankful for a friend among all these enemies, and prayed the King would spare his life.

A hand closed over her arm and ripped her away from him. The hood fell back, exposing her damp hair to the cool of night. A cloth jammed into her mouth. Her pulse drummed in her ears, but she was too weak to fight. A strong arm fastened her to a tall, firm frame. Frankincense taunted her senses, and despairing tears sprang to her eyes. She never wanted to smell or feel this body again.

Over her head, Zev spoke low into the dark. "What are you doing?"

Boz towered over them both. "What you should be doing. Let me take her out of here."

"They come for her tomorrow. Do your job, and she'll be fine until then."

"I won't stand aside and allow what happened today happen again," Boz said.

"It won't. Let's do this right. She'll be safer for it. If I let you leave, Rivka will send half the army after you. I could lose you both," Zev said, tensing. They all knew Boz was more than able to overpower him, but such a move could wake the sleeping raiders, and a far larger conflict would ensue.

Boz slumped, rubbing his head. "Swear to me. Swear you won't hurt her again."

"I swear."

It didn't matter that Mara didn't believe Zev. Boz did, and she would get nowhere without his help. The cloth left her mouth. Mara refused to look at Zev as he guided her back to the tent, a hand pressed to the small of her back. She recoiled and stumbled.

When he stooped to lift her, she pushed him away. "No. Boz will carry me."

Boz obliged. Mara felt Zev's gaze until Boz's bald head, glowing softly in the moonlight, ducked into the tent. Not long after they were inside, Donal and Arc murmured at the flap. Boz extinguished the lamp and whispered an apology. Mara was too spent to reply.

The hours passed in a series of nightmares, each one worse than the last. There was no relief at night's end. Golden rays betrayed the world.

Today, Declan would come for her. Today, Declan would die.

CHAPTER 25

The sun dragged across the sky. Plans of escape darted through her mind, each ending in an inevitable, humiliating death. Her death wouldn't keep Declan from coming, and it might cause him pain before they killed him too. She closed her eyes and wished to the King he wouldn't come.

Near noon, Zev retrieved Boz. After a cursory glance in her direction, Zev avoided her gaze. "We'll be back for you soon," he said.

Mara wasn't alone long. A portly figure ducked through the flap, exuding sweat and musk. "Loed?"

He grunted in greeting and plopped into a chair. She settled into the other. "How long have you been here? Is Selene all right? Ben? Where's Meg?" She paused, drawing back. "Wait. Why are you here?"

A wheezy chuckle shook Loed's shoulders as he unwrapped a biscuit. "If I didn't know better, I'd think you were happy to see me. You look like hell, by the way, but not as bad as I left you in Rahm-Or."

Mara glowered at him.

"There's my niece," he said. "I'm here to make sure you don't do something stupid—like try to escape. And to help escort you out."

"That's not what I meant. What is your role?"

"Oh." Loed bit into the biscuit. "I'll take Zev's place with the Ring in Rahm-Or when he takes the throne."

"What?"

A bulging eye turned to her. "What part of that was confusing?"

"Zev plans to take the throne? And what? Set himself up as king?"

Loed's jaw mirrored hers. Crumbs showered from his mouth. "Probably shouldn't have told you that. Pretend I didn't."

Zev had never mentioned wanting to be king. He'd never mentioned anything beyond revenge against his father. What was he thinking? She remembered the ships in the harbor and swore. But what could she do about them now?

"Have you been here long?" she asked.

"Came before the town evacuated."

"Selene?"

"Relax. She got out. Meg's with her."

Mara sank against the chair and then tensed. Anger flushed her face. "Did Meg—"

His jowls flapped from side to side. "Meg didn't steal the necklace. Zev assigned her to Selene after it happened. He doesn't know who took it."

"What did he promise you to say that?"

Loed shrugged. "S'true. Besides, I wanted Meg out. Saw some raider handiwork a couple seasons back. What was left of her, anyway." He shuddered.

So the man was capable of empathy. "Ben?"

He stuffed a final bite of biscuit into his mouth and wiped his hands on his pants. "With your sister. Seems determined to have one of you. Must like that Razan color."

"He's watching over her as he promised," Mara said. "She's only a child, Loed. Hills."

His face red with mirth, Loed drew a comb out of a pocket and handed it to her. "Zev said you'd want to pretty yourself before your swain shows up."

Ice filled the pit of Mara's stomach. She'd lost herself in the comfort of a familiar face, forgetting he was an enemy, forgetting he would play accomplice to Declan's murder. When she didn't respond, Loed stood with a loud grunt and began to comb her hair.

"I'll do it." She snatched the comb and plopped onto the mattress. Yanking it through her tangled locks, she scowled at the washtub, at the tent flap, at anything but him. Loed was beneath her contempt.

The tent grew hot and stuffy. Sweat soaked Loed's tunic. He wiped his face with a handkerchief until it dripped. Mara finished combing and paced, wringing her hands. It seemed to annoy Loed, which encouraged her.

"They're late." He stomped through the flap and immediately reentered. "Hills, it's hot."

"Would you like me to ask Donal to give you a bath?" she said. "It's a pleasant experience."

"That wasn't Zev's idea," Loed said.

"I don't want to talk about Zev."

Zev appeared at the tent flap, lips tight and eyes frozen. To Loed, he said, "Round up your boys."

Loed slung him a quizzical look and left to do as he asked. Zev's fingers ran through his hair, tugging the ends. Mara focused on his clenched jaw and waited.

"He didn't come."

The weight dropped from Mara's chest to her gut. One less death to answer for. One less soul to grieve. She felt giddy with relief knowing Declan would live, even as her body curled over in fear for her own life. "Good."

Zev hurled a chair through the flap.

"What happens now?" she asked.

He didn't answer.

"I'm dead, right? It makes sense. I've lost my value."

His fingers dug into her arms. "Tell me who it is. Tell me who failed you, and maybe I can save you."

"No one failed me," she said. "I endangered myself by trusting you. You're a fool to think the Council would trade one of their own for the life of a whore."

She jerked away from him, damming her eyes with her fingers. "How will it happen? Will she suck out my soul?"

"Rivka likes games. She'll offer you a choice. A choice you won't like."

Die on Zev's sword, or enslave herself with an oath. Watch Selene die, or sell her body. Betray a friend, and watch Firth burn. Shrew. "I remember."

Mara's hands were wrenched from her face. Zev buried his gaze in hers. "Don't be stubborn. Don't be brave. Choose the thing that keeps you alive."

The tent flap swung shut. With nothing better to do, she curled onto the mattress, wrapped her arms around her middle, and counted breaths. With one breath, she thanked the King that Declan hadn't come. With the next, she gave into the pain of his absence. With another, she rallied her courage. She'd need it before the end.

Zev returned with a coil of rope and resignation in his eyes. Poetic, to make him do it.

Mara resolved not to fight or scream. He hauled her up and spun her around. She squeezed her eyes shut, bracing herself. They popped open when the rope wrapped her wrists instead of her neck.

"I've done everything I can," he said as he worked. "What happens from here is up to you. Cooperate. Tell her who has Eleora as soon as she asks. You owe him nothing."

"Why bind me?"

He tightened the knot. "To keep you from running. Rivka lifted the spell she used to hide you from them."

A tail of rope swayed behind her. Zev wound it around a hand, tethering her to him, and led her outside. Boz, Loed, and several others encircled them. The entourage drew the attention of every Akaronian it passed.

Mara smelled silt before she saw the river. Any other day, the scent would've soothed her. She peered ahead, looking for signs of Rivka. Late-afternoon sun glinted off the quiet water, no mist in sight. The gathering crowd heckled and murmured. Zev tensed at her back. The raiders had glimpsed her and knew what she was.

At the boot-weathered bank, they stopped, and an Akaronian touched the water. The circle opened and fanned. Every head turned toward the river, waiting. Every head except that of Boz. His resolute gaze sent Mara courage.

Not far from the bank, the water rippled. A cloud of green-tinged mist rose from the surface, burgeoning in the air. Silence blanketed the camp. The mist converged into solid form, and Mara stood in the shadow of her lifelong nightmare. Not even Zev was as beautiful.

Rivka leered down at Mara. A terrifying smile unsheathed rows of dagger-sharp teeth. Mara fought to keep her expression blank. A low, seductive chuckle sounded in her ear. "You can't hide your fear from me, child. I taste it on the air." Her tongue extended out of her mouth and curled back in. "It's delicious."

A shudder traipsed down Mara's back.

"So your kingsman will not deign to exchange his life for that of a treacherous whore," Rivka said. "But we aren't surprised, are we, child?"

"Get out of my head."

Nearby faces stared, aghast. They looked at this loathsome creature as if she were some kind of god.

"Give me his name," Rivka said.

Mara clamped her jaw.

"Come now. Be reasonable. Your cooperation decides your fate once I'm done with you."

"What are you going to do to me?" Mara asked, hoping no one heard the tremble in her voice.

Bright-green eyes flicked behind Mara. "Stand aside, Zev."

Zev hesitated but did as Rivka asked. An invisible hand pressed Mara's back, pushing her forward. Mara dug her heels into the silt. A haze enveloped her and lifted her feet off the ground. She was carried, struggling midair, into Rivka's waiting claws. "His name, child. Give me his name, and I'll grant Zev's request for your life."

Mara gave Rivka the look Declan hated. Rivka didn't seem to mind as much.

Zev swore. "You can't save him, Mara. Save yourself."

Mara met Rivka's eyes. Rivka understood what Zev didn't. Mara's refusal to comply wasn't about protecting Declan. Rivka would find out, one way or another, in time. From childhood, Mara had given this monster everything it asked for. But not today. Never again would she surrender to the whims of a creature who knew nothing of mercy. Today, she would keep the last thing that belonged to her until she couldn't anymore.

Rivka dug her claws into Mara's neck until she gasped. Rivka's eyes dissolved. Lurid green mist swirled in their sockets. Rivka tilted her head and leaned down. A cloying odor veiled the stench of death as her cold lips pressed to Mara's and forced her mouth open. A tongue slithered inside, extending to the back of her throat. Mara choked.

Mara didn't understand what was happening. Rivka had sucked Ramzi's soul through his head, not from his mouth. The kiss—if it could be called a kiss—was a reversal of her last spirit kiss. Where the wind spirit had given, Rivka intended to take. What, Mara couldn't guess. Before long, she couldn't think at all. Death prowled the outskirts of her mind, advancing with each missed breath. But she wasn't afraid. The warm energy left by the wind spirit swelled inside, and with a snap, the foul tongue bounced off the stronger force and retracted.

Mara fell to the ground, sputtering. A shriek pierced the air, ringing her ears and echoing off the hills. When the noise faded, Mara struggled to her feet and spat a foul residue from her mouth. "What in hell was that?"

Rivka studied her.

"What did you try to do to me?" Mara demanded.

Addressing no one in particular, Rivka said, "You're no longer vacant. What shall I do with you now?"

Rivka stepped onto dry land, a flowing train of mist trailing behind her. She circled Mara, leering at the men surrounding her. "Move."

They all stumbled back.

"Bring me the raider king," Rivka said.

Two soldiers scampered off to do her bidding.

"What are you doing?" Zev said through gritted teeth.

"Hush, Zev." Rivka waved her fingers in his direction.

The soldiers returned, dragging a bulky, shirtless figure, which they flung at Mara's feet. Bruises purpled a fine jaw. Black and silver hair was matted against his head. An eerie familiarity stole over Mara as he pushed himself to standing and loomed over her. Intricate tattoos traveled up his arms and neck. A hardened face, framed by perfect brows and dusted with scruff, scowled down at her. Afternoon sun shone into ice-blue eyes. Even beaten and dirty, he was handsomer than every man there. Save one.

"What's this?" The man grabbed the front of her shirt and pulled her toward him. Eyes like flint peered down at her and then glanced up at Rivka, who cackled in delight. Mara gulped.

Zev wedged himself between Mara and the man. "Don't touch her," he said.

"She isn't a gift, Your Majesty," Rivka said to the older Akaronian, "though I can see why you might think so. The similarities are as astonishing as those between you and your son. But it isn't her or even a near relative, as far as I can tell."

Rivka smiled. "This is the girl who stole your son and helped overthrow you. Though she's oblivious to how vital she was to your demise."

Murmurs rippled through the camp. A wispy finger stroked the underside of the raider king's chin. "Your command left her an orphan ten winters ago." Rivka cocked a brow at Mara. "Whatever would she have done without Zev and me to care for her? Zev wishes to execute you for your crimes when he secures the kingdom."

Mara glared at Zev, who avoided her gaze. How long had this been his plan?

Rivka discoursed on. "But he expected a throne today, and I expected the King's magic gemstone. It simply won't do to disappoint us both."

Zev led Mara several paces away. He had the look of a lost child until he caught her expression. He hardened again.

"You were their prince. Why didn't you tell me?" she said.

He pulled the tail of the rope and anchored her back against his chest.

"Who do I look like, Zev? Who did your father think I was?"

"Watch," he said.

The raider king plummeted to his knees, coping no better with Rivka's magic than Mara had. Rivka's teeth glimmered in the sun.

Zev's breath blew on Mara's ear. "She can't use you to infiltrate the Council now, so she'll toy with you. Give her the name, and beg for your life, or this is what awaits."

"Tell me what she tried to do to me," she said.

He hushed her.

Rivka bared her teeth and latched onto the raider king's brow. He screamed and thrashed as Rivka drank his life away. Instinct urged Mara's feet forward to help, but Zev held her fast. How could he watch his father die this terrible death with no emotion at all? The body collapsed, its blue eyes burned out.

Rivka raised her exultant face and released a satisfied sigh. Bowing her head to Zev, she said, "The Akaronian throne is yours, Your Majesty."

Zev didn't move or speak.

Rivka cocked her head at Mara. "All you need now is a queen."

Rivka raised a hand, and an unseen force launched Mara out of Zev's grasp, raising her to almost twice his height. Tendrils of mist wrapped around Mara's waist and spun her to face him. Every eye in the camp turned to her. She longed for a place to hide.

"Will you accept the hand of the Akaronian king and future king of Rahm-Or?" Rivka had the look of a cat with a mouse caught in its claws. She was playing with her food. Like Jed.

"I'd rather die," Mara said.

Rounding her lips in mock surprise, Rivka raised her brow at Zev. "Tsk, tsk, Zev. It seems you've done a poor job wooing the heart of your mistress."

Riding upon a column of mist, Rivka met Mara where she dangled. "Consider, child. I've craved your soul twelve winters now. I'll take my time. Relish it." Her tongue slid across her upper lip. "It will hurt. But I'll forego the pleasure if you prove useful. Name the one who has Eleora, and I'll marry you to Zev right away."

Mara closed her eyes, drawing strength from the rage bubbling beneath her skin.

"Be reasonable, Mara," Zev said.

"I'd rather beg crumbs beneath Declan's table than be queen of your court," Mara answered him. Her voice resonated across the camp, leaving stillness in its wake.

Rivka rubbed her hands together. "Declan. I thought so. Now. Who will it be—Zev or me?"

Mara's heart failed as she realized what she'd done. "I didn't say Declan has Eleora. Zev was wrong. The stone is protected by an ordinary kingsman he's never met."

The surprise on Zev's face gave Mara hope.

"You've become quite the little liar," Rivka said. "Zev should be proud."

"He doesn't have it," Mara insisted.

"Even if I believed you, I would kill him anyway to repay you for the trouble you've caused me," Rivka said.

Mara cursed herself. She'd meant to go to her grave without uttering Declan's name, and in a fit of temper, she'd betrayed him and lost her final shred of control in the process. Shame streamed down her face.

"Choose," Rivka said.

Mara looked down at Zev. "Shall I lose my soul little by little or have it done all at once?"

Swearing vehemently, Zev retreated to the tents. He wouldn't even honor her by witnessing her death. Coward.

An odd urge curled Mara's stomach. Perched in a cloud above a throng of violent men with the stench of Rivka offending her nostrils, Mara sniggered. Rivka's mouth opened in astonished horror. The uncharacteristic expression made Mara laugh until she lost her breath. Rivka shook her, jarring her neck. Mara laughed in the monster's face. Zev paused and turned, befuddled, which made her laugh all the more.

Mara sobered and felt much better. "This isn't a choice. It's a trap. Sorry, but I won't play your game this time. I choose Declan. I choose the King."

She plummeted to the ground, gasping as her knee twisted beneath her weight. Rivka grabbed Mara's hair and yanked back her head. Rows of sharp teeth protruded from her mouth. Bracing, Mara resolved to bite off her own tongue before she screamed. A circle of tiny daggers sank into her mind, sucking. A breathtaking agony. Sweat beaded her brow. Mara thrashed and panted, praying for it to end.

Rivka drew back shrieking, louder this time, and Mara toppled. Panting, she nuzzled the cool grit under her cheek. By some miracle, she lived. A dagger sawed through the rope binding her wrists. Strong arms scooped her up, and Mara bounced with a broad, heavy gait. She burrowed her face into a chest and breathed the scent of coconut.

Boz reeled backward, and Mara careened out of his arms.

Rivka snarled. "Control your man, Zev, or I'll kill him too."

Zev delivered a sharp order. Several men converged on Boz. Mara returned to Rivka as if snatched by a leash.

"That fool of a King thinks you're safe because you're sealed. But he can't stop me from delivering you to his Council in pieces." Gripping Mara's wrist in one hand, Rivka lifted a dagger with the other. Mara clasped her eyes shut. But in place of a cold blade through her heart, she felt a tug and heard a ripping sound. A breeze rolled off the river over her bare skin. Black scraps of clothing lay in the dirt. Despite the heat, she shivered.

Rivka wouldn't simply kill her. Mara hadn't left her that option.

"Gentlemen! We have a whore for sale." Rivka thrust Mara forward on her knees, which scraped raw as they skid across the uneven ground.

A roar erupted all around, and Mara trembled. For once, she felt grateful for her long hair. She pulled and tucked to hide herself, knowing it wouldn't matter in the end.

"Bidding begins now. Don't be shy. I'll take whatever currency you have," Rivka said.

Shouts rang above the cacophony. Zev argued behind her, not that it would do any good. Closing her eyes, Mara curled over, wrapped her arms around her middle, and rocked back and forth. Guttural bellows and the stench of men drove Boz's island far away from her mind. Mara reached for a new solace. Her hair stirred, and a soft hand brushed her face.

Another wind spirit sat before her, its eyes strong and steady.

"Stay with me?" Mara asked.

The spirit nodded, and with a ripple, its face transformed into Declan's smile.

"Thank you."

The wind spirit took hold of her hand until she was filled by the warmth inside. Comforted, Mara closed her eyes again. She would die, and it would be horrific, but she wouldn't have to endure it alone. It was a better death than she deserved.

A shrill scream rose above the clamor. Rivka cursed Zev's name. "The only way to save her now is to take her place."

"Done."

Mara's eyes opened at the voice. A hush settled over the camp. Dusty boots stood before her, framed by the billowing hem of a purple cloak. The figure shrugged off the cloak, and the fragrance of earth after rain nourished her senses. The sun at his back cast his face in shadow, but she knew him.

He wrapped the soft cloth around her naked body and helped her stand. She stared at his boots, unable to meet his eyes. He lifted her chin with a gentle finger.

Hot tears brimmed over and spilled down her cheeks. "You came," she said.

Declan held her face. His thumbs wiped her eyes. "I'll always come for you."

"Seize him." Rivka's voice rang sharp.

Several Akaronians advanced. Scowling at Rivka, Declan pulled Eleora from his tunic. The air around the stone shimmered. The raiders fell backward, rammed by a force no one could see.

"That won't be necessary," Declan said. "I'll give myself up when my friends clear that ridge"—he pointed behind him to the west—"and my men signal their safe arrival. If you try to keep them here or harm them in any way, you'll all be slaughtered."

Gavan, Kenrik, and several faces Mara didn't know emerged from the crowd, their swords drawn. They assembled behind Declan and Mara.

"Tell me, Ambassador, how you and six guards plan to slaughter my army," Rivka said.

Declan smiled at the spirit. "You've always envied Eleora, but you've never understood it." He tossed the stone in his hand. "I promise you this—you won't take anything from me today that I don't give to you. And I won't give you them, and I won't give you her."

Rivka paused. Her gaze flicked from the guards to Declan to Mara.

Declan stepped forward, placing himself between Mara and Rivka. "Do as I say, and you'll have me and Eleora. That's what you want, isn't it?"

Mara had been so relieved at Declan's appearance that she'd forgotten the cost. Only now did she understand he meant to pay it. Her mouth went dry. "No."

Declan ignored her, his attention fixed on Rivka. "What will it be? You won't receive more patience from me than you gave to her."

Rivka bowed her head, mocking him.

Declan turned to Mara and pressed his brow to hers. "It's time for you to go."

She shook her head, clinging to his tunic. When he pried her hands away, she dropped and clung to his legs. Mara wept onto his boots, her tears staining the leather. "I won't leave you."

Declan called over his shoulder. "Boz, get her out of here."

Mara and Zev whirled their heads to Boz, who strode toward her. The color drained from Zev's slack face.

"Zev, you're free to go too, if you wish," Declan said.

Never before had Mara seen Zev so flummoxed. He recovered, his features returning to their natural scowl. "You stole my man."

Declan clapped Boz on the arm. "Why don't you go with him?"

"I think I'd rather watch you die," Zev said.

Boz disentangled Mara from Declan's legs. She flailed and kicked against his hold to little effect. Reaching out, she grasped Declan's sleeve but was pulled away and carried past the six guards. "No!"

Without a word, without a move to save their fellow kingsman, the guards followed. Declan looked back at her when she cried his name, but his eyes didn't send reassurance. They sought it. Mara gasped when she understood. He was afraid.

She doubled her efforts, pounding her fists against Boz's chest. "We can't leave him! We can't leave him, Boz!"

Boz held her firmly, his face grim and determined. He would not go back. Mara searched for the wind spirit, but it had fled. Declan was alone. As he disappeared from view, he turned to face his enemies. A sob wheezed from her throat.

She'd never told him she loved him.

CHAPTER 26

Mara searched for Declan's figure in the distance as Boz carried her up the ridge, but he was hidden in the crowd. A patrol of kingsmen stopped them at the crest of the rise.

"Is Ambassador Declan with you?" one asked.

Kenrik shook his head. Boz set Mara on her feet and helped her rearrange the cloak.

"How could you?" She beat a fist against his chest, sobbing. "How could you leave him like that?"

Kenrik pushed her shoulder, turning her to face him. Fury burned in his eyes. "How could you?"

Her tears stopped at the well-aimed dagger. She trembled in the shadow of the real one he'd threatened. But if Declan died, she'd be glad for it.

"You aren't helping," Gavan said to his brother and turned to Mara. "When Eleora gives an order, we obey whether we want to or not. Our mission was to bring you out no matter what."

Kenrik delivered orders to the patrol. Mara didn't take in much of what was said but heard the words, "Prepare for battle."

She looked over her shoulder at the sight below. Sprawled across the valley on the opposite side of the ridge, the King's military camp was a flurry of activity. Not only had Declan come after her, he'd brought an army.

A large hand cupped her shoulder. "Come, Mara. We must move."

She looked up at Boz. "If Declan dies for me, I will witness it."

His eyes searched the area and lit upon a nearby hill. A soldier prepared to light the thunder powder, the signal of the party's safe arrival. Permission for Rivka to slay Declan.

"Hold the signal," Boz said and grabbed Mara's wrist. Together they sprinted to the summit of the hill. She tripped and staggered, her twisted knee throbbing with each step, but Boz kept her on her feet. She did her best to ignore the pain.

At the top, Boz dove, and they flattened their bodies against the terrain. Gavan and Kenrik hit the ground at her elbow, surprising her. From her vantage point, Mara spied the entire raider camp, all the way to the Priel. A cloud of mist billowed by the bank, Rivka at its center, Declan nearby. A whizzing noise shot into the air, followed by an explosion. The boom turned a mass of heads in their direction, and a clanking racket swept over the raiders.

Rivka held up a hand, silencing the men. Declan removed Eleora from his neck and tossed it out of reach. Rivka wasted no time. Pouncing like a ravenous beast, she latched onto his brow, and the world resounded with his wail of agony. Mara squeezed her eyes shut and tore her hair, sure she was dying with him.

Half an eternity passed before Declan quieted. Rivka released him from her deathly grip, and he toppled lifeless to the earth. Time, thought, and feeling suspended in Mara's disembodied stupor. She convinced herself she was asleep and would wake in Kali's home and work alongside Declan in the garden later that day.

A victorious cackle reached their hill.

Reality assailed with fiery arrows. Mara twisted onto her back and fought to breathe around the pain. The blue sky waned to the purple of a bruise. Thunder pealed through the hills until pebbles rattled at her ears. The earth tremored. Or maybe she only thought it did.

Men shouted. "Earthquake!"

Quakes gave way to a violent weeping, which seemed right. Creation should fracture into chaos. Declan was dead.

Boz tugged her elbow and pointed to the raider camp. Men scattered in the valley below. Not far from the bank, a jagged rift opened like a mouth and swallowed the raiders nearest Rivka, including Loed and several of his men. The ground clamped shut, but the rumble continued. Earth spirits had awoken to war.

Rivka whirled her head and pointed to Eleora. Zev crawled toward the stone, which lay next to Declan's body, but when he reached for it, his hand drew back. Mara squinted as he tried again. Zev couldn't touch the stone.

The earth settled into faint shudders. Rivka moved to retrieve the stone but stopped before she reached it. Sickly green mist churned around her, brightening until it matched the hue of her eyes. Rivka threw back her head. A moment later, her laughter reached Mara's hill.

Rivka swelled in size, and her voice carried to the King's camp. 'The ambassador is dead. I've absorbed the strange magic of his soul and now possess the stone of power. The only recourse is surrender. All who swear fealty to me will be spared. Whoever brings me the Razan girl will be handsomely rewarded."

The three men looked at one another. Exhaustion weighed down Mara's limbs. What could Rivka want with her now?

Gavan offered a weak grin. "I pity the man who tries to take you from the three of us."

Boz stood with a groan and reached to help Mara up. "We need to hide you."

"Wait," Mara said.

Rivka scooped Eleora into her hand and dangled the chain. Rivka had managed what Zev had not. She could touch the stone.

Despair stole what remained of Mara's will. She buried her face in the grass. Declan, Selene, her mother, and for a while, even she had been wrong. The stories couldn't be true. Not in a world where Rivka won and Declan died.

A choking sound cut off the evil laughter. Mara lifted her head. Rivka convulsed and gagged. Pure, white light spewed from her mouth, her feet, her hands. Eleora dropped to the ground. A loud crack sounded over the alarm of the raiders, and her visage splintered like glass.

Rivka gestured wildly to Zev, who stayed where he was. A piercing shriek rang in Mara's ears. With another crack, Rivka shattered. Shards of green sailed in every direction, dissolving into mist. One large piece hit Zev in the face, knocking him backward. He lay in the dirt, motionless. Mara willed him to get up. He didn't.

Green mist hovered above the raider camp. A strong wind blew from the south, smelling rich with brine and soil. Wind spirits rode upon its train. The spirits swept the mist north toward the Akaron Mountains.

The dying embers of the setting sun warmed Mara's back. A ray shined upon

Eleora where it had fallen. Catching the light, each facet of the stone reflected a red beam until it glowed like a small blood-hued sun.

A white-clad messenger raced on horseback toward the enemy camp. Kenrik and Gavan joined the soldiers gathering below.

"Time to leave." Boz hauled Mara to her feet.

"Why fight?" Her voice sounded hollow in her ears. "Declan, Zev, Rivka. They're . . . they're all dead."

Boz supported Mara as they climbed down the hill. "They may not. The messenger will offer terms. If the Akaronians accept, there will be no battle. If they refuse, the kingsmen will fight until they retrieve Declan's body and an agreement can be reached."

Mara couldn't bear the idea of Declan's body without his soul.

A boy ran to greet them as they neared the camp, his golden-haired dog trailing behind. "Lady Mara." A proud grin lit the stable boy's face. "A tent is ready for you."

Other than a bruise along his jaw, he appeared unharmed. Relieved, Mara embraced the boy, who was old enough to blush at a woman dressed in nothing but a cloak. He looked past her, his weight shifting from one foot to the other, and told his story.

After she'd left the city with Zev, a guard had cornered and searched him. The guard stole his coin and questioned him, threatening his family, but the boy pled ignorance. He understood the importance of the information. When the guard hit him, the boy's dog attacked, and together they ran for the Quarter. He arrived earlier than Mara had requested but was afraid of being caught and forgetting the message. He searched until he found Kali's home. The younger woman who lived there wasn't pleased to see him, but Kali fed him a good meal while he waited for the healer. The best meal he'd ever had. And she gave something to his dog too. When he delivered the message, the healer and the guards left the room and went into another. When they came back, they looked upset. The healer asked the younger woman when Mara had gone. The woman frowned as she told her story, but when she finished, everyone frowned at her. Including himself and even the dog, he imagined. She'd said some not-nice things. He hadn't understood it all, but he was sure he hadn't liked it. And when he asked the healer why Mara had wanted the message to go to him and not to someone more important, he'd told him he wasn't only a healer.

"He's on the Council of Ambassadors," the boy finished with a whisper, his eyes bright.

Mara attempted a smile but felt it falter on her face. She kissed the boy's cheek. "Thank you for delivering my message. You're very brave."

The boy led her to a tent where a bath, a female attendant, and a clean white gown waited. Boz and the boy left, and the attendant helped her into the tepid bath. Mara's injured knee was swollen, and her wrists were chafed raw. Scrapes and bruises covered her skin, but the most intense pain settled in her chest. It felt like drowning, head above water.

The attendant gathered the cloak. Mara cried out. "Please. May I keep it?"

The woman's eyes darted. Uncertainty clouded her brow, but she pressed her lips together and nodded.

When Mara was clean and dressed, she took the cloak in her hands and breathed in the scent, a scent that would fade until she had nothing more of Declan than a handful of memories and a lifetime of regret. Her throat swelled, growing hot.

Boz returned with a bowl of gruel. She stared at it but felt no hunger. "They're both dead," she said.

"Mara." Boz hesitated. "Our men retrieved Declan's body and Eleora. They're bringing them now. But Zev's body has disappeared."

"What does that mean?"

"Zev's leadership brought the raiders to defeat," he said. "I fear they won't honor him."

"You loved him," she said.

"Yes."

"The Council sent you back to the Ring after your redemption, didn't they? To spy."

"To advise and protect," he said, raising his head. "And I volunteered to go. When the Council received Zev's redemption letter—the one he wrote for me— they wanted to help us both. Zev didn't make it easy for them."

Mara swallowed. "No, he didn't."

"When you came along, Declan asked me to protect you too. You didn't make that easy for me."

"I suppose not," she agreed miserably.

With a humorless chuckle, he rubbed his head. Loss, hot and strong, wrung her insides like a cloth. The cloak muffled her sobs but couldn't stay them.

"Thank you for grieving him with me. The King knows no one else will," Boz said.

"He doesn't deserve my grief."

Boz patted the top of her head. "That's what makes it special. Your grief is a gift born from love. Gifts are given, not earned."

But it was a gift she didn't want to give, not when it divided her sadness.

Gavan appeared at the tent flap. "He's here."

Outside, neither star nor moon shined through the canopy of clouds. The darkness was so thick it all but snuffed the torches. Soldiers surrounded a slow-moving covered wagon, which shuddered to a stop.

Mara hung back as a long line of soldiers passed the mouth of the wagon. Though they stood straight and tall, torchlight shone on tear-streaked faces. Long into the night, Mara waited, ignoring her exhaustion. When the last soldier left for his tent, she approached the wagon. A lamp glowed inside. Mara reached for Declan's limp foot, cold to the touch. A guard sputtered an objection as she climbed into the wagon. Someone silenced him.

Mara steadied herself with a deep breath and looked into Declan's face. Her fingers brushed his eyelids. Unlike Rivka's other victims, his eyes hadn't burned out. Peace, not pain, marked his features. He'd never looked so noble. She rested her head upon his chest. So still, so silent. Eleora's gold chain cooled her cheek. The last time she'd touched it, it had been warm and alive.

Her tears watered the stone. "Why didn't you save him?"

She traced Declan's features with her fingertips. "I should've told you long before now, and I hope wherever you are, you can hear me. I love you, Declan. I decided on you. But I was too late."

Planting a soft kiss upon unresponsive lips, she nestled beside him. The cloak covered them both. He'd always shared his warmth. Now she would share hers. Nuzzling his shoulder, she dragged in the scent of him and closed her eyes.

"Um . . . miss?"

A whispered word from Gavan hushed the voice, and Mara was left alone to sleep.

～ ～ ～

Mara woke to rain pattering canvas overhead. Wagon wheels squeaked over uneven terrain. Gavan met her eyes, his own red and weary. Clearing his throat, he pushed a bowl of gruel and a cup of water to her. "Eat, or I toss you out of here."

She glowered at his ultimatum.

He scowled back. "Don't look at me like that. I know you. I've seen all this before, remember? It'll be worse this time because he's not here to handle you. But I'll be damned before I let you scorn his sacrifice."

She pushed herself up, feeling every bruise and scrape. The gruel was tasteless in her mouth, but she ate—not to appease Gavan but to honor the sacrifice.

"We're returning to the city?" she asked.

"Some of us. Most of the army stayed behind to work out a treaty with the Akaronians." Gavan leaned toward her, raising his brow. "They'll also begin reconstruction of Firth."

Mara took it in but didn't respond.

"Aren't you going to ask after that sister you ran off to save?" Gavan asked

She lay beside Declan again. "Loed told me she made it out."

Gavan deflated. "Oh. I'd hoped to give you some good news."

A breeze unburdened the air, carrying with it the scent of rain. Mara bit her trembling lip. "Why did he come? I told him not to. I gave him reasons not to." A tear rolled off her nose.

After a lengthy pause, Gavan said, "Well, there's the obvious—he loved you. More than I think you realize. And your message wasn't the only one we received that day. Zev sent one too. Said he was taking you to Firth under guard and could guarantee your safety only if Declan surrendered himself and the stone at the appointed time. When Lazar received the same message, we realized Zev had orchestrated your abduction to find Eleora." A sharp exhale. "I've never seen Declan so angry.

"We also pieced together your fool game. In the end, the Council agreed to send Declan after you, army in tow. You're mental for thinking you could outplay Zev, by the way."

Mara didn't disagree. If she'd done things Declan's way, he and Zev would still be alive. "Don't you hate me?"

"Not possible," Gavan said. "Besides, it was his choice. One I'm beginning to understand." He blushed.

"Elise wouldn't have anything to do with that, would she?"

A grunt. "The only thing I fault you for is interrupting our courtship. I was making progress."

"Progress? Every time she comes near you, you shut up like a clam. Not that I'm complaining. It's a relief, really."

The toe of his boot dug into her ribs. "You should know—he came for you, but he went for us all. Rivka was a problem only Eleora's equipped to deal with. Action was a matter of timing, so don't hate yourself too much."

Had Declan known what bearing the stone would cost? Had he known what saving her would entail? He'd seemed to. What kind of man loved like that? Why, oh why, had she run?

Gavan yawned. "I can only give you until tomorrow morning. They need to embalm him."

And then he'd smell wrong. Mara breathed him in until she returned to sleep.

A scraping noise. Zev, with Rivka's eyes, held her underwater. She fought his hold and screamed. Water rushed her lungs.

Mara woke upright, gasping. The space around her was dim and still. A ching of metal followed another scrape. A figure sat near her head.

"Nightmare?"

Kenrik.

Scrape. "Boz told us Zev tortured you. I warned you about him."

Mara looked toward the exit, which was covered by a curtain. The faint light of dusk seeped in at the edges. No one could see inside. Not that it mattered. Kenrik was quick, she was hurt, and this was inevitable.

Scrape. "I finally understand why you don't respond to a threat like a normal person. At first, I thought it was because you're a spy." *Scrape.* "Threats are part of the job." *Scrape.* "But that isn't the only reason. You were dead already. And you knew that I"—*scrape*—"unlike Jed or Rivka"—*scrape*—"would kill you quickly.

"You wanted me to do it." *Scrape.* "You hoped I'd save you from the guilt of betraying a man who really loved you. You're counting on me to save you now."

Not even in the raider's camp had Mara felt so undressed. Kenrik saw through fabric, skin, and sinew, all the way to her bare soul.

Scrape. "Beg me to save you," he said. Something heavy thudded onto the planked floor. Her heart beat in a rapid echo. In the rosy dim, she made out the silhouette of a dagger. It trembled in the air.

She had to prevent this. For both their sakes. She whispered his name through shallow breaths. A cautious hand reached for his.

Grabbing her wrist, he snarled in her face. "I said, 'Beg.'"

The knife whooshed down. Wood splintered, and Mara flinched. Kenrik's breath huffed warm on her face. She whispered his name again, louder this time. Kenrik shoved her away and fell against the side of the wagon. She crawled beside him.

Jerking to his feet, he said, "I wouldn't save you anyway. You deserve the hell you're in. But if you want to save yourself, I won't stop you. You have until morning." He leaped out of the wagon.

Mara studied the dagger lodged in the wood. She pulled it out and touched the blade. With a hiss, she drew the finger to her mouth. Blood.

The dagger's sharpness tempted her. Death would be easy now. Selene was safe and doing well without her. Rivka was defeated. Declan gone. With a single swipe, she could lie next to him and die in his arms.

And dishonor him and hurt her friends and waste the gifts the King had given.

The choice was her own, an alluring concept in a world that tossed her like flotsam. But the man lying beside her was a monument to the fact that she was not her own. He'd bought her from Zev in heartache and silver and exchanged his life for hers. To give her real choices. A chance to live. Freedom.

The aroma of gruel woke the beast in her belly. Following her nose, she found a bowl and a pitcher in the corner. Along with the dagger, Kenrik had brought food.

She ate it all and spent the night making plans and telling them to Declan. After his funeral, she'd see about the shelter. When she was certain she wasn't needed, she'd return to Firth, help rebuild, and take back Ramzi's farm. She missed the feeling of dirt in her hands and sweat on her brow. Every storm would remind her of him. She promised to take walks in the rain and find a way to laugh again.

Wiping her eyes, she kissed Eleora. "Tell him for me. In case he didn't hear."

Near dawn, Gavan entered the wagon with a lamp and sat beside her. "It's almost time."

"I know." Mara toyed with the handle of the dagger. The blade glinted in the lamplight.

Gavan tilted his head and snatched it away. His words were careful and slow. "Why do you have my brother's dagger?"

Mara thought hard for a plausible explanation. Gavan frowned at her. His eyes lit on the groove where the blade had pierced the wagon floor. He reached over and retrieved the whetstone. His jaw hardened. "Did he hurt you?"

"No."

"Threaten you?"

Mara clamped her mouth shut.

Gavan swore. "When?"

"Can we do this later?"

His fist pounded the wooden floor. "No, Mara, we can't do this later. What did he say?"

"He won't hurt me. He could have, and he didn't. He brought me food."

"If you won't tell me, I'll beat it out of him," he said, standing.

A light, metallic keening turned him back. Eleora sparked to life, filling the wagon with golden-red light. Mara reached out to touch it, but Gavan snatched back her wrist.

The air shimmered around them. The light grew bolder until its brilliance branded Mara's vision, and all became darkness. "Gavan?"

"I can't see either. We need to get out of here." He led her away from Eleora toward the exit. He climbed out and swung her down clumsily. Feet scuffled. Horses whinnied. Voices gasped and cried out.

The ringing noise faded. Heavy feet plodded up. "Are you all right?" Boz asked.

"If your definition of all right includes blindness," Gavan said, his tone flat.

"What happened?" Kenrik asked.

"I'm not talking to you just now," Gavan said.

"We're fine," Mara said. "Eleora did something—I don't know—strange. We can't see. Someone needs to check on Declan."

Footsteps moved toward the wagon, paused, and skidded back, kicking up gravel. An unnatural stillness fell over the camp. Staccato breaths pierced the heavy air. Mara rubbed her eyes. A degree of darkness lifted. Blinking, she willed them to focus.

White-clad figures stood motionless around her. One walked among them. An orb glowed red at the center of his breast, flickering in and out of sight. Her feet urged her forward. She collided with a body. Placing her hand on a shoulder, she circled around, hit someone else, and fell. Undeterred, she crawled through a tangle of legs until her fingers touched warm skin. Two bare feet, smelling of rain. Her hands grasped ankles and took hold of a trouser hem. White linen. Her pulse quickened, and with a deep breath, she looked up. Eleora glowed above her head, its edges indistinct. A face peered down at her but wouldn't come into focus.

The figure stooped. A hand gripped her elbow and lifted her to her feet. Wind whistled over rock and hill, tossing her hair. Fingers brushed her cheek.

She knew that touch. Her hand covered his. She kissed his palm, tasting the salt of her tears. "I can't see your face."

His lips brushed each eye. "I see you."

The voice was unmistakable, and yet, when he came into focus, she gasped. Perfect, whole, alive—Declan. Her fingers traced brow, nose, and jaw. "How?"

He didn't need to answer. The evidence radiated from his chest.

Mara made herself forget the eyes looking on and latched onto the only ones that mattered. A soft heat simmered in them. "Declan, I—"

He placed a hand at the small of her back and drew her into him. His brow touched hers, lingering there, and sweet, ragged breaths blew warm into her face. Heat welled at her stomach where Eleora pressed against her bodice. There was no need to cling to him in desperation as she had before. He held her. Not even death had come between them.

"I love you." Giving silent thanks to the King for the opportunity to say it, she tilted her face to his and kissed him as he deserved to be kissed, as she should've kissed him that day in Kali's garden. Joy surged from within—bubbling, soaring— but as it began to consume her, she pulled away.

Tender eyes puzzled at her. The crowd converged, pushing them apart. When she lost sight of him, she meandered through jostling bodies and searched for a quiet hill from which she could watch the sun rise.

CHAPTER 27

Cloudless blue sky stretched beyond what Mara's eyes could see. She envied its tranquility. Her spirit swirled with the wind—wild and free but uncertain of its place in the world. Home was an ashy rubble. Her sister hid in some unknown locale. And the man she loved had magicked himself out of death, which made him something unfathomable. The pith of legend.

Gravel crunched beneath a pair of boots. Someone climbed her hill. Declan eased down beside her with a groan. "You have a choice to make," he said, his voice light.

She propped herself on an elbow and studied his profile. His plain features had become dear to her. A kind of home.

He smiled as if he knew what she was thinking. "You can return to the city or go back to Firth with me," he said.

"How long will we stay?" she asked.

His grin broadened. "A while. I need to meet with the Akaronians. Attempt a treaty."

"Why not kill them all and save the time?" Part of her meant it.

He chuckled. "Did Zev ever mention he knew Rivka long before he met you?"

"No."

Declan frowned at the river. "The Akaronians have worshipped her as a god for generations. Her games kept them violent. It was she who encouraged the poor treatment of women."

"Why would she do that when she was a woman?"

"Rivka wasn't a woman," he said. "She appeared as one to appeal to their basest desires. Real women would soften her soldiers. She had to keep them rough and hard, which is easier when men treat women like chattel rather than souls to cherish and protect. Now that she's gone, there's hope for them."

How did he always see hope where there was none? "If you say so."

"There may be skirmishes to put down. And Firth needs reconstruction. I'd like the Akaronians to help rebuild what they destroyed. Offer them some honest work."

"Lofty aspirations," she said.

"I'm not done. I'd also like you to marry me."

Hope where there was none. Hope she'd trampled when she'd left with Zev. A blade of grass absorbed her interest. "You don't want to marry me."

An exasperated growl. "Are we still here? Mara, I love you, and unless I'm gravely mistaken, you love me. The curse hanging over you, keeping us apart—it's gone."

Mara fretted her lip. It had to be said. "I slept with him every night. Did you realize that when you came for me?"

His face was inscrutable.

"And I exchanged sex with a stranger for information about the magic fire and Rivka's plans." She plucked the grass from the soil and watched the wind carry it off. "The sickest part was I told myself I did it for you."

He was quiet a long time. "Did anyone ever teach you what sex should be?"

His question wasn't the response she'd expected. "My aunt told me how babies come into being," she said.

His eyes were speculative. "So all you know, beyond mechanics, you learned from Zev. Correct?"

Hot blood surged from her neck into her cheeks. He tucked a flyaway strand behind her ear. "To you, sex is nothing but lies, drugs, and manipulation. That isn't what it's supposed to be, love."

"What do you know about it?" she asked, incredulous.

"I'll teach you." His eyebrows wriggled. "If you'll be my wife. When you're ready. Which I'm not convinced you are. Hills, you can't even kiss me properly."

Mara couldn't decide whether to feel indignant or mortified.

"Don't look at me like that." He laughed. "The first time, you attacked me. And today you stopped as it was getting good. You're afraid. That's why you ran from me. Not to protect me, not even to save Selene. You left because you're afraid to accept my love for you and enjoy it."

"I don't deserve it." She tossed a stone down the hill.

"Doesn't stop it from being yours." He drew her into his arms. "Love makes what we deserve irrelevant. The right kind, anyway."

She leaned against his chest, contemplating. "Zev's dead. Did Boz tell you?"

"He told me Zev's missing and your uncle's dead. He also told me what happened while you were prisoner." His arms tightened around her. "We have a lot to work through, you and I."

She turned her head to search his face.

"We have to forgive Zev," he said. "And I have to forgive you. All that forgiveness is hard work."

Mara scowled. "I don't want to forgive him, and I don't know why you want to forgive me. Besides, are you sure an ambassador should marry someone like me?"

She drank him in—his warmth, his smell, the strength of his body, the beat of his heart—in case he said no. He kissed her temple. "I'm sure that I love you and that I want you as my wife until the King returns."

The look in his eyes confirmed her suspicions. "You're insane," she said.

He beamed. "Is that a yes?"

She shook her head. "Yes."

His eyes danced a quick rhythm. "Yes?"

"If you're so determined to have me." She laughed at him, and he delivered a sloppy kiss to her cheek.

"Tonight?" he asked.

"Tonight?" That left him no time to change his mind, no time to recover from his wounds. "You know, most men wouldn't want anything to do with me after what I did to you."

"I'm not like any man you've met."

It was true. Most men had never cared at all, much less loved her. Zev had been ill-equipped to love. And while Ben had cared, he hadn't forgiven her for becoming a prostitute. If he had, he would've written. But Declan had loved her before, during, and after. Though she'd pushed him away, fled, and betrayed him. He'd thrown himself into the fire for her and come out again so she wouldn't have to survive a lifelong winter alone. His only agenda had been her wholeness.

"Why not now?" She grinned, teasing him.

"I'd love that. But I still have men who can't see. Others are confused. They need my attention. I have messages to scribe and send to the Council. And I'm waiting for your wedding present to arrive. It'll have to be tonight."

"Wedding present?" A pang shot through her. She had nothing to give him.

Another pair of boots crunched up their hill. Gavan addressed Declan, his expression stormy. "Sorry to interrupt, but we need to talk."

Declan stood, brushing off, and smiled down at her. "Tonight, then."

She shrugged, feigning indifference. "Tonight."

"Tonight what?" Gavan asked, interest relaxing his frown.

"Tonight," Declan said, clapping his friend on the back, "I'll have a wife, and Laeor will have a new ambassador."

Mara gulped. Ambassador?

Mara had no special gown, jewelry, or fragrances, so she settled for a bath in a hot spring a short walk from the camp. Even if their marriage wasn't made official, she wanted to smell nice. She eased jittery limbs into the warm water.

When she had agreed to marry Declan, she'd agreed to him, not an office. Last harvest, her ambitions had been simple—purchase new livestock, yield a better crop, keep Selene alive. She had no idea how to be a wife, much less an ambassador. Her eyes searched the sky. "Are you sure about this?"

She was met with silence, as usual, but silence didn't mean she wasn't heard.

Stares greeted Mara upon her return to camp. What must they think of her— the harlot an ambassador had died to rescue? The crazy woman who'd slept beside his corpse? She searched for Declan. An entire day would pass before she shared his tent, and she couldn't spend it under the kingsmen's scrutiny. She required either an occupation or a place to hide.

As she passed between tents, a tall figure cast her in shadow. "May I speak with you?" Kenrik asked.

Mara glimpsed Declan and Gavan several paces away. They slung sidelong glances in her direction. Returning her attention to Kenrik, she sucked a sharp breath through her teeth. A bruise formed along his jaw. "Did Declan hit you?"

A rueful smile. "Gavan. Will you walk with me?"

His gaze avoided hers. Whatever he had to say would be uncomfortable for them both, but it would be wrong to refuse him the opportunity. She took his arm and attempted to set him at ease. "How did Gavan manage to hit the best swordsman in the King's army?"

He was quiet as he led her away from the tents into the harvest sunshine. She nudged him. "Well?"

"I may be best with a sword, but never underestimate my brother's ability to bash heads with his bare hands," he said.

"With the pair of you for teachers, I should be indestructible. What gives?"

He faced her. "I'm sorry, Mara. It isn't enough, but I am."

"I forgive you." She patted his arm with her free hand and tried to move on.

He remained where he was. "Declan was particular that I not allow you to excuse my behavior."

"He's very bossy, isn't he?"

"Mara—"

"The thing is I understand you," Mara said. "I would've done the same for Selene, without apology. I admire your loyalty."

The toe of his boot sent a stone skittering ahead. They followed. "True loyalty extends to those he loves. That's what he told Sabra, anyway."

"You were never going to kill me."

"Oh?"

She smiled. "Nope. You brought food when you were supposed to end me. This may surprise you, but dead women don't eat."

He had no reply to that.

They rounded the last tent, returning to the bustle of the camp. Mara stopped short and swore. "Zev knew. I told him . . . he paid an assassin to kill you. It'll be someone in the army, I think." Her eyes darted from man to man. "Maybe you should leave for a while."

"I've dealt with assassins before," Kenrik said.

"No. He seemed confident. But maybe now that he's dead . . ."

"You"—he towed her forward—"have more important matters to attend. To begin, Declan has left my fate in your hands."

"What?"

His expression turned grave. "I've been charged with treason against an ambassador of the King. It is left to you to decide my sentence. The usual penalty is death."

Mara blinked at him. "That's ridiculous."

"The penalty is quite standard."

"Not the penalty, the charge."

Her eyes widened as he knelt before her. "I plead guilt and beg mercy," he said.

"Get up." Kenrik didn't move. Panicked, she scanned the camp. Declan wasn't in sight. "This isn't funny," she said.

"It isn't a joke."

"Stand up, or I will sentence you to death."

He obeyed.

"Here's your sentence. Are you ready?"

A solemn nod.

"Never make me do anything like this again. If you don't wallop Declan for this nonsense, I will. And promise to be careful. There's been too much death already."

"That isn't a sentence," he said.

"Fine." She growled. Dust clung to her skirts, and she'd begun to sweat. "Look smart for my wedding so at least one of us will."

Mara stalked away in a huff, worried she might heed temptation and slap the droll expression from Kenrik's face. At the end of the walkway, soldiers erected a trestle table and an arbor of twisted scrub. The aroma of herbs and roasted meat wafted on the breeze. Her stomach rumbled.

As she neared the cook tent, a small traveling party appeared on the road, their horses kicking up dust behind them. Mara shadowed her eyes from the glare of the midday sun. The white-clad rider of the lead horse drew her attention. Mara went still. Dark curls whipped in the wind behind a brown face. Mara's heart bucked and ran wild. Her feet flew.

The rider sighted her and coaxed her horse. Before coming to a proper stop, she leaped from the saddle, agile on her feet, and ran at Mara. Their bodies collided, and they hit the ground, each locked in the arms of the other, sobbing and laughing.

Mara kissed Selene's face, hair, and lips until they were both breathless. Selene had never smelled sweeter nor felt so good to hold. Mara drew back in wonder. Gone was the frail wisp of a girl she'd left last harvest. In her place was a woman, hearty and shapely. More so than herself. Mara noted Selene's bare neck and fastened a lodestone necklace around it.

Selene kissed the stone. "I thought I'd never see this again. How did you—"

"Never mind that. How are you here?"

Selene's eyes swung up to the side. "Why don't you ask him?"

A hand appeared between them and hauled Mara to her feet. "I take it you like your wedding present," Declan said.

Mara threw her arms around his neck and rewarded him with a kiss to rival her joy. A throat cleared behind her. She pulled away, melting into Declan's smiling eyes. "Thank you."

The throat cleared again, louder this time. Mara prepared a fierce scowl for the intruder, which dissolved the instant her eyes lit on his face.

"Ben?"

A lean arm hooked her shoulders and gave her a lax squeeze. Mara wouldn't abide such awkward behavior, not from him. She embraced him and pecked his cheek, which lifted into his signature lopsided grin. His finger swiped the scar on her cheekbone. "Looks better than I thought it would."

"I had a couple of good healers see after me."

Selene wrapped an arm around Ben. "I hope you don't mind me dragging him along."

Ben tendered as he smiled at Selene, who glowed up at him. Mara drew up her jaw and cleared her throat. "Um . . . did Meg come with you?"

Selene shook her head. "Disappeared yesterday morning. Loed's death was a shock, I think." She cocked her head. "Will you introduce us to your friends, or are we expected to invent names for them all?"

Mara presented Boz, Gavan, and Kenrik, but when she turned to Declan, Selene smiled and said, "We've met."

After introductions, Declan pointed to the tent Mara and Selene would share for the day. Inside hung a fresh white gown, trimmed in lace and pearls. Mara fingered the design, lovely in its simplicity, and marveled. Declan had prepared for their wedding before leaving the city. She could get lost in love of that magnitude and never find her way out again.

Selene hugged the fabric. "Thank the King. I would've died before letting you attend your wedding with dirt on your bottom."

A soldier delivered two bowls of gruel. As they ate, Selene explained that Declan's party had met the Firth refugees on the road a few days ago. Declan had identified Selene on sight. He'd arranged for the townsfolk to take refuge at the nearest consulate until he sent word. When the kingswoman on duty saw Selene, she mentioned a brown-skinned girl dressed in men's clothing who had delivered a message for the Council. She repeated the message to Declan, a message he hadn't received, a point which vexed him.

Mara set down her spoon. Had Zev known she'd sent two messages before he'd tortured her?

"All right?" Selene raised a brow.

Mara brushed away the thought. Zev was dead, and she would marry Declan in a few hours. "Fine."

Keen eyes, as brown as her own, considered her. "You've changed."

Mara snorted. "So have you." Her baby sister was gone.

"Not as much as you," Selene said. "You have the look of someone who's stared death in the eye and won. And I can tell you're hurting. Really hurting. So bad that it hurts me. But there's also this light in you I've never seen before. I like it."

Mara wondered if everyone could see into her soul. "It's all your fault, you know," Mara said. "Declan showed me the redemption letter."

A look of innocence. "I have no idea what you're talking about."

"How much did you know about my involvement with Rivka?" Mara asked.

A long sigh. "Enough. I saw everything that happened that night. It was awful watching her kiss you. I might've thought I'd dreamed it all except I caught glimpses of her over the years. And I saw that man's body—the one who tried to steal you all those winters ago. After I had time to think about it, I realized she must've been responsible for you selling yourself somehow."

Mara and Selene discoursed on, recounting their exploits and adventures during their year apart, until Selene remarked on the lateness of the hour and insisted it was time to prepare Mara for her wedding. Mara acquiesced but found it all rather surreal. She'd always imagined the scenario from the opposite role. Selene combed and pinned Mara's hair away from her face and fashioned it with a garland of buttercream daisies.

Mara fingered the petals. "It's beautiful."

"I learned from the best," Selene said, stepping back to admire her work. "Who will you ask to give you away?"

Mara brooded while Selene massaged rose oil into her skin. "No one."

"Rebel," Selene said with a teasing smile. She helped Mara into her gown. "All right, then. What token will you give him?"

Mara looked at Selene in horror. What else had she not thought of?

"Why don't you give him your necklace?" Selene suggested.

"What? No. The necklaces are ours."

"I think it's right for him to have it. It's your most treasured possession and a real piece of yourself." Selene embraced Mara from behind. "I'll see if they're ready for you."

Mara hadn't noticed the fading light until now. Night would soon be upon them. It was almost time to marry Declan.

Ben passed Selene on her way out, and Mara didn't miss the look he gave her. He sidled up to Mara and looked her over with a smile that didn't quite reach his eyes. "I always knew you'd make a stunning queen."

"Too bad I forgot my cornhusks," Mara said.

Ben snorted.

"You do know I'm not a queen, right?"

"That's a matter of perspective," he said and sighed. "I'm sorry I wasn't the friend you needed."

His look of misery was more than Mara could take. He'd done all she'd asked and more. Maybe too much. "You were exactly the friend I needed. But I'll be honest—" She gripped his wrist and twisted his arm. "I can't decide whether or not to pummel you for the way you look at my baby sister."

"Hills, Mara!"

Her lips pursed and brow lifted.

"I love her, all right? Are you happy?" Beads of sweat shimmered on his brow.

Mara let him go.

Ben rubbed his shoulder and glared. "She isn't a baby anymore, in case you haven't noticed. I plan to marry her, and soon, whether you like it or not."

A grin spread across Mara's face. "I like it fine. But you need to wait."

His jaw dropped. "Really?"

"Really. You're homeless, dimwit."

"No." His fingers raked through his hair, a perplexed expression on his face. "I mean—it doesn't bother you?"

"Only the way a third arm would bother me. I'm not used to the idea, that's all."

The Ben she knew returned to her then. The reserve in his smile dissipated, and conversation flowed with ease. They were both laughing when Selene returned a short while later with a small bouquet of wildflowers and shooed Ben out.

Mara ignored the extended flowers. "Are you in love with Ben?"

Selene sputtered.

"Are you?" Mara pressed.

"Yes," Selene said. "It felt wrong at first. I'd always thought you would marry him. But after I realized you were in love with someone else, I didn't think it would matter. I should've told you in one of my letters. I'm sorry."

Motherly warmth surged from Mara's belly and blossomed into a smile. "I'm thrilled. Ben's a good man. He doesn't deserve you, but you could do much worse."

Selene threw her arms around Mara and swayed from side to side. "It's strange, feeling this happy. I'm afraid something will happen, and we'll lose it."

Mara squeezed her. "So let's enjoy it for what it is. For as long as it lasts."

"Let's," Selene said. "They're ready. Are you?"

Mara took a deep breath and grasped the bouquet, grateful for something to occupy her hands. "Yes."

Selene beamed. "Follow me."

His eyes. Sweet hills, his eyes. The moment they secured hers, she forgot all trepidation. Their light faded all her wrongs, enclosed all she was inside of him.

Mara stood at the center of a crescent of witnesses, Selene at one elbow, Gavan at the other. Declan waited at the arbor with Kenrik by his side. Too tall to fit beneath, Boz loomed behind the intertwined branches, his broad white grin gleaming in the low light. Declan's image swirled.

A hand steadied her, and Gavan leaned into her ear. His chuckle sounded far away. "Deep breaths. If you faint, I won't let you forget it."

His taunts couldn't distract her tonight.

Boz's voice was as smooth and rich as velvet, but Mara couldn't make sense of his words.

A long silence. An elbow prodded her ribs. Selene cleared her throat. Mara startled out of her daze and stepped forward. "I give myself." She hoped she'd said the right thing.

His smile. She'd fallen in love with the smile before she'd fallen in love with the man. His hand beckoned and brought her near. She'd follow him anywhere. The tears in his eyes shimmered in the torchlight. Seas and sky—his eyes.

The vows frustrated her. The words weren't strong enough. Death hadn't severed them. What good was it to swear to a beatable end? "Into eternity," she modified.

"Into eternity," he said, matching her oath.

Declan took Eleora and draped it around her neck. Her fingertips caressed the stone. She questioned him with a look, which he answered with a smile. And now it seemed the lodestone wasn't enough. She unfastened it.

He breathed her name. "Are you sure?"

Her voice couldn't be trusted, so she touched her lips to his. Selene was right. He should have the necklace.

Declan sealed their vows with a kiss Mara felt all the way to her toes, which curled in her slippers. Her heart dove from a precipice and spread its wings in flight. She wished they were alone. She never wanted it to end. He withdrew, her sentiment mirrored in his own expression, and presented her to the smiling witnesses.

Selene laughed as she cried. Gavan swiped his face. All applauded.

Mara then pledged herself to the King, becoming a kingswoman and ambassador in her own right. In turn, the gathered soldiers pledged themselves to her and she to them. Pride shone from Selene's face as she knelt at Mara's feet. Boz and Kenrik spoke their vows with dignified solemnity. Gavan struggled not to laugh at Mara's discomfort, which made her less comfortable, which made him laugh all the more. When he finished, he leaped to his feet and caught her in a tight squeeze.

Declan led Mara to a table trimmed with white linens, flowers, and candles, where they were joined by Selene, Ben, Gavan, Kenrik, and Boz. Roasted meat and vegetables adorned two large platters. Mara's mouth watered at the smell, but she was too distracted to eat more than a few bites.

Everyone in their party told a story. Ben boasted of his uncanny foresight in having voted Mara queen at the previous harvest festival for, as he said, she was as good as one now. Selene mentioned the letter by which she deduced Mara's affection for Declan. Declan laughed when he learned the great clue was Mara's description of him as "irksome." Gavan gibed Declan for falling for the most difficult woman he'd ever met—a woman who couldn't even cook, for hills' sake—and both Declan and Mara kicked him underneath the table.

Kenrik cleared his throat. "I never understood how grand a thing it is for an ambassador to be a healer until I witnessed the effect Declan had on Mara. She came to us sick and hurt. She's been through things I can't bring myself to think about, and look at her. She's radiant." He raised his cup to Declan. "I can't help but be awed by the King's wisdom and your skill, my friend."

Kenrik and Mara exchanged gentle smiles as Boz began to speak. He told everyone what had transpired in the raider camp. Mara recoiled from the memories, wondering at his point and wishing him to stop, but he held everyone rapt. "And then, in the presence of her worst enemies and best friend, knowing it would cost her life, she said, 'I'd rather beg crumbs beneath Declan's table than be queen of your court.'"

He'd uttered the moment of betrayal, her greatest shame. She cringed, but Boz looked at her with pride, not condemnation. "My dear Mara, it warms my heart to see you feasting at your beloved's table."

The table fell silent.

"Mara," Selene said. "I had no idea you were so romantic."

Mara's mouth flattened as Ben and Gavan wheezed in suppressed laughter. She turned to Declan. "Can we leave?"

Tender eyes twinkled at her in the torchlight. To Kenrik, he said, "No one disturbs us unless we're attacked."

Mara avoided Gavan's face for every silver she was worth and regretted sneaking a glance at Selene, whose dimples were craters. Blood rushed into her ears. Not long ago, she'd led men to her chamber every night in view of a crowd. Without any feeling at all. What was wrong with her?

Maybe things are as they should be. The thought came quieter than a whisper.

Taking her hand, Declan led her to their tent, which wasn't far. A lamp glowed inside, revealing two bedrolls laid side by side. Her stomach fluttered. His brow touched hers. An airy laugh warmed her face. "Breathe, Mara."

She exhaled and trembled.

"Relax, love. We can sleep if you like."

Temptation to resort to habit was strong. Seduce and seize control. Take what's needed. Give nothing away. She burrowed her face in his shoulder. "I don't know how to do this."

Drawing back, he studied her. "If you need more time—"

"I need you."

Gentle fingers removed and the garland from her hair. Loosening the pins, he ran his fingers through her thick locks and kissed her mouth, tender and slow. A measure of tension melted from her shoulders. His hands, cautious at first, explored the curve of her hips. His breath shook.

Somehow, his hesitation put her at ease. Her hands slipped beneath his tunic and wandered over his chest. Smiling against her mouth, he tugged it off. Her palms traced the outline of his shoulders, broad and capable. Strong enough to handle anything. Strong enough to handle her.

His lips caressed the skin beneath her ear. "Turn around," he whispered.

A hundred beating wings flurried inside her chest as he swept her hair over a shoulder and kissed the nape of her neck. He touched the chain of Eleora but left it clasped. "It may help," he said, his fingers fumbling the buttons of her gown.

The hair on her skin rose when the chemise fell away, but not from cold. Never before had a man looked at her like he did. Lingering, taking pleasure in what he saw, in spite of every wrong her body had done. His gaze of awe and desire warmed her all over. She stared back at him until he spoke her thought aloud. "Beautiful."

Eyes bright, he swept her up and carried her to their bed. As she lay in his arms, her soul awoke to lifelong drought, but unlike others, he didn't leave her thirsty. He matched her desperation, allowed himself to be affected. Spoken adorations and tender caresses watered her until she cried in relief. The shell that had long shielded her heart cracked, opening to all he gave, and when she had drunk her fill, the excess gave her something to return. He smiled into her face, whispered encouragement, and let her love him as she pleased.

∾∾∾

Her fingers curled around his neck and wove into his hair. She bathed in his admiration. A pleasant heat radiated from her middle, luring her to sleep. But sleep was a thief, and she wouldn't relinquish a moment of this night if she could help it. "Why did Lazar have Eleora the day I was summoned to the wall?"

His expression settled somewhere between startled and amused.

"I heard the servants talking," she said.

A hand cupped her cheek. "Do you mean to say that you believed Lazar had Eleora when Rivka questioned you, and you lied to her—even after she threatened Selene?"

"Well, yes. But—"

For a time, she forgot everything but the taste of his kiss.

"So?" she asked.

"As I said before, Eleora goes where it wishes. For the last few years, it has mostly stayed with me, but Lazar required it for a specific purpose. He returned it when he learned you were missing. To help us find you." He pulled her tighter and then relaxed. Deep, even breaths.

"I thought Zev told you where to find me."

"He did. But Eleora led us to Zev."

Mara pondered the revelation until she realized Declan was too quiet. "A wind spirit came to me the other night," she said.

His eyelids lifted in interest.

"It brought a message from the King. And it kissed me."

"I knew something had changed. Tell me about this kiss."

She tried but wasn't satisfied with her recount. Language often fell short where it concerned the King.

His eyes closed, mouth curved. "I've always known you were special."

"What did Rivka mean when she said I was sealed? Was it the kiss?"

He grinned. "Surprised her, did it?"

"Tell me."

"Is that what all her screaming was about? I assumed you were being ornery," he said.

She poked his ribs.

"It happened the day we met," he said. "You were unconscious. I was working, and Eleora came alive. I placed it over your heart. That seemed to be what it wanted. And it gave this little leap. Like it had found something that was lost. It doesn't always happen like that, but as I said, you're special."

"Is that why you were kind to me?"

A finger stroked her scar. "I was kind to you because I'm kind and because the King is kind. But you definitely intrigued me."

She began to drift and started. "Where do you sleep?"

The answer came soft and listless. "Wherever I am when I need to sleep."

"Where will we sleep?" she asked, surprised the question hadn't occurred to her before.

A puff of air blew from his nose. "Does it matter when you resist it so?"

"Do you have a home?"

"Mmhmm."

"Where?"

"Would it bother you if I told you I live in the palace?" He looked at her.

She blinked. "Not as long as I'm allowed to live there too." Living in the palace meant living next to the sea. Maybe she could claim a piece of earth in one of its vast gardens.

"I'm certain the Council will consider it," he said. "You seem to have a way with them."

His mouth found hers, and she sighed, smiling. "Again."

A sleepy laugh rumbled his chest. "We have a long day of travel ahead. We should rest."

"We rested almost two days in the wagon. I'm tired of rest." How could she make him understand? He was rest. She hadn't known it could be like this. Joyful. Freeing. As filling as it was emptying.

A kiss upon her shoulder. "Sleep, love. I won't leave you. I'll be here while you sleep. I'll be here when you wake. I'll be here tomorrow, the next day, and the day after that. You're my wife, and I'm your husband."

Not father, not patron, not lover. Husband.

Mara surrendered to the soundest sleep she'd ever known.

CHAPTER 28

A horse whinnied. Metal jingled. Boots shuffled outside the tent. Wind rustled the flap, and murmurs seeped inside. The world was still dark. Something felt wrong, but an earthy scent and the steady kiss of warm breath comforted her.

Mara touched Declan's face and whispered his name.

"Mmm?"

"There's a lot of movement outside," she said.

He was so still, she thought he'd fallen back to sleep. A sharp voice carried over the noise. When he reached for his clothes, she did the same.

"You don't have to come, love. Sleep."

She fired a pointed look. He grinned and pulled a plain gown from the trunk. Awe struck her again as she dressed. He'd prepared—not only to save her wretched life but to give her a better one. With him. He adjusted Eleora around her neck, tidied her hair with his fingers, and kissed her mouth.

Gavan met them at the flap, careful to avoid looking inside. "Glad you're up." And he sounded it.

Mara fought a smile.

"Messenger from the city. Says it's urgent," Gavan said.

Gavan led them to a tent where Boz, Kenrik, and several others waited. A large map of the city sprawled over the table the men surrounded. Each bowed his head at Declan and Mara as they entered. Uncertain of how to proceed, Mara observed

Declan. She bowed when he did and took the indicated seat along the wall. The messenger's eyes darted from Declan to her to Eleora. He muttered congratulations and an apology for disturbing them on their wedding night before launching into his tale.

A man, with the help of several kingsmen, had taken the palace the morning before, captured most of the Council, and ordered the city gates to be closed. He'd also commanded the navy to engage the mist outside the harbor. The man, identified as Zev of the Ring, wore a gemstone necklace and had pronounced himself king.

The blood drained from Mara's face.

The kingsmen in Rahm-Or were divided. Many supported the imposter. The gates would be closed by now, but the naval captains wouldn't be easily persuaded to follow Zev's orders. Most of them were loyal to the true King of Laeor. The city was under martial law. Unknown officers had been awarded increases in rank while seasoned commanders had been removed.

Mara felt sick. How had Zev survived? How had he reached the city so quickly? And what did he hope to achieve? Mara heard her name and looked up. Every face stared back.

Declan stroked his jaw. "What are your thoughts?"

"I'm sure Boz knows more than I do," she said.

Boz cleared his throat. "Zev didn't confide in me as he did in you. I learned of his plans as they happened."

Mara dragged in a deep breath and focused on Declan. "The new officers will be Zev's men, of course. You know as well as I do that a number of kingsmen are employed by the Ring. I don't know why he commanded the attack of his own fleet—unless he intends to destroy the navy, which seems plausible though wasteful. I don't know his intentions for the Razans once they reach land, but the amount of magic fire they carry could raze the city.

"As for his motivations, I can't guess. Until a few days ago, I thought Zev only wanted revenge against his father and maybe the Akaronian throne."

Questions fired in a muddle, but Declan didn't seem to hear them. A thought nagged her. "Do you think this is personal somehow? He might know you're alive."

"Possibly," Declan said. "Regardless, I feel it personally. He threatens my friends and my people. Why?"

"I wouldn't have expected this move from him. Not with Rivka gone. Left to himself, he never would've sought the throne. Taking Rahm-Or was her idea. I'm sure of it."

Kneeling, he gave her a rueful smile. "But he wasn't left alone, and he's been planning and preparing a long time. All the pieces were in already place. His actions are logical, though they sadden me. I'd hoped—"

"To save him." And now he couldn't. Zev had committed high treason.

"Yes."

Looking past Declan at the arguing men, Mara caught a flash of light on metal The messenger faded behind the crowd, eyes fixated on—"Kenrik!"

Before his name died on her lips, the men fell into a thrashing heap. She tensed to spring into the fray, but a firm grip pulled her down. Declan curled over her, blinding her from the action. The noise of the scuffle faded into the rush of blood in her ears.

Kenrik choked Declan's name. Three bodies lay on the ground—the messenger, dead; a kingsman Mara didn't know, wounded; and Boz, a pool of blood darkening the earth beneath him.

Declan ran to his side, whipping off his tunic. He pressed the white cloth against the wound, which soaked red within a few breaths. Mara stared, her horror increasing with the outflow.

"Mara." Declan's voice was calm. "Can you come?"

Numb, she moved to Boz's side and looked to Declan for instruction.

"Can you place Eleora on his chest?"

Chagrined she hadn't thought of it sooner, she yanked it off and set it over Boz's heart. Her tears splattered onto his face as she bent to kiss his smooth cheek.

"There, there, Miss Mara," Boz said.

Time lost meaning. She begged Eleora to spare him. When she opened her eyes, dawn had broken. Boz's chest was still, his eyes empty.

"No." She clutched Eleora and pressed it into his chest. Nothing happened. She pressed harder and sought Declan, who was curled over in grief.

"Nothing more can be done," Kenrik told her.

She turned to him, disbelieving. A red stain at his side distracted her. "You're wounded."

"It isn't bad," Kenrik said.

Declan was beside him in an instant. Removing Kenrik's tunic, he addressed Gavan. "Please take Mara to her sister's tent. Help her to explain the situation, and bring them something to eat."

Gavan helped Mara up, but when she stood, she found herself supporting him more than he supported her.

Boz had always seemed as enduring as a mountain. How could he be gone? With a final glance at his body, she trudged out of the tent, a white-lipped Gavan hanging on her arm. She prayed for one more miracle.

The miracle didn't come. Declan found Mara and Selene on the hill where he'd proposed the day before. Eleora dangled from his hand. Mara urged him to keep it with Boz. He sat behind her and placed it around her neck.

She stared at the stone. "Why didn't it save him?"

His arms wound around her. He rested his chin on her shoulder. "Eleora is an extension of the King. I don't understand why one lives and another dies, but I know enough of him to trust it all leads somewhere good. Maybe not today. Maybe not tomorrow. But someday."

His answer may have irked her had her shoulder not been soaked by his tears. Death was evil, no matter where it led, and there had been so much of it.

Plans had changed. They would camp another night where they were. Declan needed to communicate with the commander of the northern troops without moving away from Rahm-Or. Another messenger had arrived confirming the closing of the city gates. He hadn't been able to corroborate the rest of the earlier message, but Declan refused to dismiss it despite the treachery.

It seemed the first messenger had been paid by a captain in their company to help him murder Kenrik during the meeting. With both men dead, there was no way to be certain of the full story, but a soldier had witnessed a coin exchange between the two. Though Boz had protected Kenrik and killed both men, the victory had cost his life. They would honor him with a brief ceremony at sunset after Declan and his men devised a course of action.

Mara watched Declan retreat, his shoulders sagging, helpless to help him. Helpless to help Boz or even herself. She raged at the wind, at the stone in her hand.

How could you allow this to happen? You could've saved him. Why didn't you? Again, there was no answer.

Declan and Mara left the ceremony and returned to their tent, their hearts as heavy as they were light the night before. Mara debated whether or not to voice a concern that had troubled her throughout the afternoon. But he was so weary. It could wait.

Declan sat hard upon the trunk, buried his face in his hands, and wept. Mara inventoried all she knew of comfort, but her knowledge didn't extend far beyond the man in front of her. His nearness was comfort.

Climbing into his lap, she pressed Eleora to his heart and fastened her arms around him to keep the stone in place. His sobs ebbed. She kissed his shoulder, his neck, his face, tasting his tears. She liked for him to pet her hair. She ran her fingers through his. After a time, her touch took effect, and his mouth sought hers.

So she learned she had something to give him, something no one else could give. And in the giving, a few shards of her shattered dignity were reclaimed. Something she'd known only as a drug became medicine, and with it, they healed each other.

Mara frowned as she combed her hair. "Zev sent the messenger to us. He knows you're alive and wants you to know what he's doing. I don't know his motive, but he's baiting you."

"You think this is about me?" Declan asked.

"He'll take the kingdom if he can, but he wants something from you."

"You seem certain," he said.

The comb caught in a tangle, which she used as an excuse to avoid his eyes. "Zev not only enjoys control. He likes his targets to know he has it."

His mouth turned down. "I could kill him for hurting you."

"But you won't." A truth both comforting and infuriating.

"You're so confident in my benevolence."

"You enjoy mercy like Zev enjoys power," she said. "Given the choice, you'd save him."

He didn't disagree.

When she'd made herself presentable, he led her to the tent where he and his captains would finalize their strategies. Stationed between Gavan and Declan, Mara inspected each face. Most of the men Mara didn't know had been at the meeting the morning before. The ones who hadn't, Declan trusted. She tried to trust with him.

Selene and Ben joined them. Their rosebud cheeks and gemstone eyes were a visible reminder of good in a world gone wrong. They comforted Mara, in spite of her gray mood, as did Declan when she caught his fond smile. The absence of Boz filled the tent, but the city couldn't wait on their grief. Life carried on, even when she wished it wouldn't.

Declan spread a map over the table. Mara squinted, trying to decipher what it represented. The perimeter was shaped like the city, but instead of streets, canals, bridges, and buildings, it featured crisscrossed lines and color-coded points.

Declan glanced around the table. "Some of you know this, but beneath the city lies a network of tunnels, which access various streets and alleys." He pointed to several red dots. "These"—he pointed to a smattering of gold dots—"access the palace, while these"—he pointed to blue dots—"access key locations in King's Quarter.

"There's an entrance to the tunnels a fair distance from the wall, which we'll take under cover of night. A contingent of our brothers to the north will join us. They're on their way to us now. We'll make our way to this abandoned warehouse in the Quarter." He tapped the map. "It holds a food store that will last us a few days while we assess the situation, rally the loyal kingsmen, and cause the most troublesome of Zev's officers to disappear. If our brothers at sea maintain the harbor, we should be able to take the city with a few surprise strikes. The wall may be a different matter, depending on how many men are on the Ring's payroll."

One of the captains cleared his throat. "Shouldn't the northern troops march on the city to back us?"

"No," Declan said. "The Akaronians must be dealt with. If we abandon them, we'll have a bigger mess on our hands. We've called troops from the plains."

"Gathering cold troops will take much valuable time," someone said.

Mara listened to questions and concerns until her eyes glazed. Declan began outlining specific strategies on another map. How had she come to sit in a war council? And what kept her from running as far from Zev as possible and home to her farm? Was the farm still home? She studied the man beside her, who poked the map and captivated his men.

Home was where Declan was. Whether that be a tent, a farm, a palace or a battle zone. He had changed her. He'd given her freedom, family, and a new identity. The orphaned farm girl was gone. In her place was a woman who no longer waited for things to happen but who happened to things. She would never deserve him or what he'd given her, but not once had she doubted she belonged in this meeting, despite having little to contribute. She acted as an ambassador because she was an ambassador. As such, her inadequacies were irrelevant.

Ideas blossomed in her mind. She reached for several pieces of blank parchment and a quill. She felt Declan's gaze light on her but couldn't spare time to meet it. Her mind wasn't a tight enough sieve to catch every falling thought.

Salvation came through ink and a good quill. The feather danced a furious waltz into the afternoon. She stopped for neither food nor relief. Thirst was an unavoidable nuisance. A frustrated sigh escaped her lips each time she reached for her goblet. Nothing distracted her until she heard her name. Snickers whispered all around.

Her head snapped up. Declan, Selene, Ben, and Gavan all stared in amusement. Everyone else had gone. Declan peered at her scribble. "What has you so entranced, love?"

She scowled at the interruption, sliding the papers closer to her body. "Do you need something?"

Gavan swiped the pages, save one. He side-stepped out of his chair and moved out of range of her swinging arms. "A coronation ceremony. For all women and girls at the recovery shelter. Goal: To alter perceived identities from prostitutes to daughters of the King. Program: Read redemption letters. Stories of the King. Individual coronations. Refreshments. Supplies: Thirty-six flower garlands, new gowns . . ." He rifled through the pages. "Plans, more plans, a speech." Gavan raised a mocking brow. "So while we were slaving over battle strategies, you were planning a party?"

Mara crossed her arms. "It's battle strategy. Just different from yours. I can't save the city, but I can help a few women the way I've been helped."

"What a neat idea," Selene said, peering over Gavan's shoulder. "I want to help."

Ben's grin faltered.

Mara shifted cautious eyes to Declan and lost herself in the warmth of his gaze. In her peripheral vision, Gavan sidled toward the piece of parchment he missed. She pounced, protecting it with her body. "This one's personal."

"Let her be, Gavan," Declan said and turned back to Mara. "About the women you'd like to help—will you organize a team to clear the brothels? I don't want them to become barter tokens once the strikes begin. I won't be free to make compromises."

"The more princesses to coronate, the better," she said.

Declan turned to Ben and Selene. "Will you join us?"

Selene squirmed, her eyes darting up to Ben's face. "We need to talk it over."

Mara watched them leave, Gavan trailing behind. "I remember when she talked things over with me. It's strange not to be needed."

Declan kissed her ear as she stacked her work. "If Selene indicates anything at all about your mothering skills, our children will be delightful."

Her head whipped to him. "You want children? With me?"

Humor sparkled in his eyes as he cocked his head in mock inspection. "You are the woman I married, are you not?" He pulled at her collar and peeked down her bodice. "Yes." He kissed her agape mouth and moaned. "Definitely the woman I married. Ten seems a good number."

"Ten? Have you forgotten my temperament?"

He set her upon the table, drawing her legs around him. "You're perfect for ten children. Clever, adaptable, devoted, tireless, strong willed. Of course, we'll have to employ someone to teach them to cook."

Draping her arms around his neck, she threatened him with a glare. "I wonder if our children will be as sassy as their father."

"No, love. They'll be far worse." His brows teased her. "For you will be their mother."

Laughing, he muffled her retort until she could no longer pretend to be angry.

CHAPTER 29

Mara's knees gave way at the fervor of Declan's kiss. Her fingers twisted into the fabric of his tunic. A throat cleared. "Turn around, if it bothers you," she said to Gavan.

Torchlight flickered across Gavan's flat stare. His boot tapped the stone floor, echoing off the tunnel walls. The noise rolled down each section of the crossway, loosening dust from weathered crevices. Selene sneezed again and swore.

Mara raised a brow. "Language."

"Because you're so careful with yours," Selene said with a roll of her eyes. Growling in irritation, she dug a finger in each ear and scratched.

"Are you certain you won't take Eleora?" Mara asked Declan.

Declan fumbled through his pockets. "Yes. It's yours until Eleora must go elsewhere, at which point I'll have to give you another wedding token, I suppose. Here it is." He handed a handkerchief to Selene.

His gift reminded Mara of her own. From her pouch, she extracted a roll of parchment and a small bundle wrapped in a handkerchief. She offered the parchment first. "This is a note for Zev. Should you meet him and decide to spare his life, I'd like you to give it to him. If you feel inclined. Once you've read it."

She gathered her courage as he tucked it away, aware that Gavan watched every move with a ready taunt. She'd intended to give Declan the handkerchief earlier, but the rush of the past few days had driven it from her mind. "This is my wedding gift to you."

His fingers unwrapped the soft, palm-sized bundle. "Dirt?"

Gavan sniggered.

Mara focused on Declan. "I've never told you what you smell like to me." She held a pinch to his nose, rubbing it between her fingertips. With a deep breath, she tried to temper the frenetic beat of her heart. "Earth after rain. It's my favorite smell in the world—like a beacon calling me home to you. But it's more than that. Your smell is what you are to me.

"When you first met me, you saw past everything—my bad decisions, my moods. You saw potential. Which is what I see when I look at a seed. And you planted me." Her hand rested over his heart. "You watered and sunned me until I burst open. You brought me to life."

His hand closed around the handkerchief, and he drew her into his arms. His lips caressed her ear. "I'll come as soon as our spies report. I'm going to make love to you in the garden between the fruit trees we planted."

A wave of heat washed over her. "Don't be long."

Answering with a springtide smile and a final kiss, he spun on his heel and jogged to catch up with his men.

"You know," Gavan said, "I remember a time, not so long ago, when guarding you wasn't gross. I miss those days." He heaved a nostalgic sigh.

Mara watched Declan's white uniform fade into the darkness.

Gavan sniffed. "Of course, few things are as romantic as the gift of dirt."

She glanced at Kenrik. "How much farther?"

Kenrik squinted at the map.

Gavan elbowed her ribs. "And wow. You smell like dirt. Now that's a line. Have you been taking lessons from Kenrik?"

Kenrik frowned. "Stop moving the torch."

"It's a fair question considering your success with women. I mean, look at you. Tall, handsome, a vision in white. And yet tragically bereft of my charm and romantic know-how."

Mara snorted.

Kenrik whacked the side of his brother's head. "We're almost there."

"Thank the King," Selene said through a stuffy nose.

Congestion had troubled Selene since parting ways with Ben. The handkerchief she held now was the third Declan had given her. Selene hadn't been willing to give up Mara so soon, and Ben had needed to return to Hedya and the townsfolk who might require his services. He'd encouraged Selene to accompany Mara to the city, but not before admonishing her to keep as far from danger as possible. Mara had mocked the idea of Selene near danger. If Declan wouldn't allow her to go with the rescue team to the brothels, she certainly wouldn't allow Selene.

Without the company of kingsmen, the tunnels seemed larger and darker. The echoes of their footsteps and even Gavan's wisecracks rang ominous. Mara missed Declan already and also Boz's hulking figure and gentle way. Judging the droop of Gavan's shoulders between jokes, she suspected he did too.

Mara collided with Kenrik's back. Before she could mutter an apology, he said, "This is it," and pounded the metal covering with the hilt of his sword.

No answer. He knocked again.

"They're sleeping well tonight," Gavan said and handed the torch to Selene.

Kenrik knelt, and Gavan climbed onto his shoulders. Kenrik lifted his brother's solid figure with a loud grunt, a sound Gavan reiterated as he pushed against the metal covering. With a loud scrape, dust spilled from above. Mara rubbed Selene's back as she recovered from a giant sneeze.

"Almost out, Selene." Gavan caught a bit of falling dust and wiped his hands. Grinning, he grabbed the lip of the opening and disappeared.

After a few bumps, light glowed from above. Kenrik called for Mara and lifted her into a dank, unfamiliar room with a low ceiling. In the corner, she spotted a stair, which led to a trapdoor.

The trapdoor opened. Mara smiled, expecting Kali. A masculine figure lunged and shoved her aside, slamming her shoulder into the wall. Gavan spun, unsheathing his sword in time to meet the man's blade. Gavan fought well in the tight-footed space until two more figures dropped into the room.

Mara screamed a warning to Kenrik and Selene, which distracted the men long enough for Kenrik to climb through the hole on the opposite side. The scuffle turned into a precarious dance. The men closed in, herding her friends toward the hole, but Gavan and Kenrik pushed them back.

A cold blade pressed against Mara's neck. She gasped, and sharp metal bit into the delicate skin. "Enough." Mara recognized the voice of Arc, one of Zev's henchmen.

Gavan and Kenrik froze, assessing.

"Throw down your swords, or I slit her throat." When they hesitated, a harsh laugh blew on Mara's cheek. She cringed. Blood dripped, tickling all the way to her neckline. "Or keep them, and give me an excuse to kill the bitch."

The swords clattered onto the stone floor. One of the men collected them. Arc said, "Let's all go upstairs to chat. I don't like it down here. Donal, bind 'em. If you boys give us any trouble, the girl dies."

Mara scowled into the dark hole, worried for Selene but relieved she hadn't come up. Kenrik hadn't brought the map, which was hopeful. Maybe Selene would find her way to Declan. If the torch didn't burn out.

Arc held Mara in place until everyone had gone upstairs and then prodded her with the knife. "You're like an unlucky copper. Turning up when I thought I was rid of you."

They surfaced in Kali's bedroom. A lamp and vase lay shattered on the floor. Browned blood stained the planks. "Where's Kali?" she asked.

"Not here," Arc said and pushed her ahead of him into the sitting room and onto the couch. The others tied Kenrik and Gavan to a pair of wooden chairs across from her. The arrangement unsettled Mara, and she didn't like the dark look that passed between the brothers.

"Let's chat." Arc slouched at her left, resting an ankle on his knee. Donal loomed over her right shoulder.

Mara fought a shudder. "Shall I make tea?"

One arm draped across her shoulders as his free hand played with his knife. She recoiled. His smile mocked. "Maybe in a moment. I'd like to play a game first," he said.

Torture. Mara had experienced a lifespan's worth of sadistic games in the previous weeks and was sick of them, but she had no idea how to avoid playing. Her protectors were bound, and Arc's blade moved like an extension of his arm. It would be impossible to pry from his grasp. But even a plan doomed to fail was worth a try.

Mara sprang to her feet, drawing Kenrik's wary eye. "I'll tell you everything you want to know when I've had a cup of tea and something to eat."

As she stepped toward the kitchen, Donal pushed her back onto the couch. Eleora swung at her neck. Arc leaned forward, transfixed. "Is this—"

His fingers brushed the stone. He snatched them back as if they'd been burned. It wasn't much of an opening, but it would be the only one she would get. Mara dove for the knife, landing on the floor. With a quick roll, she escaped Arc's pounce. Knife in hand, she slashed the legs of another assailant and crawled frantically toward Kenrik. The knife hadn't sliced all the way through the ropes when she was yanked back by her ankle.

Twisting, she kicked as hard as she could. Her boot connected with a jaw. Arc grunted. By the look of him, he meant to kill her, but she wouldn't make it easy. She slid the knife toward Kenrik. As Arc wrestled her down, the heel of her palm slammed into his nose, which gained her enough leverage to deliver a knee to the groin. Arc released her, groaning. Another attacked, receiving an elbow to the face and thumbs in his eyes. Only Donal was left. Dread flooded her lungs as she remembered his strength.

Free the boys, and let them take care of him.

She scanned the floor for the blade. A flash of movement. A boot slammed into her ribcage. Tears sprang to her eyes. She'd forgotten the man whose leg she'd slashed. Stunned by pain, she couldn't crawl away. Her nails sank into his wound. A scream. Cursing, he hit the floor beside her. A hand closed over her throat.

She scratched and kicked, but his hold didn't give. Long arms kept his furious eyes safe from her claws, eyes that began to blur. A large boot smashed into his head, reshaping his face, and air rushed her lungs. The man collapsed on top of her, heavy and limp. Too weak to push him off, she coughed and panted, tasting sweat and blood on the sticky air. Metal clashed in her ears.

The noise stopped. The body slid off, and she blinked into Kenrik's concerned face. "Are you hurt?"

She shook her head, but as he pulled her up, she hissed, clutching her side. She waved him away. "It's not bad."

After Gavan bound the men still breathing, Kenrik told him to check her over and dashed to Kali's bedroom. Gavan cleaned the cuts on her neck with a frown, but a wide grin broke across his features as his fingers inspected her ribcage.

"What?" she asked.

He shook his head, laughing. "You. The way you fight."

She winced at his touch.

"Probably a cracked rib or two. Kenrik'll make you a poultice. I'm as good at poultice making as you are cooking." He challenged her glower with a rare serious expression. "For once, I'm not mocking you. If I hadn't been scared spitless, I would've cheered you on. You're so scrappy. Why haven't you ever fought me like that?"

"You've never made an earnest attempt on my life," Mara said, somewhat appeased.

Mischief danced in his eyes. "Hmm . . ."

Remembering Declan's parting promise, she smiled. "And I really wanted to survive."

"Taking on four armed men by yourself without a weapon isn't often conducive to survival, but I'd say you did well considering."

"I have good teachers." She rubbed her throbbing shoulder.

"We taught you to defend yourself, not attack like a wildcat. If Declan wouldn't ham me, I'd take you to a bar and start a brawl for the entertainment of it," he said.

Kenrik reappeared, panting. "She's gone. But I think she went in the right direction."

Selene. "You think?" Mara said. "That's my sister down there."

Kenrik's scalp shifted back. "Yes, well. There are no footprints leading in the wrong direction, at least."

"Do you think Zev has Kali and Sabra?" she asked.

Kenrik's pained gaze met her own. "I hope not."

They discussed options while Kenrik made a poultice from Kali's stores. Kenrik thought they should take the tunnels to rendezvous with Declan and the others. He and Selene would worry. Mara wanted to check the shelter first in case Kali and Sabra were there. Gavan sided with Mara, fear flickering in his eyes. They waited for Selene until dawn. When she didn't reappear, they left for the shelter.

An eerie silence blanketed the quarter. Even in the early morning, some traffic should pass through the streets. Gavan and Kenrik flanked Mara, eyes darting, but they saw no one. At times, she glimpsed movement in the corner of her eye, but nothing concrete.

Snap. Rustle. A bird flew from a bush, startling her. She expected a rib from Gavan, but he said, "Yeah, I don't like this either."

They rounded the corner and stopped cold. The shelter was a blackened frame. Mara staggered up the stone steps, impaled by the sight. Her boot kicked a sooty doll. Shattered glass tinkled underfoot as she waded through ash and debris to the garden. Late summer vegetables lay rotten in the grass where she'd played with the children. Her only comfort was that they found no corpses.

"I'm going to kill him."

"Mara—"

She wasn't sure which said her name, so she whirled on them both. "He did this to hurt me. There's no other reason—" Her voice broke. She sat hard on the ground, barely breathing. "Why? This isn't his way."

Kenrik sat beside her.

"Assuming we manage to rescue the rest of the women, where will they go? And where are the ones who live here?"

"I'm sorry," Kenrik said.

Gavan knelt on her other side. "We'll rebuild. Don't you worry. The important thing is they aren't here, which means they're alive somewhere. Now, let's go find Declan."

A flash of movement pricked her senses. Hair rose off her skin in response to a sensation she knew well. "We can't," she said. "We're being watched."

CHAPTER 30

Kenrik and Gavan agreed the safest option was to return to the house and take the tunnels to Declan and the troops. Curtains stirred in windows as they went. Footsteps thumped behind doors, but no one stepped out to speak with them.

Mara rounded a corner and stopped short at the point of a blade. Kenrik and Gavan drew their weapons as kingsmen surrounded them. Mara counted eight.

Kenrik spoke behind her. "Braddok."

"State your business," said the man with the offending sword.

Kenrik sheathed his sword and pulled Mara away from the man. "Council business. I'm not at liberty to disclose details."

Braddok squinted. "The Council are guests in the palace dungeons. How did you escape?"

"Sorry, but that's confidential. Allow us on our way, and we'll clear the street," Kenrik said.

Braddok's eyes rested below Mara's bosom and sharpened. She grabbed Eleora in a belated attempt to conceal it. When Braddok stepped toward her, Kenrik tucked her behind his back.

"Let me see it," Braddok said.

"Put away your sword," Kenrik replied.

Blade slid into sheath. Kenrik guided her to stand in front of him but left a hand on her shoulder. Gavan edged closer.

Braddok leaned to the side, inspecting but not touching. "Why does this girl have it?"

"It was a gift from Ambassador Declan," Kenrik said.

Interest sparked Braddok's eyes. "Declan is outside the city. Were you of his party?"

Kenrik answered nothing. The lack of progress annoyed Mara. She frowned at Braddok. "Who do you serve, kingsman? The true King or the imposter?"

Gavan grumbled under his breath. Mara caught the word "subtle."

"Well?" she said.

"I serve the King and his appointed leaders," Braddok said.

"Good." Holding his gaze, Mara stepped out of Kenrik's reach. "Take us to your headquarters. I require your assistance." Even as she said it, she was amazed by her own gumption.

"Who are you, miss?"

Gavan hissed a warning. Mara looked into Braddok's eyes and decided to trust him. "I'm the wife of Ambassador Declan and an ambassador in my own right, and for now, I carry the Spirit of the King."

Braddok glanced behind her at Kenrik and Gavan. Relaxing, he offered a solemn bow. "Come with me," he said and led them down an alley. A soldier removed a metal grate and disappeared. Braddok turned to her. "Down you go, Ambassador."

Before Kenrik or Gavan could stop her, she took Braddok's hand as a show of trust and dropped into the darkness below.

"What if you'd been wrong?" Gavan said through his teeth.

"I wasn't, and I don't see how my actions could've made things worse. Had I left it to you two, we would still be standing on that corner at an impasse."

Gavan growled. "You can't go around telling people you're Declan's wife. Not while we're in a state of emergency. You'll become a target."

"Leave her be," Kenrik said. "She did well."

Gavan did as he was told, but sent his irritation to Mara in silent waves.

The soldiers stopped. One used his sword to pound the metal disk above. This time, someone answered and extended a ladder down the hole. Braddok climbed out first. Mara followed Kenrik, beads of sweat forming on her brow. She paused, clutching her side.

"All right?" Kenrik asked.

Gritting her teeth, she nodded. Braddok led them out of the cellar into a large but modest home. The rooms bustled with activity. Mara looked around, taking it in. "Elise?"

A petite figure whirled, paused, and then ran at Mara. Unexpected tears sprang into Mara's eyes as she nuzzled Elise's silky hair. Mara blinked up to see Gavan's relief. Elise surprised him when she left Mara's arms for his. Blood rushed from his neck, turning his face as red as a tomato. He forgot his irritation.

"Is everyone here?" Mara asked, fighting a smile.

Elise released Gavan and nodded. "Thanks to Lazar."

"Mara?" Lazar stared as if he didn't believe his eyes. Then he sighted Eleora. His gaze was slow to travel back to hers. He stepped toward her and kissed her cheek. "It's a great relief to set eyes on you, my dear. I'd very much like to hear your story."

A child scurried by, chased by another. Mara smiled, her hand brushing a passing head. "As long as you promise to tell me yours. Are Kali and Sabra here?"

"Captured with the rest of the Council, I'm afraid. But there are no reported deaths yet," Lazar said.

Mara released her anxiety to Eleora, which lent its comforting warmth to her middle, and launched into a censored retelling of the past few days. It wasn't necessary for Lazar to know everything. His eyes shone with happy tears when Mara recounted Declan's resurrection, and he proved his goodness again when she told him she was Declan's wife. His wince went no further than his eyes, and his congratulations were sincere. All he wanted was her happiness, or so he said.

His disappointment made her ache, but there was no comfort she could give, and there were urgent matters to discuss. "How did you escape Zev?" she asked.

"Give me a moment, and I will tell you." Lazar guided them to a table framed by several chairs. Mara sat carefully, feeling all her bruises, and yawned. A nap was long overdue.

Wenny served steaming mugs of tea as Lazar gave orders to Braddok and his men. Mara felt a rush of warmth when she saw her, but Wenny returned her smiles with as many quizzical stares.

A mug clopped onto the table. "Hello, miss," Wenny said. "I don't think we've met."

"Wenny, it's me. Mara."

Wenny narrowed her eyes and leaned down in study. "You're mistaken. But it's pleasant to meet a fellow kingswoman nonetheless. Lovely necklace."

Wenny walked away, her wild hair bouncing. Mara shook her head. She'd grown to love the crazy old bat.

Lazar joined them at the head of the table with a sigh. Dark circles shadowed determined eyes. Everyone wanted sleep. Mara made herself focus as he began his tale.

Because Lazar lived on the outskirts of the city, he'd received word of the Council abductions before Zev's men had come for him. Familiar with the tunnel system, he'd escaped with his servants to his family's city home, which he kept for operations the Council preferred to remain secret. Few knew its location, and it appeared to be abandoned from the outside, making it the perfect hideout. Once he'd arrived, he'd gathered the loyal kingsmen he knew and formed plans to rescue the Council members, plans yet unrealized due to unexpected developments.

An inexplicable concern for Mara's shelter had nagged him until he brought the women and girls to his home. The following night, the shelter had burned to the ground. He also worried for the women at the Ring's brothels, which Zev's men used as command centers. Lazar feared the men wouldn't permit them to leave if they wished and might abuse them with less restraint. Furthermore, he didn't want them used in some malicious scheme. He and his men had raided all but one brothel, rescuing every woman who'd agreed to leave.

"Which brothel is left?" Even as Mara asked, she knew.

"Yours."

She nodded. "What's the situation?"

"It's the most active and heavily guarded," Lazar said. "We can't raid it. Even stealth would prove risky."

"Is there an access to the tunnels nearby?" she asked.

Lazar called for a map. It was like the one Declan had shown her. "The access is here in this alley. Unfortunately, there are no exits on this side of the compound."

"I think my old room has a window that faces this alley." Mara pointed "If someone can get inside and upstairs, the women can climb down."

"Too slow," Gavan said.

"No one ever used this alley," Mara said. "If there were men to catch them, the women could climb down partway and drop the rest. It would save time, and I can't think of a better way."

"Joss will hate it, and Levanna will like it too much," Elise said.

Mara drummed her fingers on the table. "We'll need a thick rope with big knots."

Lazar jotted a note on a piece of parchment. "Getting in will be a problem."

The silence thrummed with spinning minds. Eleora pulsed. Mara shut her eyes and said what she must say. "Not for me."

"Absolutely not," Gavan said.

"Gavan's right," Kenrik said. "Declan asked that you restrict your role to planning."

Lazar scratched his beard. "I agree with my comrades."

Odd—they thought she wanted to go. "Do you have another kingswoman at your disposal?" she asked.

"Ah, no," Lazar said.

"Then we must abandon the mission. Because I assure you, no man will get up those stairs. They creak when supporting a man's weight, and someone is always listening. But I can go before the morning staff arrives, after the patrons are gone. If I'm seen, I know of places to hide. And while my friends trust me, they may hesitate to leap out of a window for a complete stranger."

The men were unmoved.

She held out a hand. "Parchment, please."

Lazar pushed a piece to her with a frown. Mara scribbled a note and slid it back. "Add whatever you like to this, and send it to Declan. Tell the messenger not to return without an answer. I'd like to get this done tomorrow morning before dawn."

Gavan peered over Lazar's shoulder, his expression incredulous. "You're asking permission? How . . . unlike you."

Kenrik arched a brow. "What will you do when he says no?"

"He won't."

Gavan scoffed. "How do you figure?"

"Because"—she warmed her hands on the crimson stone—"Declan answers to a higher authority than my safety, and he says I'm going."

CHAPTER 31

From her perch on Kenrik's shoulders, Mara peeked out of the tunnel into the dark alley, checking after the soldier who had declared it clear. The danger of what she was about to do made her tremble inside, but Eleora comforted her with its heat.

Eleora was an extension of the King, which meant the King wanted her here, and if the King wanted her here, she had nothing to fear. She couldn't lose.

Kenrik shifted beneath her. "If something goes wrong, run. If you can't get back, hide. Gavan and I will find you."

"Nothing will go wrong," she said.

Selene, who had returned to Lazar's hideout with the messenger and Declan's written permission, sneezed. "Be quick. This makes me nervous."

"See you soon," Mara said, hoping she sounded more confident than she felt.

Her hands hooked the edge of a cobblestone, and with a groan, she pulled up her weight. Kenrik pushed against her dangling legs, and she rolled onto the pavement, clutching her side. Her eyes darted down both ends of the alley. The scrape of the heavy tunnel cover thundered in the silent street. She paused again, alert, smelling the sharp scent of rust on her hands. When her heart quieted and no one came, she crept through shadow to the back of the compound.

Mara lifted her skirt, grabbed the satchel secured on the trouser belt underneath, and pulled out a hook and rope. Staring at the tall garden wall, she gulped. Her ribs throbbed in dread of the climb. With a sigh and a prayer, she tossed the hook. To her surprise, it bit into the wall on her first try.

"Thank you," she whispered to Eleora and shimmied up the wall. When she was halfway to the top, her side twinged in pain, and she slipped. Clinging and gasping, she made it up and over to the other side. A miracle.

A hen clucked in warning when her boots hit the ground. Mara froze and looked around. Only the chicken stirred. Holding her breath, she tried the kitchen door. It creaked open, and firelight spilled onto the grass. A quick step and she was inside. The room was empty. She breathed.

Mara slipped out of her boots and climbed the stairs on tiptoe, tense as a bowstring. Pausing on the landing, she listened around the pulse in her ears. No one was working. She scooted inside her old room and jumped.

A naked woman stood at the basin, cloth in hand, too stunned to speak. Mara closed the door behind her, racking her brain for something to say. The woman glanced at the pull rope.

Mara held up a hand. "Please don't do that. I'm here to help you."

The woman stared, eyes wide.

"You don't know me, but I worked here two seasons ago. My name is Mara. Maybe Cadha or Joss mentioned me," Mara said.

A cautious nod.

"I've come to take you away from here. The Ring is at war, and the Council wants to keep you out of danger. There's a safe house in town. Will you come?"

"How did you get in here?" the woman asked.

"I'll tell you everything when we're out. For now, I need to use your window, and you need to dress."

The woman glanced between Mara, the pull rope, and the window. It terrified Mara to place her fate in the hands of this stranger, especially with her friends still inside. She almost heeded temptation to truss and gag her. But that was what Zev would do. Every thought became a prayer. Every moment stretched into two.

The woman relaxed and nodded. Exhaling, Mara strode to the widow, which stuck to the wooden frame. The woman, wearing a chemise and robe, brought a butter knife. Too grateful to question why the woman would keep a butter knife in her room, Mara smiled and wedged it beneath the window. It opened with a groan.

Mara took one of the five stones she'd stored in her apron pocket and tossed it at the metal disk in the street. It missed and skittered across the cobbles. The third stone struck with a loud ting, and the disk slid away from the hole.

Gavan climbed out and helped Kenrik up. Others followed. The woman stared at them and then at Mara. "I thought you were insane."

"Don't absolve me until we're safe," Mara said.

Gavan threw the rope, which Mara caught and fastened to a bedpost. After he tested it, Mara turned to the woman. "You first. Are you the only new girl?"

"There's one more. The room next to Cadha," she said, staring down the drop.

Mara patted the woman's back. "I'm going to help you out. Climb down partway, and let go. The men will catch you and take you to safety. Tell them there'll be five more before I come down."

The woman gripped Mara's hand and climbed onto the ledge. Trembling, she grabbed the nearest knot, swung over, and eased down. Gavan was right—it was slow, but a slow escape was still an escape. Mara waited until the woman was safe on the ground before crossing to Cadha's room.

A dim lamp glowed on the vanity. Shadows hovered thick around it. A snort from the lump in Cadha's bed told Mara she wasn't alone. Cadha didn't stir. Mara almost left her for last in case the man woke, but Eleora drew her forward. She tiptoed to Cadha's side and clamped both hands over her mouth.

Cadha's eyes flew open. Another miracle—she didn't scream. Mara whispered in her ear. Cadha rose, wrapped herself in a robe, and followed Mara across the corridor. Clutching her chest, Cadha said, "What are you doing here?"

"I've come to get you out."

Cadha's lips quivered, and then she threw herself on Mara's neck and sobbed. Mara rubbed her back until she calmed. Straightening, Cadha dabbed painted eyes with her fingertips. "I'm sorry. But you don't know how awful it's been. When Zev came back, he left the place to a horrible woman who lets almost anyone upstairs. We're treated like common whores now. And she stopped Nuri's schooling and makes her sleep in the pantry." Cadha dissolved again.

Mara explained the plan. "Can you talk to the other new girl while I fetch Nuri?"

Cadha nodded, and they parted ways. Mara slipped downstairs again, praying the kitchen would still be empty. It was, but it wouldn't be for long. Kitchen staff would arrive to make breakfast soon. When Mara opened the pantry door, Nuri bolted upright, clutching a frying pan. Mara shut her eyes, sinking at the reasons a child would sleep with such a thing. Why hadn't Zev made provisions for her safety?

"Mara?" The little girl leaped into her arms.

"Come with me," Mara said, taking her hand.

Mara spun and froze. A man glared into her face. "Stand aside, wench." His breath was thick with whiskey.

White-hot rage set Mara in motion. She glanced at the man's waist and boots. He carried no weapons. His advantage would be limited to strength.

The man scowled, tilting his head. "Why're you wearin' white?"

As Mara poised to defend herself, something cold brushed her fingers She grabbed hold and slammed Nuri's pan into the man's face with a loud clang. With a grunt, he slumped to the floor, blood spouting from his nose. Afraid the noise might draw unwanted attention, she sent Nuri upstairs while she dragged him into the pantry.

Her room was empty when she returned. Mara peered out the window. Cadha and Nuri scurried to the tunnel access. The sky faded from black to gray in the east. She smelled dew.

"Hurry," Gavan called from below.

"Two more," she said and darted to Joss's room.

Mara eased the door open and found Joss alone, reading in bed. Her eyes narrowed when they focused on Mara but relaxed into interest as Mara explained her business.

"I'll fetch Levanna while you dress," Mara said.

"Wait," Joss said. "Let me talk to Levanna. She won't accept your help even if she wants it."

"True. I'll wait for you, but don't be long. The sun is rising," Mara said.

Back in her room, Mara reclined on the black settee. Considering the number of particulars that could've gone wrong, the plan was already a success. Mara held Eleora to the lamplight. None of this would've been possible without it, nor would she have found the courage apart from its help.

"What's that?" Levanna reached to take Eleora from Mara's hand and drew back with a hiss. "It jolted me. What in hell is it?"

"Nothing from hell, I assure you. Are you ready to climb down?" Mara stood to help her.

"I'll manage," Levanna said. She slinked to the window and hesitated.

Mara crossed her arms. "Get on with it, or let me help you. We need to clear out. I've got one unconscious man in the pantry and another in Cadha's—"

Levanna whipped out a dagger. Mara gasped as the blade sliced through the rope. Shouts rose from below. Mara ran to the window and spun Levanna to face her. "Why would you—"

A puff of mist showered her face. Mara clawed at her eyes, which itched and burned. Losing equilibrium, she fell hard on the floor. Her limbs slackened, indifferent to her will. Recent horrors flashed through her memory.

Joss called out the window. "I've sounded the alarm. There's no time to rescue her. Leave now, and I won't tell them how you came."

A shadow knelt over Mara. "Hold still," Joss said. A finger applied salve to her eyes.

Relief was instant, but Mara still couldn't see. "Why?"

"I'm sorry," Joss said. "It isn't personal, but you keep forgetting one very important fact. I'm not a slave."

"You are, though you don't know it," Mara said.

Joss hushed Levanna's cackles. "The reward for your capture allows me to leave with enough coin to buy my vineyard. I'll leave as soon as I have it."

"What about Levanna?"

"Why do you care, whore?"

"Shut it, Lev." Joss softened her tone. "She's coming with me. So you see, you saved us all. And we both know Zev won't hurt you. Everything will be fine."

Mara was ashamed of the fear she felt at his name.

Several pairs of boots plodded up the stairs. The planked floor vibrated beneath her. Mara hoped the others were safe in the tunnels.

"Good work, Joss. How did she get in?"

The voice shocked through Mara. "Meg?"

"I'm not sure, but the others climbed out of the window on a rope," Joss said. "Lev cut it. By the time I arrived, they'd all gone."

A boot prodded Mara's cracked ribs, causing her to gasp in pain. "Did you act alone?" Meg asked.

"Yes."

"You're lying. Don't suppose it matters. Zev'll get it out of you." A sharp breath hissed in Mara's ear. "Why do you have the stone?"

Mara said nothing and received a kick to the ribs. She cried out. The assailant ignored Joss's protest and kicked again. Meg must've touched Eleora because she swore violently and barked an order. A stranger lifted Mara, careful to avoid the stone.

Mara moaned. "Please, Meg. I'm your niece."

"You were my husband's niece, and he's dead." To someone else, Meg said, "Take her in the carriage. Arm yourselves. They may attempt a rescue."

"I'm sorry about Loed," Mara said before they took her away. And she was. Sorry for a wasted life. Sorry for an untimely death. Sorry for Meg's loss and bitterness. But Meg didn't seem interested in condolences.

Mara was carried downstairs and shoved inside a carriage. The carriage lurched, throwing her onto her injured side. Pain stole her breath, but worse was the prospect of seeing Zev again. He'd changed. The old Zev would've been daunting enough after all he'd done, but this new Zev, who forgot Nur and burned her shelter, was a stranger. Mara didn't share Joss's sentiment. The old Zev had hurt her plenty. This Zev might murder her with a smile.

And yet she couldn't shake the feeling she was where needed to be. Mara couldn't see Eleora, but it hung around her neck. It soothed her aching side. A wry laugh escaped her throat as she recalled her plan to steal it from her friends. Eleora couldn't be seized or controlled, even by the bearer. She finally understood what Declan had meant. It went where and with whom it wanted.

"So you want to go to the palace," she said aloud. "Well, if you insist on taking me with you, I need to know why and what you want me to do. Because I don't want to go to the palace. Not without Declan. This wasn't the plan."

Eleora was still and silent. No wind spirit materialized. No new insight came, offering assurance.

"Suppose I'll have to trust you."

CHAPTER 32

By the time the carriage arrived at the palace, Mara's vision had cleared, and she could wiggle her fingers and toes. Voices exchanged outside. The door opened, letting in the sea breeze—a small gift on a difficult day. Mara was relieved to be greeted by someone other than Zev.

"What's wrong with her?"

"Drugged. You'll have to carry her."

"Is that—why does she have it?"

"Won't say, but Boss Lady didn't try very hard. She's hurt on her left side. Nudge her a time or two, and she'll talk."

A kingsman gathered her in his arms, taking care with the side he'd been warned of. She couldn't guess the reason for his kindness. He carried her through an unfamiliar section of the courtyard to a long, squat building and called out. "I need an extra set of hands, please."

A door squeaked open. Someone chewed something gummy and spat. A fat man with a pronounced underbite came into view. "You got a pretty thing there."

The kingsman's tone flattened. "It's the girl he asked for."

"I meant the trinket." The man reached for Eleora and released a string of curses.

"It's the real thing, and it's magicked. You won't be able to touch it." The kingsman's voice dropped to a low grumble. "Or her, I imagine."

"Shame." Keys jangled ahead. A bolt clacked open, and the stench of mildew and urine overwhelmed the scent of brine. The low ceiling, cracked and tinged green, made her feel anxious. Trapped. A gate opened with a loud keening, and Mara was laid on a pile of sour hay.

Her name was spoken as a question. Someone shuffled to her side. Kali's face, purpled and swollen, came into view.

"Kali?" Mara reached for Kali's cheek. Her arm was heavy and difficult to control, but it moved. "What have they done to you?"

"Never mind me, dear. Are you all right?" Light hands checked for injuries.

Mara raised her head. "I will be. Is Sabra here?"

"Yes. She's . . . sleeping at the moment."

Kali fetched Mara a cup of water. While Mara waited for the drug to wear off, she recounted all that had happened since she'd left the city with Zev. Kali laughed when Mara told her she'd married Declan. Tears ran from joyful blue eyes. "Oh, I'd hoped you would. Did you wear the gown I embellished for you?"

Mara kissed Kali's hand. She'd scold Declan later for forgetting to tell her. "I did. Thank you. But how did you find time to make it?"

An abashed grin released her dimple. "I began some time ago."

"When?"

"Oh, you'll whip me when you can stand. Not long after you came to us." Kali peeked at Mara between her fingers.

"How could you have known back then? I was always fighting him," Mara said.

Kali's dimple deepened. Instead of answering, she began her story. A few days ago, a group of men had entered the house during the night. Sabra had killed two before being taken. Before Kali could reach her weapon, one had knocked her unconscious. Upon waking in the palace dungeon, they'd been questioned, which Mara understood to mean "tortured." Zev had known about the tunnels and had hoped to obtain a map. In a moment of weakness, Kali had divulged the existence of the underground room.

"Is the Council here?" Mara asked.

"Most. Have you heard from Lazar?"

"Safe and well."

Kali sighed. "Thank the King."

Mara pushed herself up to sitting. Sabra lay curled in a dark corner, her face splotched with bruises. "Has the devil shown his face?" Mara asked.

Kali pursed her lips. "He comes and goes. I'm surprised he hasn't already come to see you."

"This isn't the Zev I know. Nothing and everything he does surprises me."

Kali drifted to sleep. Mara stared at the ceiling, going over memories of Declan one by one, until Sabra awoke. Her eyes lit on Mara, widened, and dropped. Mara rose, stretching. Pieces of hay drifted to the floor around her. She refilled the drinking cup she'd emptied and placed it in Sabra's hand.

Sabra stared at the chipped stone floor as she drank. "How are you here?"

"Look at me," Mara said.

Cautious eyes lifted to hers.

Mara detected a softness in them that hadn't been there before. "Let's skip the awkward apologies and forgiveness speeches and be friends. The story's too long as it is."

"Sounds good to me," Sabra said.

Mara pressed Eleora to Sabra's chest. The stone glowed and began to hum. "Do you want a synopsis or the full epic?"

A pair of traitor kingsmen came for Mara near sunset and bound her wrists in leather cuffs. They didn't hint at the kind of torture she should expect. She followed the lead soldier up the stairs and into the courtyard. The fresh air revived her, and for a moment she forgot her fear.

Instead of heading to the room above the dungeon as she'd expected, the men guided her to the wall overlooking the sea. The steepness of the stairs tired her long before she reached the top, but she trudged on. In the end, she was glad she did.

Breathtaking gusts from the sea made her feel she had wings. Had her wrists not been bound, she would've lifted her arms in mock flight. The sun hung large and heavy in the western sky. Its fiery light stained the clouds, reflected off the waves. A rainbow crossed the heart of the cloud hiding the Razan ships.

"I thought you'd like to watch the sun set with me." A tall figure appeared in her peripheral vision.

Her smile dissipated. Taking a steadying breath, she looked into Zev's perfect face, which remained in shadow. An ordinary gemstone hung around his neck—to fool loyal kingsmen, she supposed.

When she didn't reply, he said, "I see you received my summons." He smirked. "But I must say, it's bad form to kill the messenger."

She turned back to the panorama, drawing strength from its beauty. "What will it be? Torture? Or will you fling me off the side?"

He leaned against the wall two arm's lengths away and peered down at the rocks below. "There's no point. My informants have apprised me of the facts."

But of course he had spies among the loyal kingsmen. He always had. A lump formed in her throat.

"Declan lives and mobilizes enemy troops as we speak. You're his wife, an ambassador, and the new keeper of Eleora. If you were to take a nasty fall, what would keep an earth spirit from catching you or that stone from piecing you back together? Your death won't solve my real problem anyway."

"Which is?"

He nodded to the steam cloud. "The navy attacks the Razans at daybreak."

Mara indulged the abrupt change of topic. "I don't understand. Why bring the fleet all this way and go to the trouble and expense of hiding them only to attack them?"

"With any luck, the navies will destroy each other."

The belly of the sun dipped into the sea, and the clouds sighed purple and rose. The Razans' last sunset, and they wouldn't see it for the haze.

"You make no sense," she said. "Do you hold a grudge against Razans you never told me about?"

He didn't answer.

A humorless laugh barked from her throat. "At one point I thought you might use them against Rivka. Maybe send a fire spirit after her or something."

"Do you really believe I would double-cross Rivka?"

"I did."

He scowled.

"The Zev I know is the perfect combination of cunning, daring, and good to do such a thing."

"Good?" he scoffed. "Will you still think so when you experience the delights of magic fire?"

Mara sensed danger even if she didn't understand his full meaning.

"I need to destroy that stone," he said. "If I can't use it, I'll be damned before I let it be used against me. Tomorrow, it burns."

"It won't work." Her voice shook, shaming her.

"Of course it will. Magic fire burns everything. Even spirits."

Darkness gathered in the east, and Zev faded into night. Mara turned from him to watch the sun slip over the edge of the earth.

"I'm willing to spare you. All you have to do is throw it into the flames," he said.

"I'll die first."

"I thought so."

What had happened to him? Zev had never been soft, but neither had he been callous. Not where it concerned her.

He stood still, head cocked, watching her. "It's not the way you look that makes you like her. It's your fire."

"Like who?"

"My mother," he said and strode away into shadow. "Return her to her cell," he called over his shoulder.

"I'll take her from here."

The voice jerked Mara back to reality. Her eyes focused on the kingsman who'd carried her from the carriage. The one who'd tried not to hurt her. The dungeon door stood open behind him. She had no recollection of her descent from the wall. Aware now, she stumbled down the dungeon stair. The kingsman steadied her. At the cell gate, he removed the binds from her wrists and pressed something into her palm. Her fingers closed around it.

The kingsman tilted his head toward a guard snoozing on a stool at the opposite end of the dungeon. At the creak of the gate, he startled awake. The kingsman nodded to him and guided Mara inside.

"Did he hurt you?" Kali asked when the kingsman was gone.

"Not with his hands." Mara opened her fingers, uncovering a tiny roll of parchment, and locked eyes with Kali. Stepping as close to the torchlight as possible, Mara unrolled a message.

Coming for you. Tell others. Eat.—D

Tears filled Mara's eyes. She showed the message to Kali and then popped the parchment into her mouth. It melted on her tongue. Its sweetness surprised her.

"Honey paper," Kali mouthed.

Mara wondered how to alert the others with the guard on duty. Kali patted her chest and mouthed again. "Leave it to me." But instead of some clever act of espionage, Kali lay down in the hay next to Sabra and closed her eyes.

Mara opted for the solitary corner. Tired though she was, sleep wouldn't come. The encounter with Zev had been too upsetting and strange.

She reached for Eleora, which twinkled in the gloomy dungeon. Eleora had led her here, which meant something important was happening but she stood on the wrong side of the magic glass and couldn't see what it was.

What did the King mean for her to do?

Resting her head against the mildewed wall, she waited for inspiration to come.

Taps resounded in Mara's aching head. One eye slid open.

Kali sat at the opposite wall, stone in hand. *Tap, tap, ta-ta-tap, tap.* She paused and tensed. Taps answered several cells away. The guard snored, unbothered. Sabra didn't stir.

Through the barred window overhead, the pitch of night waned. Declan hadn't specified the time of his arrival, and morning carried death on its wings.

Kali crawled to her side. "They're ready."

Mara entwined her fingers with Kali's. It was time she knew. "I'll be executed at dawn. Zev thinks magic fire will destroy Eleora, and I refused to hand it over. If Declan's late, tell him I love him and that I'm sorry for being such a nightmare."

Kali seemed unworried. "You'll be able to tell him. You'll see."

But the sky lightened, and still he hadn't come.

An idea materialized as the kingsman's torch descended the stairs. She had no power to stop her own death, but maybe she could stop the deaths of others. The Razans' motives may not be innocent, but they shouldn't be condemned until they committed a punishable crime. Why further deplete a dying race? And the King's navy shouldn't waste their lives destroying men who might be friends.

The gate opened, and Kali curled over Mara in protest. The kingsman pushed her away with a firm hand. Mara stood and leaned toward him, a message perched on her tongue.

The night guard passed in front of the cell. "I'll follow you up," he said, scratching his backside.

Mara revised her plan. It wouldn't do to oust the Council's only ally. She flung herself at him, clutching his tunic with wild eyes. "Please. You can't let him kill me."

The kingsman squirmed, grasping for her wrists. Mara retreated and leaped again, this time falling onto him. Before the guard could intervene, she put her lips to the kingsman's ear, blocking the guard's view with her hair. "Declan must stop the naval attack."

The kingsman rolled and pinned her. Leather cuffs bound her wrists behind her back. His beard grazed her cheek. "No time."

"He must," she said softly. He hauled her to her feet and pushed her out of the cell. She wailed. "Please. Talk to him. He can't allow this."

The night guard scowled. "Shut it, wench. Give him any more trouble, and I'll return the favor."

The kingsman drew his baton and prodded her forward. Mara shot Kali a staid glance before climbing the stairs. "Thank you for everything, Kali. I'm truly sorry about the wine."

Kali grabbed the bars, tears graying her eyes. "The King be with you, darling girl."

A half dozen white-clad brutes met them on the palace lawn. Oafish with nothing but violence in their eyes, these buffoons had little chance of fooling loyals. But maybe that didn't matter to Zev. "We'll take her from here," the leader said.

The kingsman tensed. Whatever he'd planned, it hadn't included these men.

Mara remained intent upon her mission. "May I give him my last words?" she asked the leader.

He grunted what she took for permission. She faced the kingsman's regretful eyes and understood. *No time.* He'd meant to get her out, and had she not delayed him, he might've been successful. "It's too late to save me," she said. "He must try to save his kinsmen and my people. The King will take care of me. He should entrust me to him."

The kingsman nodded, his mouth flattening into a resigned line.

"Strange last words," the leader said, flinging her into the center of his men.

The sinking moon testified the dwindling hour. Even now, light seeped into the night sky. She wished the kingsman spirit-speed.

The sight of the pyre drove all other thought from her mind. The wooden platform reached as high as her neck and stood at the center of a sand pit twice the size of Kali's garden. A thick stake pierced its heart. Judging from the amount of wood, Zev would reduce her to ash. Fear washed over her, cold and fierce.

A dark figure emerged from shadow and slinked to the edge of her guard. Frankincense wafted on the breeze. "It'll be quick," Zev said. "Magic fire burns hot."

Her knees gave way. One of Zev's henchmen dragged her through the sand and lifted her onto the pyre. He held her still while another climbed up, a coil of rope in hand. As they bound her to the stake, the sky brightened, heralding her end. Ceramic pots scraped open. A dark liquid with a honey-like consistency poured onto the wood. Mara wrinkled her nose at the sour smell.

The rope tightened at her ankles. Zev climbed the pyre and loomed over her. She willed herself to meet his gaze. If he murdered her in this cold, calculating way, there would be no absolution. No matter how much Declan wanted to save Zev, he'd kill him.

She dismantled the dam of pity she'd built for him. The scowl dropped from her face. "Don't do this. You'll become your father."

He reached out, swept the hair from her face, and took a handful in his fist. She turned her mouth away as he leaned in. His lips brushed the skin beneath her jaw. Sighing into her neck, he pulled away. When she shook her head in disgust, his mouth twisted, and his blue eyes misted green.

Green eyes. Zev's erratic behavior.

Before she had breath to curse the name on her tongue, he poured the sticky liquid over her head. "Good-bye, Mara."

The goo clogged her nose and made her dizzy. Mara wiped her face on her shoulder so she could breathe. An acrid flavor drew up her tongue. Spitting made it worse. Boots clambered off the pyre and shuffled through the sand. Frantic now, she blinked down at Eleora and wished she hadn't. Liquid seeped into her eyes, scalding them.

All the while, Eleora pulsed warmth and serenity. Accepting its peace, Mara spoke to her friend. "I don't suppose my belief or lack of it ever made a difference to you. You're what you've always been. It's me that changed. I was strong, but you were stronger. You have to be stronger than magic fire too. You're the Spirit of the King. Show that bitch a bit of real magic."

"Mara!"

Her head jerked in the direction of the shout. Selene shouldn't be here. Ignoring the pain, Mara opened her eyes. A company of kingsmen rushed the garden, Selene among them. Kenrik and Gavan ran at the front, clashing swords with imposters in King's white, until archers emerged from the parapets surrounding the garden. An arrow embedded in Kenrik's back and brought him down. Mara couldn't hear her own scream above the rush in her ears.

Others fell. Zev called for surrender. Armed swordsmen, superior in number, rushed from the palace doors, encasing Mara's would-be rescuers. Zev strode among them, his head darting from one face to another. "Where is he?"

A trap. Zev had known of the loyal kingsman all along and had allowed him to work both sides to serve his purposes. No one bested Zev. No one except Rivka.

Swirling fragments of information froze in her mind and zipped into place. If she was right, Zev had been fool enough to double-cross Rivka. He'd hired the Razan fleet to eliminate her once she reached the city. To cut her out. To kill the one behind his mother's death. Which was why Rivka wanted to destroy the fleet. Because they were a real threat. Because magic fire burned everything. Including water. Including spirits.

Rivka had to burn. Which meant Zev had to burn. Mara cringed.

"He's not here," she called.

Zev's face whipped to her, but the eyes were all Rivka.

"He's at the harbor stopping the attack."

Green eyes flashed. Rivka-Zev held up a hand. "Pity. I'd hoped he'd hear you scream."

The hand came down, and a fiery arrow landed at her feet. With a roar, the liquid turned to flame, consuming the pyre, the stake, and the sand around it.

Mara burned, a human torch.

CHAPTER 33

She should be dead. The fire burned on her skin, in her hair, even inside her mouth. The heat should've melted the flesh from her bones. Flames and smoke formed a solid wall around her, blocking her sight from the events outside. The ropes burned through, freeing her from the stake. At her middle, Eleora glowed so brightly she couldn't bear to look at it. A conspiratorial smile curled her mouth. "Want to help me set a water spirit on fire?"

This time, Eleora answered—not with words but with a fire of its own. Magic fire raged all around Mara while Eleora lit a fire within, possessing both spirit and bone. Its ruby hue tinted her vision until the world bled.

The King didn't want to set Rivka on fire. The King wanted to heal Kenrik.

Mara waded through the burning rubble and walked out of the flames. The sticky liquid had burned away. Her hair and skirts undulated in the breeze, whole and unsinged. When she emerged from the smoke, no one saw her. No one looked in her direction. Selene sobbed nearby. The kingsmen were being corralled and forced to their knees. Mass execution. Rivka would stain the cobbles red.

Kenrik had been left to die where he lay. Mara wrenched the arrow out of his back and rolled him over. His blood watered the grass. Unfocused eyes drifted over her, resting on Eleora. Mara pressed the stone to his chest. Its power surged through and out of her, filling his lungs with air and waxen cheeks with color. His gaze sharpened and turned wary. Mara placed a finger at her lips.

Now to save the others.

The enemy archers had to die. Mara leaned forward, planting her palms in the soil. Eleora nestled in the grass, humming a battle anthem to the earth spirits below. Coin-sized stones rose from the ground and tilted back, awaiting her command. One for each archer.

Mara stood and scanned the courtyard. She drew her hands to her chest, palms facing outward, and channeled Eleora's fire into the stones. Her palms thrust forward. The men on the parapets dropped with fleshy thuds.

One plummeted to the ground behind Rivka-Zev, drawing his attention. He puzzled at the vacant parapets as Mara stalked toward the thugs who dared to point blades at her people. At her baby sister. Kenrik followed at her heels. Uncertainty pulsed from his body like a heartbeat.

Mara selected an imposter. At Eleora's touch, he dropped. Collecting his sword, she marched into the circle. Every head turned to her. Faces fell slack. Selene choked on a sob. Rivka-Zev failed to mask his naked horror.

The fire in Mara's bones rose to her throat and engulfed her tongue. "Let it be known to you, Rivka, enemy of old, there is no higher magic than the King. All magic belongs to him, even yours, and today he will take it from you."

The fire evaporated, and the red world faded into a golden morning. Breathless, Mara supported her sagging frame on the hilt of the sword.

Rivka-Zev ran for the palace. A stone slab jutted from the earth, blocking the door. Spinning on his heel, he ordered every man to attack Mara.

Fear detained them long enough for the loyal kingsmen to retrieve their weapons. Now herself, Mara was too winded to stand straight, much less fight. Gavan and Kenrik stood on either side of her, ready to fend off attackers.

Selene threw herself on Mara's neck. "You don't even smell like smoke. How can that be?"

"I'm not sure." Mara offered a weak smile.

Gavan spoke out of the side of his mouth. "So you're alive. And you saved my brother. I'll tell you later how thrilled I am, but first—what was happening with your eyes?"

What did they look like?" she asked, curious.

"Flames," Selene said. "Red flames."

"Huh."

"That's all you're going to say?" Gavan engaged an enemy who came too close. "'Huh'?"

Kenrik felled an attacker at her left. "We need to move you to the tunnels."

"Can't," she said. "I need to herd Rivka to the pyre. Magic fire will end her for good."

Kenrik frowned. "Someone else can do that."

"They'll need Eleora. It's the only thing that scares her more than magic fire. She wouldn't even touch me unless I was restrained." Mara reached to take it off.

Kenrik held up a hand. "Leave it. Are you certain it's her?"

"Yes," she and Selene answered simultaneously.

Selene shook her head in Rivka-Zev's direction. "That isn't Zev."

Rivka-Zev engaged two kingsmen midway between the sand pit and where Mara stood. Sweat trickled down her neck from the heat of the fire. Kissing Eleora, Mara pulled her blade from the ground. "Get me close, and I'll manage the rest."

Together, they slogged through a mire of fallen and fighting men. Gavan and Kenrik did most of the work, but once, several men converged on them, forcing Mara to defend herself. Despite her fatigue, she parried each blow. Her heel knocked against something solid. A body. Her opponent was so intent upon the kill, she doubted he noticed. She allowed him to gain ground and then distracted him with an offensive sequence, turning his feet just so. When she retreated, he tripped over the corpse.

Kenrik delivered the killing blow. "Well done." He patted her shoulder.

Gavan said, "Now what?"

Mara looked up from the gore. Rivka-Zev fought two new kingsmen a few strides away. The first two lay still behind him.

The stench of death suffocated every thought, save one—the bloodshed had to end. But the only way was to shed more. "Kenrik, help the other two. Herd her toward the fire. I'll help if I'm needed. Gavan and Selene, cover me."

A man lunged for Mara when Kenrik moved away, impaling himself on Selene's quick blade. Selene blanched and lost grip of the sword as the body fell.

Her horrified expression grieved Mara. "Wait for us in the tunnels," Mara said.

Selene took the sword from Mara's hand and set her jaw, moisture glimmering in her eyes. "I'll keep hold of this one."

Mara opened her mouth to argue, but Gavan said, "Let her stay. She's far better with a sword than you. And every bit as stubborn."

Not long after Kenrik joined the scuffle, another kingsman fell dead at Rivka-Zev's hand. Kenrik and the other backed Rivka-Zev into the sand pit. An enemy rushed them, and a well-aimed dagger sank into the other kingsman's thigh. He collapsed, crying out. The enemy joined Rivka-Zev against Kenrik, who now stood alone.

"Help him, Gavan," Mara said.

Gavan shook his head. "You need me more than he does."

And he was right. Splendid in form and speed, Kenrik defeated the newcomer without losing ground. But Rivka-Zev realized the ploy and shifted direction.

Mara cut him off, extending Eleora. He shrank from the stone. The backward motion reset him in the right direction. Mara followed, Gavan and Selene at each side. When he saw he was cornered, Rivka-Zev howled in frustration. Or so Mara thought.

The howl was a summons. Gavan and Selene turned to fight.

The clash and clang of metal punctuated the roar of magic fire. Kenrik and Rivka-Zev soaked their tunics in the heat. Sweat ran into their eyes—Kenrik's focused, Zev's turning helpless.

Eleora kicked, and Mara's vision altered again. She gasped. This time, rather than a change of color, her sight underwent a change of perspective.

A magic glass materialized between her and Rivka-Zev. She stood on the right side, seeing what she hadn't seen before. A presence filled the space over her shoulder, but the thing meant for her to see was ahead, not behind. To turn and look would be wrong.

She studied the image. It was a picture of herself—hair flowing wild, features fixed and intense, red flames in her eyes. Eleora had taken her over, but she hadn't disappeared. She'd remained herself, her will intact, only she'd been improved by the Spirit of the King.

The presence behind her radiated satisfaction.

The image shifted from one scene to another. A glowing green shard impacted Zev's face. Rivka kissed her, nearly choking her with that foul tongue, but she was no longer vacant.

Next, the wind spirit's kiss. It was the King's answer to her request. He'd filled the emptiness, and Rivka hadn't been able to possess her. On the day Rivka shattered, a piece of her had survived. She'd needed a home and had claimed residence where she'd found a vacancy.

Zev was still in there.

The presence affirmed her conclusion.

If Zev was still in there, Mara couldn't let him burn. As much as she hated him, she loved him. He was part of her, and though she'd changed, they'd begun the same. She was no better than him, no more deserving of redemption. She couldn't withhold the mercy shown to her.

Maybe Declan was right to hope. Maybe Zev could be saved.

The presence bucked.

But Rivka mustn't be allowed to go on raping his mind and sowing discord in the world. She must be dealt with.

There was only one power present that could save Zev and end Rivka.

Yes. The word rang clear in Mara's mind.

A lump lodged in her throat. "It'll be dangerous."

Yes.

"Do you know what you ask of me?"

A smile.

"Do I have a choice?"

The image and presence disappeared. Clarity faded from the world.

A paradox—the choice belonged to her, and it didn't because it did. The choice had been given, not earned.

What real choice did Zev have? Who had ever cared enough to give him one? Maybe he deserved to burn with Rivka, but she loved him. The King loved him too.

"Love makes what we deserve irrelevant." She spoke Declan's words aloud.

Clammy fingers wrapped around Eleora. She peered into its perfect radiance. "I'm staking everything on you."

Neither Kenrik nor Rivka had gained ground. Gavan and Selene were busy with the same foes. It was as if time had held its breath for an interlude only Mara was privy to.

A proud smile formed on her face as she watched Selene in action. Mara could wait for assistance, but the longer she waited, the greater the danger of losing someone she loved. If she risked a life, it would be hers.

Her heart drummed a brisk rhythm as her feet crept forward. Kenrik and Rivka-Zev were so focused on staying alive, neither noticed her approach, which was just as well. If she distracted Kenrik, it could cost his life. If she drew Rivka-Zev's attention, she'd lose the advantage of surprise. She prayed for an opening.

Their blades locked above their shoulders. Mara ran. Maybe time drowsed. Maybe Eleora gifted her with preternatural speed. Either way, Kenrik and Rivka-Zev hadn't moved when she wedged between them.

Mara pressed Eleora to Zev's chest and pushed Kenrik away with her free hand. A mighty jolt burst from Eleora. Mara gasped at a sharp pain as Kenrik flew backward several strides and slumped to the ground. She then gave her full attention to Zev, startling at his victorious sneer. The jolt hadn't affected Rivka.

Mara chose trust over panic. Slowly, the familiar warmth of Eleora flowed from the stone, through her hand, and into Zev's chest. Rivka-Zev thrashed against the magic but was held captive by its power. The luster of Rivka's eyes intensified.

Mara's chest wrenched. She cried out, but she wouldn't release Rivka for anything. Not until Rivka released her friend.

Green faded to blue. Zev's eyes rolled in his head, and he toppled onto the grass. Mara staggered to her knees. Pain drew her gaze downward. A crimson stain blossomed from the dagger hilt buried in her chest. The sight stole what was left of her strength. She dropped with a cough, tasting metal.

Mara searched for Eleora only to find she'd never let go. Clutching it with both hands, she asked the King to save her one last time.

The dagger annoyed more than hurt now. Fatigue drifted over her like winter silence.

Zev knelt beside her, eyes wide. Reaching up, she touched them. Blue. As they should be. Like the sky.

She smiled, and the sky became sea. Boz's sea. Warm and clear. The air smelled of coconut. Palms rustled in the wind.

Floating on the placid water was a boat. In the boat was a man—a man with the face of a father. A real one who fills empty chairs and doesn't abandon daughters for gems. The man was the presence. The one who'd looked with her through the magic glass. The one who had stayed with her in the Akaronian camp. The one who had spared her life time and again and had helped her in impossible moments.

He was the King.

Finally, she could see him. Touch him. His tender smile was an invitation she couldn't refuse.

CHAPTER 34

Zev sat upright, himself again and somehow more. He rubbed his chest. Warm. The clash of blades and smell of blood sharpened his mind. A memory jarred him. Not a memory. A nightmare.

A liquid cough corrected him. Not a nightmare. Memory.

Distrustful of his legs, he crawled to Mara's side. Her fingers clung to the glowing stone as if it was life itself. There was too much blood, and it kept coming.

She brushed his eyes with stained fingertips and smiled at him. He'd killed her, and she smiled. Her hand dropped. Her brown eyes arced to the sky, their light fading.

Ripping off his tunic, he spoke to her, unconscious of his words. Lifting her, he wrapped the cloth around her chest and applied pressure to the wound. The cloth soaked through with alarming speed. His bloodied hands pried the stone from her grasp and placed it over her heart where he'd driven and twisted his blade. "Come on, Mara."

Declan appeared like a miracle and crumpled to his knees. Zev searched for the calm assurance he now expected from him.

"What have you done?" Declan choked.

Zev wasn't sure who he'd asked. His stomach turned inside out.

Mara stirred, lashes fluttering open and closed. Blood dribbled from her smile. Declan took her in his arms and covered her mouth with his. Why didn't he do something to save her?

Someone seized Zev by the arms and dragged him away. They cuffed him. Declan pulled the dagger from Mara's chest, which had fallen still. He kissed her brow, her cheek, her mouth again. Then he buried his face in the curve of her neck and sobbed.

Selene fired arrows of wrath from her eyes, but they weren't for Zev alone. One launched every time she looked at her sister. The short brother walked away. The one he'd fought looked on, white lipped and stricken.

A swift execution was the only possible verdict. He'd murdered an ambassador. His friend. The child he'd sworn to protect. The only person in the world who'd loved him.

Declan lifted his head. His fingers traced her features.

A kingsman cleared his throat. "Sir, what should we do with the imposter?"

Declan raised bloodshot eyes. "Dungeon. But don't harm a hair on his head until I've questioned him."

Zev scowled in confusion. Why not throw him in the fire? Behead him? Unless Declan wanted him to suffer as she'd suffered. Which, of course, he deserved.

To be taken away was a relief. One more moment with her bloody corpse and he would've gone mad.

The dungeon was empty, the Council gone. A bucket of water stood in the corner of the cell. Zev scrubbed his hands with grit again and again, but her blood clung to his skin, unwilling to wash clean. The water stained red.

Three days later, Declan brought Zev's evening meal, the look in his eyes stealing all residual hope of another miracle. Declan unlocked the gate, plopped onto the floor, and stared through the bars at the opposite wall. He blew out a long, heavy breath. "The fleet is gone. Dispersed this morning. We recovered our lost ships and men. The Razans weren't interested in diplomacy, but an interesting thing—they wouldn't leave until they were assured Rivka had been destroyed and the city was secured against Akaronian attack."

Zev stared at the steaming bowl of food. Its contents ranked far above normal prison fare, but he had no appetite.

"When Mara sent word of them, I was sure you intended to destroy the city, but she didn't assume the worst. She understood you. Knew you were working some kind of angle."

When would he go away? Or better—order the execution?

"No one can explain to me why she did it. Enlighten me."

Zev didn't want to do this. Not now, not ever. His eyes flicked to Declan's haggard profile. "Because she's a damn fool." He didn't care how it sounded.

Declan's fists clenched. His jaw went rigid. Zev decided to let him hit him, but Declan shut his eyes and relaxed on a breath. "We both know how clever she was," Declan said. "What was her reason?"

Now Zev wanted to hit him. How could Declan speak of her as a thing of the past while she still breathed on every thought?

Zev remembered he'd killed the man's wife. The very least he owed was an explanation. "That day by the river . . ." The day Declan had done what Zev should have.

"Rivka latched onto me. Got in my head. Made me my worst self. Made me my father. Mara knew something was wrong. When the stone—"

"Eleora." Declan's voice rumbled low and dangerous.

After a leery silence, Zev continued, "All I know is that when Eleora touched me, I could think for myself again."

Declan was quiet a long time. "Her original plan, the plan they were prepared for, was to burn you alive. At some point, she must've decided you could be saved." He banged the back of his head against the wall. A dark gaze settled on Zev. "What I really want to know is was it worth it? Did it make a difference?"

Losing his head would be preferable to this conversation. "It made a difference. But it wasn't worth it."

Declan turned back to the wall. "I didn't know her long, but I feel her death like I've loved her forever."

"What will you do with me?" Zev asked. He didn't want to think about how long he'd known and loved her.

"Release you. You're pardoned."

"What?"

"You're free to go."

He'd gone daft. "I killed your wife. I murdered an ambassador. I remember enjoying it. I deserve to die."

A faint smile passed over Declan's face. "What does it mean to deserve something?"

"I committed treason."

"Yes, and the ambassador you killed pardoned you at the expense of her life. The Council honors her sacrifice. I hope you will too." Declan stood. "You're welcome to attend her burial tomorrow morning. East garden. Selene agrees that you should come."

Zev scowled at the open gate, hating it.

A slip of beige turned his head. Declan had left behind a small scroll. He knew better than to open it. The parchment, which smelled of flowers and fertile soil, unfurled to Mara's wild scrawl.

Zev,

I forgive you for everything, past and future, and hope you might one day be free. In spite of everything, I still love you. I think the King does too.

Mara

Zev observed the burial as far from the crowd as possible. It was an understated affair for an ambassador, despite the number of officials who'd come. Scattered among them were the women Mara had rescued. Some faces were familiar. Selene stood next to Declan, leaning on a tall, skinny fellow Zev didn't recognize.

The ceremony was misery. Romanticized speeches about her life and character made her seem deader than she was. No one spoke of her spitfire temperament or doggedness, the traits he'd appreciated most.

Flowers, dirt, and grain rained upon the box she slept in. He tossed ten silvers onto the pile and left before they lowered her into the ground. He couldn't bear to watch.

CHAPTER 35

The ledger and inventory lists were complete and checked. Zev's work was done. Tomorrow, the old headquarters would belong to the city, and he could leave the place and its ghosts behind. The window displayed a crisp springtide sky. If tomorrow was as fair, travel wouldn't be unpleasant.

The scent of jasmine wafted into the room. Joss. A rap upon the doorframe. He turned from the window. "Come in."

Joss and Levanna, dressed in new traveling gowns, rustled into his office. Each took her old seat across the desk. He sat and tried to appear pleased to see them.

Joss looked him over, lingering on his unshaven jaw and disheveled hair. "We came to say good-bye."

Levanna shot him a "bed me now" look. "And to be sure you won't come with us."

Joss rolled her eyes.

"I have business to attend to," he said.

Polite chat faded to awkward silence. The women stood to leave. Rounding the desk, Joss stooped and pecked him on the cheek. "Try not to punish yourself forever."

It'd be nice to see her punish herself a little.

Levanna went for his mouth and pulled away scowling when he didn't return the kiss.

"Safe travels, ladies." He waved them out.

Zev retrieved the last bottle of whiskey from the cabinet and poured himself a generous glass. He gulped and listened. Three pairs of boots traveled the corridor. Heavy footsteps. Men. He groaned.

Declan and Mara's guards entered his office. No swords. Two daggers each. New uniforms. The dark circles below Declan's eyes and a light dusting of silver told the truth of things.

With him, Zev wasn't compelled to pretend. He gulped down the rest of his glass. "What do you want?"

An inexplicable smile tugged at Declan's mouth. "To ask if you'll come to Eleora House's grand opening and coronation ceremony tomorrow."

"I received the invitation." Zev indicated the parchment with his empty glass.

"Will you come?" Declan's tone was patient. As if he spoke to a child.

Annoyed, Zev looked past him at the brothers. The tall one worked hard to avoid Zev's gaze. He wasn't as bored as he appeared. He simply hated him. The short one glowered back as if Zev had bedded his sister.

Hell—maybe he had. After Mara had left him for the Quarter, there had been a lot of women. Lately though, having a woman in his bed for the night felt . . . wrong. He blamed Mara and that cursed stone.

Zev shot Declan his flattest stare. "I'll think about it."

"It would mean a lot to Nuri," Declan said.

Zev poured another drink. "I leave the city tomorrow."

"Stop by on your way out."

Zev pushed the ledger and inventory list across the desk. "Finished these. Take them, since you're here."

Declan accepted them with an indifferent expression. "The Council thanks you for your donations. The renovations at Boz House are almost complete."

"Didn't do it for you."

"Oh, I know."

How Declan grinned like that when she was no longer in the world was beyond him.

Declan continued. "And Sabra has improved Jed's old properties. She'll have them open to residents soon. You should see them if you have time."

"I won't."

Declan stood and shook Zev's hand. "See you tomorrow. And thank you again."

"For what?"

"For reminding me of her," Declan said.

Zev scowled after them. He needed to put the city and that walking symbol of his failures behind him. As soon as possible. At daybreak. Before even. Nuri would understand.

Morning broke cool and cloudless. The horses twitched in their stalls, eager for exercise. Having packed a few belongings and what was left of the whiskey, Zev mounted his black mare and guided her to the street entrance.

A new sign hung above the doors. *Mara House.* Within a few days, the city's most vulnerable women would make a home in the newly renovated and furnished compound, where they would learn skills to keep them out of slavery and poverty.

Zev, Lazar, and Sabra, to whom Zev had endowed all of Jed's holdings, had converted the other brothels into similar homes. Zev smirked. What would Jed say if he knew more than half his properties housed destitute women for the purpose of empowering them? Bastard.

Clicking his tongue, Zev pointed the horse northeast. An early start allowed a comfortable pace and would give him time to conduct business at the first outpost before dinner.

By next springtide, the Ring would be dissolved, a project already begun in the city. A new Ring was sure to take its place, but that wasn't his business. He couldn't right his own wrongs. He wouldn't concern himself with the potential wrongs of others.

At the foot of the bridge, he turned his head southeast toward King's Quarter. The coronation ceremony would begin soon. At this moment, Nuri watched the door for him. He swore, turned right instead of left, and picked up speed.

The reconstructed Eleora House boasted a small whitewashed stable. Mara's stable boy took Zev's horse. His golden-haired dog panted after him, wagging his tail. After several startled blinks at Zev, the boy led the mare to a stall. Zev liked his innocent face. If the boy was fortunate, he might keep it for a time.

Nuri ran to him the instant he walked through the door. Zev patted her head and met Cadha's cold stare. She accepted Nuri's ongoing affection for him but hadn't forgiven what had happened. Nor had he.

"How can I help you get ready, Princess Nuri?" he asked, kneeling.

Grinning, she held out a flower crown made of daisies and violets. A lump formed in his throat. It was like the ones Mara had made for Selene.

Pinning a flower crown to a bobbing head without swearing was more difficult than managing a kingdom-wide spy ring.

Elise approached when it was done, her face glowing. "Have you heard my news?"

Zev waited, trying to look interested.

"I marry Gavan this summer." She said it with a relaxed sort of happiness, different from the giddiness he remembered.

Gavan. The short brother. Well, that explained the look. "Congratulations," Zev said.

As Elise chattered, a familiar shade of brown drew his eye. Selene busied herself in a corner, pinning multiple crowns to moving heads with ease and a smile. Grown now, her figure was like Mara's before he'd broken her and she'd lost all that weight. The commonalities ended there. Selene's features were soft and pretty. Mara was the most striking woman he'd ever met. Selene was sweet. Mara had been compelling.

No one ever liked Mara. They either loved her, hated her, or avoided her altogether. And when a community lost that, the void was palpable. Like today. Her absence was a presence.

Declan nodded to Zev before calling everyone out to the garden. Nuri snatched Zev's hand, hauling him behind her. He was glad he'd come and sorry to leave her.

As the audience assembled, he spotted Lazar in a quiet corner, the brothers, Kali, and Sabra. They'd all come.

The girls and women formed rows at the center of the green. Selene stepped forward, facing them, and read from a parchment covered in Mara's handwriting. "Today we put our past lives behind us, and celebrate our newfound freedom as daughters of the King . . ."

The speech was long and poetic with farming metaphors few would understand, but he welcomed the sound of Mara's thoughts. After the speech, Declan told the story of the King, and Elise led a "Princess Pledge," which Zev endured without rolling his eyes.

The women dispersed and began passing out something too small for Zev to identify. Nuri rushed him with a wide grin and dropped a bean in his hand. "For Mara."

One by one, each guest planted a bean in the freshly turned soil. Zev waited until almost everyone had finished. Without ceremony, he pressed the bean into the dirt and covered it.

"Did Mara ever give you a lesson in growing beans?" a voice behind him asked.

Zev ground his teeth. "Don't think so."

"You would remember if she had." Declan planted his bean, smiling. "I have something for you." He extended a cloth bundle.

It weighed heavy in Zev's hands. Wary, he unwrapped it. Gold and crimson sparkled in the morning sun. A shock pulsed through him. He offered it back.

"She gave it to you. That makes it yours."

"I can't travel the kingdom with a priceless object in my possession," Zev said. "What would I do with it, anyway?"

Declan took a breath, as if about to say something, but hesitated. Absent fingers adjusted Mara's lodestone pendant around his neck. "Eleora has chosen to go with you, which means no one can take it from you. As to what you'll do with it, I imagine that will be quite the adventure. Accept the gift, Zev."

Declan strode away from Zev's outstretched arm.

Musicians tuned their instruments, adding to the cacophony. It was time to leave. But when Zev told Nuri good-bye, she begged him to stay for the dance. He reluctantly agreed. After today, they may not see one another again.

Zev took refuge inside while the musicians and dancers assembled. In the quiet foyer, he unwrapped Eleora. It pulsed warm and alive in his hand. Half his life, he'd searched for it. Now that it was his, he had no idea what he would do with it. Ruling Akaronians no longer appealed to him. And the cost of the gift—well, he would give it back if it would do any good.

Voices hushed outside. Zev rewrapped Eleora and tucked it in a pocket. He leaned against the doorframe, snickering at Nuri and her wiggly companions. With the opening chord, the girls posed and proceeded with an elegant dance.

The audience applauded at the end. The key changed, and the tempo sped. The women joined the girls on the green, laughing, clapping, and twirling.

Zev turned to go, and a flash of white stopped him cold. Eleora warmed his pocket, vibrating until it hummed. He peeked over his shoulder, terrified what he thought he saw wasn't real.

Long, black hair glistened in the sun. He swallowed. A brown face passed between heads and was hidden again. The crowd thinned.

And there she was, healthy and whole, arms outstretched, palms to the sky, twirling in a gown so white it hurt his eyes. In all the time he'd known her, she'd never smiled like that. Not even Declan smiled like that. Laughing, she leaped into the air, higher than should be possible, and spun again.

He stepped toward her. The stone jerked him back. All he could do was watch. But it was enough.

Declan appeared at his side. "You see her too."

"How?"

"I'm not sure."

She stopped midtwirl and smiled in their direction. Did she see them? Her head whipped over her shoulder, tossing her hair. The smile relaxed, but her eyes stayed bright. Like a happy child's. Then whirling midair, she burst into a shower of rose petals, which fell on the dancers and dissolved on the ground like snow.

A raindrop splattered on Zev's hand. Confused, he glanced at the sky. Blue and clear. Declan pressed a handkerchief into his palm. Zev blinked, stunned by the moisture in his eyes. He'd been a child the last time he'd cried.

Declan's voice dropped low and reverent. "We'll see her again someday."

Zev frowned at the piece of earth on which she'd danced.

"One day, the King will return, and she'll be with him."

The words warmed his chest like a flame. Zev shook Declan's hand and made his way to the stable. Work awaited outside the city gate. After the Ring was no more, he had no idea what he'd do. For the first time in a long while, he could choose.

Eleora pulsed in his pocket. He took it out and hung it around his neck, tucking the stone into his shirt.

As Zev peered down the road ahead, the loneliness that had been his lifelong companion couldn't be found. In its place swelled a sense of belonging. And something else, equal parts thrilling and terrifying—freedom.

A NOTE ABOUT SEX TRAFFICKING

Sex trafficking is a worldwide multi-billion dollar industry fueled by pornography, drugs, and consumerism. Trafficking occurs wherever there are people. Victims can be any race, either gender, and from any socio-economic class. Many victims are children.

Survivors of sex trafficking suffer from posttraumatic stress disorder similar to that experienced by war veterans and need long-term intensive care, a part of which should be a strong, loving community and as much exposure to the presence of God as possible. But even that may not be enough to keep them from going back to "the life."

While Mara shares many common struggles with sex trafficking survivors, her experience doesn't represent that of a real survivor. I accelerated the timeline for her healing and assimilation back into real life to accommodate the pace of the story. Six months is an unrealistic time frame for anyone to go from a life of constant trauma and abuse to managing city-wide projects. And for the record, survivors should stay as far away from their pimps as possible. Honey, you can forgive him, but you can't save him.

If you would like to learn more about how to fight sex trafficking, go to www.rebeccabender.org, www.A21.org, or www.enditmovement.com. To support Project 41, a ministry for sex trafficking survivors in Melissa's hometown, visit www.p41ministry.com.

ACKNOWLEDGMENTS

First, I must thank my husband, Brandon, who was my first reader and has believed in this story since its inception. I love you. I must also thank my mom, who called *Eleora* her "favorite book ever" before I'd worked out the kinks, and other early readers—Nona, Linda, Eddie, and Jennifer; and Lindsey Nadler of Project 41, who offered her invaluable knowledge about sex trafficking and its survivors. Your input made a better book. Thanks to Stephanie Chou, my editor extraordinaire; to Misty McKeithen, who designed my map and story-related art—you are amazing; to Len Woods and Talena Winters, who assisted me with decisions about loglines, book blurbs, marketing, and cover design; to Kristen Lamb for her forty-page Death Star treatment; to my mother-in-law, Debbie, who made research runs to the library when I was too sick to go myself; to my dad, who can make a brilliant headshot on the fly; to Torey Morgan, my childhood friend and logo rock star; to my high school English teacher Linda Wilson, who fed my love for writing and good literature; to Danielle, the only sex trafficking survivor I know who continues to choose abundant life again and again—you are my hero; and to Jarrod Richey, who is the busiest person I know and yet made time to typeset my book, design the cover, and advise me on marketing.

This book began as a vision of a girl learning to wear her robe of righteousness, an image inspired by Sarah Young's devotional *Jesus Calling*. Several scenes and sections of dialogue are the fruit of books and sermons by Timothy Keller, which I consumed in mass quantities during my years of illness. Readers familiar with his work will recognize his thoughts. I cannot thank these authors enough for their contributions to my walk with God.

BIOGRAPHY

Melissa has loved writing since she learned how to use a pen. After years of journaling, blogging, and crafting short stories for her own entertainment, she decided to write a novel. It was terrible, but she didn't let that discourage her. In 2012, Melissa became very ill with an allergic disease called mast cell activation syndrome, which caused a wide range of symptoms including regular episodes of anaphylactic shock. When she could no longer safely leave her home even while wearing a mask, she became a shut-in. During that time, she wrote and revised *Eleora*, much of which is a symbolic record of her personal journey. Beginning in November 2015, Melissa experienced progressive miraculous healing through prayer ministry and is now able to leave her home and eat any food she desires without reacting.

Melissa is a wife, mother, music teacher, writer, and minister with the healing prayer ministry that changed her life forever. She lives in north Louisiana with her husband, Brandon (a.k.a. Superman), and her two favorite red-heads, Micah and Sara.

You can find out more about Melissa on her website,
www.melissakeaster.com.

9 780099 884930